FLOW AS WATER

EARTH STONES TRILOGY BOOK ONE

FLOW AS WATER

LISA CRAM

THUNDER
ROAD
PUBLISHING

For Dana and Derek
The world is what you make of it.

N
Sea
of
Meura
Winterlands
(Arctakai)
City of Ice
Desertlands
(Seakai)
Forestlands
(Terrakai)
Inception
Great
Ocean

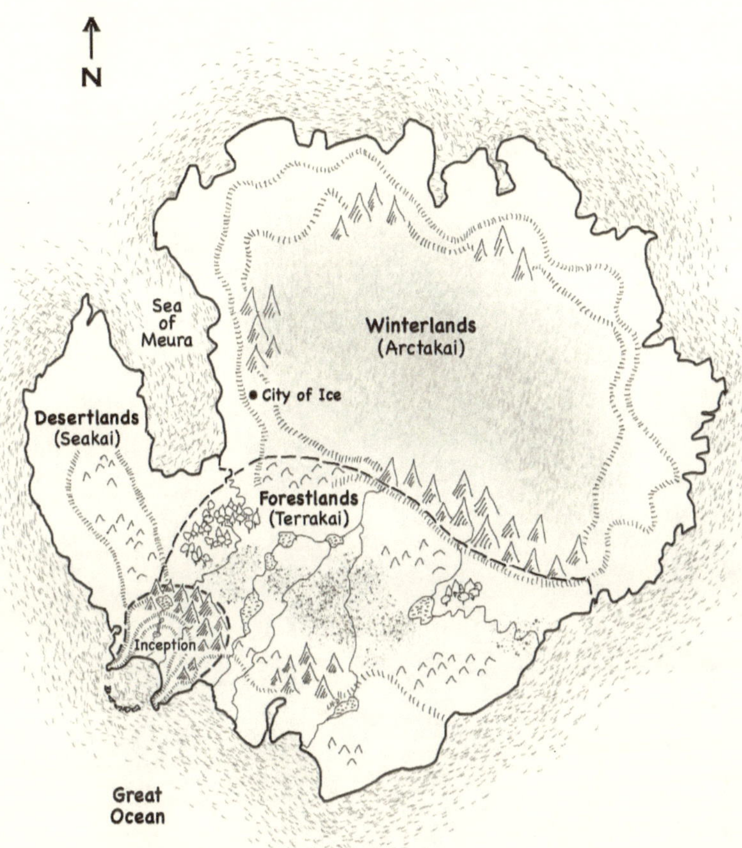

MERLUMA

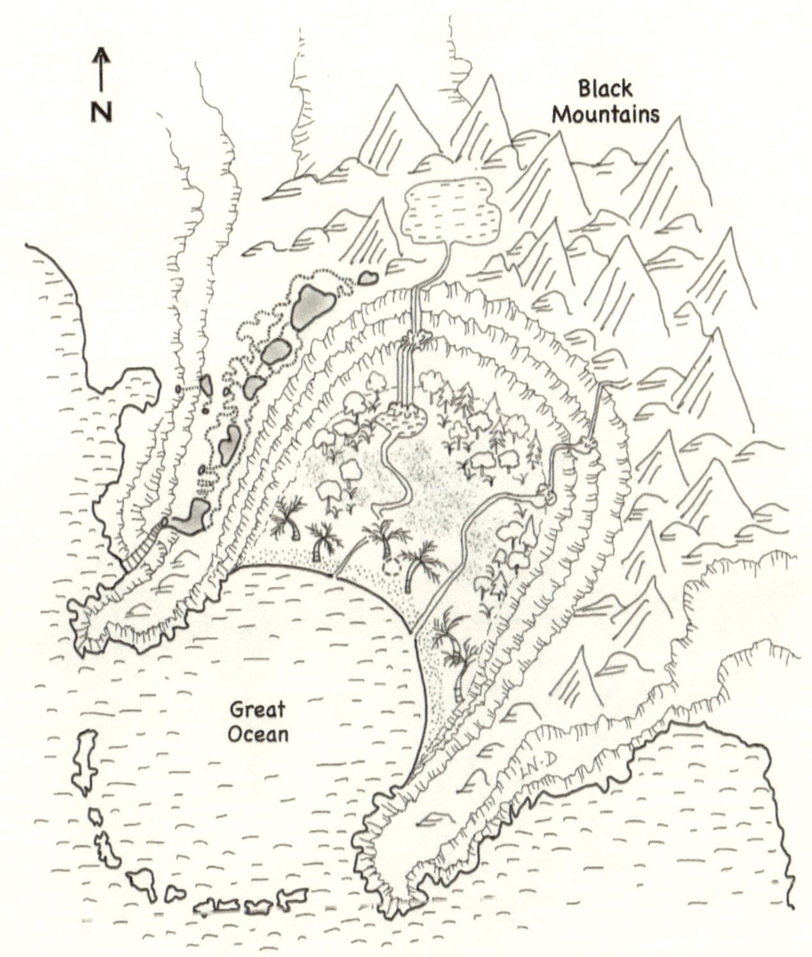

INCEPTION

TALLAMURE

PART ONE

1

Stirring Secrets

THE NIGHTMARE VISITED LATE in the night, the same as always; the shrill scream of anguish and despair, the body of her mother limp and unresponsive in her father's arms, bronze skin pallid, sea water trickling past lips painted a sickly shade of blue; a green fishnet tangled around her neck and torso, twisted and tattered as if she had struggled mightily to free herself; the dive knife safely tucked in its sheath and strapped around her thigh... unused.

Why didn't she use it?

Audrey Grey woke from sweaty restless slumber, tearing away the wisps of the nightmare, the unanswered question as puzzling today as it was every time the night terror presented itself. But something felt different about this morning. She drew a shaky breath and raised a trembling hand, resting it on her chest where her heart beat with anticipation. Not in a bad way, but oddly, the same way it had early that fateful morning: her tenth birthday, bursting with excitement, dreaming of a day that should have been filled with love and laughter, silly games and cake.

Ten years had passed, and she lie in the darkness with the mystery of her mother's death ever swirling in her waking thoughts, as it had most mornings. *How could it have happened?*

Her mother was a strong swimmer and free diver with intimate knowledge of the shoreline and reefs surrounding their tropical Pacific island home. She had promised to teach Audrey of the many wonders of the ocean, to embrace its secrets, and to respect the danger of this otherworldly realm, without fear. "*Move in harmony with force of life, flow as water, like stream around rock,*" she often said.

But what should have been never came to be, and Audrey grew up afraid of the ocean.

Yet here she was, waking to a gray morning in the Pacific Northwest, about to venture onto the waters of the Salish Sea as a newly minted marine biologist. And as she had every time, she clung to hope that, eventually she'd unravel the mystery, the nightmare would end, and she would find peace in her heart and soul.

A knock on the door.

It was still dark outside. She checked her phone. Blake was early.

"Coming!" she yelled, hopping out of bed and flipping on the light. She gathered her clothes and got dressed, took a quick trip to the bathroom to wash her face, brush her teeth, and braid her long wavy hair. Back in her room, she slipped her phone in her back pocket, stepped into her canvas shoes, donned a thick polar fleece jacket.

Before opening the door, she wound her long braid across her shoulder and gave it a gentle tug. She whispered, "Move in harmony with force of life, flow as water, like stream around rock." Then she grabbed her backpack with one hand, opened the door with the other.

Blake Goodfellow was a ray of sunshine on a dark dreary morning. His eyes were bright, every strand of dark hair set in place. He wore freshly pressed khaki-colored chinos and topsider boat shoes, fresh from the box. Not a single pill marred the soft knit of his navy cashmere sweater. She shuddered to think of how she looked beside him with her messily braided hair and puffy eyes, dressed in jeans and t-shirt thrown together without much thought. A fright, compared to him.

His gaze dropped to her mouth. "What's that on your chin?"

She wiped it with the back of her hand. Toothpaste dribble. *Peachy.*

He reached for her pack. "Want me to carry that?"

She smiled. Blake was a true gentleman, a rare breed in the twenty-first century. He always offered to open doors, or carry her bag, or point out embarrassing things no one else would, like white slime dribbling down her chin.

Good-fellow indeed...

"That's okay, I've got it." She slung it across her shoulder. "But thanks for the gesture."

"My pleasure."

She shut off the light to her single-room cabin and locked the door.

He walked beside her. "Looks like it's going to be calm. Good day to be on the water."

Her step stuttered. *Be on the water...* "Uh, sure."

He stopped walking. "Are you certain you're ready for this?"

Was she? She sucked a deep breath. "If not now, when? You know I must do this. Besides, you won't let anything bad happen, right?"

He squeezed her shoulder and gave her a reassuring smile. "Of course not."

It was still dark when they reached his Pathfinder parked in the student lot of the Friday Harbor Labs. He opened her door and she climbed in. Two cups of coffee sat in the cup holders. Steam escaped through slits in their tops and filled the interior with a fresh-brewed scent.

Her heart swelled with gratitude. "You are the best friend. Ever," she said, reaching for hers.

"Had a feeling you might need it, and this too." He handed her an energy bar.

"Peanut butter, my favorite."

"Still having the nightmare?"

She didn't answer right away, tore open the energy bar. It hovered in front of her mouth. An image of *herself* wrapped in the green fishnet, lips colored blue, flashed in her mind. She took a bite, answered with her mouth full. "Always, you know, whenever a day with water is involved."

"Maybe today will be different," he said with a smile.

She swallowed down that last bite. "Maybe."

"Maybe today we'll unlock the secret we've been hoping for."

Audrey thought about that. *Secrets.* Since her mother died, her life felt full of them. That tingly feeling struck again. Not of anticipation but uncertainty.

Maybe some secrets are best left where they lay.

2

Promise

AUDREY AND BLAKE WALKED in silence along the docks at Roy's Marine and Shipyard located at the south end of Friday Harbor. They stopped at the berth of a classic thirty-foot lobster-style powerboat named *Annabelle*. Audrey marveled at its well-maintained clean lines, pristine as the day it was first splashed. Roy often offered *Annabelle* to students at the Labs whenever on-water research was necessary. A safe and stable boat armed with the latest electronics. With Blake as an able and experienced captain, she had nothing to fear.

"Where to first?" Blake asked.

Audrey was glad she took the effort to look it up last night. "K Pod was last sighted in Haro Strait, north of Andrews Island."

"Then Andrews Island it is."

Blake unlocked the door and handed her a self-inflating life jacket. She slipped it on, adjusted the straps until it was snug, then hopped off the boat to the dock. Blake fired up *Annabelle*'s diesel engine while Audrey coiled up the power cable. Lines were cast and they were on their way. Blake slipped behind the wheel inside the warm cabin and pulled the door shut. Audrey remained in the cockpit, breathing deeply the briny sea scent, taming her fear.

Move in harmony with force of life, flow as water, like stream around rock.

Once clear of the harbor, the Salish Sea sprawled between the many islands of the San Juan archipelago, steely gray under an awakening sky. *Annabelle* skipped across the glassy surface heading west at eighteen knots. To the east, the silhouette of Mount Constitution on Orcas Island loomed in a soft and fiery sky and the evergreen hills and solid rock shores of San Juan Island grew distant.

Water stretched in every direction as they entered Haro Strait, a large body of water separating the United States from Vancouver Island in British Columbia. A thick bank of fog lay in their path. *Annabelle* burst through. The temperature plummeted and the world turned gray and misty. Dew gathered quickly on the oiled teak deck and freshly varnished bright work. A tangled mix of brine and diesel exhaust billowed from the transom, trapped in a cloud of oppressive damp gloom.

Audrey slid the aft cabin door open and poked her head inside, cheeks prickling from the sudden blast of heat.

"How much farther?" she asked.

Blake looked up from *Annabelle*'s radar screen.

He said, "We're nearly there."

The Turn Point Lighthouse emerged from the gray mist lit by a golden beam of sunshine. The fog lifted above the sea but lingered atop evergreens furring the rocky peaks and desolate shore of Stuart Island like strands of cotton snagged by prickly Velcro.

Blake spun the wheel hard to starboard once *Annabelle* cleared the kelp-strewn reef, skirting the point. The boat leaned into a smooth arc, heading northeast, out of the protection of the San Juan archipelago into the open waters of Haro Strait.

Audrey braced herself in the cabin's doorway. Normally the sea changed here, where the opposing current collided with wind-driven waves rolling up the strait, but this morning the water was smooth and oily.

She gazed at Blake's profile when he raised a set of binoculars and focused them on a pod of seals lying on the shoreline north of the lighthouse. He noticed her watching and lowered the binoculars. "What?"

Her heart swelled. "Nothing, really, just super jazzed to be doing this, thanks to you."

He gave her his lopsided grin. "Then let's get to it."

She grinned, gave him a salute. "Aye, aye, Captain!"

It was Blake who came up with the brilliant idea to continue their post-graduate studies together, along with their good friend Ryan. *I've heard rumors that strange new sounds in the Salish Sea are puzzling researchers at the Friday Harbor Labs on San Juan Island. They're overwhelmed with existing studies and hope to resolve the rumors and offer a logical explanation for the phenomena, with potential for a breakthrough discovery in orca and dolphin language. We should seriously consider it for a research project.*

Blake used his contacts in Seattle to secure funding and pushed through their application to the Labs for a research apprenticeship with a fully funded research project, which was readily accepted, locking down spots for the three of them at the prestigious institution. It was the push she needed to approach her over-protective father to let her stray farther from his ever-present radar. Blake accompanied her to the tense meeting to help overcome all of her father's objections. To her surprise, he agreed to let her go. Autumn courses began two weeks ago.

She grabbed the duffle loaded with their gear, and got to work. She plugged the hydrophone—a microphone adapted for capturing sounds underwater—and two sets of headphones into the amplifier mounted to the aft cabin wall and switched it on. Satisfied all was in working order, she stepped out into the cockpit with the duffle slung over one shoulder, hydrophone and headphones in hand, carefully uncoiling cords in her wake.

The last of the fog lifted. The morning sky melded from pink to gold; the sea bloomed teal green. The rocky shore of Andrews

Island emerged, its steep slopes a rough cloth of evergreens dotted with golden bigleaf maples.

Blake slowed *Annabelle* to a crawl and shut down the engine.

She expected silence but blood sang in her ears. Her scalp prickled. Once again, something felt different. *Off.*

Her mother believed humans once possessed a psychic sense of the natural world. That if Audrey practiced, she would learn how to use it, like her Polynesian seafaring ancestors. She taught Audrey that clues abound in the most unlikely places—the sky, the water, the bountiful life surrounding her. *Look without eyes, listen without ears. Only then will you understand.*

She tried to understand what her mother meant, pretended even, but now...

Something *was* stirring her in a profound way. Her thoughts cast to her father and the fear he instilled after her mother died. His fear that something bad would happen to her too. Her heart quickened. She scanned the sky, the sea, and the shores of Andrews Island, searching for clues in all those unlikely places. The air was crisp and still, the sea flat, the sky a dusty rose. An eagle twittered from a dead snag at the pinnacle of Andrews Island. Picture-postcard perfect. She blew it off as residual paranoia.

From the cabin Blake whistled and circled his finger, his signal for her to drop the hydrophone into the water. She tied it to a cleat and lowered it beneath the calm surface. But still. She couldn't stop obsessing. Something felt *odd.*

She jumped when Blake popped his head out of the cabin and said, "Hear anything?"

She donned her headphones. Silence. "Try turning it up."

He ducked inside and a moment later a glorious symphony of high-pitched squeals, rat-a-tatting ticks, and deep-rumbling growls filled her ears. Maybe what she was feeling was the collective energy of the orcas, nearby and gathering.

Blake stepped out and put on the other set of headphones. He gasped when he heard their many varying voices. His eyes found hers, pools of cerulean blue framed by dark brows—a startling contrast to his pale skin and pink cheeks, flushed from the sudden cool air. They grinned at each other, listening to the ticking purrs and joyous song of the warm-blooded beasts of the sea.

Audrey slipped her headphones sideways, Blake did the same. "So many! K pod?"

"Sounds like K pod… fifteen, maybe more."

Audrey dug the tablet out of her backpack and scrolled through the notes she took the night before. "Three native pods travel between Washington and British Columbia. At last count there were seventy-three resident orcas in the Salish Sea." She set down the tablet. "K pod is the largest."

Blake pressed the headphones to his ears as his brow hardened in concentration. "Wait—Did you hear that? Some conversations are clipped… That's odd. Sounds like transients. Residents and transients don't usually travel together."

She grinned. "Only one way to know."

Blake grinned back. "Markings."

They reached for their binoculars and began a slow sweep along the horizon, starting in opposite directions.

"Half mile, group of three," Blake said.

"Closer in, two, wait—oh my." She swung her gaze one-hundred and eighty degrees. Dozens of black dorsal fins rose like periscopes. Mountainous bodies broke the surface, feathery plumes of salty mist exploded into the sky. Several groups of two, three. Five! Her eyes watered from not blinking. "They're all around us, too many to count! And to think we might have missed this if you hadn't been in such a—" Blake slipped the headphones off her head, plucked the binoculars from her fingers "—hurry this… morning."

He set them on the deck.

"What are you doing? We need to record this."

He curled his hands around her chilled fingers, warming them. "We have plenty of time. Whale-watching season is over and they're likely to be here for hours enjoying the peace and quiet. Like us. Close your eyes. Listen, and imagine what they're saying by the way their bodies pass through the water."

"You sound like my—"

"Shh."

Her eyes slid shut. In the distance, the whales broke the silence with loud bursts of air, the slap of fins, and whispered splashes as they dove. She imagined an underwater ballet of tuxedoed bodies surrounded by green.

Blake cupped her shoulders and pulled her closer. "It's just us and them. You and me."

When she opened her eyes she was struck by the full force of his gaze. She wanted to say something poetic or clever in reply, but her tongue was glued to the roof of her mouth.

He dug something out of his pocket. "I made this for you." He held out his hand. "It's a friendship bracelet." It was made from a trio of thick strings—green, orange, and purple—and tied into series of square knots. In the center was a larger knot that looked like a shamrock. He pointed to it. "For luck, and to us." He held out the bracelet. She held out her arm and he tied it around her wrist. "Wear it until it falls apart, and after..."

She smiled. "You'll get your wish."

He smiled back. "I hope so, or maybe before." His gaze fell to the bracelet around her wrist. "I need to ask you something."

She swallowed. "Sure."

He reached up and fiddled with the nylon tube of her life jacket, lying flat across her shoulder, his gaze darting between her eyes and his fingers. "You've been an incredible friend, but I was hoping that maybe we could, that I could..."

He was staring at her mouth like he wanted to kiss her. Her heart suddenly thundered. "Could what?"

He leaned in, lining up for her lips.

Her eyes fell to his mouth. She always thought of Blake as a friend, not because she couldn't imagine him as something more, but because she assumed he wouldn't have been interested if she had. She'd never made out with anyone or had a boyfriend, not that she didn't want to, but because of the long shadow her father cast over everything she did and questioned anyone she befriended. She did sneak a kiss with a guy, once, during a party her freshmen year of college, but it ended awkwardly and nothing more came from it. The guy quickly lost interest, probably because she had no idea what she was doing. Like now. She pressed a hand to Blake's chest.

He leaned back and blinked. Surprise rippled across his features.

Peachy. He's probably never been refused, until now!

"I'm sorry, that was—" His hands fell to his sides. "Inappropriate."

"No! It's okay, it's just—I wasn't expecting this—and—and I'm not real practiced at—um." She touched his lips. "*This.*"

His face brightened. "Would you consider me to be your teacher?"

She gazed back in shock. His sudden gambit. The surge of strange feelings coursing through her body. *Why not?* She smiled and nodded. This time he didn't hesitate and his mouth found hers, wet and wonderful. She was amazed at how a simple kiss could spark fire in her belly, and startled when his tongue slipped past her lips and explored inside her mouth, an odd yet pleasant sensation. She quickly responded, swirling her tongue with his. She wound her fingers through his hair, savored the smell rising from his skin.

Blake pulled back and grinned. "You're a fast learner."

"And you're…" She felt her cheeks flame. "Well-practiced."

"Perhaps." He smiled, twined his fingers between hers, and kissed her again, less urgently and tender. All lips, no tongue. She liked that too.

"What I really wanted to ask—" He drew a sudden breath, holding it for a moment. "I want to be with you."

Audrey was speechless. At first she felt a flare of excitement, followed by a sinking feeling in her gut. She may have been inexperienced with relationships, but was well aware of what men typically wanted.

Blake's brow quirked, having sensed her apprehension. "I mean, exclusively." He offered a sincere smile. "As in... I want to date you, Audrey Grey. If you'll have me."

A gasp escaped Audrey's lips. For all the ways she imagined this day to unfold, this certainly wasn't what she was expecting.

She gazed at him with fresh eyes, that last kiss vividly fresh in her mind. How much she appreciated his kind gestures. How natural his hand felt in hers. How easy he was to talk to. How nice it might feel to snuggle with him on the sofa... She laughed. "Yeah, sure."

"Promise? No one else?"

"No one else. I promise." Her heart untethered and bounced around inside her ribcage.

What just happened?

An eternity seemed to pass, breath held, gazes locked. They both grabbed for the clips securing their life jackets, which fell in a heap at their feet. Blake kicked them aside, wrapped her in his arms, and kissed her. One kiss morphed into another. Whale songs drifted from their abandoned headphones; distant splashes grew closer.

Audrey and Blake clung to each other laughing. She said, "We really should get back to work."

"But teacher isn't through with his lesson."

3

Orcas

BLAKE LEANED IN FOR another kiss, his gaze flitting between Audrey's eyes and her lips, making her stomach flutter. The sound of parting waters and the *hiss* of an orca's vapored breath interrupted them, drawing their attention to the side of the boat. Enthralled, they stole a hurried look.

Audrey gasped when a second orca burst from the depths and breached. A geyser of water rained down in the cockpit. Her hand slipped from Blake's grip when she reached for her eyes and wiped away salt spray, clinging to her lashes. Her heart thundered. "Wow! This is unbelievable!" She faced Blake, laughing. "First your confession, and now... *this?*"

She leaned over the side. Dozens of orcas surrounded the boat, circling beneath the mirrored surface of the water, flashing their white bellies and stealing curious glances with their jet-black eyes. Mothers nudged babies close enough for Audrey to reach over the side and touch their rubbery noses. Ever-watchful males circled on the perimeter, six-foot-high dorsal fins and bodies as big as *Annabelle*'s hull. She had never seen an orca this close before.

With shaky hands she tried to jot down every detail on her tablet, the size and shape of each orca's dorsal fin, nicks and scars, unique markings she would compare with records on file once they returned to campus.

The orcas slipped away as quickly as they had approached until all that remained were three males circling *Annabelle's* hull. Together they dove and disappeared beneath the oily surface of the water, popping up a hundred yards off *Annabelle's* port side. The speed at which they fled was mind-boggling.

Audrey's brows knitted as the males circled back around, lining up in a V formation. She felt the blood drain from her face as wonder and excitement tilted toward confusion and horror as the trio raced atop the surface with startling speed toward *Annabelle*, dorsals raised like steel swords rushing into battle.

That unsettled feeling she felt earlier sparked into a full-fledged fire.

Audrey's tablet slipped from her fingers, landing on the deck with an ominous crack.

Blake stepped up behind her, threaded an arm around her waist and pulled her protectively against his body.

Panic rose in her throat, stifling a scream. Her body tensed and coiled from the image of three black-and-white warriors racing in for an attack.

The sound of rushing water grew louder. Blake tensed behind her. Both anticipated a sudden impact.

But none came.

The orcas slipped beneath the surface of the water a mere fifty feet before contact, diving deep. Their wakes slapped violently against *Annabelle's* hull.

Blake released her and leaned over the other side of the boat, peering into the depths of the water. Seconds passed before the orcas surfaced on the other side, in fast retreat.

She frantically searched for the others, sweeping the horizon with her binoculars, hoping it wasn't true.

A minute passed, then five, and the water lay down as before, gently swelling as if *Annabelle* rested upon the chest of a sleeping giant.

Reluctantly she slipped on her headphones. Silence.

"They're gone—we missed our chance!"

She pulled off her headphones. Picked up her tablet lying on the deck.

The screen was cracked. The notes she had taken were unreadable scribbles. In all of her excitement—Blake's unexpected question, that kiss, the sheer number of orcas—she had forgotten to take videos or a single picture. *Stupid!* Now they were missing the vital information they needed to complete the research paper due next week.

She fell to her knee, shoved her tablet into her backpack, and pinched back tears of disappointment. It had taken all week for her to muster the courage to take this trip, to venture out in Roy's boat onto the open water.

"I was hoping they could have stayed a little while longer," she said, choking down a sob.

"I'm sorry—I shouldn't have—I didn't think that—"

Audrey turned to tell him it wasn't his fault, but the words died on her lips.

An orca rose from the sea, its massive body clearing the surface of the water, darkening the sky. It arched toward the transom where Blake was standing, eyes glaring, dark and menacing.

Audrey screamed, "Watch out!"

Blake jumped forward in the nick of time.

The orca landed on *Annabelle*'s transom; fiberglass splintered like balsawood. Blake sailed into the air, arms and legs flailing, and landed in the water. Audrey hovered airborne before slamming down to the deck on hand and knee.

The orca slithered off the back of the boat and disappeared beneath the surface. *Annabelle* bucked from the sudden shift of released weight. Audrey grabbed a cleat on the port gunwale, but it ripped from her hand as she was tossed into the air like a ragdoll and landed on her tail bone, biting her tongue. Pain reverberated up her spine. Blood filled her mouth.

She scrambled to her feet.

Another jarring strike to the hull.

She flew backwards and slammed against the cabin door. Air was knocked from her lungs, stars filled her eyes. She slid to the cockpit floor, dazed.

She lay on her back, unable to breath, unsure how she came to be staring up at the brightening sky. Pain shot through her head when she rolled onto her hands and knees. She sipped air until she could see clearly, until she was gulping ravenously. She swayed to the motion of the boat rocking haphazardly.

Get up! Take stock!

She rolled to her feet.

The sea around the boat was frightening. Whirlpools swirled in random patches, boring fathomless holes in the sea. Confused sharp waves collided into one another and violently slapped against *Annabelle*'s hull. Beyond, the sea lay calm and flat. The commotion surrounding *Annabelle* came from nowhere. It made no logical sense.

But it was the water flooding the cockpit that raised a prickled warning across her spine.

Audrey fell to her haunches, back pinned against the gunwale, eyes glued to the water swirling around her feet. Panic rose swift and sure. Cold water filled her shoes, its icy fingers encircling her ankles. She tried to move, tried to scream, but couldn't, frozen by her deepest fears.

Submersion. Entrapment. Drowning. Like her mother. The pallor of her skin and unseeing gaze. And since Audrey matured, her features forged into a younger version of her mother's, what she saw vividly in her mind's eye at that moment was the pallor of *her* face, *her* unseeing gaze...

Water trickling past my blue lips!

Her vision narrowed. All she saw was water. Water coming to take her. She heard its taunt, felt its icy grip. Like irons locked around her ankles, their watery taut chains running across the deck and disappearing through the hole in the transom. Chains wound around the wrists of souls lost at sea, coaxing her to join them, to join her mother, in the icy depths of the green abyss...

A seagull screamed.

Audrey gasped and looked up. The shock of cold air filling her lungs broke her breathless trance. She gained a tiny edge against the fear.

Dozens of seagulls circled the boat, screaming and diving where she cowered in the cockpit. Helpless. Like—

Blake.

She scrambled to her feet but was knocked down by another strike to *Annabelle*'s hull. The boat rolled and she lost her footing as sea water sloshed in the cockpit. The bow rose and the stern settled deeper into the sea.

Audrey looked down at her chest. No life jacket. She cursed, remembering how she and Blake had carelessly cast them aside. Now they lay in the far corner of the cockpit pinned beneath the crushed transom.

How much time had passed? Blake had fifteen minutes, maybe less, before hypothermia set in. Unconscious, he would sink without a life jacket.

She grabbed the hydrophone's cord pinched in the cabin door and pulled herself hand over fist up the sharp slope of the deck toward the life ring mounted beside the cabin door.

Beyond the gunwales, the sea boiled.

"Blake!" She screamed his name until her voice was raw, scanning the water's surface for a mop of dark hair, a flash of pale skin or blue eyes. All she saw was water and menacing beasts circling.

Annabelle groaned and settled dangerously low in the water.

Audrey ripped the life ring from its mount, slid open the cabin door, and groped her way to the steering station. In the bilge, pumps labored.

She tapped the GPS screen. It came to life. She pressed the MOB button, triggering the "man overboard" feature. *Annabelle*'s current GPS location flashed on the screen, burning it into electronic memory.

She grabbed the VHF radio transmitter. "Mayday! Mayday! Vessel *Annabelle* calling. Man overboard. Taking on water. Repeat, *man overboard*—help me! I'm sinking!"

Her whole body trembled, not knowing what to do if they didn't reply. She reached for the phone she thought she had slipped into her jeans back pocket. Gone, like Blake. Gone...

The water had taken him. Soon, it would take her too.

Fear knotted in her chest. Gasping, she repeated her distress call. "Please answer!"

A crackled reply, "Coast Guard calling vessel *Annabelle*. State your location."

Annabelle's bow rose suddenly. Oily water swirled past her legs. She heard a sizzle and a pop. The GPS went blank as did the radio. Then she was tumbling through the aft cabin door and down the steep slope of *Annabelle*'s cockpit.

She landed against the belly of an orca lying in wait where the transom used to be. It wrapped its slippery black fins across her chest and dragged her into the sea.

Water flooded her throat when she opened her mouth to scream.

4

Feathered Distraction

AUDREY WOKE VOMITING SALT water. She heaved until her eyes nearly popped from their sockets. She struggled to catch her breath between fits of coughing up water. Her throat burned and tongue swelled from lingering salt.

A high-pitched ringing filled her head, growing louder and louder with each passing second as if her head was about to explode. She clawed at her temples, tugged on her ears. She wondered if this was what it was like to go crazy. She opened her mouth to scream.

Her ears popped.

The ringing stopped and pressure subsided. She worked her jaw and her fingers. Every joint in her body was stiff and achy, every muscle felt overstretched. But she was grateful. It meant she was alive.

A tangle of braided hair blocked her vision. She pulled it aside and was blinded by the sun. She cradled her face, blinking away sun spots. Her eyes stung from the sudden brightness and salt clinging to her lashes.

What she saw made no sense. She sat on white sand peppered with black shiny granules, legs partially submerged in a turquoise sea. She was soaked through but didn't feel cold. Sweat beaded on her brow and the air was warm and sticky. The water lapping around her legs was as warm as her skin.

She looked around, taking in her new surroundings. A crescent-shaped beach, palm-like trees stretching from a thick jungle toward an electric-blue sea. Glistening black cliffs hemmed in the land at both ends of the beach like the open side of a horseshoe. Ocean swells crashed on their rocky shores and frothed across submerged reefs offshore. A frenzy of seabirds swooped and dived, their screams announcing a bountiful feast. Puffy clouds dotted the sky across an infinite blue ocean, bending with the curvature of the earth. Bird song drifted from a wildly textured jungle butting up to the top of the beach. Fronds clacked in the gentle breeze. A pleasant succulent scent permeated the air. A tropical paradise.

Beyond the jungle were cliffs smothered in green and streaked with dozens of waterfalls. Above the cliffs lightning bloomed within dark clouds that lay atop elevated foothills. Poking above the clouds stood a majestic range of jagged black mountains, dusted with snow. A fast-running river carrying snow-melt cut a swath through the jungle, across the sand, and down to the sea, muddying the clear waters on the right side of the bay.

The air was shockingly clear. No smog or smoke or haze. It was difficult to gauge distances. The mountains could be a hundred miles away, or only a few. The air was so clear that everything reflected intense color; the water, the jungle... The white sand beneath her glowed. The sun burned a rich gold.

The scents and sounds emulating from the jungle were pleasant yet foreign. The vegetation varied in small degrees from anything she had ever seen, as if she had been plucked from the Pacific Northwest and dropped into a world vastly different from the one she called home.

But that would be impossible. Only moments before she—she...

She pondered her situation, her mind racing for an explanation.

This must be a dream.

If it was a dream, it was more intensely real than any dream she'd had before. A dream with acute tactile feel and all five senses running in overdrive. She shivered though the air was hot and humid, the rays of sunlight piercing. Not a dream. It felt *real.*

Her mind reeled. She dipped her fingers in the warm water engulfing her legs, trying to remember the recent events that preceded her waking—or finding her way into this realistic dream—in a very strange and very real place. She remembered an orca pulling her into the Salish Sea, every muscle constricting from the shock of cold water engulfing her, seawater pouring down her throat, and then—

Then she remembered nothing.

Movement beneath the water's surface caught her eye. Dark shadows slithered by. Real or imagined, she felt the sea's liquid tentacles winding tighter around her legs. Her mouth filled with the metallic taste of rising fear and panic. Her vision narrowed. All she saw was water. Water where strange and not-so-nice creatures lurked. She imagined rows of sharp teeth framed in black, a pink gummy smile, and soulless black eyes surging from the depths to steal her from the shore.

Move in harmony!

She scurried back on heels and palms, up the rise of spongy sand, with no intention of stopping until she scaled the cliffs and climbed to the top of the distant mountains, far from the sea.

Audrey gasped when she bumped into something solid.

A black bird larger than an eagle and fierce as a raven stood solidly in her path. It stood firm and fixed her with its iridescent blue-and-white eyes. It thrust its long narrow beak forward, stabbing the tip of her nose with its sharp point. A hair-raising rasp rose from deep in its throat.

She froze, fearing that if she moved, the bird's beak would slip past her nose and stab her in the eye or pluck it out. Neither gave way. The tense standoff ensued for several heart-pounding seconds.

The bird retracted its beak and cocked its head. Its strange eyes sized her up, head to toe.

Something drew its attention in the sand. A pea-sized sand-colored flea hopped between its feet. The bird plucked it from the sand with its sharp beak, tossed it in the air, and swallowed it whole.

More flea-like things materialized from the sand. The bird stomped and fluffed sand with its large talons, riling them up, drawing more of them to the surface. It feasted, ignoring her completely.

Audrey watched, intrigued by the bird's sudden change in demeanor, from fierce to indifferent to feeding frenzy. But most intriguing was the combination of features. Slick-bodied and thick-necked with curved eagle-like talons. A tuft of red feathers rose from its head like an unruly cowlick. A raptor of massive size, towering over her as she sat on the sand. But the most unusual feature was its eyes. White and reflective irises that flickered an iridescent blue with each twitch of its head. Like moonstones embedded in black velvet.

Audrey lifted her hand to assess the tip of her nose, startling the bird. It crouched suddenly, the red feathers atop its head retracted. It looked more like a harmless duck then the fierce bird it first seemed to be. But then it slowly rose to its full height and spread its massive wings. A span of glistening blue-black feathers nearly twice as tall as she, casting a long dark shadow. Its brow furrowed and eyes slitted. A growling rasp rose from its throat.

She cowered, fists protectively guarding her face.

Both froze. Another strange standoff.

The bird screeched, fearsome and deafening, shattering the silence.

Flee!

Audrey leapt to her feet and ran. She cut toward the shoreline where the sand met the sea, hard-packed where her feet could gain better traction. Running to escape the strange bird, running to the next unknown. Running because it was all she could think to do.

Her legs felt heavy and cumbersome and she tripped over her own feet. Her legs flew out from under her. Diving forward she tucked, hit the sand and rolled on her shoulder. Forward momentum brought her to her feet. Without missing a beat she kept running. She easily fell into a rhythm, ignoring the pain where her shoulder struck the sand. She willed her legs to move, one in front of the other. Levitated by sheer will and adrenaline, she gained speed, driving from the pads of her feet, arms and legs scissoring.

She heard the whisk of wing. Looked back. The bird descended; talons aimed for her head.

She dove for the sand, rolled to her side and curled into a tight ball with her back to the sky, hands clasped behind her head, elbows tucked to protect her face and neck. A protective posture, just like her father taught her.

The bird struck from above. Whipping wingtips slipped through her defenses, ripping hair from root and skin from ear. The bird grabbed her arm with its talons, snapped its wings, and yanked it up. Every muscle in her body tensed and she coiled tighter into a ball, resisting the fierce bird. All she could think of was protecting her jugular.

She screamed.

The bird released her arm and rose up, wings whipping like swords slicing air. She rolled onto her back, kicking and punching the air between them wildly. "Go away! Scram! Shoo!"

The bird wobbled as if her words packed solid punches. It swooped to the right, then the left, then fell to the sand with a *whamp*, wings splayed as if it had been shot down by a rifle mid-air. The bird lay on its stomach, silent and unmoving.

Audrey rolled to a squat. Crouched low, she sidestepped toward the stilled bird, fists protectively drawn to her face. She wondered if the bird had broken its neck, if it was still alive.

She poked the bird with a toe.

The bird opened it eyes. They gazed at each other in silence. It rolled to its side, breaking the connection. Its chest rose and fell with a raspy gasp. Defeat?

Audrey stepped back to a safe distance, fists still at guard, in a warrior stance ready to bolt or fight, waiting for the bird to make the next move.

The bird slowly rose to its feet. It wobbled, stumbled forward, taking drunken steps toward the water.

Audrey relaxed her fists to her side, released a ragged breath.

A clicking sound came from the jungle. The bird bolted upright. Its gaze swung toward the sound. Audrey's gaze followed, curious as to what had drawn the bird's attention. She saw nothing but jungle.

The bird burst into a complicated song of lilting tweets peppered with staccato chirps. A long pause, then a drawn-out caw and more chirping. Another long pause as the bird continued to gaze intensely at the greenery of trees in the jungle gently swaying in the breeze. It swung its cool gaze in her direction and nodded, then glanced back to the trees and chirped.

A chill zipped down her spine.

Who is the bird talking to?

The bird approached, gingerly setting one foot in front of the other, head bowed, gaze cast to the sand, like a messenger coming to bear bad news. It stopped just out of reach, looked up. A copper chain with an opaque pale green stone hung around its neck. She hadn't noticed the chain until now.

Someone's pet?

The bird chirped softly, stealing her attention from the stone to its lively blue-and-white gaze. It stepped forward and swiveled its neck, exposing a ring of red feathers underneath. Teasing her to reach out and scratch it.

She had fallen for a trick like this once with a seemingly harmless parrot, the inch-long pale scar on the back of her finger a painful reminder, like the fresh puncture wounds on her arm inflicted by this bird's sharp talons.

She firmly tucked her fingers into a fist at her side. "Not a chance."

The bird lifted its head, as if it understood what she had said but was having none of it, and tried to seduce her once again, brushing the top of its head on the back of her fist.

She crossed her arms, burying fists in pits.

The bird straightened, drew a long slow breath then released it, clearly disappointed. It turned its back to her and took flight, disappearing into the jungle.

Hair rose on her arms. She knew better and cursed herself.

Shit! This place, the bird... merely distractions.

But from what?

The magnitude of her predicament struck full force. Shaking, she scanned her surroundings with fresh eyes, gulping down rising panic.

Where am I? How did I get here? What happened to Blake?

They both ended up in the water. Did he wash up on this same shore?

I knew something was wrong. Why didn't I warn him?

She cast her fear aside and searched through debris washed ashore for clues, flipping over clumps of seaweed, dead palm fronds, chunks of tree bark, broken coral, and various seashells. Some with their last occupants still inside, rotting. She found no garbage, or anything remotely man-made. No backpack, or duffle or life jackets or pieces from *Annabelle's* hull. No sign of Blake. No footprints, except her own.

She gazed up, shading her eyes from the intense brightness of the sun. On the horizon a faint sliver of the moon hung low in the sky. Last night it was three-quarters full.

Everything was wrong. Moon phase off. A turquoise sea so brilliant it hurt to look at it. No logical explanation of how she got here.

She bristled, surveying her surroundings again. Think! Some things appeared familiar, yet not. The fronds on the palm trees were thicker and barbed, the bark white and peeling, exposing smooth red trunks beneath. The black cliffs glittered like cut crystal when the sun struck them just right. A sky brilliantly clear. A huge half-eagle, half-raven with a crown of red feathers. Like one or the other, but not exactly. Most unnerving were its eyes. The chain and the stone. Its conversation with something in the jungle. A pet.

Her heart pounded and scalp prickled, like that moment on *Annabelle*, right before her world exploded.

A troubling thought struck but she crushed it before it took root, and instead focused on the waves crashing on the far shore, lifting and scattering rocks littering the base of the cliffs, clacking and rumbling like distant thunder. The air stirred up pleasant scents coming from the jungle. A frond fell and stabbed the sand beneath a palm tree.

This can't be real. Her mind back-peddled. *I must be dreaming.*

But the way her hands trembled and her stomach knotted she knew it was as real as the friendship bracelet Blake had tied around her wrist.

That troubling thought returned and grated, like a metal fork scraping a steel pan, until she could ignore it no longer.

Maybe this is where you go after you die.

She didn't believe in such things. Dead was dead. Body and soul. Though she questioned if she really knew anything at all.

The bird burst from the jungle and circled. It landed at her feet, hopping and flapping its wings, cawing excitedly. It rose up, dipped a wing, and flew back into the jungle.

A warning? An invitation?

The beach held no answers. Beads of sweat rolled down her cheeks. The sun beat down relentlessly. The shaded jungle emitted a coolness that beckoned.

Follow the bird.

Stepping into the jungle was like stepping into another world, exploding with the chaotic and vibrant song of life, rich with the sweet scent of spring. Birds twittered in the treetops. Bees buzzed and dipped drunkenly among tropical flowers. Iridescent-shelled beetles marched across her path. Giant sword-like ferns stabbed the sky. Thick vines wound up and around tree trucks as wrinkled and gray as an elephant's hide, their bright green and pink leaves indistinguishable from their hosts'. Luscious fruits hung too high to easily pluck. Beams of sunlight cut through the dense canopy, lighting up a swarm of gnats stirred to life by her passing.

Her feet sank into the rich dark soil, shot through with a pale network of micro roots. Her footprints comingled with those of smaller creatures scurrying beneath a sea of sprawling ground cover. She ventured deeper into the jungle searching for the bird, pushing aside ferns intermixed with a variety of exotic flowers. Their cloying scents hung heavy in the air.

She found the bird sitting on a low-hanging tree branch, casually preening its feathers. It stood up once it saw her, then flicked its beak toward a break in the foliage. A game trail like the one she had been following led deeper into jungle.

She drew a deep breath. Took off her coat and tied it around her waist. Deciding against whatever better judgment she could muster.

She felt alive not dead, though she was unsure if she was safe.

But...

There was a quivering sense of curiosity building in her chest. One she could not ignore.

She looked up at the bird. "Promise you won't lead me astray?"

The bird gave a merry chirp before disappearing down the trail.

5

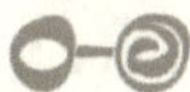

Dead End

THE TRAIL WAS CHECKERED with an array of many animal prints. Some fresh, some old, some cloven with dewclaws, some without. Some with three pointed tapers. Some she didn't recognize at all.

Foliage on either side of the trail was stripped clean of leaves, grasses mowed by herbivore teeth. As curious as she was to continue, she kept her wits sharp and stepped lightly with eyes glued to the dense foliage. A game trail offered easy pickings for hungry predators.

She fell into rhythm with the jungle, growing accustomed to the unique bird songs, the spicy scents wafting from herb-like plants growing in the crooks of forked branches, the spongy feel of loamy soil beneath her feet, the bird with moonstone eyes guiding her way. It gave her something to dwell on other than the event that led to her current plight and the way her salty damp clothes chafed with each step. It felt right to keep moving, seeking an explanation of where she was, and why she was here.

She was certain she was very much alive, although why or how she could not fathom. She distinctly remembered the sensation of drowning. Of water rolling down her throat. The darkness that followed.

And if she was alive, Blake could be too.

The trail rose in elevation. The easy hike became a strenuous climb through the thinning jungle and uneven ground. Soil turned to rock, a dry river bed of it. She squatted and picked up a softball-sized rock. Graphite gray with sides like sandpaper. She smashed it against another at her feet. It cleaved neatly into two halves, the exposed edges sharp as a razor, the new surfaces black and smooth as a glass. By the way the cliffs at the beach glittered in the sunlight, she guessed it to be obsidian from the distant mountains. If true, it was rare but not unusual.

The jungled thickened, the high canopy offering a reprieve from the sun. The trail steepened. Coiled roots sprang from soil between rocks buried and strewn along the trail. She feared twisting an ankle or tripping and falling on a sharp edge of rock. Each step calculated, making agonizingly slow progress. The ever-present bird patiently waited when she fell behind.

The trail intersected a solid wall of obsidian towering overhead. Somewhere to her right in the thick of the jungle was a nearby sound of fast rushing water—the upper portion of the river that ran across the beach from the jungle to the sea. The bird led her in the opposite direction along the base of the cliff to a fracture in its mighty wall. Boulders were serendipitously placed in a zig-zagged stair-step fashion. She scurried up the well-worn path, tiny bits of black glass finding their way inside her shoes. By the time she reached the top she was panting, her neck slick with sweat.

She paused briefly to rest and shake tiny bits of glass out of her shoes, thankful for the thick protective socks she wore.

The jungle canopy spread below like a cool green pond she could easily step into. She memorized the subtle changes in the topography she passed. The cut of the dry river bed in the trees. The rushing river racing for the sea. In her mind she tried to calculate the direct distance from where she stood to the ocean by how long she had been walking. Minus the zigzags, it was a couple of miles at least. She visualized in her mind's eye landmarks along the trail that she had traveled thus far; every turn, every crossing, every slight change in elevation. She quickly mapped an overlay of the trail on the vast space of jungle below. She analyzed the position of the sun. Noted that the ocean lay to the south, the mountains to the north. It was a habit instilled at a young age, just as her mother taught her, and her father after her mother was gone.

Always know where you are, how to find your way back from where you came, the fastest and safest route for escape, he preached.

She gazed at the vast and unending sea spread beyond the beach and black cliffs.

If only I could find my way back to the Salish Sea.

The harrowing reality of her situation swelled, threatening to overwhelm her. She forced down her despair.

Stay in the present. Focus on the bird. Focus on where it's leading you.

Woodlands stood between her and the distant mountains and she felt a noticeable change in climate. The air was less humid and cooler. She untied the coat hanging around her waist and put it on, still damp from her plunge in the Salish Sea. It offered little warmth but the thought of another layer across her shoulders helped to calm her unease.

The forest at this elevation felt more like the island she recently called home. Mild and hospitable. Lacy ferns, waxy-leaved ground covers, and spiky greens grew along the trail. Evergreens and deciduous trees intermingled and towered. Berry-packed shrubs dotted the spaces in between. The scent of sun-baked greenery filled the air like the last days of a warm dry summer in the San Juan Islands, though the plants and trees differed from anything she had seen before. Like being on an undiscovered continent with no idea how she got there. Unsettling.

The trail intersected a fast-running stream. Seeing the water reminded her how parched her tongue felt. She dropped to a knee and splashed cold water on her face. She bent to take a sip but stopped when a flicker of movement caught her eye. The bird waded in the water on the other side, gorging on something wiggling and eel-like it had plucked from the water. It paused to look up at her before swallowing it down in a single gulp. It stomped its feet, flapped its wings, and spun around with glorious pomp, then lifted its tail and pooped. The cloudy plume swirled at its feet before curling its way into the current and dissipating in the clear waters running downstream. Her gaze swung upstream where the rush of water disappeared around a bend. The bird chirped. She suddenly lost her thirst. The bird's message was clear.

Moss-covered rocks dotted a path across the rushing water. Midstream she slipped and her foot dipped into the freezing cold water. Something slithered around her ankle. Not wanting to linger and find out what it was, she bolted to the other side.

The bird hopped along the trail skirting the stream, eyes flickering and merrily chirping after consuming its slimy meal. Audrey's stomach rumbled and she stewed at the injustice of not knowing what the forest might provide that would be safe to eat or drink. She shoved these thoughts aside and focused on the bird and not so much on where it was leading.

Keep moving.

Another trail merged with the one she was following. One recently used by large and heavy animals. Horses, she guessed, based on the shape of their hoof prints. Big hoof prints, and recent. She had to step over a large pile of moist manure, fresh and nose-burningly pungent.

The forest thinned. Sunlight cut through broken rain clouds and slanted in the thinning canopy. Lush grass surrounding the trail glistened with dampness from a recent shower. Steam rose where sunlight reached the ground. A rainbow arched across the sky.

The bird called to her from atop a large boulder that was part of another rocky area rising above the treetops. Eagerly, she scampered up the rocky trail. She stopped to catch her breath halfway to the top on a wide ledge fifty feet above the ground. Thorny sages grew from fissures and cracks in the sharp black rock. She plucked a tuft of thick matted fur snagged by a branch. Dingy-white, course to the touch, with a strong musky scent. She tucked it into her pocket to analyze later and kept climbing, zig-zagging through loose rock and sage.

At the top of the cliff, she breathed in the vista, exhilarating in its natural beauty. The crescent-shaped beach, a gemstone-colored ocean. The blackest of black cliffs extending into the ocean to the east and the west and merging into the mountain range to the north. A giant horseshoe of steep ridges with a wild jungle and cool woodlands trapped in between. The river that cut across the beach, along with a second much smaller one she hadn't noticed before.

She hadn't thought about it before—the cliffs and dual rivers—barriers for someone traveling on foot. For someone deathly afraid of the water.

No contrails marred the sky. No passing ships disturbed the marbled surface of the ocean. No sign of Blake or of another human being.

It started up again, that deep sinking feeling of despair. Curiosity stifled. Hope withered. Reality gripped her heart with an iron fist, refusing to back down no matter how hard she pushed it away. A dead end, nowhere else to go. The sheer stupidity of believing something good was to come from this. Trapped by mountains, rivers, and an endless sea. A nature-forged prison. Lost and alone with no idea as to why, or *where*.

The bird landed at her feet. It cocked its head, staring at the tears tracing her cheeks, at the braid of hair twisted into knots around her fingers.

The bird brushed its head against her thigh and twittered softly.

She squatted until their gaze was even. "Why am I here?" she whispered.

The bird twittered and flicked its head toward a grove of trees with smooth mustard-colored bark and delicate white leaves. Like aspen trees with the colors reversed. Like everything in this place, all mixed up and backwards. The breeze ruffled the treetops and white withered leaves twirled to the ground like snowflakes. It was there that the trail resumed.

Audrey stubbornly continued.

As if sensing her despair, the bird strode beside her with its wing outstretched behind her, gently coaxing her along toward a thundering roar in the distance. Falling leaves brushed past her tears, settled on her shoulders, snagged in tangled strands of wild hair. The white carpet crunched beneath her feet, stirring a rot-sweet scent of autumn.

The roar grew louder with each step.

Dutifully she followed her guide, sensing her tour was nearing its end, bracing for whatever fate awaited.

6

Things Mythical

THE TRAIL ENDED AT a grassy meadow ringed by an evergreen forest. Sunshine cut through a hole in the clouds, lighting a mighty waterfall feeding an emerald-green pond. Thick moss and lacy ferns smothered the surface of rock where mist swirled and hovered in puffy clouds. A stream flowed from the pond, disappearing into the dark recesses of the forest.

The game that made the trail were gathered. She gasped at the magnificence and a startled flock of bright yellow birds took flight, drawing the gaze of several strange creatures. Heart pounding, she dropped to her haunches to hide in the knee-high grass.

She had never seen anything like these creatures before. Horses with a single pointed horn, long and straight and narrowed to a sharp point like the horned head of the mythical unicorn. Not the bubblegum-sweet pink unicorns of childhood myth, but wild and scruffy and frighteningly huge ones that stoked fear in the heart. The youngest stood eighteen hands tall, maybe more. Their gray-and-white coats were caked with dirt and uneven with a new winter's growth coming in or falling out. Their manes and tails were unkempt and matted, like the tuft of hair she found along the trail and had stuck inside her pocket. Wild and untamed.

The alpha broke from the group and charged, barely stopping before crushing her where she squatted, frozen in fear. He rose up and slashed the air with his mighty hooves, landing with terrifying weight. The ground trembled beneath the violence. He pranced back and forth as if held back by an invisible fence, teeth bared, mouth frothing, eyes wild and fiery gold. She crouched lower, cradling her head, wondering if she had made the right decision to cower not flee, fearing how it would feel to die under the foot of such a wild beast.

The alpha stilled and whipped its wild gaze across the meadow to the far forest. There was a brief moment of calm. Then a whinny, a pawing of the ground, a final glance in her direction. Calmly he retreated with a parting snort and the sharp smell of him.

He joined the others gathered in a circle, communing. Ears twitched, matted tails swatted; there was a brief round of neighing and nervous white-eyed glances in her direction. Then they broke from the circle and resumed grazing. Nary a care to her presence.

She rose to her feet ever-slowly, mindful not to raise the alpha's ire. He paid no notice and sidled up next to an equally large mare, nuzzling noses.

Willowy trees lined the pond's edge by the waterfall, their spindly branches swaying in the breeze generated by the wall of falling water. Bright pink lilies and orange berry bushes grew next to a gently sloping beach. Camouflaged by the shadows were miniature black-and-white speckled goats with giraffe-like elongated necks, rearing up on their hind feet to feast on the low-hanging willows.

A trio of heavily-laden fruit trees offered a patch of shade in the center of the meadow. Monkey-faced sloth-like creatures hung from their branches. Long-haired rabbits tucked their bodies into tight balls and rolled around the meadow, randomly stopping to unfurl their floppy ears and limbs and nibble on wildflowers. On the far side of the meadow, giant butterflies with bioluminescent wings flitted among bushes covered by a blanket of flowers bleeding from purple to pink, peach to yellow.

Like the jungle and the forest she had previously passed, the foliage in the meadow was different from anything she had ever seen before. The shape of the leaves, the size of the trunks, the color and texture of the fleshy fruits. Like horses with horned snouts, bunnies that rolled instead of hopping, and glowing butterflies. Parts familiar, yet put together in strange and different ways. Though here it felt natural, cohesive—like pieces of a puzzle that produced a beautiful and balanced ecosystem. One that felt familiar yet looked nothing like the world in which she belonged.

She sidestepped along the edge of the meadow toward the small beach at the pond's edge and away from the horned horses quietly grazing in the grass.

The pond's water was crystal clear and free of algae. The entire bottom was peppered with bright green pebbles flecked with white spots, giving the pond its emerald color. A school of rainbow-sided fish swam against a consistent current running from the falls to the stream cutting a swath through the forest.

She suddenly felt weak and rubbery. From vomiting a gallon of sea water, from the exhausting hike, from the slithering fear coiling in her belly. Her tongue swelled with thirst as she weighed her options. She pinched the skin on the back of her hand. It was slow to bounce back; dehydration already setting in. How long could she hold out?

Drink now or hope to find another source.

Based on the volume of water rushing through the pond and the clarity, she surmised it was heavily diluted and most likely safe to drink. Bordering on desperation, she dropped to her knees and took a sip. The water was shockingly cold and hurt her teeth. Deeply she drank its sweetness till her throat grew numb and her belly was full.

Satiated, she sat back observing the smaller creatures moving around her—vole-like things covered with spines, shimmering gold-shelled snails expelling a trail of steaming red liquid, foot-high stick bugs wandering aimlessly along the branches of the willowy trees. Bat-winged flying things with whip-like spiked tails and bull-frog mouths swooped over the lake, gobbling up smaller flying things, that in turn gobbled up even smaller flying things until all that was left were the ugly bat-winged bullfrog things. The more closely she observed of the little things moving around her, the more alarmed she became.

Ten-legged spiders? Dancing mantis? Migrating lumps of sod?

She startled when a swarm of the bioluminescent-butterfly things appeared out of nowhere and swirled above the pond. Their wings were as big as her hands and painted in a riot of color and abstract shapes and lines to the likes of Kandinsky, Picasso, Pollock. Their black child-like slender bodies had human-like arms and legs, and three fingered hands with opposable thumbs. Their expressive faces had tiny pert noses and lips, and extra-large upwardly slanted eyes, glowing in a multitude of colors like their decorated wings. Their ears were elongated and pointed, and they lacked any form of hair, except for a pair of thread-like spiraled antenna that randomly unfurled and twitched for no apparent reason.

She was mesmerized by the way they frolicked in updrafts generated by the waterfall. One mischievously tried to trick another into swimming through the deadly wall of falling water. Others danced mid-air, giggling and singing songs with their whispery voices and indecipherable lyrics.

One split off from the others and circled around Audrey's head, its bright yellow gaze appraising every inch of her, its pointy fingers tugging at her braid and poking at her clothes, spouting questions in a breathy language she didn't understand.

Curious, she held out her hand. The winged creature readily landed, squatted back on its haunches with its elbows perched on knees and chin propped in cupped palms. One tapered finger tapped its cheek, presumably thinking.

Audrey giggled at the absurdity.

Unicorns and faeries?

The faery-butterfly smiled and winked, as if it had read her mind. It jumped to its feet and flapped its wings, emitting a cloud of dust that swirled around Audrey's head.

She suddenly felt giddy and lightheaded—the world around her blurred and sharpened, stretched and shrunk. The faery-butterfly was zipping around her head, adding more dust to the cloud. Audrey began to hear strange voices, someone giggling. Then she realized that the someone giggling was her, that the finger writing her name in the glowing cloud of dust was attached to her arm, and that arm was attached to her body. A reality she questioned. Was she hallucinating? The faery-butterfly burst through the "A" and each subsequent letter she had drawn. She was surprised by the tears of joy she was shedding when her name fizzled to the ground.

Audrey sneezed. The dust cloud scattered and she drew a fresh breath of air. Her mind cleared and vision sharpened.

The faery-butterfly hovered just out of Audrey's reach, wings ablaze with movement, fists perched on child-like hips, studying her with a coy smile on its face. It turned to the others and whistled, high-pitched and piercingly loud.

Dozens of tiny heads swiveled in response. All at once they darted forward. Dozens of faery-butterfly creatures circled, stabbing their pointy appendages in her direction, whispering to each other in a rapid succession of breathy whistles while their leader silently observed. Dust spilled from their wings and landed at her feet in a circular glowing rainbow.

Audrey laughed, startling the swarm. They fell silent and cowered together in pairs like frightened children. The leader whistled and began waving and pointing. Eyes rolled and tiny mouths frowned before they dispersed to the other side of the meadow.

"Come back!" she screamed, louder than she had expected. Her voice reverberated across the pond, the meadow, and echoed off the cliff.

Chaos ensued. The unicorns reared up and spun in wild circles before fleeing. Rabbits bounced and rolled across the meadow. Giraffe-necked goats darted surprisingly fast into the white-leaved grove from whence she came. Monkey-faced sloths dropped from the trees and, very slowly but deliberately, slunk into the forest. Spiky voles dove into holes and the faery-butterflies slipped into the flowering bushes with their wings wound around their bodies, perfectly camouflaged.

Alone and abandoned, she whispered, "Please, come back."

7

Reprieve

AUDREY HAD NO CHOICE but to embrace the gravity of her situation. Nothing about this world was familiar except for the water she drank from the pond, the sun burning in the sky, and the fact she found herself in an ecologically balanced environment. And in a balanced environment everything was prey to something. Plants to herbivores. Herbivores to carnivores. She dreaded the thought of discovering what kind of predators lurked in the shadows or why the creatures in the meadow were so quick to startle and flee.

She returned to the pond and crouched under the cover of the willowy trees tucked along the shore where she could hide and observe the meadow and watch for movement in the forest.

Her teeth worried the inside of her cheek, her fingers spun the knotted bracelet on her wrist, and worrisome questions swirled: Where am I? How did I get here? Had Blake been rescued? Had Blake made it to shore? Or had Blake... her breath faltered. She simply refused to accept the other possibility.

He's somewhere. Alive. Safe.

She dwelt upon that hopeful thought watching the giant disc of the sun arc across the sky.

Soon, her butt fell asleep, her feet cramped, her skin chafed. She stood up and stretched. She needed to move, to do something other than hide from something that might not exist, waiting for something that might not happen.

She kicked off her shoes and socks, peeled off her coat, wriggled her toes in the soft sandy soil, knelt and took another sip from the icy pond. The dirt felt like dirt, the water tasted like water, cold was cold. These were things she knew for certain. She rolled up her jeans, waded into the water, and lingered there until she could no longer feel her feet.

The black bird circled overhead, dove down, veered, and disappeared behind the waterfall.

Curious, Audrey followed, stepping around the pond's edge, through the ankle-high grass, and onto a flat boulder slick with a sheen of algae. The curtain of water fell from the sky with a deafening roar. Updrafts of mist and the strong smell of sulfur swirled. She followed a footpath that wound around the back side of the waterfall.

It took a moment for her eyes to adjust to the dim lighting. A steaming pool of water was cradled inside an open cave carved into the cliff wall. A beam of sunlight cut along the path she had followed, illuminating rising mist. Moss carpeted the ground at her feet. A riot of shade-loving ferns and vining flowers grew up the cave walls, their sweet scents competing with sulfur.

The bird hopped down a set of rocky steps that disappeared beneath the surface of water and began bathing.

Her salt-encrusted clothes chafed and her scalp itched, to the point she wanted to scream. A dip in the pond was tempting.

She hesitated, stealing a glance back to the path, then to the wall of thundering water, worrying the inside of her cheek. While the cave was well-hidden, she had few options for escape. If the bird hadn't shown her, she never would have guessed it was there. She gazed back to the bird who was joyously splashing in the warm water, feeling a pang of jealousy. She sniffed a noseful of steamy sulfur. Surely it would easily mask her scent should a predator pass by. At least that is what she hoped.

The bird hopped up from the water's edge and burrowed into a bed of moss. Tendrils of steam rose from its glossy feathers. It chirped before burying its beak under its wing. So far the bird had not led her astray and appeared at ease in its current surroundings.

Audrey descended the rocky stairway and dipped a toe. The water was hot but not scalding, and she craved more.

But paranoia rose swift and sure when her father's warning threaded: *Always be aware of where you are, of your fastest and safest route for escape...*

His warning warred with the mantra from her mother. The one that guided her through times of uncertainty and past the wall of fear:

Move in harmony with force of life, flow as water, like stream around rock.

She took another step. Water swirled around her ankles, solid and comforting, then she dropped to her knees. She splashed water on her face and the back of her neck. Steam billowed. It felt good against her skin. Her scalp itched as if a thousand fleas nested. She wanted more and stole a glance toward the far side of the waterfall where sunlight beamed, then to the bird soundly sleeping.

I can do this. Just a quick dunk. In and out. Easy peasy. No harm, no worry.

She dipped her head, but slipped and fell head-first into the water.

She burst to the surface from the shock of it, flailing and gasping, splashing water everywhere. Her scrambling feet found the solid bottom and she stood, neck deep.

The bird glared from its perch above her. A crown of red feathers she hadn't noticed before rose from the top of its head, quivering. It didn't seem too pleased to be disrupted from a pleasant nap.

She gazed from the bird to the surface of the water lapping against her chin. Her heart thundered as unfounded fear reared its ugly head. Fear of the water. Fear of drowning like her mother. Her father tried to rid her of this fear, forcing her to swim in the saltwater pool he had installed. Holding her down beneath the surface until her lungs threatened to suck a watery breath. Therapy, he called it. Abuse, was more the truth. It was her mother's mantra that helped her control her fears, not her father's unorthodox ways. Yet, she endured, to prove to him that she wasn't a coward.

The bird gave her a raspy hiss.

She glared back. "I am not a coward."

It hissed again, tucked its crown of red feathers along its neck and stuck its beak under its wing, its strange blue-and-white eyes locked on hers in a fiery gaze. It reminded her of her father. The disapproving scowl, a tsk, and words unspoken but message clear in his icy gaze:

Yes you are.

I. Am. Not. A. Coward.

All worked up over the kerfuffle, she stripped to her bra and underwear. She gave her salty clothes a good dunking, then rolled them tight and squeezed as much water as possible out of them. Then she chucked them over the bird toward the opening of the cave where the sun pierced through. She would deal with them later.

She found a well-placed perch opposite the stairs where she could sit chest deep in the hot water with her gaze locked on the path and the jungle beyond. Her heart settled and skin prickled from the heat. Tiny bubbles rose from the pebbles below her feet, tickling her toes and rising to the surface of the water like freshly poured champagne in a tapered flute.

The bird resumed its nap and she began to relax.

She released her braid and finger-combed waves of long dark hair, then re-braided it and tied it atop her head in a tight knot.

She soaked until her face was flush from the heat and her fingers turned to prunes.

Audrey quietly slipped from the water, using care not to disturb the bird. She tiptoed to where she had tossed her clothes and laid them across a low-lying bush cast in sunlight, beyond the waterfall. Then she tiptoed back and curled up on the moss next to the sleeping bird.

There she lay cocooned by the warm steam filling the cave, a welcoming womb for the weary.

Exhaustion steamrolled.

8

Thing In The Shadows

AUDREY WOKE WITH A start. The bird was no longer sleeping beside her. A faint imprint in the moss was the only clue it had been there. The cave was much darker than before. Her skin was dry and hair mildly damp. She had no idea how long she had been sleeping, or the time of day. What she knew for certain was that it would be dark soon.

She stood, feeling the sudden need to hurry. She stepped over to the low-lying bush where she had laid her clothes to dry. They were gone. She glanced around the cave. The bird was gone too.

Wearing only her bra and underwear she felt vulnerable. Not that a layer of cotton would help protect her from a dangerous beast or a heavy night chill. Cautiously she emerged from the cave and peeked around the waterfall. The sun was much lower in the sky, its late afternoon rays brushing the tops of the trees.

Suspecting a critter stole her clothes to use as a nest, she searched the immediate area around the edge of the waterfall and along the shore of the pond for tracks, lifting up ground covers, rummaging through bushes. She thought of the faery-butterflies, that maybe they had pulled a trick. But the faery-butterflies were on the far side of the meadow, wings aglow and nestled in the trees.

Their whispery voices floated across the water, singing a joyful song in their strange language.

There was a subtle shift of the breeze and she caught a whiff of wood smoke. Heard the crackle of fire.

A flattened path in the grass led to a clearing near the forest where a small fire burned within a circle of black rocks. Her clothes hung next to the flames, draped across a vine strung between two stakes buried in the ground.

Goose bumps rushed up her arms. The bird. The chain around its neck. Her earlier thought remembered.

Someone's pet!

She fell to the ground, tight lipped, breathing through her nose, trying to not make a sound. She scanned the meadow, the depths of the jungle. No one. She crawled across the flattened path like a lizard, belly skimming earth, hidden as best as she could in the ankle-high grass.

She paused at the edge of the clearing, the fire a mere body length away. She dropped lower, eyes gazing over blades of grass. Another scan. Nothing, no one. All clear.

She lurched, body crouched, toward her clothes hanging by the fire, grabbed a pant leg and yanked. The vine snapped. Her clothes fell to the ground with a *thwump*!

She rolled to her back. Grit bit into her skin. Her hands shook as she pulled on her jeans. Her shirt sleeve lay in the fire and began to smolder. She grabbed it before it caught.

A twig snapped.

She froze, then said, "Who's there?"

Silence.

She hugged her shirt across her chest and rolled to her knees. "Who's there?" she asked more forcefully.

Silence.

"Please answer me! I mean no harm."

Silence.

The breeze shifted; she caught a whiff of something cooking over the fire. In her haste to retrieve her clothes, she failed to notice the pile of wood, or the log perfectly positioned for sitting upon, set beside the fire. Enough wood to burn for hours and a handy place to sit. She was stirred by hunger and the taunting fragrance. She crawled low to the ground toward the fire.

Lying beside a bed of coals, steam rose from a vent in a pouch woven from wide-bladed leaves. The sweet scent of poached fish filled her nostrils. On the ground next to the fire was a platter carved from a slab of tree bark, with a conch shell stuck upright into the dirt. It was filled with a pink liquid.

Her mouth watered and heart pounded. She was starving and vulnerable. Before her was the perfect distraction for an attack. Maybe it wasn't a distraction and was just someone else's dinner. Someone who might not think kindly of her if she stole it.

A someone who took my clothes and hung them to dry...

The top of her head prickled, that same sensation she felt on the beach when the bird was gazing at something in the jungle. That distinct feeling of being watched by another intelligent being.

She slipped on her shirt and buttoned it up, all the while scanning the meadow, the pond, the forest. Her gaze locked on a break in the trees between the pond and the fire where a path in the grass had been flattened. A chill washed over her. She thought she saw something peculiar.

Something in the shadows.

She closed her eyes, willing her heart to calm, drawing slow, deep breaths. She stood with her hands loosely fisted at her sides. She hoped whoever was hiding in the trees couldn't see that they were shaking.

She spoke with purpose, "I know you're there! You have nothing to—"

She saw a flicker of movement and gasped. The mottled skin of a tree trunk shifted, brownish spots rearranging on the white surface, leafy shadows stirred by the breeze lagging behind and out of sync, like a heat wave, rippling the air. She blinked in disbelief. She could swear the outline of the apparition matched the shape of a human body, standing from a crouched position.

Everything has a scientifically logical explanation—eyes play tricks—a stress-induced ocular migraine for instance—and stressed I am...

Eye tricks aside, she realized she was an invader in someone else's camp, bathing in their hot spring, salivating over their food. Regardless of what she thought she saw, she thought it best to leave, and quickly.

The trailhead from whence she came was not far. She reached for one of the stakes next to the fire and yanked it free from the dirt, eyes glued to the trees. Someone had taken great care to whittle away the bark and hone the tip into a sharp point. A spear. A useful weapon she knew how to use with deadly accuracy thanks to dear-old-dad.

She gripped the spear with both hands against her chest and slowly stepped back, eyes glued to the break in the trees where the air intermittently rippled as if someone or something was fidgeting.

Stress. Ocular migraine. No other explanation.

Peachy.

She paused briefly by the pond where she left her shoes and socks. She slipped them on, hugging the spear to her chest with her knees as she tied them. She grabbed her coat, slipped it on one arm at a time, spear held firmly in the other. She glued her gaze where she last saw the rippling air by the forest as she sidestepped across the meadow to the trailhead, spear held at guard against her chest.

Once she reached the forest of white-leafed trees she turned and ran.

9

Brown-Eyed Girl

Sinto crouched in the shadow of a mukai tree, gleefully watching his guest discover her coverings hung to dry and the meal he left for her on the fire.

He was confident she had not yet seen him: while conversing with his companion, Rave, on the beach; following her as she journeyed to this safe place; observing her reaction to the docile creatures gathering in the meadow.

Like a chameleon in the jungle or a cephalopod in the sea he could change his appearance to reflect the world surrounding him—color, texture, movement—like the pocked white surface of the tree he leaned against, the leaf-shaped shadows dancing at his feet.

His heart leaped when she called to him. He had eagerly stood up to greet her but came to a sudden halt from the harsh glare she cast in his direction when she took the stake, carefully crafted to help dry her coverings on the vine, and held it as a weapon.

He held his camouflage fast in place, watching for clues of intention in her dark features; face of soft brown skin, the long dark braid springing with untamed waves knotted atop her head, and warm brown eyes like the shell of the ku'uah nut he nervously worked in the palm of his hand.

Her body had filled out and her face had pleasantly matured from the first time he had met her.

But the menacing gaze in her eyes startled.

Is this the same girl I once knew?

Audrey. He never forgot her name. The girl who would not harm a spider even if it was crawling up her leg. That same girl was now casting that menacing gaze in his direction.

He gleaned from her body language, the sound of her pounding heart his acutely sensitive ears could hear, and the bright orange flair of her aura that she was afraid. He disturbingly concluded, by the way she held the stake honed to a sharp point, that she knew how to use it as a weapon, and by the look in her eye, would not hesitate to draw blood.

Not the girl he remembered.

Puzzled, he sniffed the air, capturing the lingering scent of her. Sweet and spicy, an indescribable mixture different from anything he had ever encountered in nature. A scent uniquely her own. Honey and cinnamon and peaches.

He had nearly dropped his camouflage and chased after her when she started her determined scamper across the meadow. Then she ran off without eating the fish he had caught and cooked for her. Did she not know it was a gift?

Other than Rave's blunder on the beach where he mistakenly attacked her, everything he had asked of Rave afterward had proceeded as they planned. She found the fresh pond of water, the cave behind the waterfall, the warm soaking pool. She even laid out her cleaned coverings for him to hang by the fire to dry.

He knew she must be weak with hunger. He certainly was, having spent every moment observing her every movement, anticipating her needs, preparing for the next step, waiting for the right moment to make a proper reintroduction.

And now?

His carefully laid plan had completely unraveled.

Sinto followed Audrey at a discrete distance as she picked her way back to the beach, remaining camouflaged to fade into his surroundings. Not necessarily by choice but because revealing himself now might be quite a shock.

Sinto was in his natural form unencumbered by material coverings. The Merahvu had no physical need for such coverings. Beneath his skin was a layer of insulation, to provide warmth or cooling depending on the environment, wet or dry. Coverings among his people were used as a form of ornamentation; as representative of one's tribe or to show off a recent kill, and, on special occasions, coverings were worn for entertainment. Such coverings were more common where great numbers of Merahvu gathered such as in their cities, or when the leaders of the three tribes of the Merahvu formally met. And most certainly, coverings were a requirement whenever the Merahvu ventured into the Sapiens' world because of some slight differences in their anatomy that Sapiens might find alarming. There they wore coverings common in the Sapien world so they could easily assimilate, coverings like those Audrey wore.

Sinto relished the opportunity to shed coverings whenever he ventured in his native lands, like here on Merluma. Because of that he had forgotten to retrieve his animal skins in his haste to follow her to the meadow from the beach, and again, to retrieve a second set in his haste to chase after her when she fled the meadow.

He could only presume that a naked male chasing her through the forest might be misunderstood as aggressive, and she would use that weapon comfortably held in her hands before he had the chance to explain why he was chasing after her.

Entrenched in these thoughts, he had not noticed that his guest had stopped walking. He had just hopped atop a large log lying across the trail. If he had continued down the other side he would have run straight into her. Instead he froze atop the rotting log with one foot dangling in the air.

She turned and took a tentative step toward him, eyes wide and darting to and fro, from the air above his head to the gap below his dangling foot. Each time her gaze passed over him, it felt as if he had been stung by a bee because of her probing intensity.

She passed the stake to one hand and slipped gracefully over the log to the other side, her head passing a mere inch from his dangling toes. She took two steps back up the trail toward the meadow, stopped, and turned abruptly.

Tentatively, she leaped onto the log and stood up facing him, the rapid pulse of her heartbeat visible on that soft spot of her neck. Her gaze swept around him, up down, left, right—everywhere but directly in front of her, everywhere but at *him*.

She gripped the stake he had painstakingly striped of bark and sharpened to a fine point, as if readying to strike at any moment.

The air filled with the acrid scent of her fear, and her aura danced jagged and hostile red. She drew a ragged breath, held it, pinched her eyes shut, then slowly opened them, her gaze locked on his chest where his heart thumped loudly. Slowly her gaze traveled from his chest, up to his neck, across the slits in the side of his throat, over the curve of his chin, up the plane of his nose. Her brow furrowed when her gaze settled on his camouflaged eyes.

A mad itch crawled up the inside of his nostril. He dared not scratch. His eyes burned from not blinking. He dared not blink.

She bent, studying the place where his foot dangled, craned her head left, then right, as if trying see what was behind his foot. Only she was not looking at things behind it. She was looking *at it*. He was confident in what she would see—trees, succulent leaves, sticks and twigs—an exact rendition of the jungle, adjusted to match her perspective and curled around the curves of his body. Many years of evolutionary refinement were on his side.

Calm, he told himself, *she cannot see me.*

His standing leg cramped. He buried his toes into the moss and rotting wood of the log to better steady himself. He nearly flinched when she straightened suddenly, breathing harder with her gaze locked on his chest. He held his breath, fearing the slightest amount of movement would cause his disguise to flicker.

Had it happened already?

She crouched with the stake's tip angled toward his chest, coiling like a snake readying to strike.

His merlux charged. An innate defense mechanism. She was cast as a lethal threat to his reptilian brain. An evolutionary refinement that at this moment was *not* working in his favor since his common-sense brain and reptilian brain rarely interacted, and when they did, they usually disagreed.

Electricity coiled in the merlux nestled beneath his heart and charged flueox flooded his bloodstream, spreading to the receptacles rising to the surface of his skin, electrifying every inch of it. The process of which secreted the acrid scent of danger meant to warn whatever was threatening his reptilian brain to back off and immediately.

But that was not what she did.

Her brows knitted into a confused dark line. She leaned closer, sniffing the air, angling her ear closer to his chest where his merlux crackled and buzzed within. She leaned back with a gasp. She lowered her weapon and reached for his electrified chest.

His eyes locked on her outstretched fingers. Frozen by panic, he was helpless to stop her.

Rave dove from above and clipped her hand with his sharp talons.

She fell off the log and rolled to the ground. Sinto's cramped leg buckled and he fell beside her, his skin a quick-shifting montage of leaves, moss, dirt. While what she saw he could control, what she heard was another matter. Twigs snapped and leaves crunched under his sudden weight.

She scurried backwards and away from where he lay, back slamming into a tree trunk. Her gaze swung to see what had stopped her, then swung back in his direction. Their eyes locked. Electricity burned through his irises and for a brief second revealed their true green color. Her mouth gaped and eyes widened in bewilderment. She grabbed the stake, jumped to her feet, and bolted down the trail toward the beach, her footfalls quiet as a panther's.

"*Rave, follow her!*" he silently commanded his trusty Scout.

Rave took to wing and chased after her.

Sinto collapsed with his back propped against the rotting log, gasping. He stifled a scream, then punched the hollow below his sternum where his merlux sparked and sputtered before settling and going back to sleep.

If it wasn't for Rave...

How close he came to shocking her!

And it wasn't the first time.

He was perplexed. His merlux never misfired. Except once ten years ago, when he first met her. She was playing alone in the sand on a beach. He had been curious about the girl he saw while hiding in the shallow water offshore. It took time to muster the courage, but eventually he did and approached her, rendering a pair of tattooed nipples on his chest—another feature of his camouflaging ability—and wearing a stolen pair of swim coverings, confident she would not see him as different.

He summoned the memory of their first encounter, one he played over many times in the past ten years. Of meeting the brown-eyed girl and the uncontrollable misfire of his merlux. It was happening all over again. A memory as fresh today as it was then reeled in his mind, searching for clues as to why...

~ ~ ~

The dark-featured Sapien girl intently focuses on a creation she is forming in wet sand. She must not have heard him approach. She startles when she sees him, her mouth forming a perfect O. A strand of hair from her braided hair snakes along the curve of her neck. The temptation to tuck it back from where it escaped fevers. He bends to his knee, reaches to point out a part of her sand creation he particularly likes. Before a word slips from his mouth she grabs him around the wrist.

"Stop! What are you doing?" Her eyes sweep across the ragged swim shorts he wears. Her brow crinkles. "Who are you?"

His gaze falls to her dark sandy fingers clamped around his wrist. His tongue feels like lead. He couldn't think of a logical answer to such an open-ended question. What part of "who" could he tell her without getting into trouble? He merely stares back tongue-tied and mute.

"Tell me your name," she demands.

"Sinto," he finally says. "My name is Sinto. Please, let go of my wrist." He tugs against her grip. She squeezes tighter. His merlux fires, provoked by her stubborn and firm grasp of his arm.

"Where did you come from?"

"Me?"

"What are you doing here?"

"Doing?"

His reptilian brain takes over, driving his merlux to defend against the girl who will not let go. His thoughts scramble, words slip from his reasoning mind's grasp. All he hears are nonsensical questions. Doubt fills him. Why did he approach her? What did he want to accomplish?

Flee! Flee before I kill her!

He tugs against her grip.

She holds fast.

"Answer me," she says firmly.

Flueox rushes through his bloodstream like a fast-running tide; the receptors on the surface of his skin engage. His eyes blaze with electrical fire in warning. The air crackles and blooms with a warning scent. The soft downy hair on her arms rise to the sky; the loose strands escaping her braid follow.

She gasps. "What is that smell?" Eyes dart to the hair standing on end. "What's happening?"

He knows all too well. He is about to shock an innocent Sapien girl. How could he possibly explain? He doesn't know why his merlux has gone crazy! He can't control it. Can't stop it. But he must!

He thinks of his younger sister, the way she teases him, launching stinging bolts of fire from her eyes at his chest. She knows how to channel it to her eyes and frequently uses Sinto for target practice. Every time he tried to get her back, she laughed at his clumsiness, called him a neophyte. She laughed harder when he asked her what a neophyte meant.

Determined and frightened, he wrangles control over the current looping through his bloodstream and rising to the surface of his skin and imagines it racing from his skin receptors to his eyes. There is a second of uncertainty—what if I fail and strike her defenseless fingers? Would she die instantly or would she slowly burn from the inside out?

He gazes upward, summoning all of the energy roiling inside, and imagines it escaping in one giant bolt through his eyes. He looks up to the sky.

A crackle and a snap. He is momentarily blinded.

She gasps and releases his wrist. "How did you do that?"

"Do? What?" Panting, he jumps back, far from her reach. His knees threaten to buckle.

"Flash your eyes!"

"My eyes?"

"A bright green light exploded into the sky." She points to his face. "It came from your eyes and they're—they're still glowing bright green."

"It is a secret. I—I have to go."

"No! Come back! I want to be your friend. Tell me your secret!"

"Another day, I promise!"

~ ~ ~

...he sighed once the snippet of that memory played to the end, recalling the days that followed.

Sinto did come back the next day, and the day after that. He learned her name was Audrey, born in the same year as him. She introduced him to her Pacific island home. They made mermaid and dolphin creations in the sand, hiked through the jungle collecting bugs and climbing trees, lingered for hours observing the many birds that nested there. They swam among coral heads chasing fish, and when the sun reached its zenith in the sky, they huddled in the shade of a palm tree sloping over the beach while she read him stories from a thing made of paper that she called a book. And every time they parted it was with the promise to meet again. Both saying, "Salamora."

Their brief friendship lasted the course of a full moon's cycle. They never spoke of the day his eyes shot bolts of green fire that fizzled in the sky. She never touched him again, though she tried. Whenever she reached out for his hand he always pulled away afraid he would shock her. An unspoken understanding formed between them.

He never told her his secret. He never got the chance. She was Sapien, he was Merahvu. A forbidden friendship cut short by tragic circumstance.

After that, he never saw her again until today.

Sinto opened his eyes and dug his fingers into the damp soil where he sat, breathing the scent of the forest. He felt weak and wrung out from their nearly fatal encounter, and revisiting the past memory of when they first met, remembering his promise.

One he intended to keep, now, ten years later.

He stood up and calculated the time remaining here on Merluma before he had to return her to Earth. He calculated several hours of daylight remained there, which meant he had the same number of days here before someone would notice her missing.

He ran toward the beach, limping from the lingering cramp in his leg.

10

One-Who-Clicks

By the time Audrey returned to the beach, the sun hovered low over the sea, a bright ball of orange fire readying to slip below the horizon.

She paced the shoreline where the sea lay flat and reflective, masking whatever creatures lay beneath. She chewed her nails to the quick, stealing nervous glances toward the jungle, reflecting on what just happened as she raced back from the meadow.

She was certain of what she saw, once in the meadow and again in the woodlands on her trek back to the beach. A ripple in the air the size and shape of a human, camouflaged to look like the jungle.

The gash on her hand finally stopped bleeding; beads of congealed blood speckled the skin. She had the distinct feeling the bird had saved her from harm. But saved her from what?

The thing in the shadows.

She jumped when something brushed against her.

It was the bird with her coat held in its beak. A trail of smooth sand tracked from the place she had stripped it off once she reached the beach, sweating and gasping for breath.

She knelt and took her coat from the bird's beak. "I suppose this means I should trust you. Thank you for…" She raised her hand. "Earlier."

She wanted to ask, if only she could: *What was it? What does it want? Is there more than one?*

The bird merely chirped and lay its head against her leg.

She scratched its neck with her fingers, warming up to their odd companionship.

The sun kissed the horizon, molten fire smeared across a cloud-layered sky. A breathtaking sight. It was what came next that terrified. It would be dark soon.

The air was rapidly cooling. She slipped on her coat and zipped it up to her chin. Stiff with lingering salt but thankfully it had dried; she was going to need it. The mountains and their snow-tipped peaks loomed, seemingly much closer than before.

Heavy hearted, she sat with her knees tucked to her chest, fingering the bracelet Blake had tied around her wrist. The fact she'd seen nothing to indicate his presence in this strange place sank any hope of finding him alive and well, deepening her growing despair.

The bird leaned against her shoulder. Together they watched the sun slip into the sea.

"What should I call you?"

The bird cocked its head, flashing its blue-and-white eyes.

"Your eyes remind me of a moonstone."

The bird chirped.

She smiled. "It's settled then, I'll call you *Moonstone*."

Moonstone cawed softly in approval.

She raised a curious brow. "Male or female?"

Moonstone cocked his wings and fluffed his feathers. A mohawk of red feathers rose from his head. Then, he pompously stomped about like a king surveying his kingdom.

She laughed. "*Clearly* male." She was intrigued that the bird seemed to understand her questions. Her gaze fell to the chain around his neck. She poked the pale-green stone dangling from the copper links. "Who gave this to you?"

Moonstone flicked his beak toward the jungle. Her gazed followed.

Wood smoke wafted from the greenery. She stood up for a closer look. The flames from a contained fire cut through the trees—a fire that wasn't there earlier.

She looked at Moonstone, then back at the fire lighting the sand at the top of the beach. "The thing in the shadows... is that your *master*?"

Moonstone cawed and took flight toward the fire. Audrey followed, scanning the shadows for movement or rippling air.

A crackling fire burned within a ring of black rocks. Firelight glinted along their smooth glass edges, sparkling like the cliffs she had climbed earlier and the cliffs hemming the beach. Pure obsidian.

Next to the pit was a pile of wood in various lengths and sizes, ends splintered. Scavenged, not cut with hatchet or saw. Plenty to keep the fire going for hours.

Moonstone circled, stirring smoke with his wings, stealing her attention from the flames. He swooped and landed on top of a shelter fabricated from a circle of bent saplings, forming a dome shelter covered by woven fronds to protect from weather and offer privacy. A small opening faced the ocean, capturing the briny breeze. Within was a bed of ferns covered with a woven mat and a thick, woolly black hide.

The wood stacked by the fire, the shelter, clearly planned. But for what reason?

The top of her head prickled. She spun on her heel. Saw no one or nothing peculiar. She looked up. Braided vines hung from a ceiling of greenery lit by the fire and dripping with fragrant flowers. One of the vines swayed gently, maybe from heat waves rising from the fire. Maybe something else.

Her heart hammered. "Hello?"

Her greeting was answered by a myriad of nocturnal creatures awakening in the jungle.

Darkness fell quickly and she added more wood to the fire. Her tongue swelled with thirst and stomach rumbled with hunger. She regretted not doing something about it while it was still light. Resigned, she sat, gazing into the flames, poking the fire with a stick. Mesmerized, her eyes slid shut and head dipped.

She woke with a start. The fire had dwindled to a bed of glowing coals. The stick she had held in her hand was a line of ash that nearly reached her fingers. She tossed the remainder into the fire and rubbed the crick in her neck. She stood to stretch. Her leg buckled, asleep from where she had been sitting on it.

The stars were out in full glory and she wandered a little way onto the beach to get a better look. She looked up. Spiky fronds from a nearby tree were stamped against the glittering sky. The quarter-moon hung across from the Milky Way. Its light danced along gentle swells rolling past the froth line of offshore reefs. The sound of rushing water from the river emptying into the bay permeated the darkness, reminding her of her thirst.

She debated venturing onto the beach in the dark for a chance to steal a drink from the river. Both prospects were risky. The question of potential predators lingered in her mind.

She decided to wait until morning and returned to stoke the fire. Minutes passed and it seemed to grow even darker.

She heard a sound different from the cacophony coming from the jungle.

There it was again. Coming from the beach.

Click-click-click. Pause. Click.

The sound was clear and consistent like that of a critter or a bird calling a mate, but there was something very distinct about it. Like a tongue striking the roof of a mouth.

A human mouth.

Click-click-click. Pause. Click.

Click-click-click. Pause. Click.

Silence.

She clicked three times.

A lone response. *Click.*

She drew a sudden breath, clicked three times again.

Again, in response. *Click.*

She ran onto the beach, aglow from the moon and the stars. She clicked three times.

Silence.

She did it again.

A single click came from the direction of the fire. Cautiously she returned, scanning for any kind of movement, saw none. But found a hollowed hunk of tree bark piled with various fruits—none of which she recognized—as well as strips of dried seaweed and a large abalone-like shell filled with chunks of white fish floating in creamy liquid.

Beside the platter were three conchs, stuck in the ground pointy end down just like by that first fire in the meadow. Two were filled with water, the third a pink liquid. She grabbed a water and drank greedily, the liquid spilling down her chin to her chest until it was drained completely. The empty conch fell from her fingers as she gasped for air.

The sand at her feet had been wiped smooth. Whoever left the meal had used care to cover their tracks. She tried not to imagine why.

Spinning, she shouted, "Who are you?"

From the direction of the water came a single click.

She ran once more onto the beach, a flawless expanse of white sand bathed in moonlight except for a darkened spot she hadn't notice before.

She drew closer. It wasn't a rock or flotsam or anything solid. Just a muted patch of sand. Like the patch of sand extending from her feet. A shadow.

She clicked three times.

A soft click came from the shadow.

The air wavered and the shadow shifted. She was tempted to reach out and touch it, but took a step back. The scratches on her hand were an itchy reminder of Moonstone's earlier warning.

The shadow began moving toward the water and faded into the shoreline. Messily scattered sand was left in its wake, as if someone was trying to cover their footprints, or they dragged their feet with each footstep.

She looked closer. Whoever it was had missed one. A perfect specimen. A very large and very wide human footprint. She placed her foot inside it. Being tall she had larger than normal feet for a woman, but the foot that made the print was three inches longer and half again as wide.

She knew she should be frightened but came to believe that whoever it was had no intention of harming her.

She retreated toward the fire, putting all that she had observed together. Whoever it was must have the ability to camouflage, and quite perfectly. Based on the shape of the shifting air and the shadow on the beach they were taller and a little fuller than she was. They had huge feet with a heel and five toes, clearly human. She scratched her head confused. A human that can *camouflage*?

She wondered if they understood English. Moonstone clearly had understood her questions which meant that whoever it was must understand her. Maybe they were unable to speak. A mute? Maybe the clicking sound was a form of another language or the only possible way of expressing themselves. A mute with a tongue?

What should I call this discovery?

Hard to know without visual observation. She could only draw a conclusion by the footprint, the shape of wavering air, and by the way they attempted to communicate...

Ah ha! One-who-clicks!

Moonstone was clearly the one-who-clicks' pet. From her observation earlier, they clearly have a unique way of communicating, not just simple commands, but what seemed to be long drawn-out *discussions*. A form of silent communication.

Telepathy? If that was the only form of communication possible with the one-who-clicks it would be a lonely conversation.

She stooped to pick up the platter. Paused when her gaze fell upon the conch shell filled with a pink liquid. She took a sip and winced. Something fermented and very strong. She tasted it again. It was sweet and packed a punch.

Despite feeling unnerved about the elusive manner of the one-who-clicks, and Moonstone's earlier warning when she tried to touch whoever it was, and the fact that she was starved, she wolfed down the food. The fish was sweet and tender, the fruit exotic and juicy.

After finishing the last bite, she stole off to find a bush to take care of some business, then retreated to her shelter with the water and pink liquid in hand.

Tempting as it was, she decided not to drink any more of the pink liquid and set it aside. Best to keep her wits sharp. Besides, she had an idea; one that might flush the one-who-clicks out of hiding.

Two can play this game.

Audrey worked under the cloak of darkness, carefully removing the fronds along the back wall of the shelter until it was wide enough for her to slip through. It wasn't the first time she had sneaked out in the middle of the night and knew how to fool anyone into thinking she was tucked into her bed, soundly sleeping. She mounded up sand and ferns to look like the shape of her body. Then fluffed the wooly hide's fur for extra loft. Made a quick examination of her work.

Perfect.

She grabbed the conch containing water and quietly slipped out into the darkness, wove the shelter's fronds back in place, and carefully smoothed the sand to hide her footprints. She had scoped out a place to hide in the jungle while peeing before going to bed. A place where she could spy on the entire campsite. She would hide as long as it took, anticipating that the one-who-clicks would be curious and come forward first thing in the morning. Maybe to check on her, maybe to light the fire...

She waited, spine pressed against the smooth trunk of a tree amongst soft ferns. Knees bent, feet wide. Coat zipped to her chin, braid tucked inside, hood over her head. She set the conch of water in the sand beside her for later.

She shivered in the chill air. She planned to nap lightly, tucked behind the bushy foliage. The cool air would help. She had done it before, as her father insisted as an extension of her martial arts training—like soldiers in the military, stealing whatever slivers of sleep they could afford amidst battle. What for, she had questioned at the time. Now she was thankful.

She laid her hands by her side and closed her eyes, imagining herself floating, relaxing every part of her body starting with her toes and working her way up to the top of her head. She inhaled deeply and slowly. The sound of air rushing in and out of her lungs was a soothing lullaby.

Sleep came fast but not for long.

She was abruptly woken by a flash of lightning and crash of thunder, heralding the first of many thunderstorms that rolled through during the night. Her perfect hiding place became a puddle. She crawled in the dark, seeking higher ground. Damp and shivering, she slept fitfully, curled around a tree trunk, out of the worst of the tree's drip line. By the third deluge, she nearly crawled back to the shelter.

But she held firm, gritted her teeth, and rolled to the other side.

11

Courage Summoned

Sinto slept restlessly and woke long before dawn.

Why had he not shown himself to her when he had the chance last night on the beach? He had made contact, though not the way he had planned, but by the simple act of clicking. It was a fine start. He had felt her unease fade, observed her aura softening to a warm yellowish glow. She had been receptive and ready. He could have dropped his camouflage there and then and introduced himself like a proper human.

Instead he panicked, tongue-tied, with his merlux abuzz in his chest, pumping flueox through his bloodstream. Electrically charged and armed to kill. He wanted to murder his reptilian brain.

Throughout the night he fumed. He could tame wild creatures and command the sea to do his bidding, but he could not summon his tongue or control the erratic misfiring of his merlux whenever she was near.

She is a harmless Sapien girl I once knew! What have I to fear?

He ground his teeth in frustration. It was not his lack of coverings that gave him pause. Although it might have been an untimely distraction, and there would have been much to explain, along with everything else, all at once. His mind boggled at why he had not thought of these compounding complications. No wonder his tongue twisted into a knot. He struggled to find the right words, to put the tale he hoped to tell into a relatable and clear story.

One thing he remembered quite clearly about Audrey was the way she demanded answers to her seemingly random questions. Surely she would demand to know why she was here, first and foremost. The answer to which was complicated and requiring proper context to make sense. And, most importantly, he wished to avoid a nasty confrontation.

And once he spun his story, what if she didn't believe him? What if she refused to truly listen?

Do I hold her against her will until I can make her see reason?

What if she runs away screaming once I reveal where she is and what I am?

Maybe it would be better if I waited, gave her more time to settle...

Why am I making excuses!

He knew exactly why. The singular reason for all of his ridiculous bumbling.

What if she doesn't remember me?

In the end, it was the memory of a wise lecture from his mentor, Wantemo, one he gave Sinto the day he entered adulthood, that snapped him from his stupor: *Once a man you may feel things, newly stirred emotions that might be difficult to control. The boy acts on emotion. The man channels his emotion, acts on instinct and wisdom, both learned and intertwined with wisdom and experience passed down through blood and bone from his ancestors.*

He was not a boy. Time to act like the man he was.

In the darkness, he crept to the shelter he had made for her and peeked inside. The animal skin was heaped into an oblong ball. He heard not a peep. He imaged her soundly sleeping inside and smiled. Finally, something was going as he had planned.

So he crept into the jungle to find a sweet treat to present to her upon rising.

Electrified flueox coursed through his veins, lighting his irises and casting a pale green path at his feet to a tree with ripened fruit. Drifting down from the lacy foliage of the mangeleno tree was the soft suckling sound of busheetails feasting on the exotic fruit.

The ground at his feet was peppered with mangelenos in various stages of ripeness, many marred by busheetail teeth and bruises from a long fall. Not a one was acceptable for his Sapien guest.

He dimmed his eyes and gazed up. The suckling sounds abated and dozens of beady red eyes set in round white faces turned in his direction. The mangeleno tree was impossible for a man or large beast to scale because of its smooth white trunk and sky-high branches. A tree whose fruit was fiercely guarded by the busheetails. The only way to obtain the best fruit was to negotiate. Knowing this, Sinto came prepared.

He held out a handful of shelled peakle nuts.

A young female was tempted, swinging back and forth among the branches, uncertain. Peakle nuts were another favorite of the busheetails, unshelled even better. Sinto waited patiently, certain if the young female did not move quick, another would soon take interest.

She accepted his offer, slipped down the smooth white trunk and leaped to the ground at his feet, the coarse, white plume of her bushy tail held high.

Sinto forged the image of exactly what he wanted and slipped his message inside the little monkey's mind—a ripe mangeleno, firm but with a slight give to the touch, with even color and flawless skin.

The little monkey snatched the nuts from Sinto's outstretched hand and shoved them all into her mouth. With her tiny white cheeks bulging, she scaled a neighboring tree and leaped across the wide expanse of air to the uppermost top of the mangeleno tree.

The young busheetail took her time and Sinto grew anxious as pink fingers of dawn stretched across the sky. Busheetails were stubborn tricksters and not always cooperative. But his newly recruited minion obliged, taking painstaking time to inspect *every* mangeleno on the tree she could find with her small human-like fingers.

Finally, she found one and dropped it to Sinto's open hands.

With the sweet gift for Audrey in hand, he took a shortcut through the foliage, stirred to life by the rising sun.

He stopped before reaching her shelter to make sure the animal skins he had hidden in the trunk of a hollow tree were ready to go.

Then he sat in the shadow of the jungle against a rock hidden within the leafy foliage. With a clear view of Audrey's shelter, he waited for her to awaken.

He hoped his gift would suffice as a proper apology. And while her mouth was full of the sweet fruit, he could regale her with his story before she could ask any questions.

12

Escape

AUDREY WOKE TO STIFF joints and muscle spasms. A new day cracking. The horizon a faint line against a pale pink sky. The sun yet to rise. She lay still for a moment, listening for movement, sniffing for wood smoke. All was quiet and still. The air was smokeless.

As she rubbed the crust from her eyes and cleared cobwebs from her mind she questioned her original plan. That the one-who-clicks would reveal themselves, answer all her questions, and promptly take her home so she could begin a full-blown search for Blake. But doubt had planted seeds between thunderstorms during the night. Maybe the one-who-clicks didn't have answers, maybe she merely washed up on their beach and now was their captive, maybe what either side may have to say would be lost in translation. How do you convert clicks to English?

Most concerning:

What does the one-who-clicks want from me?

She decided not to stick around long enough to find out. While she was itching to learn who and what this stranger was, there was that unsettling quiver of fear tightly coiled in her belly that she had felt ever since she woke in this strange place.

I must find a way home.

But how did one find a way home when they didn't know where they were?

She felt stuck. She had to keep moving. Staying in one place made her vulnerable. Determined, she decided she had to find a way over the black cliffs, to the mountains, and beyond. Surely there must be other people—a city, village, or homestead. Something to give her hope. Someone to give her answers.

A warm ocean breeze stirred the scent of charred ash from the campfire. The first golden rays of light broke the horizon. Already the temperature was rising.

She rolled up her jeans and tightened her shoelaces. She removed her coat and tied it around her waist. She didn't intend to stroll. She quickly stretched, warming up her muscles. She picked up the spear she had stolen from the meadow and cast aside upon returning the night before. She meandered to the beach.

The bay was alive with movement. Sea turtles emerged from the sea, dozens of glistening domes lumbering up the sandy shore as far as she could see. A line of shark fins hovered several yards beyond the surf line, trolling the fresh waters dumped by the nearby river, cutting across the beach. A young turtle hesitated before riding in on the surf. A shark swiftly took the prize and seized it in its mighty jaws. The sea boiled red. A frenzied party of thrashing tails and gaping jaws ensued.

Great balls of herring-sized fish formed large dark shadows below the surface like black fabric twisting in the current. Seabirds swooped in from the far cliffs and descended, their war-crying screeches adding to the cacophony and the spilling of blood.

She had never seen anything like it. The sheer volume of sharks and turtles, bait balls, and birds all in one place. She could spend hours studying the wild spectacle of nature unfolding before her.

Why was she leaving? Regretfully, she knew. Curiosity could be deadly. Nature was unpredictable. Best not to hesitate, to linger, like bait.

Like that poor turtle.

The words her father preached rang loud and clear:

Keep moving or die.

But these words stifled the opportunity to learn something new. To observe and learn, stillness was required. That was what scientists did. Sit, observe, learn. A feat that was impossible while running away from unfounded fear.

Her desire to study and learn had been inherited from her mother, and she hated how her father fought so hard to crush this piece of her. She had no reason to be fearful, other than the fear of some unknown danger *he* had instilled in her. He warned her of it, told her it lurked, always waiting for her to turn her back, for her to be still and let it take her. But he never produced evidence of such danger, or exactly what it was and why it existed; not through lessons, or lectures, or his stilted expression of love. But she knew that, with enough repetition and gaslighting, the mind bends to the will of the one manipulating it. Hers was no exception.

That ever-present fear her father planted and cultivated over the years coiled in her belly as she viciously pawed at her braid, bits of hair breaking away in her fingers.

Damn him.

In the end she found compromise:

Keep moving. Observe. Find a way across the river. Find a way through the mountains.

13

Hide And Seek

SINTO DROPPED TO HIS haunches next to the opening of Audrey's shelter. He painted his skin to match the coarse grains of sand at his feet mottled by the moving shadows of fronds above. He did not want to scare her but he was burning with expectation. Once he confirmed she was stirring he would leave and wait for her to emerge, rested and receptive to meeting the one eluding her. Him. Then he would offer her the mangeleno, his tongue would untwist, and everything would be set right.

He heard rustling around inside, imagined her rummaging for her coverings, for her shoes, tying the strings in neat bows. He fought the urge to steal a peek inside, but having learned how much Sapiens cherished their privacy decided that would not be wise. Satisfied she was awake, he tiptoed to the hollowed tree stump where he had hidden his animal skins. He crouched, waiting for her to emerge, skins in hand, drawing circles in the sand with his finger.

The sky radiated a rosy glow. Bird song reached its final crescendo as light bled through the jungle's dense canopy and the birds began the day's foraging frenzy. The air was crisp and scrubbed clean by last night's unsettled weather.

Time passed. Silence descended on the camp. Sinto grew impatient.

How long does it take to tie a shoe?

Silence continued to come from Audrey's shelter. He concluded the sounds he heard earlier had been her merely shuffling in sleep and not waking. He sat back, took advantage of the moment to calm his nerves and recite the brief and simple greeting he had decided upon during the night. Then, once proper greetings—and a long overdue apology—were dispensed, he would tell her where she was and why she was here.

His thoughts were interrupted by a bout of labored wheezing coming from the shelter.

He bolted upright at the unexpected sound. What if Audrey had been exposed to a virus, one her body had yet to be introduced to, and she was burning with fever? What if it was something he fed her? Could something nutritious to him be poisonous to her? That might explain why she was taking so long to wake.

He leaned toward the shelter, opened his mouth and inhaled. Expecting the taste of her rolling across his tongue, he startled at the unexpected taste of something else.

He hopped to his feet and poked his head inside.

The fern bed he had made was scattered, replaced by a deep hole where a huge female turtle was busy laying eggs.

He gaped, dumbfounded.

He surveyed the ground around the shelter and found a hand print pressed into the sand around the backside, opposite to the opening. Torn leaves and twigs littered the ground at his feet where she had torn a hole in the woven foliage and tried to fill it back in. Other than the hand print, the sand was wiped smooth just as he had done to hide his footprints on the beach. Farther away he observed more disruption, flattened ferns growing up against a large tree, then the space between it and another tree as if she had crawled from one to the other in the dark.

Beneath one tree he found one of the conch shells he had left for her, emptied and cast aside. Under the neighboring tree he found an indentation where she had lain coiled into the fetal position around its trunk.

Frustration mounted.

He frantically scanned the ground scattered with moist leaves loosened from trees during the night's squalls. Toe-less footprints circled the campfire, then along the edge of the jungle heading toward the river that cut through the beach to the sea, flowing swiftly and too deep to pass through. She had stopped, dropped to her knees. Moisture spotted the soil where she scooped water, to drink or wash her face. He tracked her prints running beside the river and deeper into the jungle.

She had found his path—frequently used but well hidden. How she knew puzzled him and decided it was pure luck or a sharp eye. The path led to an old tree bridge he had used many times to cross. The wide trunk was worn smooth from years of use. He ran across.

Fresh footprints marred the path that meandered back to the beach. Running, he burst onto the sand. Widely spaced footprints zigzagged around resting turtles and faded at the water's edge where the sand hardened from the ebbing tide. He ran along the shoreline hoping he was not far behind her.

To his relief he spotted her. The dark wavering outline of her body, distorted by the reflective sand and sunlight hitting it just right, was retreating in the distance. He altered his skin to reflect his surroundings and sprinted.

Once she reached the cliffs, she meandered along the face, stopping to reach up and climb. She fell, hugging hand to chest. The ridge was mostly glass and unforgiving to tender flesh, sharp and nearly impossible to scale without protective skins covering hands and feet. She found out the hard way. He winced sympathetically.

But that did not deter her. She ran up the beach toward the jungle, pausing before slipping into the thick foliage. By the time Sinto reached the cliffs she was gone and he was huffing mightily.

He scanned her footprints where sand met flora. She had paced back and forth along an impenetrable wall of carberry thick with thorns and sap wasps stripping the bark for their nests. He searched for crushed greens or broken branches, anywhere she may have muscled through. On his second pass, he saw it, as she must have, based on the number of times she passed by it before stopping to observe. An overgrown trail cut through the carberry in zigzag fashion, created by the great white bears who journeyed from the Winterlands beyond the mountains for berries and to fish the ocean when the days began to shorten.

The trail ran parallel to the ridge, towering four times his height. A solid wall of obsidian spewed from the Black Mountains, cleaved and chipped by the passage of time. Razor-sharp edges glinted in beams of sunlight stealing through the trees.

Audrey ran on the balls of her feet, making her footprints difficult to spot. But to his well-trained eye he could see clearly where she had passed, where the ground was dry from the displacement of dew-moistened leaves, the darker side of a rock carelessly overturned, and a disrupted line of redspot ants on the march. Signs that marked her recent passing.

The temperature dropped as the ground rose in elevation. The jungle thinned and canopy rose. Tall prickle pines and skunk leaf scented the air.

He quickened his pace. The creatures that dwelt in the foothills this side of the river would not welcome his Sapien guest like the docile creatures in the meadow and jungle skirting the sea. There she was considered a pest; here she was prey.

Audrey's footprints came to an abrupt stop near the tangled root ball of a recently toppled mangeleno tree, leaning against the cliff beyond the forest canopy. Dirty footprints led a path up the smooth white trunk.

He scaled the tree with fevered purpose. When he burst through the protective canopy into the blinding sunlight, his face shifted to reflect the sea of green from which he emerged. The cliff rose before him, steep and jagged. The forked top of the tree was wedged on a small ledge a body length from the top. Fresh blood glistened in the sunlight from a protruding shard of glass in the cliff face; a trail of drops led to the top.

She must be near!

He crawled onto the ledge, back hugging the cliff, listening.

He heard weeping.

He silently cursed the busheetail for delaying his return earlier and slowly scaled the last few feet of cliff. Razor sharp glass cut through finger and toe. His blood mingling with hers.

Before he crested the top, a sudden avalanche of small rocks rained down, bouncing off his shoulders. Slivers of glass clung to his hair. He froze and mimicked the sharp contours of the cliff, reflecting black, jagged, and shiny.

Audrey stepped to the cliff's edge, gaze locked to something in the far distance, tugging on the braid lying across her shoulder, the stake tightly clutched in her other hand. Tears stained her cheeks, blood trickled from a cut in her knee; the tangy scent of her blood was strong.

She stomped her foot. A rock bounced off his head.

Her voice quivered, "What do you want?"

She began to waver, leaning dangerously over the edge. He wanted to answer her plea but dared not move or drop his cover for fear the sudden sight of him would cause her to startle and fall. She stepped closer to the edge, toes claiming air.

He gasped. *Oh no, she's going to jump!*

Audrey knelt and leaned over the edge with her face so close to the top of his head that her ragged breaths parted his hair. He knew what that meant, but there was nothing he could do to stop it; the movement would cause a flicker in his flimsy disguise. His merlux buzzed and crackled. He couldn't look up, for surely she would see the electrical fire bleeding through the black coloring of his eyes from the surge of flueox flooding his bloodstream.

"I know you're there," she whispered. "Click if you understand."

He sensed her despair, yet his tongue remained firmly rooted to the top of his mouth, like his body clinging to the wall like a stubborn tuft of desert grass.

Agonizing seconds passed where neither moved or spoke or clicked.

Then, a noisy breath, a smothered sob, the drop of something moist on his shoulder. He heard her stand and take a step back and pick up the stake he had honed into a spear.

He bit his tongue, ashamed it had come to this.

"I'm not an animal. Find someone else to observe and stick in your zoo."

A large rock struck him on the shoulder, bounced, and disappeared in the sea of foliage below. He heard the crunch of footfall, fading in the direction of the Black Mountains.

Sinto scaled to the top of the cliff. He was rubber-kneed and gasping; from holding his breath, from the excessive hammering of his heart, from producing an overabundance of flueox in his merlux.

From this vantage point he understood her despair. He had learned the meaning of a zoo from Scouts who ventured into the Sapiens' cities and from Sapien books the Scouts gathered for him from their tours. It was true. Audrey was caged by the Black Mountains that spanned the land from sea to sea on this protected and cherished part of Merluma known as Inception. That was why he chose refuge on this side of the Black Mountains. He knew he could keep her safe and away from prying eyes. Anywhere else she would not be welcome, especially on the other side of the mountains where Terrakai still dwelled.

He had not intended to keep her here for very long. Sinto had been given the secret and important task of seeking her help for a particularly sticky situation that affected them both, of which this was merely the first step.

He beat feet and chased after her.

14

Lost

Audrey ran across a lava field sprinkled with glass boulders and loose rock, spear firmly gripped at her side. To the west, the ridge climbed even higher, blocking her view of what might lay beyond. To the east was the side she had scaled from the densely forested basin. The jagged peaks of the mountains towered to the north, the direction she was running. Steep, snow-covered, and seemingly impassable.

Her only choice was to continue forward, toward the heavily forested foothills looming at the foot of the mountains where the lava field ended, with hope of finding a hidden valley through the mountains. Optimism strained as she ran headlong, fueled by blind faith.

Dark clouds squatted atop the forested foothills, with thickening wisps stretching overhead as she approached the tree line. The smell of imminent rain.

Her encounter on the cliff unnerved her, like her encounter in the jungle on her way back from the meadow, and the strange shadow cast by the moonlight on the beach. She nearly stumbled off the cliff when the one-who-clicks' head burst through the green canopy. She knew it was there by the unnatural movement of light and texture and a slight waver in its camouflage whenever it moved. And the rock she threw bounced off solid nothingness instead of falling to the ground.

She believed the one-who-clicks to be human.

But what kind of human?

She stopped to catch her breath and stole a look back. A black and shiny humanoid shape was in aggressive pursuit, arms and legs scissoring and drawing dangerously near. Gasping, she bolted across uneven rock and through scattered bushes as the rocky rise began to sink into a dense forest.

Raindrops pelted her face, first as a few random drops, then followed by pea-sized hailstones. A layer of ice quickly covered the ground. Every step was dangerous and she was forced to slow down or risk slipping or twisting an ankle. Gratefully her pursuer seemed to struggle as much as she was.

The cliff melted into the forest floor carpeted by a dense layer of bright green moss. She didn't bother looking back and ran deeper into a forest shrouded in mist.

The storm settled overhead. Lightning streaked beyond the treetops and the ground beneath her feet shuddered with thunder. She cowered behind a boulder, shivering and waiting for the storm to pass, confident she had lost the one-who-clicks.

But a new problem arose. She had failed to memorize her route or note which way was north or south. In the gathering gloom, she realized she was utterly lost.

She ran blindly through the forest, crashing though bushes and ferns. Moss grew equally on all sides of trees, rocks, and bushes, eliminating her best hope for distinguishing north from south. A flash of lightning saved her from blindly running into the side of a giant fir tree and a group of large black birds hunched over something on the ground. She swerved as they took flight for the treetops, screeching from the sudden interruption of their gathering.

She tripped over something squishy. Caught a whiff of a sickly, sweet smell. Reluctantly she looked, hand pressed over her nose and mouth. The carcass of a large animal, an elk or something large like it, was lying on its side, ripped open and in the process of being picked clean by the sharp-beaked scavengers peering down from the treetops. She swallowed down the urge to heave.

A wolf howled in the not-too-far distance.

She stumbled back from the carcass, planted her back to a nearby tree, and imagined herself melting into it like the one-who-clicks. The vulture-like birds descended on their prey and resumed feeding.

Move in harmony, flow as w-w-water—stop panicking!

She decided to go back, to take her chances with the one-who-clicks. She would play its—his or hers—game, whatever that was. Confront it, find another way to escape, concede—whatever made sense. She had to keep moving or else become like the dead carcass of that beast. A meal.

She spun, trying to make sense of her surroundings, searching for her tracks. She had made many in her haste to flee and easily found her way back, thankful to put the rotting corpse behind her.

Her confidence waned when she lost sight of her earlier footprints in a carpet of thick moss. The moss bounced back with every step. The trees looked the same whichever direction she turned, enshrined with moss.

Hopelessly lost, she clicked three times.

She was answered by a flash of lightning, the crack of a treetop toppling, and the thundering rumble of hooves fast approaching.

15

Bluestripes

Sinto berated himself for being careless, for being a coward and not stopping Audrey when he had the chance.

A graywolf howled; an icy reminder they were not alone in the forest of Merluma and the animals here were not docile like those on the other side of the great river running from mountain to sea.

Wind whipped through the tree tops. Thunder rumbled. Lightning lit the sky. A rain of tiny prickly cones bounced and settled within indentations in the moss from Audrey's footprints.

He pursued her with purpose, hopping over fallen trees, crashing through thorny grapeberry, crushing tender fungi.

He found a fresh disturbance by the scattered remains of a dover elk, recently slain. Uprooted moss and the strong scent of stirred earth. He squatted down, touched the disrupted earth. Saw her tracks retreating away from the mountains toward the beach, running in a full sprint.

Sinto followed, quickly and discretely. She was wily and unpredictable, and she clutched the stake in her hand like a weapon. He would not be surprised if she popped out from behind a tree and whacked him on the head. Not that he didn't deserve it. He proceeded with determined caution and paused periodically to listen for her labored breaths, to scan the darkening forest for the pale bottoms of her shoes kicked up as she ran, to watch for the braid of dark hair bouncing along her spine.

Storm clouds moved in and sap-scented rain slipped through the evergreen treetops, splattering and irregular.

The sky exploded with a thunderous *boom* and a bolt of lightning, striking a tree beside him. Sinto was blown off his feet and landed on his back. Shredded and burnt bark rained. He lay, stunned and momentarily deafened beside a deep hole, blackened and smoldering. The air was thick with its acrid and electrical scent. He touched the side of his head where it throbbed. A clump of singed hair disintegrated in his fingers.

A herd of dover elk crashed through the trees. He sat up. The world spun. Luckily, he had enough sense to crawl out of their way and press against the smoldering tree before being trampled.

Why are they running?

It took an exorbitantly long and dizzying moment to realize why. The answer arrived rather quickly.

A pair of bluestripe tigers slipped through the forest, quiet as a whisper in pursuit, their silken blue-gray fur rippling. They paid him no notice with his body haphazardly painted to blend into the smoldering tree.

He was unsure how or when he got to his feet, but suddenly he was running, eyes glued to Audrey's footprints. His heart skipped when he saw the bluestripes' paw prints cross his path and join hers, before veering off into the woods, each in an opposite direction.

The bluestripes must have caught a whiff of her blood from the cut on her knee and were setting up for a sneak attack. A human was a much easier kill than a large dover elk.

Sinto slid to a stop where Audrey's footprints disappeared. He crouched, analyzing every sound, scanning every irregularity in the forest in every direction.

Where is she?

He heard rustling and quickly zeroed in on its source. The female bluestripe crouched in the bushes, growling below a rooted-pillar tree. The stake Audrey had carried lay on the ground beside it. The bluestripe's fiery-orange eyes fixated on something above.

Sinto followed her gaze.

Audrey clung to a large horizontal branch above Sinto's head. The male bluestripe clawed his way up onto a branch above her, distracting her from the female bluestripe lying in wait below.

Sinto knew the ritual. As part of his lessons, Wantemo had him witness bluestripe tigers in action, attacking the unsuspecting docile creatures of the forest. The male distracted their prey while the female lay in wait. Female bluestripes were the dominant ones in the pair and made the fatal strike, feasting first.

Sinto had never negotiated with a bluestripe, though he knew it was possible. Bluestripes were highly intelligent creatures, potentially open to reasoning, but usually with a terribly high price. Wantemo claimed he had successfully negotiated himself out of a potentially deadly situation once, by offering himself instead of their intended prey. He had survived, the bluestripe had not.

Sinto suspected many of Wantemo's heroic tales were embellished, translating them into important life lessons meant to make a specific point. But in this case, Wantemo had outlined exactly how one could win in this situation with bluestripes, an important lesson Sinto struggled to recall in his current distress. He remembered something about maintaining calm and seeking precision, and that a slight miscalculation in the use of his merlux could backfire with deadly consequences. But that seemed to be the basic lesson behind all of Wantemo's tall tales turned into lessons.

Why can I not remember the one about bluestripes?

Sinto didn't have time to ponder and readied for action, relying on his instincts.

Maintain calm. Check. Heart pounding, but breath under control, he secured his camouflage, fired up his merlux, and quietly circled the scene, rounding up behind the female hiding in the bushes.

The male inched closer to Audrey.

Sinto swiftly slipped onto the female's back and drove his elbows, fully weighted, between the tiger's scapula and spine. Her chest collapsed to the ground. He clamped his hands around her skull and revved up his merlux. Electricity flowed through his fingertips, administering a mild but painful shock to her temples. Her hind legs melted and belly dropped to earth. The sharp smell of urine pooled beneath her.

His confidence bloomed, and he slipped the female bluestripe an image of his stern warning; one where she and her mate retreated, leaving Audrey unharmed, versus another where he blew up her head with a surge of electricity if they didn't comply. He sent a jolt through his fingers to add credence to his warning.

Quivering, she acknowledged and chose the option where everyone lived. Sinto loosened his grip, then realized too late he had been tricked. She roared, warning her mate, and suddenly rolled, pinning Sinto beneath her massive body. He poured whatever electricity he had to the surface of his skin in defense. Leaves crackled on the ground beneath him. The bluestripe's fur was merely singed, enraging her more.

Sinto had underestimated her mass and the protection her thick pelt offered, wasting precious merlux reserves. The bluestripe weighed twice as much as him and had him stubbornly pinned. He fought to free himself and for every breath, his merlux crackling and popping under the strain. She anticipated his every movement, matching it with an equally forceful adjustment.

Sinto gazed up. Audrey stared back, eyes registering shock and disbelief. Somewhere in all the commotion his camouflage had slipped, flashing erratically. At some point, she must have seen him, fully exposed. But he had much bigger worries to care about now, and focused on keeping them both alive.

He wrapped his arms and legs around the bluestripe's belly. Residual electricity in his bloodstream rippled across the surface of his skin, but his merlux simply sputtered, the weight bearing down on his chest not helping. He had burned his initial reserve of electrical energy and needed time to recharge his merlux.

Audrey had crawled out of reach of the male, who was momentarily distracted by Sinto's struggle with his mate. A large stick with a splintered tip dangled within reach above Audrey's head. Sinto pointed a finger and with what little air he held to keep his lungs from crushing under the weight of the bluestripe, gasped, "Weapon."

Audrey's eyes widened upon hearing his voice but was quick to look up. She reached for the stick.

Sinto struggled to breathe. His vision winked, his merlux sputtered, and mind spun toward unconsciousness. He loosened his grip and the bluestripe shifted just enough for him to grab a lungful of air. He wound his arms around her chest and squeezed with all his might. She rolled to her side, pumped her legs. Sinto held tight. Bound together they spun in circles in the dirt. Sinto knew if he let go, he was as good as dead. Audrey too. The bluestripe swung her head from side-to-side, snapping her teeth, aiming for Sinto's neck. Fire erupted in his shoulder when her canines grazed his flesh.

Sinto raged at the thought of Audrey lying dead at the feet of the bluestripes, feasting. Anger fueled him. Anger at his weakness, for letting Audrey escape the safety of the beach, for letting emotions drive him.

For acting like a boy, not a man.

His merlux came to life and rumbled, chest swelling from the power rising within. His head cleared and he finally remembered Wantemo's lesson. The power his merlux generated was deadly and it could backfire and kill him instead of his intended victim if not properly channeled. It was why he failed the first time—the fear to channel it into something fatal, to himself and the intended victim. But that was not the whole of it. Sinto had never used his power to kill. He was at war with his moral conscience, a mistake he wouldn't make again.

Electrical fire coursed through his veins and danced below the surface of his skin. The trick was to concentrate the flow to a singular target with precision, with just enough wattage. His chest was pressed to the bluestripe's spine and thick pelt, but the inside of his arms were wrapped around her more vulnerable underside where it was soft and fleshy. He focused on the points where his forearms held fast and where his hands lay splayed across her ribcage, above her heart and vulnerable internal organs.

Electrical fire flowed from his merlux through his brachial arteries, radiating out through veins to the surface of the skin on his inner arms, hands, and fingers. He visualized the blue strands of electricity encircling each of her internal organs, but mostly her heart. He upped the voltage.

The bluestripe jolted and convulsed. The strands of current intensified, looped back, and rippled up Sinto's arms, reaching back toward his merlux revving beside his wildly beating heart. Gasping for air, he released her, breaking the connection.

A final spasm and the female bluestripe stilled, eyes glazed, a swirl of smoke escaping from her gaping mouth.

The dead immovable mass of her body held Sinto's arm and leg pinned underneath. He gritted his teeth and pushed with all his might, but the body was too limp and heavy.

Audrey screamed.

The stick he had pointed out to her now lay on the ground. Audrey had crawled to the end of the branch, precariously bouncing under her weight. The male bluestripe leaped to a more stable branch directly above her. He coiled, ready to pounce.

Sinto had no recollection of how he wrestled free from the dead mass lying on top of him, only that he suddenly had. He sprang to his feet, ignoring the throbbing pain racking the side of his body. He fired up his merlux and channeled every bit of voltage to his hand. He punched the surge toward the bluestripe.

A bolt of lightning exploded from Sinto's fist just as the bluestripe leaped. The branch disintegrated. Sinto's aim was true but the bluestripe was faster, landing atop Audrey. The flimsy branch she was clinging to snapped. Audrey rolled mid-air and landed atop the bluestripe in a rain of splintered wood and ash. She rolled off the beast and crawled away in a blur of arms and legs, but got tangled in thick foliage.

The bluestripe roared in frustration, crawling after her with one strong hind leg, the other dragging limp and broken behind him.

The bluestripe pounced, awkwardly, but his reach was sufficient and he snagged Audrey's shoulder with flexed claws. Audrey screamed when they cut into her flesh. She fought to escape but the bluestripe dug his claws in deeper and dragged himself on top of her, pinning Audrey on her stomach. She writhed, fueling the bluestripe's blood thirst. He roared and pawed the ground beside her neck with his free paw, claiming victory.

Sinto's merlux sparked weakly in his chest; he had used too much, too soon, in his fevered haste to blow the bluestripe out of the tree. The side where he had been pinned by the bluestripe's mate was numb and unresponsive and his fists were no match for the beast.

Sinto watched helplessly as the bluestripe slavered over his catch, burying his nose into the braid of hair at the base of Audrey's skull, grazing the skin with his sharp canines where her jugular thrummed. Audrey wisely stilled.

Blood flowed from her shoulder. The air was rich with the smell of it. Soon the bluestripe would not be able to resist and would finish her off.

The bluestripe raised his head and roared again in victory, then swung his gaze toward Sinto, eyes ablaze with blood lust. The image the bluestripe pushed in Sinto's mind made his heart clench;

Audrey ripped open from neck to groin. Justice for Sinto killing his mate.

The image shook Sinto to his core. Something bloomed inside of him; adrenaline, thick and hot; rage raw and empowering. He leaped, grabbing the bluestripe's head as he landed on his back. Sinto melted into the bristled contours of the bluestripe's body, grabbed his head, and yanked it sideways so Sinto could gaze into his eyes.

Sinto pleaded for Audrey's life, sending a stream of messages—reasoning, an apology, threats—anything to distract the bluestripe from killing Audrey, to buy more time to recharge his merlux.

The message he got in return turned his blood cold. The bluestripe could easily overpower Sinto even with his injured leg, and they both knew it. Then something important occurred to him, and he cut off the string of thoughts flowing between them.

The bluestripe had a weakness, and it was staring Sinto in the eye.

Sinto jammed his fingers into the bluestripe's eye-sockets; fevered eyes popped like ripe tomatoes.

The bluestripe roared and freed Audrey from his deadly grip. He thrashed blindly, kicking his good hind leg, clawing the ground, rolling side-to-side. Audrey slithered away and lay on her side convulsing, blood flowing freely from her shoulder, shock registering in her eyes.

Sinto's fingers held fast within the bluestripe's sockets and held his mount atop the bluestripe's back. He spread his legs, locked them into a V, drove his toes into the earth, and clenched every muscle in his body. He released his tail from his spine and flattened the flukes between his spread legs, using all his might to hold the bluestripe belly-down to the ground.

Sinto drove his fingers deeper into the bluestripe's skull, grazing the soft gray matter within. The bluestripe jerked in spasm. Sinto's merlux fired, weakly but enough.

Precision.

He visualized a concentrated stream of current flowing to the palms of his hands clutching the skull and his fingers pressed against the bluestripe's brain. He increased the current, slow and steady.

The bluestripe jerked, appendages extended, paws fisted, jaw clenched. Wisps of smoke escaped from his nostrils. The bone beneath Sinto's fingers heated.

Pop.

The bluestripe's skull cracked into several pieces. Hot liquid leaked past Sinto's fingers. A soft sack of fur, crumpled bone, and sizzled brains fell to the ground. The jaw fell open revealing the bluestripe's massive canines.

Sinto rolled off the bluestripe's body.

Audrey lay at his knees, soaked in blood, unconscious. Her aura was dangerously dim.

He felt for her heartbeat. Weak, but still beating. He rolled her to her stomach and tore away her shirt. Blood gushed from the wound on her right shoulder, her bronze skin turning deathly pale. She had lost a lot of blood.

His heart shuddered.

Please, don't die.

He gently pressed his palm to her shoulder, captured the last of the current flowing in his bloodstream, and whispered an apology for what he must do if she was to live.

Audrey screamed when her skin caught fire, cauterizing the wound and stopping the flow of blood.

16

I Am Fire

AUDREY STANDS ON A *tropical beach wriggling her toes in the sand. The water brilliant and clear. Fish, dolphin, and turtle fill the bay. Black birds hang on wings in the sky like specks of dirt stuck in balls of cotton.*

She is a dolphin in the sea. An eagle in the sky. God of her dream. Time zips forward.

The sea is flat. The sun sets on the horizon, kisses the sea; unmoving, it hovers. A ball of life-giving fire stuck at a crossroad in mirrored reflection. Sun of earth. Sun of sea. Alien worlds entwined as one for a glorious moment.

She is not alone. Her mother and father approach, holding hands, drawn to the shore by the mesmerizing beauty of twin suns.

She raises her arms to embrace them. Yet they pass through her as if through air.

Her father stands a head and half taller than her mother, a handsome man with dark hair shot gray at the temples and a body honed from years of rigorous physical training. His pale chest is bare and blushed from too much sun and deeply scarred from some long-ago trauma. He wears a traditional Hawaiian pā'ū batiked in a thousand shades of blue like his eyes, ever changing.

Her mother wears a sheer white dress with nothing underneath. Audrey can clearly see her tapered waist and the generous curves of her breasts and hips beneath. The dark skin of her Polynesian heritage cuts through the whiteness. Her hair hangs to the top of her buttocks like a sheet of black silk. A large mole marks her face just beneath the corner of her mouth. Anywhere else would have been a flaw, but next to her mouth accentuates her exquisite beauty.

The lovers share a whisper, a kiss, musical laughter.

~ ~ ~

The dream shifts from make-believe to a distant memory...

Audrey is nine years old and back on the Pacific island where she was born. Her mother is still alive.

The sound of reggae music drifts on a tropical breeze. It makes Audrey happy. She hums along, spinning in circles, wearing her favorite red dress. The sand beneath her feet is silky and warm from the late afternoon sun.

Her mother and father raise a glass of red wine and toast. A special Bordeaux he imports from France and only opens on special occasions.

Audrey asks, "What's the occasion?"

Her mother hands her a small box wrapped in white tissue and tied with a grass string.

"Your birthday, soon." She kisses Audrey on the cheek. "An early gift. No need to wait till tomorrow. Open it."

Inside is a small glass figurine, a man with a fluked tail and green eyes. The tenth to add to her collection of mermaid figurines. Each gifted on her birthday by her mother.

Her mother's wine spills down her chest, staining the white dress. It spreads into the shape of a heart. They all laugh at the irony.

~ ~ ~

Time sputters and speeds up. Reality wavers. Memory turns to dream again...

The sun slips beneath the horizon. The sky darkens. A sudden gust whips through fronds and Audrey's untamed hair. Swells roll into the bay and race up the beach. Rain and thunder follow.

A bolt of lightning strikes.

Her mother looks up, mouth agape and eyes wide with fear. The heart-shaped stain on her white dress turns to blood, gushing from a hole in her chest where her heart once was. Blood pools at Audrey's feet, sticky and hot between her toes. Audrey feels dizzy from the smell of it.

A second bolt of lightning strikes and ignites the blood gushing from her mother's chest. Her hair is first to flame, then her dress. The fabric clings to her skin on fire. Her flesh blackens and sizzles beneath. Screaming, she reaches for Audrey but her fingers crumble and turn to ash before she can touch her. Then the rest of her crumbles, until she is but a pile of gray ash on white sand.

Fire engulfs Audrey, licking her skin, lifting the tips of her hair, dancing across the tiny white flowers printed on her red dress. Yet she doesn't catch fire or burn. She feels no pain or fear, but a deep hunger; for what she is unsure but it festers and demands immediate attention.

She opens her mouth, draws the fire inside. It satiates her hunger.

Fire ignites the blood in her veins but it doesn't kill her. It makes her stronger. Invincible.

Smoke rises from her skin and swirls, blotting out the moonlight, smothering the sound of her father screaming until all she hears is the sound of water lapping on the shore—shush-shush-shush—and the click of a tongue—click-click-click.

She turns toward the source of the sound.

A boy with pale hair and green eyes emerges from the smoke.

She knows him.

Knows him by the green fire in his eyes.

He whispers a word she doesn't understand, over and over, sala-something. Just as she begins to remember the word and grasp its meaning his voice is overpowered by a scream.

Her father: "Run, baby! Run from the fire!"

But she is confused.

How can she run?

I am the fire.

17

Boy With Exploding Green Eyes

AUDREY OPENED HER EYES. Smoke filled her lungs and clouded her vision. She lay on her stomach, cheek pressed against something soft and slightly scratchy—a mat of woven grass lying on the sand. Her gaze settled on the curled fingers of her left hand, so close to her face they blurred. Her other arm was straight and tucked flat beneath her right thigh, numb from her weight and lack of circulation.

Thick smoke swirled all around her.

Not a dream! I must get away from the fire!

She couldn't breathe. She felt dizzy and confused. She could feel the heat of the fire along her right side, opposite from where she was looking.

She tried to roll over. Pain shot across her back and seized her chest. Dark spots danced before her eyes. She dangled on a thread of consciousness.

A sudden gust of wind cleared the air. She heard the crackle of a fire, caught the taunting whiff of meat cooking.

Memory of the dream slipped away like the wisps of smoke disappearing into the thick foliage of the jungle.

She was back on the beach from which she had escaped. She was unsure of exactly how she got there. What she did remember came back in a fuzzy mix of memory. She remembered tigers chasing her, the smell of blood and searing pain, and staring down death's corridor. There had been a great struggle between a tiger and a man; the one-who-clicks, revealed and certainly human—a young man with gold hair and fiery green eyes, his body flickering between reflecting the ground and being naked. He spoke, said the word "weapon," which she clearly understood.

Determined to see what was cooking on the fire, she tucked her chin and rolled her head onto her forehead, inch by agonizing inch, until her nose was pressed flat against the mat. She clenched her teeth and cried out, rolling her head the rest of the way over. Pain ripped through her right side and she fought to overcome the darkness that threatened to overtake her. It won. Momentarily.

The leg of a large animal hung from a spit over a smoky campfire. Juice dripped from lean muscle to fiery coals with a hiss and a puff of steam. Beside her was a conch filled with water like those the one-who-clicks had left for her before her attempted escape.

Fueled by thirst she wriggled her right arm free, punching through the pain, fighting to stay conscious, but her arm was limp and useless. She tried again, gathering her other arm beneath her chest.

"Stop," a deep voice said, "else you'll open the wound."

The golden-haired man stepped into view carrying a bundle of sticks and set them next to the fire. He wore a short tan animal skin around his hips and a matching vest loosely tied by a leather string across his chest.

He knelt by the fire and spun the meat on the spit. An explosion of moisture struck the coals. He jerked back to avoid a burst of steam to the face.

"You're the one..." Audrey clicked her tongue three times.

His gaze fell to his fingers. In profile she could tell he was smiling. "Yes, I..." He never finished the sentence. He mumbled something she couldn't decipher, shook his head, and started pinching the meat with long tapered fingers.

After closer inspection she wondered if he was a little older than her because of his size, or maybe he was younger by the way he avoided her eyes. Maybe an early bloomer or maybe just shy. Hard to know for sure by watching his actions or by the deep sound of his voice.

If only he would look at me, she thought. *Eyes tell secrets.*

As if he knew what she was thinking, he turned to face her. Their eyes locked and she gasped. These were eyes she knew. Eyes alive with green fire. Like the boy in her dream. Like the boy she met long ago.

She wanted to ask, to confirm the truth, but her tongue failed to move. Her eyes darted to the conch filled with water.

"Thirsty," she croaked.

"Oh, sorry! You need water but I didn't want to wake you." He moved with the grace of a dancer, strong yet lithe, and closed the distance between them as fluidly as a wave crossing the sea. He smelled of mesquite salted by the sea.

He picked up a leaf the size of his hand. It was not yet fully sprung. The smooth edges curled inward toward the thick vein running down its center, forming a straw. Her cheek was still glued to the mat, unmovable. Understanding his intent, she opened her mouth. He stuck the pointed end past her lips. She curled her tongue around it. He poured a trickle of water from the conch to the leaf, then pulled the leaf from her mouth so she could swallow. He repeated the process several times, which worked splendidly until he poured a little too aggressively and she felt like she was drowning and coughed up a mouthful of water.

"Enough," she could barely whisper between coughs. It hurt to cough, to breathe, to talk. It took her a while to recover.

He rose to his feet, grabbed something next to the fire, returned to her side. In his hand he held a kidney-shaped bladder tied shut at the top with leather string. Slightly translucent, it appeared to contain a thick red liquid.

He untied the string, slipped the tip of the leaf between her lips, poured. "Drink."

Fiery liquid filled her mouth. He pinched her lips together, forcing her to swallow. It happened so quickly. Some of it puddled against her cheek pressed to the mat. It felt cool against her skin but smoldered in her stomach. She could feel the heat seeping through her bloodstream from head to toe. Tingling followed, a cool relief from the fire. Her body fell under control of this new master coursing through her bloodstream and she melted into the mat on which she lay. Soothing numbness followed.

A heavy sigh slipped passed her lips, sticky with whatever he had forced her to drink.

"Is the pain gone?"

She tried to answer but her lips were too numb. So was her brain. She slipped a lazy glance to his eyes and blinked.

He smiled back, acknowledging, then hopped up to tend to the meat cooking over the fire.

Her gaze wandered to his unusually large feet and odd toes, flared and connected by a translucent web of skin. Her gaze continued up his legs to his chest. His skin was flawless and iridescent like the surface of a cultured pearl. Legs, arms, chest, even his armpits, smooth and hairless. His face seemed normal if you ignored the eerie glow emanating from his eyes. Handsome, with an angular jaw and high cheekbones, eyes wide-set and upwardly slanted with smooth mono-lids. His brows were dark with thick lashes to match. His golden hair was streaked with touches of fiery copper and a dark bronze the same color as his brows. Some of his hair was missing on one side.

Nordic meets Far East meets something not of Earth. Kind of like this place; tropical meets Pacific Northwest meets creatures not of Earth. Alien.

He extracted something shiny and black fashioned into the shape of a knife from a leather sheath tied around his thigh. Honed sharp as a razor, it easily cut through the meat cooking over the fire.

In one swift motion he came to her and dropped to his stomach with a thin slice of meat in his fingers.

His other arm lay on the sand next to her hand. Curious, she ran a finger across the skin at his wrist. It felt slick and rubbery like the skin of a dolphin.

Scratch Nordic or Far East. He was from somewhere else altogether.

She gazed into his eyes. The tight black beads of his pupils were in motion, pulsing like a heartbeat, pounding faster like her own. A memory sparked but fizzled before she could grasp it. So familiar, like the rubbery feel of his skin. Could it be?

He quirked a brow and gestured for her to take a bite.

She shifted her gaze to the slice of meat pinched between his fingers. The surface of his skin flickered, and for a moment his fingers were indistinguishable from the slice of meat.

She blinked. "How do you do that?"

"Do what?"

"Your skin it..." she closed her eyes, opened them, focused on his fingers. They looked perfectly normal. She was certain his skin had changed to look exactly like the meat. She recalled the strange apparitions she had seen earlier. Indistinguishable movement of patterns and shadows in the jungle, the bodiless shadow on the sand that night on the beach, the shiny black figure chasing her across the lava field. The flicker across his skin whilst he fought a great beast.

Superior ability to camouflage. Definitely alien.

"Uh, never mind."

He pressed the meat against her lips.

"I'm not hungry."

"Pain steals hunger but you must eat to heal."

She opened her mouth to object, but he shoved the meat inside. She spit it out, tried to roll away.

Mistake!

Tears burst from her eyes. Her mouth gaped like a beached fish. He gently rolled her to her stomach with her face toward the fire.

After inspecting the wounds in her back, he released a grateful breath and placed one hand at the base of her neck, the other on her lower back just above her buttocks. He tipped his head back and closed his eyes, concentrating. He drew a sharp breath, and a low hum rose from the center of his chest. She felt a slight vibration radiating from his fingers. Warmth flowed from his hands. It felt like icy hot liquid was flowing up and down her spine, melting bone and muscle. Her scalp prickled and the world went black momentarily.

He released her. It stung where his hands had been. He brushed away a wisp of hair pasted by sweat to her cheek. His eyes glowed brighter than before.

"Better?"

The pain was now more annoying than intolerable, with a deep burning and itching sensation in her right shoulder where she remembered a tiger had dug in its claws.

He offered another bite of meat. She heeded his advice and began chewing.

After the meat, he fed her some kind of root vegetable wrapped in leaves that he had dug from the fire's ashes and mashed up with his fingers. Bland, but he insisted. She ate until her stomach felt ready to pop.

"No more," she begged.

He held up the kidney-shaped bladder. "Just this, that's all, I promise."

"What is that?"

"Sucuvita." His gaze shifted to the bladder. "What you might call a form of medicine."

He employed the leaf straw like he had before. She took a gulp, made a face. Sickly sweet and potent, more like the shot of

Jägermeister her friend Ryan made her try once. It made her feel the same way—loopy, only sucuvita was much stronger.

"More," he said.

She managed two more gulps. Her eyes watered from the fire erupting in her stomach. He smiled with satisfaction, tied the top tightly with the leather string, and propped it up in the sand beside him.

It felt as if her body was a beehive, buzzing and tingly all over. "I feel funny."

"Good," he stood up, "that means it's working."

The sun set in fast motion with clouds smeared across the sky in strands of gold and crimson. The chitter-chattering of myna-like birds faded deeper into the jungle. The wind died. Waves gently lapped the shore.

He stole a glance over his shoulder and gave her a reassuring smile before resuming his chores. In the growing darkness, she watched him wrap the remaining meat in a large supple leaf, dismantle the spit, and stoke the flames of the fire with dried wood gathered and neatly stacked.

The pieces finally came together. He looked the same but grown up. The boy who helped her make sand mermaids on the beach. She remembered his name, strange to the ear, but easy on the tongue.

Sinto.

"Do you still have the book I loaned you?" Her voice was weak and came out barely a whisper.

He stopped what he was doing and turned to face her. Half his face was lost in shadow, except for one glowing eye. Slowly his lips curled into the shy smile she remembered. He nodded.

"Why didn't you come back?" she asked without thinking.

It didn't matter whether he had or not. She wasn't there to greet him. The day she gave him the book was the last day she saw him. The day before her tenth birthday. They had huddled together under the shade of a palm tree, reading, while her mother swam off shore as she had every day.

Sinto had never seen a book before and marveled at the way the pages were glued together at the spine, at the feel of the paper made from wood, the smell of the ink, the hidden meaning behind the story. She had felt sorry for him, believing he was the son of a poor fisherman, too poor to afford a book, so she gave it to him with the promise that he would return it another day.

The next day her mother died and her father whisked her away from their island home. She hadn't been back since.

"I'm sorry I left," she said.

"I'm sorry too."

18

Infection

Sinto had no idea how long he had been sleeping. Stars canvassed the sky. Embers smoldered from the ashes of the fire. The waxing moon hung high. His mind's clock guessed midnight.

Before settling he had rolled Audrey to her left side and propped her right arm atop a rolled mat of grass to relieve pressure from the wound in her shoulder. He lay at her back.

"Help me," she whispered.

He crawled to her other side and faced her. Her eyes were glassy and distant; her skin was slick with sweat.

She drew a shuddering breath. "It hurts to breathe."

He jumped up and stoked the fire so he could see better. He peeled back the leaf dressings he had applied before he lay beside her to rest. What he saw alarmed him. The skin around the wound was dark and swollen. Grayish pus oozed from a slit, releasing the putrid scent of death.

Necrosis!

"I'm c—cold."

He pressed his cheek to her forehead. Her skin was on fire, confirming his fear.

The infection seemed to spread before his eyes, purple veins branching across her back.

She panted, "What's—happening to me?"

"Infection—spreading fast, much too fast."

She grew quiet, then whispered, "Am I—am I going to die?"

Sinto wrestled with the answer. He needed her trust if he was to save her.

He weakly bleated, "We all die, eventually."

A unique toxin excreted from the bluestripe's claws had poisoned the flesh surrounding the wound—a tenderizing of a prey's flesh which restricted circulation in the surrounding tissue, in effect killing it. Like the bite of a venomous spider. He thought he had flushed all of it out but must have missed some. The flesh where it festered was too far gone for the body to naturally heal.

Sinto grew anxious. This was not supposed to happen! In just a few days' time he was to return her to her Earth world. Untouched and just as she was the day she was borrowed. The infection left unchecked would kill her before dawn.

Stuck in the sand beside him was a half full bladder of sucuvita. A rejuvenating elixir for aiding cellular regeneration, for warding off inflammation, and increasing cellular longevity. Sucuvita couldn't stop the infection spreading from Audrey's wound. Nothing could at this point, except to remove the infected flesh entirely. And if she survived, she would have limited use of her arm and be horribly disfigured.

His ancestors had mastered the art of rejuvenating damaged or missing tissue, like a lizard growing a new tail. Sinto had practiced on injured animals and mammals of the sea under the full supervision of his mentor, Wantemo. His lessons involved setting broken bones and healing non-life-threatening punctures or cuts with the aid of special tinctures that numb the pain and distract the mind.

Rejuvenating flesh was unpleasant and extremely painful. So much so that it regularly led to sudden heart failure. Even the most hardened of warriors during the Forever War failed to survive when Healers attempted to repair their ravaged bodies without the aid of painkilling relief.

Sinto had neither Wantemo—who was a practiced Healer—by his side, nor did he have immediate access to special tinctures to ease pain. Audrey's wound was far worse than anything he had attempted to heal before, considering the extent of infection and the sheer size of it. While Sinto was confident he could overcome this lack of experience, he had much less confidence in dealing with the trauma inflicted by intolerable pain.

To overcome that complication, the Merahvu had discovered another option as the result of tending to the wounded in the thousands of years of tribal conflict. One he had not practiced with another human—an advanced form of what the Merahvu called *sharing*.

It was second nature for his people to share memories or experiences, to debate or communicate quietly and privately through a form of telepathy known as mind-speak—an advanced form of communication that was unique to his species of human. It was how Sinto communicated with living things in the natural world without requiring knowledge of a vast number of different languages, spoken or otherwise. But the advanced form of sharing he was considering went well beyond the sharing of thoughts and ideas.

The Merahvu had discovered one way to minimize the trauma of rejuvenating flesh—to disassociate the mind from the injured body. It was a learned skill, for which Wantemo had taught Sinto the basics, to coax a conscious mind to leave its nature-given body and enter another's for distraction and safe-keeping. A disassociation that proved tricky to control, depending on the mind, and worked only temporarily.

To be successful, unfailing trust must be established between the Healer and the one being healed. A detached mind can be a delicate thing. One misunderstanding could lead to potential madness, or worse, permanent disassociation. A body without a conscious mind cannot survive, nor can a conscious mind survive without its body for very long. It was a slippery proposition with a Sapien unaware of such possibilities.

The simpler the mind, the easier it was to control. Audrey was human, complex and independently minded. His skills were unrefined and his confidence shaky on this particular form of advanced sharing.

He gazed down at the festering wound growing worse by the second, at her pleading eyes.

If I fail she will die. If I do nothing she will die.

The choice was clear:

I must try.

Sinto grabbed Audrey's hand. It was hot and clammy. Her face glistened in the glow of firelight. He brushed a clump of damp hair from her forehead and gently massaged her temple. Her pulse raced below his fingertips.

"Look at me."

Her eyes burned with fear, but rooted in the fear was a fierce determination to live.

It gave him hope and boosted his confidence.

"You must give me your absolute trust and do everything I tell you. No matter how strange the request. No matter what you feel or not feel. This will be like nothing you have ever experienced. *Do you understand?*"

She nodded. "I don't want to die."

He gave her a tight smile. "You might, before this is over."

"Please—f-fix me. Whatever it—takes." She struggled to say the words but her grip around his fingers was firm.

He held up the sucuvita. Her eyes fell to the bladder in his hand. She blinked, acknowledging she understood.

There was no time for sipping small mouthfuls. She needed all of it, now. To help calm her mind for what was to come and to attack the inflammation spreading throughout the healthy parts of her body.

He slipped his hand beneath her head and lifted, elevating her chest higher than her stomach. She screamed when her wound tore open. Blood and pungent, viscous liquid oozed to the ground.

He shoved the tip of the bladder into her mouth.

"Drink! All of it."

Tears burst from her eyes but she faithfully drank, stopping only to swallow and grab a sip of air.

19

Me You

AUDREY'S VISION BLURRED WHEN the strange liquid hit her stomach. It ripped through her veins like a wildfire racing across a field of dry grass. She felt heavily drugged and strained to keep her eyes open.

The world moved in slow motion, stopping and stuttering like a filmstrip grinding around the reels of a broken projector. The flames licking air, a beetle crawling up a stem, and Sinto, hair waving gently in the breeze, the slow blink of his eyes, the nervous dart of tongue sliding across lip.

Sinto took her hand and leaned closer. Her vision spun like a kaleidoscope. A thousand Sinto faces circled and spun.

"Gaze into my eyes." His voice was odd, deep and drawn out, slow-motion distortion. "Tell me what you see."

She blinked until she could focus on a single face. Sinto's eyes burned like whirlpools of green fire.

"Green fire," she slurred.

"And beyond the fire?"

She dared not blink and gazed deeper. "A—pupil. No, a tunnel..." She felt a pull, of every inch of her body dissolving into a wisp of smoke. "Pulling me inside."

"Do not resist. Let it take you, swiftly. Flow, as if you are water rushing downstream."

Flow as water like stream around rock.

She slipped past the green fire into darkness and through a cool mist. The tunnel brightened, and beyond, a warm golden light beckoned. She was captured by that light and was cast into a weightless unseeing state. She reached for her chest, her legs, anything to ground her, but she had no hands. She tried to breath, but had no lungs to draw air. She was...

Bodiless.

She sensed a beating heart, steady and strong; the flow of breath, circulating in and out of lungs; the vibration and buzz of a thousand bees, gathering. How she sensed these things boggled her mind, for she had no eyes or ears or nerve endings.

She played back Sinto's instructions, odd to her at the time, but that now produced a heightened sense of uncertainty and fear.

You must give me your absolute trust and do everything I tell you. No matter how strange the request. No matter what you feel or not feel. This will be like nothing you have ever experienced. Do you understand?

She certainly felt strange, nor had she ever experienced anything like it, and she struggled to understand but knew one thing for certain:

I am no longer in control.

She determined she was bodiless but fully conscious, merely an observer—but could such a thing be possible, and if it was, where was she?

She tried to speak, desperate to ask the question, but had no mouth to form the words, no voice to project them. She grew anxious, thinking the question, over and over.

"Where am I?"

She got an answer. *"You are safe and with me."* Sinto's voice echoed through her mind as if a thought of her own. He added, *"There is no reason to be afraid. It need not be for much longer."*

"How did you do that? How are you in my... head?"

"I'm not in your head, you're in mine."

There was a movement in the void, the silhouette of someone approaching. Sinto in his animal skins, with an outstretched hand, walking toward her.

Gravity claimed her feet and she was standing before him. Her braid lay across her shoulder, wild strands springing up. She had eyes that could see, ears that could hear, and hands that could feel. She was dressed like the day she ran away, before she was attacked by that tiger. The place that greeted her was an open void, with nothing but the two of them filling it.

He smiled, "Remember what I told you?" His voice was soft and real, not a passing thought.

Afraid that her voice would fail her, she nodded.

"I need you to stay calm. No matter what you see or feel or not feel. *Do you understand?*"

She realized she didn't understand any of this. "I'm afraid."

"As I would expect. But you must trust me and accept what is happening. It's the only way I can save you."

The weight of his words reverberated. "Save me?" She felt her chest heave. Rising panic narrowed her vision; a dark tunnel, a warm light, an out-of-body consciousness.

"Am I dead?"

"No! You're not dead. I have no time to explain, not now. Be patient; you're safe, for now, here with me. Please, take my hand. I must put you back." His hand was warm and solid.

Back? Back to where, she thought.

A dark oval doorway suddenly appeared beside them and he pushed her inside. She was back in that state where she felt weightless and disembodied, like a wisp of smoke.

Sinto? she thought.

She received no response.

It wasn't the first time she found herself alone. She recalled her past, of the old wood-and-stone house where her father took her after departing their Pacific island home. Transplanted to Seattle, a green, rainy place with short mild summers where your bones never fully warmed from the perpetually damp winters. He ensured every need was fulfilled except one: The freedom to venture beyond the sprawling walled-in grounds surrounding the house. She had been trapped, emotionally abandoned much of the time, and powerless to do anything about it. Her overly protective father claiming to save her from a danger he never clearly articulated. He too asked her to trust him.

A flash of panic and anger overcame her.

What's happening to me! Tell me. Now!

Nothing.

Sinto! Let me go!

What happened next stunned her to silence.

Audrey knelt next to the fire, hovering over her body. In her fingers was a knife of obsidian, black and shiny, with a honed sharp blade.

But these were not her fingers wielding the knife. The fingers belonged to Sinto, the knife the one he had used to carve the meat roasting over the fire the previous day.

His fingers moved quickly and with the precision of a trained surgeon, carving away gray rotting flesh from her shoulder. She felt the nausea roiling his belly and the heat of the coals along the side of his body. Through his ears, she heard the hiss and sizzle as he tossed her rotting flesh into the fire. Through his eyes, she saw the wave of darkness when it momentarily smothered the flames. And through his olfactory, she smelled it burning.

She gazed with horror at the bloody scene unfolding through Sinto's eyes. Blood swelled from the cuts made with the knife and flowed in rivulets down her ribcage, pooling beneath her cheek where it lay on the mat. She helplessly watched as he swiped his fingers around the edges of cleanly cut muscle and severed tendon, across the exposed scapula gleaming under the moonlight, inspecting his work.

My blood, my bone!

She felt nothing from the things he was doing to her body. She only felt Sinto's elevated heartbeat, the rush of air flowing in and out of his lungs, the cool smoothness of the obsidian knife in his hand. Blood clung to his fingers that felt like her own. She observed other sensations, like the strange taste in her mouth, the effortless liquid-like movement her body made, the snap and crackle of electricity flowing though her veins...

Me you.

She gazed at her face through Sinto's eyes, calmly sleeping. *Her body* missing its mind, unaware of her rising panic. Of the battle raging. Of a mind trapped where it didn't belong. She had been warned. Had readily agreed, even though she had no idea what Sinto had implied.

He had not lied: *This will be like nothing you have ever experienced.*

But this? How many rules of nature were being broken? What if she couldn't find her way back? What if it killed her?

She tried to remain calm. To be strong. To overcome the irrational. She warred. But her rational mind was losing control. The primal one took over. And the reptile won.

She imagined the door Sinto pushed her through...

Imagined reaching out and turning the knob...

Bursting free...

Seeking escape...

But she saw and felt... nothing.

She fought to stay calm.

Trust him... be strong.

But the harder she grappled for control, the deeper she sank into despair.

She couldn't gain a sense of up or down, solid or nothingness, real or imagined.

Lost. Stuck. Out of control. *Dying...*

She replayed everything that had happened—How she ended up in this blind and weightless and panicked state—Sinto asking her to gaze into his eyes—to flow past the fire—into the darkness. Into a tunnel.

Let it take you swiftly...

It finally struck her. The how.

To escape.

To flee, as the lizard was screaming for her to do.

Eyes!

She focused every bit of will to her eyes, not her mind's but her body's.

She imagined them opening...

Suddenly, she was lying on her stomach overwhelmed by a tidal wave of pain and the sickly smell of blood, watching the last of her flesh sputter and smolder in the fire.

She felt a stab to the shoulder, a glance off bone, a tug. Exposed nerves undulated hot and cold, like a thousand hot needles piercing her skin. She felt a splash of cool liquid, then a sharp, stunning sting. A silent sob slipped through her lips. She felt the blood at her cheek, hot, sticky, and nauseating. She felt Sinto's hands grasp her and roll her to her side.

A trifecta of pain shot through her core and reverberated down her spine to her toes, sharp, throbbing, and stinging. Her mind hit overload.

Stars. Darkness. Peace.

Consciousness eventually returned. She again felt that deep ache throbbing, and other new sensations: the flow of warm liquid; fingers poking, then—a jolt of electricity, undulating and very hot; sharp needles knitting; a maddening itch. On it went—wriggling fingers, fire, needles, itch, itch, itch—a repeating cycle over and over.

She quietly suffered until she could take it no longer and opened her mouth to scream.

Sinto shoved a stick between her teeth. "Bite!" It tasted of blood.

He returned to his work, eyes on fire, intensely focused on her shoulder.

A splinter of wood stuck in the roof of her mouth. She spit the stick out. "Stop," she whimpered.

Sinto stopped what he was doing and placed a bloodied palm across her forehead, and gazed into her eyes.

She thought. *I don't want to die!*

He answered as clearly as if it was her own thought. "*You're not going to die.*" He gave her a slight smile. "*Stay strong, you're healing nicely.*"

Then, his voice looped in her mind—

"*You feel no pain. Imagine this is just a dream.*

"*No pain... a dream...*"

She focused on his reassuring voice, looping in her mind. She succumbed to his words and drifted far from the pain and the stink and the terror, and into a dream about a boy with exploding green eyes who she befriended long ago.

20

Gift

AUDREY WOKE TO DAYLIGHT, lying on her side, facing the sea, breathing freely. Fronds clacked in a gentle breeze. Waves lapped on sand. A dark bird circled.

She had no idea how long she had been lying there. All she had were fuzzy memories of time passing. Of the sun rising, moonlight and stars, passing more than once. Of Sinto's hands gently coaxing her to lie in different positions. Of water and strong liquids passing through a leaf straw into her mouth. Of fire and wood smoke. Of Sinto helping her relieve herself into a coconut shell as she lay on the ground. Of pain, much more tolerable but intense at times, and a persistent itch radiating from her shoulder.

But now was different; she felt alert and no longer felt pain. Though there was that itch, as maddening as ever.

She reached around to scratch it. Where she expected a hole down to the bone, she found soft skin and firm muscle, tender to the touch as if mildly bruised. She gasped in disbelief and brushed her fingers across the smooth skin and felt no scar. She wondered if what she thought had happened truly was a hallucination, a vivid nightmare, brought on by the strange liquid Sinto forced her to drink.

"Sinto?"

A rustle of bushes. He came from somewhere behind her, hastily tying his wrap around his hips and vest across his chest.

"How do you feel?" He sank effortlessly cross-legged beside her and gazed into her eyes as if the answer was buried somewhere deep inside. She remembered gazing into his eyes that painful night and in a dream when she became him, then she became her, again...

She squirmed uncomfortably, remembering how intimate it felt, how real, to be occupying his body.

"I feel good but my shoulder, it itches like crazy, and I need to..." She realized she had to pee rather badly. "Can I sit up?"

"Of course, let me help you."

He easily lifted her into a seated position and gently brushed his fingers across her right shoulder. A cool wave of relief. No more itch.

She diverted her eyes, aware of the close proximity of his body. An awkward silence fell between them.

That was when she realized her bra barely covered her modest breasts, the right arm loop held together by a knotted thread. When she looked up their eyes met and she detected a slight flush wash across his cheeks.

"Uh, your coverings were torn and quite bloody, but..." He quickly reached around for something behind him. A piece of silken blue-gray fur with a single dark-blue stripe running through it. "Perhaps you will be more comfortable wearing this."

He shook it open, held it up. An angle-cut top with one armhole. He had sewn it together with stiff string from something organic, like strands of twined vining or, something else she didn't want to think about, perhaps intestine.

"But how can I..." She glanced over her shoulder at her back, reluctant to move her right arm.

"You may move as you like. Your shoulder's fully healed." He grabbed her right elbow, placed his other hand firmly atop her shoulder. He raised her arm and gently rotated it around the shoulder joint, forward, back, and around in a circle. He beamed. "Just like new."

She reached forward, bowing her upper back and flexing the scapula. Then spread her arms and stretched back, expanding her chest. She felt a little stiff and sore but in a good way, like the day after a rigorous workout.

Images of blood and bone and burning flesh flashed through her mind. She glanced at the pit where it had burned, the charred bones of a log, the pile of gray ash. Ashes of her flesh buried beneath the many fires since. She reached around with her opposite arm and fingered the smooth skin amazed there wasn't even a hint of a scar.

"How was I able to heal so quickly?"

He grimaced. "With much determination, and a lot of luck." He picked up the fur. "Hold up your arms."

He rocked forward on his knees, his chest coming inches from her face. He smelled like he had been rolling around in newly cut grass. He pulled the top over her head, rocked back, then tugged at the ragged bottom, ran his fingers across the seam at her left shoulder and along one side, inspecting every detail, like a tailor proudly verifying his handiwork.

"Perfect!" Clearly pleased with the fit he reached behind and grabbed a second bundle of fur. "I also made you a matching wrap."

That's when she realized she wasn't wearing her jeans, just her underwear with a blood-stained waistband. She attempted to cover herself with the corner of the grass mat she sat upon.

"I cleansed your pants. If you would prefer, I can fetch them."

She bit her lip. "That's okay," and reached for the wrap.

She buried her face in the silky folds, breathing its pleasant woody scent and marveling at the silken feel. She held it to her waist. It too would fit perfectly. She tried not to dwell on how he knew. "Thanks."

"You use the ties to adjust the fit."

He pointed to his wrap and the five leather ties that held it together along his left hip. He untied the top one and pulled it open, exposing the skin from waist to thigh, his abs smooth and toned, clearly muscular, but not comically rippled. A wild pattern of swirls and dots adorned his hip. Embossed as if painstakingly carved by a fine-tipped knife to make the skin scar and pucker. He threaded the strand back through a loop sewn on the other side, tied it in a half bow. It was obvious he wore nothing underneath.

He said, "Go on, give it a try."

She gazed at the fur lying in her lap, twiddled with the leather ties knotted along one edge, and stuck her pinky finger through each of the holes in which they were intended to go, hoping he would get the hint. Finally, she looked up and met his gaze. He was sitting cross-legged with his hands casually resting on his knees, waiting.

"Um, Sinto, do you mind?"

His eyebrows rose. "Mind?" He grinned. "Not at all, I am not squeamish."

Squeamish? She bit her lip, unsure exactly how to tell him to go away without offending him, so she could find a leafy bush to squat behind and relieve herself.

His grin faded. "Oh, I thought you meant, *did I....*" After a beat he hopped to his feet, brow furrowed in confusion. He raised a finger as if preparing to make an important announcement. "You know it need not matter, I already have seen every—"

Her cheeks flamed and spread like wildfire down her neck. She knew what he was about to say, that he had seen her as she lay helpless, when he pulled down her underwear so she could relieve herself into a hollowed-out coconut husk he held in his hand. It was his fingers that had tied her tattered bra to cover her exposed breast.

He pointed. "Uh, I'll wait for you, on the beach." He retreated and stood by the shoreline, respectfully looking out to sea.

Audrey stood up on shaky legs. She hadn't eaten since Sinto forced her the day before her wound became infected. She was unsure how many days had passed since then.

She found a bush and squatted, releasing a long drawn-out sigh of relief. She laughed at Sinto's choice of words, like "squeamish" when related to seeing someone of the opposite sex naked and "cleansed" for washing her clothes. Legitimate use of the words but a little out of context from what she was used to. She had forgotten that about him from when they first met as children.

She wrapped the fur around her hips, tying the leather ties along her hip as Sinto so clearly demonstrated. She tugged the arm loops of her bra off her shoulders and over her arms and dropped it on the ground. She opted to leave her underwear on, *uncleansed* as they were.

The inside of the hide felt like butter against her skin, and she found herself instinctively petting the outer silky fur covering her thighs. She stole a glance at her backside. Giggled at the absurdity of the situation, where she was, how she must look.

Me Jane.

True to his word, Sinto patiently waited on the beach with his back to the jungle and eyes on the curved horizon of the sea, turning to face her as she approached.

"Well, what do you think?" She spun and realized too late that spinning was a bad idea.

Sinto caught her before she fell to the sand.

"I'm okay," she assured him, blinking away the dizziness. "I think I just stood up too quickly."

He felt her forehead, pressed his fingers across the smooth skin on her back, peered deeply into her eyes. "Perhaps you should stay out of the sun."

"Really, I'm okay, just hungry, and—I'm a little confused about how you healed me. From what I recall, what happened—how you—how I—" She made a mixed-up gesture with her hands. "Surely that was not possible."

"Would it matter if it was?"

He had a point and she pondered, *Would it?*

"You're whole again. That's all that matters." He smiled. "Which reminds me. I have something for you." He held out his hand.

Lying in his palm was an exquisite necklace. Pearls, crystals and other stones hung from hammered and twisted loops of silver. Hanging in the center of the necklace was a claw, two inches long from root to tip, stripped of soft tissue and polished to a high sheen.

"A token to remember me by."

"You made this?"

His cheeks colored and he nodded.

"When did you possibly find the time?"

"I needed something to stay busy while you slept. Several days have passed."

She pointed at the claw. "And this was…"

He gave her a pained smile. "Unfortunately."

He slipped behind her and clasped the necklace around her neck.

The necklace felt alive, silver links undulating hot and cold, the claw vibrating against her chest as if pulsing with the life of the deadly beast it once belonged to. She fingered the sharp tip that had recently parted her flesh and planted the seed of infection that nearly killed her.

She looked down at the fur clothing Sinto gave her, shimmering blue-gray fur with a broad stripe of dark blue. The same blue stripe that ran down the back of the tigers that chased her.

"The fur of the tiger who tried to end you, a bluestripe" he confirmed.

She gazed toward the campfire, and swallowed, "And the meat?"

"You needed nourishment. It would have been a waste otherwise. I respectfully shared the rest with the creatures in the forest."

She gasped.

He placed his finger on her lips. "Before you object, please answer me this. Do you like the necklace?"

He retracted his finger. Her lip tingled where he had touched it. He gazed back, eyes wide and glowing like bright-green light bulbs, anticipating her answer like a child seeking approval.

He had wrongly assumed she had meant to object. She was in thrall with what he had done. Forcing her to eat the flesh of the animal that nearly killed her to make her strong, for giving her something to cover her nakedness. Clothes that clearly meant much more to her than to him. She imagined him returning to the place where she was attacked. Dressing the kill, extracting the claw, skinning the carcass, hauling part of it back to the beach to roast over the fire, sick with worry over whether or not she would die. Sharing the rest with other creatures in the forest. Raptors, small mammals, maggot and worm. Nothing wasted. She was alive and healed as if she had never been attacked.

She fingered the claw hanging around her neck. And now this.

A token to remember me by.

Token or not, she would never forget what he had done for her. She would never forget him again. A simple thank you seemed trivial and insignificant. But that was all she had to give.

Tears threatened to spill. "Thank you for everything. For saving my life." Her fingers curled around the claw hanging around her neck. "And for this thoughtful gift. I can't imagine anything more beautiful."

His eyes lingered on her face, dropping to her lips for a brief moment before flicking back to meet her gaze. A touch of a smile tugged at his mouth. "I can."

21

Splintered Earth

AUDREY AND SINTO SAT in the shade of a prickly fronded palm tree nibbling on fruit and nuts. The jungle was alive with a typical day's movement—ants scavenging, leaves rustling, birds twittering. Moonstone stomped around on the beach, gobbling up sand fleas.

Sinto sat across from her, cross-legged, blissfully ignorant of the ruckus taking place in her ribcage. Her heart pounded and lungs quivered with each breath.

"No need to be afraid, just ask." He shoved half a banana-like fruit into his mouth.

The pent-up question burst from her lips. "What *are* you?"

He stopped chewing for a beat, then swallowed.

She continued, "You made me a promise once and, up until now, I believed it would never come true. The fire in your eyes, the way your skin feels so different from mine. I've waited ten years to learn of your secret. So, tell me, what *are* you?"

A smile slowly spread across his face and with each millimeter of movement his eyes grew bright and fiery. "I'm a human, just like you, but my ancestors traveled a different evolutionary path."

She gazed around the jungle, brushed her fingers across purple six-leaved clover growing beside her. "A different evolutionary path like the flora in the jungle and the fauna I observed in the meadow?"

He nodded.

"How can that be?"

He looked down at her knotted fingers in her lap.

"Are you afraid to learn the truth?"

She splayed her hands across her thighs, released a nervous laugh. "No—I mean, yes, a little, but mostly I'm curious. Everything here is different than I'm used to, like I've been transported to a small undiscovered island in the middle of the ocean. Are there such places left in the world?"

"Depends on what world you're referring to."

"Earth. What world are *you* referring to?"

"The other one."

Her heart skipped a beat and her voice squeaked, "Other one?"

He stood, rummaged for a small stick, then squatted with his chin on one bent knee, his other tucked beneath him. He smoothed the sand between them.

"The ancients tell us that roughly forty-two thousand years ago Earth's magnetic field flipped for a brief period of time before shifting back to its previous state—a geomagnetic excursion that registered barely a blip of geographic time. That event is documented in Earth's scientific texts as insignificant, but unbeknownst to your scientists, something very significant happened."

He drew a circle, tapped it with the sharp end of the stick. "Earth." He drew a second circle in the sand. "Earth was replicated. One became two." He tapped the original circle, then the new one he had drawn. "Earth, and the other one, *Merluma*."

"Replicated? Like cells dividing with identical DNA—er, I mean, obviously not with DNA, but hypothetically?"

He pondered, then smiled. "Yes, hypothetically, kind of like that, or maybe—"

She gasped. "A parallel universe?"

He smirked. "I find quantum physics puzzling, but anything is possible, I suppose, until proven otherwise."

"And this place, this is *Merluma*?"

"Yes."

"A separate *planet*?"

His brow quirked. "Not exactly."

He erased one of the circles and drew a diagonal line crossing through the remaining one, like the universal "no" symbol. "Imagine two worlds meant to be separate, but for reasons yet to be discovered, are stuck together, say... like conjoined twins." He ran a finger along the line. "One planet, splintered but seemingly independent. Picture one side as Earth, and then turned inside-out, the other as Merluma. Each with different personalities, but linked and inseparable. The fate of one dictates the fate of the other."

He tapped several places along the line. "Along the splinter are cracks. *Portals* that allow passage between the two worlds. We've been passing between the earth sisters for thousands of years, secretively and peacefully."

"And by *we*, you mean *you*—you're from Merluma?"

"I was born on Earth, but my ancestors were from Merluma. They tell us that when the event occurred, Homo-Sapiens were in the process of a great migration, across many frozen landscapes. Several tribes—as well as many other species—slipped through cracks within the ice and discovered Merluma."

"So what I have witnessed is how these species diverged over time."

"Yes!" He set down his stick and sat back. "Initially Merluma was like Earth, following the same geologic patterns, but eventually they diverged. Merluma became violently unstable as Earth settled. Merluma fevered and flooded; the seas rose from melted glaciers as well as water released from Merluma's layers of underlying mantel. Land masses were buried within the sea permanently, stranding many species on what tiny speck of land remained." He tapped the ground where they sat. "Here, on this lone island in the Great Ocean. What species remained were trapped, their access to Earth buried beneath the sea. Many died off, new ones were spawned, and those that survived did so by adapting. My ancestors called it the Great Upheaval. With a limited landmass to build up ice and with Merluma's mantel transformed, the water never retreated. Merluma was forever rendered as vastly different than its sister, Earth. Merluma is essentially an ocean of water."

Audrey scanned the treetops where rays of sunlight pierced the thick canopy full of vitality, occupying a sliver of land that rose above an otherwise water-based world. Life here progressed day after day oblivious to new and bewildering discoveries humans may make. She had no reason to doubt Sinto's story, yet struggled to free herself from doubt, instinctively rejecting these new facts because they defied her own beliefs. As a scientist she was well aware that once something was discovered, it was very likely that something new would be unearthed and shatter what was previously considered as scientific fact, with the new discovery taking precedence. The ground never rests beneath the feet of science. As long as humankind observes, more is revealed.

"So if Earth and Merluma are indeed one, one might assume they share the same solar system, and if they share the same solar system, why have our satellites not discovered Merluma from space?"

"That is a conundrum. One for which I have no answer. We observe none of your satellites in Merluma's sky. And Earth's satellites are unable to 'see' Merluma. How and why remains a deep mystery."

A deep mystery indeed. What Sinto described shattered every scientific theory of the universe. A single planet sharing the same solar system yet acting as two very separate worlds, with one unseen from space and undiscovered by the greatest minds and continual technological advancements. Connected but not. Did this turn quantum physics on its head, or confirm it? Or was this something else entirely? Her mind reeled and heart pounded at the possibility of a breakthrough discovery that would turn everything she knew about her world upside down, or more accurately, as Sinto had described, *inside out.*

"Tell me more about these portals."

"They are simply connections between Earth and Merluma."

"What other things might slip through these portals?"

"Mostly us, but sometimes other species find their way, unintended."

Audrey recalled the strange and wondrous creatures she witnessed in the meadow, how humans celebrate creatures like them and others in novels and movies and at fantasy conventions. How would the world react, learning they were real?

"Like unicorns and faeries?"

He chuckled. "Actually, yes. Your myths might be truer than you know. Those particular creatures are prevalent here. We try to retrieve whatever crosses over accidentally and put them back in their rightful place in an effort to not upset the natural balance."

"These portals, how many and where?"

"Ah, that is a secret that must remain so."

An awkward silence descended.

Why is he telling me this? Why am I here?

She thought back to the orca attack on *Annabelle*, of suddenly plunging into the Salish Sea and remembering nothing afterward. How she felt after she woke on the beach; the body aches, the ringing in her ears, the way they popped when she opened her mouth to scream. It made sense now. Effects from a sudden transition between worlds, like sinking to the bottom of a lake—a dramatic change in atmospheric pressure, or maybe from something else entirely.

She picked at the bracelet Blake had tied around her wrist. "How did you find me?"

He swallowed. "I followed you into the forest—"

"Not here, I mean, before. Did I accidentally slip through one of these cracks?"

His eyes cut to his fingers, kneading his kneecaps. It took him an awkward amount of time to answer. "I was passing through the Salish Sea and I found you floating on the surface, unconscious, clinging to a large white ring."

She took a deep breath. "Did you see a man with dark hair and blue eyes? He was with me right before I—"

He looked up, shook his head. "Just you."

Tears pricked behind her closed lids. She thought of the life ring she had clung to. She should have thrown it to Blake as soon as he fell overboard. Instead she panicked and, most likely, cost him his life.

"So why did you bring me here?"

"I recognized you. I thought you were dying, needed aid. So I brought you here, the safest place I could help you, without drawing unwanted attention."

"And ditched me on the beach *dying*?"

His eyes grew brighter and shifty. "By the time we reached—you seemed okay—uh, what exactly is the meaning of *ditched*?"

"Abandoned."

"Oh." His cheeks bloomed red. "I didn't abandon you."

"Then why did it take you so long to come forward? I mean, you could have said something before I took off my clothes in the meadow."

"I was retrieving my skins when you woke." Then he pointed toward Moonstone stomping around on the beach. "My companion, I had asked him to welcome you but he—he..." His eyes fell to his fingers wound tightly around his kneecaps.

He sighed heavily. "The truth is, I was afraid you wouldn't remember me." He suddenly looked like that boy she met long ago, a little unsure of himself. "I was planning to greet you when you woke up the next day, but you were gone."

She bit her lip. "I guess I should have been more patient."

"And I more bold."

She believed his reason as to why he had been hesitant. It was true, she had forgotten their childhood friendship under an avalanche of grief following her mother's untimely death, just as he feared.

He was a mystery then, as he was now. But mystery or not, she felt genuinely safe in his presence. After all, he did save her life. Twice. He hadn't taken advantage when she was at her most vulnerable, and he genuinely attended to her every need while she was unable. The necklace resting against her chest and the fur covering her body was testament to his compassionate and thoughtful character. And what he revealed about Merluma was the scientific discovery of the century, the *millennium.*

But she suspected Sinto wasn't being entirely truthful. Especially about her presence here, and why. And he seemed nervous when she asked about Blake. Yet she sensed there was more to Sinto's story, and he was anxious to finish it, she anxious to learn why.

His eyes glittered like cut emeralds anticipating her next question.

She cast her gaze to his hairless legs and funny toes, how the edges of his extra-large feet blended seamlessly into the sand. She traced the edge of his foot with her finger.

"Homo-Sapiens can't do that."

She gasped when he faded seamlessly into the background. Everything except his fiery green eyes and leather vest and wrap.

"Sapiens can't, but my kind can." His voice cut from the space below his disembodied eyes.

She reached out, finding purchase on his shoulder. Her fingers slid across deltoid and she marveled at the way the illusion wrapped around the curves of his body. She released her hand as he slowly faded back into view.

"If I am a Sapien, what should I call you?"

"I am a Merahvu. Long ago there were three distinct and warring tribes; Seakai, Terrakai, Arctakai. We fought for thousands of years in what we called the Forever War. It ended out of necessity, before we drove ourselves out of existence. Peace was struck, and all three tribes were unified under a common governing circle and a singular name, *Merahvu*. We're still fiercely protective of our tribal roots, but share an understanding of respect and compassion toward one another. And we equally submit to the ruling Circle of Representatives, upholding the symbolism of a common name. I am a bit of a rarity being of dual-tribe; half-Terrakai and half-Seakai, but I proudly describe myself as Merahvu, as do all, regardless of which tribe we were born into.

"The Merahvu extend this respect to Sapiens of Earth, as we hope Sapiens would to us, should our existence, and that of Merluma, ever be exposed."

She looked up, capturing Sinto's gaze. In that moment she realized the significance of what he implied. She knew exactly why Sinto never told her his secret, even though he had promised to long ago. If Sapiens of Earth discovered Merluma, both their worlds would be impacted in profound ways. The threat of violation, a potential land grab, a shift in geopolitical power. Earth's history reveals over and over that discoveries such as Merluma could only lead to one thing; exploitation, territorial conflict—war.

"Oh no. No, what you're telling me, if this ever came to light, this could be bad. Very bad."

Sinto took her hand. "It doesn't have to be. Merluma has been a secret my kind have honored and fiercely protected, through tribal war and now peace, as we have for thousands and thousands of years. It is possible to forge new alliances, peacefully. It happens every day, without you knowing it."

She thought back to how easily his skin shifted. His ability to camouflage shockingly sophisticated. "And the Merahvu have been living among us secretly, potentially camouflaged as you just demonstrated?"

He shook his head. "It is much easier to hide in the open. It's not a stretch for us to pretend to be Sapien."

She flashed back to the mythical creatures she witnessed in the meadow, back to that day they first met as kids. How he came to the beach from nowhere, watching her form sand creatures. The inclusion of "mer" to describe where he came from and what his kind called themselves. The use of "sea" in one of their tribal names.

She leaned forward. "And what about venturing across the sea?"

He made a funny face, like the answer to her question should be obvious.

"Are you implying you're a *Mer*-man?"

His lips pressed into a thin white line. "We are not half-fish beings or seals with magical cloaks, nor are we bound to the sea as your myths may lead you to believe—wild embellishments of the truth. We are Merahvu. We prefer to live on land and travel by sea, although, if necessary, we can survive underwater for quite some time. We are not sea creatures—we are human, and we are amphibious."

So it was true. Her mother told her fantastical stories passed down by her Polynesian ancestors of a mysterious tribe that frequently visited their Pacific islands long before the Europeans arrived. Strange beings with eyes of fire and hair that shimmered like gold, who had no need for a canoe because they were strong swimmers. After she died, Audrey's father told her that her mother made up those stories to teach her simple life lessons in a fun way, that they were merely fantasies.

If only he knew.

But there was a troubling problem with Sinto's story.

"If what you say is true, it would take tens, maybe hundreds, of thousands of years for Merahvu to evolve so dramatically different from Sapiens. How is that possible?"

"A quirk about Merluma. Time sweeps at a different rate, much faster here than on Earth. Currently, one day here equates roughly to one hour on Earth. It didn't start out that way. At first it was the same, until Merluma was covered by water. The advance of time accelerated on Merluma while time remained unchanged on Earth. Because of that, my ancestors evolved for hundreds of thousands of Merluma years, surpassing Homo-Sapiens, and becoming an entirely new epithet within the genus Homo."

"Homo-*Merahvu*."

"Does have a nice ring to it."

Audrey pondered for a moment. "Do you...do you have a tail?" she asked sheepishly.

The tension in his shoulders eased and he gave her a sly smile. "Of course."

"Well?"

"Well, what?"

"Show me, show me everything about you that's different."

22

Anatomy Lesson

Sinto grinned ear to ear. "I thought you would never ask."

Audrey trembled with anticipation. So many things about Sinto were a mystery. From the light emitted from his eyes to his oddly shaped toes. He helped her stand up and he took a step back so she could see him fully.

He splayed his fingers. Between each was a translucent web of skin, nearly invisible to the naked eye, and thin and resilient to the touch. He wriggled his toes to draw her attention. His feet quivered and from his toes emerged flexible bones about six inches long connected by translucent skin like the webbing between his fingers.

"Retractable fins! That's why your toes look funny and feet are so big!"

He retracted them with a sudden snap. Then he turned his back to her and removed his vest, exposing his broad shoulders and thickly muscled back. The skin atop his shoulders peeled back. Tips of a fluked tail rose and unfurled, extending twice the width of his shoulders like a pair of wings. The muscle along his spine puckered and swelled and with a soft sucking sound his tail was released, and curled toward her. She stepped back, giving way to his unique and fascinating appendage. With a gentle thrust of hip, it flopped to the sand, fluke spread between them. Decorative markings ran down the spine of his revealed back, along the ridge of his tail, and on to the fluked tips. The markings continued around his hips and disappeared beneath the front side of his wrap.

She gasped at the beauty displayed. Embossed swirls and dots laced together, some dots laid out in trios forming a triangle. The combined effect was exquisite and wild. The swirls looped like the pounded silver of the necklace he gave her, with dangling stones and pearls like the dots in between. The necklace mimicked his unique markings.

A token to remember me by.

She lost all sense of decorum. Like the gravity grounding her feet, her fingers were drawn to touch him. Her fingers swept across the top of his shoulders where the fluke lay when tucked. She traced the swirls and dots along his spine and around the curve of his hips.

Sinto drew a sudden breath when her fingers reached the top of his wrap. She quickly withdrew her hand, shocked by her brazen action and the fact she was so absorbed by the feel of his skin and the embossing of his markings she didn't realize how close she came to touching him in uncharted places.

"No need to stop. It's just—I'm not used to being touched... like that." She bit her lip. He smiled and placed her hand back on his hip. "It's okay, I know you're curious."

She moved her hand to his upper arm, smooth and free of hair. Her fingers slipped effortlessly across the surface to his shoulders as if he was coated with a layer of silicone. But when she rubbed her fingers together, they were void of any kind of residue; the slickness was a natural feature of his skin.

The muscles beneath his skin hummed like coils of live wires. And the more she touched him, the more her fingers began to tingle.

She stepped around to face him, stifling a gasp. His pectorals were merely smooth rounds of solid muscle. No nipples. No scars from them being forcefully removed.

He grinned. "There are many pesky aquatic creatures that tend to latch onto things that protrude. Females are as you would expect, though their breasts are covered by a protective layer of skin—as are other parts of our anatomy—embellished by markings like the ones on my back. Merahvu males are born without mammary glands."

"Are you all marked like this?"

"Yes, but in our own unique way. The swirls I inherited from my mother, the dots from my father."

"And your skin, it's different too."

"Thicker than yours with a dense layer of fatty tissue for insulation."

She pressed a finger to his chest. It felt like there was a layer of neoprene just beneath his skin, and under that, the muscle was hard as rock. Once as a child, she swam with a dolphin. The feel of Sinto's skin and the density of muscle underneath reminded her of the massive power that dolphin packed in a small package. When she withdrew her finger from Sinto's chest, it took a while for the indentation to fade.

He placed her hand to the hollow of his sternum, below his heart beating strong and in rhythm with his pupils. "This is where we differ the most," he said. "My merlux. It charges a fluid which flows through my bloodstream and electrifies my skin. It is my greatest weapon for defense."

His merlux was the source of the subtle buzz that emanated from his chest whenever his eyes glowed. The skin beneath her fingers crackled and sparked. She tried to pull away but her palm was stuck by the weight of his hand atop hers. Her heart pounded its way up her throat and fell into rhythm with his. They stood like that for a while, her hand stuck, gazing into each other's eyes. When he let go, her palm felt pleasantly numb.

"Is that why that bird stopped me from touching you in the jungle?"

He blushed. "Sometimes my merlux reacts on its own when I'm threatened. The way you were wielding that stake set off a primal instinct. If you had touched me then, I could have accidentally electrified you. I was most grateful that didn't happen."

"Me too." The words came out barely a whisper, having lost her breath. Electrified skin. How dangerous a simple touch could be! "Is that why your eyes exploded with green fire?"

A wave of confusion rippled across his face, then vanished with sudden understanding. He nodded. "The day we met, the way you held onto me—my merlux reacted as if I'd been threatened. Especially by the fact you wouldn't let go... I panicked and did the only thing possible to not shock you. I vented the voltage through my eyes."

"Now I understand why you never let me touch you after."

She knelt at his feet pretending to study his odd toes. Her hands knotted, afraid to touch him.

"I won't shock you, if that is what you're afraid of."

She looked up, gave him a shaky smile. He extended his foot fins and wagged his toes, teasing her to touch them. Finally, she did, tracing the boning protruding from his toes, the meshing in between resilient but translucent as a fine lace.

He flinched. "That tickles."

"Sorry!" She looked up and without thinking, her gaze fell and lingered where his wrap hung across his groin, where his markings slipped underneath. She felt her face fever, both by curiosity and the sudden image her mind conjured as to what was hidden beneath. She stood and turned away from his curious gaze, pretending her eyes and mind had not probed that part of him, and began fiddling with the tie on her hip.

He spun her around. "That part of me works the same, though there is something that differs." He reached around to untie his wrap.

Audrey grabbed his hands. "Er, maybe you don't need to show me *everything*."

"Are all Sapiens so modest?" He brushed a wisp of hair from her eyes.

A bead of sweat trickled down her ribcage. Her curiosity treading into more dangerous territory.

Think of something else quick!

"Show me your gills."

The skin on his neck flickered and a trio of narrow slits flared. He held them open so she could peek inside. The edges were translucent, the inside a dark-red meshing. He snapped them shut, the openings invisible and nestled perfectly within the curve of his neck where the jugular vein lie, invisible to the naked eye.

She reached for them but he stopped her. "That, uh, might not be such a good idea. Our gills are extremely sensitive, in an intimate sort of way. Physically, and in our culture, touching me there is a clear gesture of intention and consent."

She tucked her hand under her chin. "Oh."

"No need to be sorry, but please try not to forget."

She quickly changed the subject. "Wow, I'm speechless. Your adaptations are exquisite. I—uh—"

"Do you trust me?"

"Trust you to what?"

"Show you my world."

23

Underwater Fantasy

SINTO GRASPED AUDREY'S HAND and pulled her toward the water.

She dug her heels in the sand. "Wait!" She wriggled her hand from his grip.

He cocked his head in confusion.

"I'm afraid of the water."

He gently spun her around, pressed her back to his chest, slipped his feet beneath hers, and coaxed her to move forward in that liquidly graceful way. "Why do you fear the sea?"

Her eyes were fixed on the water, brilliant blue and intoxicatingly mesmerizing. "It's not the sea I'm afraid of, it's..." She was close to spilling tears. She desperately wanted to see his world but couldn't overcome the fear of drowning.

"There's nothing to fear as long as you're with me."

She nervously petted the fur lying across her chest, trying to ignore the fact he was leading her to the edge of the water. "But this beautiful fur... it will get wet."

"Do you feel wet?" That was when she realized they were waist deep in the water, and true to his word she didn't feel wet.

"See, you can trust me."

Then he pulled her under.

Despite his assurances and the fact her head felt dry, fear consumed her, fighting to escape the confines of her chest like a giant moth trapped inside. Her mind went blank, trying to recall her mantra, afraid to open her eyes, afraid of what she would see.

She felt covered by a thick blanket, soft and squishy beneath her feet and warm and humid pressed against her skin, like the tropical air on the beach.

"Open your eyes," he said.

His voice was crystal clear and when she opened her eyes her cheek was pressed against his chest, her arms wound tightly around him. She had no idea that she had spun around and was hugging him like a lifeline. Regardless of how bold it felt she had no intention of letting go.

A thick transparent gel engulfed their bodies, separating them from the surrounding sea.

Sinto loosened her arms from their death grip around his torso. The stuff covering their bodies stretched outward like a giant bubble, opening the space between them. They were several feet below the surface, hovering above the corrugated sandy bottom. The water was crystal clear. She could see at least a hundred feet in all directions.

She held her breath, afraid to breathe. The stuff inside the bubble felt dense like water, but her hair and the fur covering her were dry. Her lungs began to burn. As much as she wanted to trust him, her instincts did not. Air escaped her lungs and hovered between them like soap bubbles.

Sinto shook her gently. "Breathe." She didn't understand. He wasn't breathing through his gills but through his nose. But how?

The burning in her chest became unbearable, dark spots stealing snippets of her vision. Her fear of drowning was doing just that; she was suffocating herself.

He shook her more forcefully. "Breathe!"

Her knees buckled. Sinto said something else, but the ringing in her ears drowned out his voice. Then she heard a whisper, weaving through the ringing like a thought.

Trust me.

She didn't remember opening her mouth, but her lungs suddenly filled with a fizzy liquid, startlingly cool and satisfying to her oxygen-starved lungs. It tasted like the sea, sweet and briny. Her eyes widened from the shock and pleasure of it. She gulped down several breaths, laughing at the tiny bubbles tickling her nose.

"Careful, what you're breathing is highly oxygenated. It will make you feel amazingly good." His grin stretched to the outer limits of his cheeks.

Her senses sharpened and mind cleared. "More like... Wow!"

"Pure water has that effect."

"I'm breathing water?"

"Oxywater, a breathable liquid whipped up to trick your lungs, like breathing a warm misty air."

A school of rainbow fish swam by. Curious, one stopped to nibble on the outer surface of the bubble engulfing them. It sparked. The fish twitched, then flickered away to rejoin the others. Audrey cautiously poked the bubble with her finger. It flexed and bounced back, strong and resilient. Ripples and sparks skittered across its surface.

"How did you—where did this—" She poked the bubble again. "Come from?"

He held out his arm. A thick bead of an oil-like substance rose from a tiny pore in his skin. He pinched it between his fingers and rubbed it in the palm of her hand. It spread like oil, lingering for a moment before evaporating.

"An oily excretion from special glands in my skin. It thickens once exposed to water to form a protective shell."

She pressed her palm to the side of the bubble. "There are creatures from the deep sea that form a protective cover like this, *lorica*."

"Yes, lorica." He smiled. "My lorica provides a layer of thermal protection and siphons oxygen from the water. The result is oxywater." He took a sip and rolled it around in his mouth as if sampling a fine wine.

Her fingers tingled. The spark, the fish. She withdrew her hand. "Electrified?"

"A defense mechanism."

"And you always venture into the water protected like this?"

"Only when we descend to deeper depths where there may be little or no oxygen or we require additional thermal protection." He eyed her with curiosity. "And, as you have just proven, it is sufficient enough to host a Sapien guest."

She gasped, clearly remembering his promise to trust him. "You didn't know?"

He grinned mischievously. "I thought you were studying to be a scientist? Are scientists not eager to test new theories?"

"Yes, but..."

He hooked his finger. "Come here."

She hesitated, wondering what other theories he wanted her to test.

He laughed and grabbed her hand. "I don't bite." Then he spun her around and pressed her back to his chest.

The bubble contracted, hugging their clasped bodies like a second skin. When she opened her mouth in panic, it went no further than her lips and she was able to suck a lungful of oxywater.

Sinto flicked his tail and they were off, flying through the bay in a blur of whipped-up bubbles.

An underwater metropolis unfolded like a living Monet painting, bursting with color and movement and a din of pops and ticks. Sea creatures of all kinds swam by, big and small, thin and fat, smooth and prickly, thin-lipped and plump-lipped and no lipped at all. Some had teeth, others baleen. Some scurried along the bottom with spiky long legs, some floated on wings and soared above their heads, others struggled to keep their bellies afloat. Some darted from holes, devouring unsuspecting prey passing by, while others nibbled along the gills of monstrous hosts or stole shredded bits of flesh spilling from their toothy jaws.

Strange scents filled Sinto's bubble, sweet and spicy, mouthwatering and vile. She wanted to stop and discover what made these scents of the sea, but Sinto insisted they press on, claiming there was more to see.

Beyond the reef, sea grass spread across the sandy bottom like a field of tender young barley. Sea turtles feasted. Hatchlings dove between blades of grass when Sinto and Audrey swam by. Juveniles chased after them, brushing their wrinkly noses against their outstretched hands. Along the sandy fringe adult males mounted females in pockets of frenzied orgies.

Sinto noticed Audrey was gawking. "They started mating all the time, not just in season, as are all the other creatures. We're not sure why. Recently, it began in earnest."

They continued toward the bay's outer reefs where the sea surged and boiled from ocean swells crashing over them. He swam along the base of the reef poking inside dark holes where things with glowing eyes lurked, then he dove inside one of those holes, a cave barely big enough for the two of them. He swam deeper and deeper until they burst through the other side and into the dark open ocean.

A school of sharks as big as great whites circled above but one in particular outsized them all. It made the great whites look like minnows.

"Is that a megalodon?" she gasped.

"One of the last of her kind."

The megalodon was prehistoric and considered long extinct, and this one looked every bit the part—covered with giant barnacles and ancient battle scars. Remora swam alongside its massive body, equally impressive in size. The megalodon circled and swam up beside them. Audrey could see the entirety of their bodies reflected in the megalodon's platter-sized fathomless eyes.

Sinto swam alongside, touching the megalodon's head. "She is a magnificent and misunderstood creature." He gave Audrey a mischievous smile once he withdrew his hand.

The megalodon bolted and disappeared in the murky distance, the other sharks following in her wake.

Audrey sighed in relief but a moment too soon.

The megalodon exploded from the abyss like a jet bursting from a cloud, bearing down on them with mouth agape and endless rows of teeth flexed and ready to shred.

Audrey struggled to escape from Sinto's grip, but he held firm, placing her between the megalodon and his body. He was laughing hysterically, like a madman who had saved her only to feed her to this mighty shark!

A scream froze in her throat as she watched the megalodon bear down. She imagined her bones crushed and flesh shredded, the sudden gush of blood staining the water; of her dying—cold and alone—in the dark, slimy belly of this "magnificent and misunderstood" beast.

The megalodon arched back and veered, snapping her mighty jaws shut before she reached them. Audrey's head slammed against Sinto's chest from the surge of water exploding from the megalodon's mouth. The massive shark circled, mockingly grinning as she passed by before lazily swimming away with the others, trailing behind.

"What an adrenaline rush! What is not to love about such a magnificent beast!" Sinto's eyes were on fire as he struggled to catch his breath.

Her voice was still stuck in her throat. She wanted to tell him she loved it so much that she had nearly peed all over the beautiful wrap he had made for her. She punched him in the chest, not hard but enough to get his attention. "Was that some sort of demonstration? Scheming with that monster! Could you have not picked a dolphin or a turtle or something less menacing?"

His jaw snapped shut and he fixed her with an incredulous stare. "I thought you would find that exhilarating." He was dead serious.

Once she regained her voice and her wits, she apologized for hitting him and confessed; it *was* quite a thrill, and goaded for more with a finger to his ribs, but maybe not with something so deadly.

Laughing, he said, "Of course." Then he swam farther out to sea, until the color of the water shifted from indigo to turquoise. The sandy bottom gave way to a barren reef in the middle of nowhere, swept clean of life by the relentless flow of violent water.

A swell swept across the ocean, tripped on the reef, and rose up. A wave was born. They hovered beside the reef on the deep sandy bottom, watching the magic unfold. A wall of liquid stretched toward the sky like a skyscraper, until finally it toppled under its own weight and continued on its way, like a massive barrel banded by glistening vortices. The sea rumbled and roiled; whirlpools stirred sand and tugged at their bodies.

Sinto grew solemn, intensely studying each wave form and die, each growing bigger and fiercer. He drew deeper and fuller breaths, oxygenating his blood like a runner preparing to sprint.

"I need your help," he said, then twined his legs around her ankles and sandwiched them against his fluked tail. "Flow with me. Together, we swim!"

She gasped when he burst into action—legs, tail, and core pumping in a graceful rhythm like ripples rolling across a pond. Up they climbed as an integral part of the growing wave, building in height and strength. A race to the top before it toppled and died. She struggled at first, trying to grasp the timing of Sinto's intricate rhythm. It was a whole-body affair, conjoined with another in a foreign dance, bodies melded stem to stern. A physical intimacy to which she was accustomed; like the tangled holds she fought to escape during her martial arts training. But this physical connection was kinder and gentler, like the healing night when she had shared his body—as if she were a fetus in the womb, or a child cradled to a mother's bosom.

Not once had Sinto taken advantage of her. He saved her life and administered the caregiving that followed, no matter how unpleasant. He had respected her modesty, and, throughout, her dignity and need for independence. He encouraged her to overcome her fear of the water and brought her to the brink of heart failure for the sake of a thrill. And now this. It felt like taking that first breath upon waking from a coma, like feeling a cool mist rising from the ocean and the explosion of sweetness when tasting a mango for the first time. Like the blossoming of deep and selfless love between lovers or a parent and newborn child.

Heart palpitating, breath bated, it struck her.

This is what it feels like to be truly alive!

It felt strange to let go, to release years of guardedness, to extinguish the fear and paranoia instilled in every lesson, every lecture, day after day, as her father insisted—loveless teachings without passion and for questionable purpose.

She melted against Sinto's body and gave into the heat and vibrations radiating from his chest, the slick feel of his skin where it touched hers, his breath grazing her cheek. And when she gazed up to meet his eyes she saw a future bright and hopeful. All she had to do was open her eyes, her heart, her mind; to trust another.

Was it fate that Sinto found her, first on that beach ten years ago and again in the Salish Sea? She had learned to fear fate. Fate took her mother and turned her father into a cold and heartless man. Fate knocked Blake into an unforgiving sea... Was fate a thing to fear or seek? Surely it was fate that brought Sinto back to her after all these years.

Faster they swam, fiercely pumping combined muscle as one body for fear they would fail to reach the top and fall, crashing on the reef below and being ground to bits under thousands of pounds of churning water.

They moved with the speed and strength of a dolphin gracefully slipping through the sea. Up, up, up they rose till they could go no further. Sinto veered and suddenly they were zipping along inside the top of the wave, through a crystal hallway, rays of sunlight bleeding through its walls and refracting into a rainbow of color.

I'm surfing inside a wave!

When the wave reached its zenith, they burst through the top and rode the cresting lip on arched bellies, arms spread wide, soaring through the air like a seagull hovering atop a thermal.

In the distance were the lands of Sinto's ancestral world, a speck in an endless sea; slivers of pale yellow and green, and black craggy teeth covered with gleaming snow and topped with a misty cap. In that magical moment, Audrey breathed deeply of Sinto's world, free of noise and pollution and the frustration of Sapien-made things that don't work right, or technology that drove humanity into isolation. A world filled with natural beauty, danger, and hidden potential.

In that moment, perched atop a liquid mountain, vulnerable to the whims of a selfless being from a strange world she never knew existed until this day, she had never felt so real and alive.

Sinto rolled into a ball, their bodies spooned together, and they tumbled down the face of the wave. The sea rushed up and swallowed them whole. The wave followed like a fist from the sky and punched them down to the depths of the sea. Deeper and deeper they sank beyond the froth and chaos to a dark silent world aglow with alien creatures.

Tears of joy streamed and her voice quivered. "Can we do that again?"

Sinto eagerly obliged.

Over and over they climbed, whizzed, and plunged. A pod of dolphins joined them, dodging and racing. Soon it became a game; the goal to climb higher and hang in the lip longer. Sinto kept winning, of course, whipping the dolphins into a frenzy with his frantic laughter. Audrey watched in awe as the dolphins strategized and formed tag teams; one dolphin would nip at their heels while another tried to nudge them aside. Audrey didn't care who won or lost—she was too busy marveling at their grace and antics.

They finally succumbed to exhaustion, and pressed together as one body, lazily swam back to shore, breathlessly chattering, regaling in their underwater adventures.

The sea churned violently the closer they came to shore. The bottom rose up and turtles swayed in the surge, nibbling on algae growing on black rock. The water swirled between boulders where giant whirlpools drew figure eights in the sea with a fizz of aerated water. Sinto dove inside one, taking advantage of the current. Around they swirled and were launched to the surface at breakneck speed. Then they were airborne, like a troublesome seed spit from the mouth of the sea.

Sinto's lorica liquified and rolled off their bodies. Salt spray filled Audrey's eyes and wind whipped through her hair. She blinked away tears from the sudden shock of it.

Still entangled, they flew toward the rocky shore, arms spread like wings, past glinting knife tips stabbing the sky and ringing a black pool of still water. Sinto released a giddy war cry and dove. Her muffled scream drowned when her head went under.

Sinto burst to the surface elated. Audrey clawed up his chest, gasping and coughing up water.

She splashed water in his face. "Why did you do that?"

His glee fizzled. Sinto said nothing and dragged her to the edge of the pool and lifted her onto a shallow ledge. She stood, heart pounding, sucking air. Beads of water rolled down her body, like pesky ants crawling across her skin.

With the flick of his tail Sinto leapt from the water and landed gracefully on his feet beside her. She cowered and turned away, arms hugging her chest, ashamed.

He reached for her, but she pushed his hand away, not entirely sure why. She burned with anger and humiliation, not because of him but because of her baseless and stupid fear.

He stepped back, mouth gaped as if trying to say something. His gaze fell to his fingers pumping into fists. A clenching of jaw, then, "I'm sorry. I made you a promise, I let you down. That will never happen again."

Seeing the disappointment in his eyes made her want to cry. After all he had done for her, she had acted like a helpless child. She was the one who should apologize.

Her heart quivered when she fingered the bracelet around her wrist. "You've nothing to be sorry about. It's me, my hopeless fear of the water. And because of it I've lost a good friend. My friend Blake he's—he's gone because of my fear." She sucked down a sob. "Oh god, I feel so sick inside!"

Years of pent-up grief bubbled up. Sinto reached for her but she turned away and sat, hugging her knees to her chest. Jittering sobs shook her body and erupted from her mouth. Tears rolled down her cheeks. Tears for her mother, for Blake, for the man who was once her loving father. Tears for the hopeful and trusting girl she used to be. Tears for Sinto having to apologize...

Tears are for the meek. Words spoken by her father whenever she cried from exhaustion, from the bruises and sore muscles, from the brutalized bones in her feet and hands, teetering on the brink of shattering from smashing stacks of wood he held in his hands. *Again,* he would say, over and over. *Again.* She despised that word. Never had he said, *enough.* All the grueling lessons, the isolation, the tests she had endured. All that, and yet, she failed to save her friend.

She didn't know how long she sat there, gazing at the water lapping at her toes. The sun was much lower in the sky and the fur covering her body was nearly dry.

Sinto came up from behind, crouched and offered her a conch shell of water.

She took a sip, poured some in her hand and rinsed the salty tears from her face. "I'm sorry you had to witness that."

He took her hand and squeezed it. "And I'm sorry about your friend, and for..." He shook his head, having decided not to continue.

Then he gave her a sad smile. "But mostly, I'm sorry that it's time I take you home."

24

Salamora

AUDREY GAZED AT HIS outstretched hand, eyes rimmed red from crying. She looked so small sitting there with her long legs folded and knees tucked beneath her chin.

"I don't want to go," she whispered.

Sinto cradled her hand with his. "You don't belong here."

She looked up. "I don't care!"

He would swallow the Great Ocean to keep her here or go with her, if he could. "I don't belong in your world any more than you belong in mine."

He pulled her to her feet.

"Will I ever see you again?"

He felt a pang of regret. "Someday."

"What do you mean? Years from now? Tomorrow?"

"Soon."

He had made the connection he sought. Earned her friendship and, he was quite certain, her trust. He had enlightened her with the truth of Merluma and of the Merahvu. She had accepted the token. Goal achieved, assigned task dutifully accomplished. It was time to set her free. How much time would pass until their next meeting was entirely up to her.

Yet here he stood, feet deeply rooted like a snaggletree in the Desertlands on the other side of the ridge, reluctant and requiring great effort to move. It was time to gather her things and do that last thing he must, something he knew was profoundly wrong and insensitive to her privacy.

Her gaze fell to his mouth and she touched his lips with her fingers. A daring move, unexpected, and much more intimate than he anticipated from such a simple touch, finger to lip. It was only yesterday he had touched her more than that; finger to bone, stitching her back together, forming new muscle, tendon, nerves, vessels, the connective threading encapsulating all. Then the final act, wrapping it all up with a layer of soft skin perfectly blended to match the rest of her. Like the skin at the tip of her finger lying gently against his lower lip.

His breath hitched and merlux buzzed in an unsettling way to which he was unaccustomed. Not to defend himself from her, but to draw her closer. He felt tangled strands of electricity reach out to embrace her. He puzzled over this new and thrilling thing.

Without a thought he cradled her jaw with his fingers, more skin touching, like magnets clicking into place. He could feel her tremble and when she parted her lips a breath escaped her mouth. He breathed deeply the soft and subtle smell of her; sweet like honey, with touch of cinnamon spice.

He memorized every aspect of her face, the dark peachy glow of her skin. A jut of dark lashes framing her dark innocent eyes. The dramatic slash of wild brows, slightly askew from the day's adventure. The faint line in between that deepened when she thought no one was watching.

His gaze froze on her mouth. Where her top lip was slightly fuller than the bottom, the way it curled up like a cresting wave, temping him to ride it with his own. He wanted to kiss her, deeply so, to discover how well her lips would fit against his own.

But duty snapped him to the present. The consequences too great. He had vowed to gain her trust and friendship. Nothing more.

He broke the magnetic pull of his fingers from her jaw and tucked a loose strand of hair curved against her neck back into the messy braid from where it had escaped.

Her lips parted in surprise and disappointment. It pained him to see the sadness that filled her eyes, the sudden crease deepening between her brows. She turned away, wiping away a tear. Not the way he envisioned their parting.

His throat was a knot and he was afraid his voice would fail him. "Do you remember the meaning of *salamora*?"

She gave him a sad smile. "A promise to meet again."

He nodded. To the Merahvu, "salamora" didn't represent mere words or a simple promise. It was so much more. A sharing of deep and profound understanding born from the heart and that thing that defines who one truly was—of that thing Sapiens call a *soul* and the Merahvu call *essence*.

He looked into her eyes and pushed the true meaning toward her conscious mind, a word carrying the weight of a blood promise, never to be spoken lightly and never to be broken, a word encapsulating the commitment and depth of one's respect, love, and friendship. A spiritual message from one to another, a message beyond words. A promise of more. To share in joy and sorrow, support and sacrifice. An unconditional expression of selfless caring for another.

He had not expected her to acknowledge, lacking the understanding or experience necessary to interpret the non-verbal communication of *sharing*, as the Merahvu frequently do, with *salamora* being one of the more common expressions passed between family, friend, or lover. Like a kiss or hug goodbye, only so much more. Only in the height of the healing, when she had opened her mind for him to save her life, had they made small steps toward sharing simple thoughts.

He was surprised when she reached for her temple and shivered. "Was that you?"

His heart pounded in delight. "Yes! Salamora. More than a simple promise spoken in words."

Her cheeks bloomed and she nodded in understanding. Then he wrapped her in his arms and held her, gathering the strength to let go, to take her home. He imprinted every detail of this moment to memory; the smell of her hair, the feel of her skin, the sound of her fluttering heart. He held her, helpless to let go, to look her in the eyes and do that thing that he deeply regretted.

To violate her mind without her permission.

He gave a silent apology when he released her, pulling back enough to gaze into her eyes, innocent eyes filled with trust and wonder. Trust he had won, but did not deserve. Not after this, and certainly not after she learns the truth she has yet to discover and her innocent understanding of his world is crushed.

And here she stood, unaware of her fate. Unaware of how vulnerable her mind was, how vulnerable she was to the seed of suggestion, how near to the surface her secrets bubbled, tempting him to take a peek. It was not his place to seek what he yearned. He was to complete his task, nothing more. Bliss was blind.

What she would feel next was a slight tickle, like a drop of water rolling down her ear canal, a tiny prick to the ear drum, a gentle squeeze of the vagus nerve resting at the base of her skull, linking the mind to the body.

She twitched upon the initial contact, and he hovered at the gates of her mind. What he was about to do was far more intimate than the kiss she had desired or when he had distracted her mind by sharing his body during the healing of her wound. He would be privy to her deepest secrets threaded amongst innocent memories.

He delved inside, riding neuron pathways, sifting through recent memories, plucking only those that included her last few days; of waking on this very beach, of their fateful meeting, the bluestripes' attack, sharing his mind, of his beginnings, of Merluma. Memories he bundled and buried alongside his message. A message that would manifest once her subconscious mind digested everything he had told her, when the overwhelming knowledge he shared cooled from a boil to a simmer, once rational thought and acceptance ruled over the shock and hysteria of these newfound truths and what they meant to her future. And finally, once she accepted the fate of her friend and gained a safe emotional distance, then and only then would she discover the key to unlock his message and the flood of memories he hid from her.

As an afterthought, he decided to plant a small and harmless suggestion, one he hoped she would be thankful for, the next time she encountered water.

When it was done, she fell limp in his arms, fast asleep. He gently lay her on the sand so he could retrieve her things.

He respectfully stripped her of the fur coverings and the necklace he had made for her, then clothed her in her original things, slowly and methodically, all but for the shirt shredded in the attack. He clasped the hooks on her tattered bra, buttoned up her jeans, zipped up her coat, pulled up her socks one at a time, then her shoes, using care to tie neat even bows like the ones he had watched her tie as he hid in the shadows.

He zipped the necklace inside her coat pocket and slipped the life ring she held when he first retrieved her through his arm, scooped her up from the sand, and carried her to the water's edge where the sea was painted fiery red by the echoing rays of the setting sun.

Encased by his protective lorica, he dove with her cradled in his arms to the dark depths where the crack between Earth and Merluma lay.

He broke through the first of two membranes separating their worlds, to that place the Merahvu called the *between*. The sudden transition in time and space made her gasp in her unconscious state, and Sinto—having passed through cracks between the worlds many times before—clamped his teeth against the bone-crushing pressure filling his head and the joint-aching tug of limb and appendages throughout his body. Then they shot through the second membrane to the other side. She would endure no long-term consequence from their passing, only brief discomfort that would subside, as it did now for Sinto—joint pain and nausea and an unbearable ringing filling his head.

The teal-green waters of the Salish Sea brightened and filled with movement. He circled a sunken ship—a Sapien-made reef abundant with sea life—until he reached the thick linked chain sprouting from the bottom of the sea, anchoring a large buoy floating on the surface.

That was where he left her, lying on the buoy near the shore of the island not far from the waters where he took her, seven Earth hours prior.

He slipped back into the sea with *salamora* planted in her quieted mind.

25

Rescue

AUDREY LAY ON A buoy among crusty piles of seal scat, shivering in fits and starts. Her head pounded and an incessant ringing filled her ears. Clutched to her chest was *Annabelle*'s life ring.

Discontinuous memories bobbed in her mind like weightless pieces of a puzzle. She imagined reaching out and sorting them into piles of like colors and patterns, to make sense of the chaos, but her mind was as numb as her fingers.

The noise in her head grew intolerable and her eardrums felt as if they were about to burst. She closed her eyes and began drawing deep controlled breaths through her nose, focusing on the air flowing in and out of her lungs.

To her surprise it worked. Her ears popped and the noise eventually subsided, as did the ache in her head and every joint of her body.

A flood of memories followed: of Blake's kiss, of orcas surrounding *Annabelle*, and then mayhem and Blake disappearing beneath the surface. The last thing she remembered was *Annabelle* sinking as she slid down the cockpit before falling into the water. She didn't remember climbing onto the buoy or how she came to find it.

She sat up, using care not to slip from her precarious perch. Mounted to the top of the buoy was a sign: "Andrews Island Marine Preserve: Fishing or Anchoring Prohibited. Diving by Permit Only." Nearby, two mooring buoys dotted the rippled surface of the water.

A memory sparked. Something Blake had recently told her. Below the water's surface was an old sunken ship, creating a prolific reef. He said that Andrews Island was a privately owned preserve, and was the only island in the San Juan archipelago that had been left in its native state and was never logged. At the heart of the island, old-growth trees grew to the size of a house.

Fifty yards from the buoy and marking the east-most point of the island was a low-banked pebble beach facing southeast.

She looked at the life ring in her hands, then the surrounding waters. There was no trace of *Annabelle* or any other boats in the vast stretch of Haro Strait, wrapping around the island. To the north, the Gulf Islands of British Columbia winked in the distance. To the south, Stuart Island.

A gust of cold wind shook the buoy, cutting to her marrow. A ray of sunlight peeked through the clouds, covering the mountainous peaks of Vancouver Island to the west. She was surprisingly dry but chilled to the bone and freezing. Nightfall was coming. She had to find shelter, and soon.

She faced her dilemma with dread. Swimming to the beach was risky. With the life ring she could keep her head out of the water, but not her entire body; hypothermia would quickly set in, and she was already cold. Or she could stay put on the buoy, hoping a boat would pass by before dark—an unlikely scenario this time of year.

In the murky water was movement, light and dark shadows darting across the reef. Her heart hammered, remembering the orcas and their violent attack. She forced down that memory. This movement was merely fish, not mammals of heightened intelligence.

She gripped the life ring and focused on the beach, mustering courage. Much to her surprise, she didn't hesitate, not for one second, about what she was getting ready to do.

It's only water. I'm strong. I can swim. I've nothing to...

She was suddenly taken aback by those last thoughts, realizing something very strange had happened. She gazed into the water.

I'm not afraid!

Her only fear was how cold the water would be, which was a genuine concern. But she didn't feel that rising panic she felt before: the fear of drowning. What scared her most in this moment was being stuck on this buoy all night, and learning exactly whose scat was scattered on its flat surface. Seals were cute and friendly so long as you kept your distance. They weren't so cute or friendly if you invaded their territory, which was exactly what she was doing by staying there.

Move in harmony with force of life, flow as water, like stream around rock.

She hugged the life ring to her chest, rolled off the buoy, and landed on her back.

Every muscle contracted when she briefly went under. The life ring popped her to the surface and she gasped from the sudden shock of cold, sucking a mouthful of water. She wasted precious moments coughing and thrashing.

Swim!

She willed her legs to action, heavy as lead. Arms and legs flopping, she fought for every stroke, focused on the shoreline.

The buoy retreated. Making progress, her spirit revived. She had made the right choice.

She pushed harder, but as she drew closer to the beach she realized her mistake. The current ran parallel to the shoreline, away from the beach. It rounded the east point and curled north toward open waters.

She panicked, swimming against the current, losing ground against a force much stronger than she. The closer she came to shore, the faster the current ran, dragging her away from the island.

She cursed at her stupidity, failing to see the telltale signs; confused waves, seals feeding, and seagulls circling above.

The tip of the island inched farther from her reach. Going, going...

Gone.

Her body fell limp as blood withdrew from her extremities to pool around her vital organs. She was tired... so tired. She wrapped herself around the life ring praying to gods she never believed in, calling out to Blake, Ryan, her father, anyone...

Fate called and she accepted.

Sorry, Daddy, I'm just like Mom, in life and in death.

She stared at the friendship bracelet Blake had tied around her wrist. She wanted to cry but her tear ducts were dry. She angered at the unfairness. Did Blake face this same fate? Did he think of her before his end? Did he blame her for not saving him?

Warmth filled her chest and cold numbed her extremities. Her eyes fluttered shut. She felt no pain and her fear quelled. Hypothermia set in, more peaceful than she imagined once enduring the shock of the cold. She was ready to succumb, to let fate take her. To slip into a deep and everlasting sleep...

She heard a whisper, "*Hold on.*"

She smiled and whispered back, "Blake is that you?"

"*Wake up! They're coming.*"

Her eyes jerked open when she heard a growling rumble. Was she imagining that too? She rolled her head toward the sound. A boat was speeding toward her; a white speck of hope on a dark cold sea. She tried to wave but her arms failed her. It didn't matter; they saw her, someone was screaming and pointing at her from the cockpit. Someone who would know where to find her.

Ryan!

Her best friend leaped into the water and swam to her. He grabbed her by her braid and swung her around. The tension surrounding his eyes unwound when she gazed back.

He waved to the driver of the boat. "She's alive!"

"'b—b—bout t—time." Her teeth chattered.

The boat came alongside of them. *Annabelle*'s owner, Roy, emerged from the cabin, cheeks puffed and brow wrinkled with worry. Ryan wrapped his arm under the life ring frozen in her grip and swam hard to the swim step. Roy yanked her up by the armpits while Ryan shoved her up from behind. She tried to stand but her legs buckled.

"Whoa. Take it easy," Roy said.

Ryan grabbed her feet, and the two of them dragged her over the transom. She flopped into the cockpit like a prized catch.

Roy dropped to his knees, pried the life ring from her hands, and tossed it aside. "Hurry, get the blankets," he told Ryan, then he rubbed her hands between his. Tears welled in his crinkled blue eyes. "Do you remember your name?"

"A—Audrey." She tried to smile, but her lips were too numb.

His face bunched up several times, fighting back tears. "You're safe now."

Ryan returned from the cabin and dropped a stack of blankets beside her.

Roy stood up. "Get her clothes off and warm her up."

Ryan pulled the cockpit bench cushion onto the floor and rolled her onto it, dropping to his knees beside her. "Hey kid," his throat caught, "it's not what you think." His hands shook as he unzipped her jeans.

The boat's engine roared to life and the boat lurched forward when Roy kicked it into gear.

Ryan unzipped her coat. His eyes widened. "Whoa, what happened to your shirt?"

"My shirt?" she slurred.

"Yeah, like it's *gone*, and your bra—it's tattered. What happened out there?"

"Blake..." She began shivering uncontrollably. "H—Have you found him?"

Ryan paled. "The others are still looking."

He covered her with blankets and stripped down to his boxers before snuggling underneath with her. He faced her and wrapped her in his arms and legs, pressing his body against hers.

Audrey writhed and screamed and fought to escape the heat radiating from his body. Her skin burned and itched as if she had been wrapped in nettles, not the arms of her best friend. When she could take it no longer, she punched Ryan in the chest, but he took it in stride, rolled her over, spooned his legs and chest against her backside and resumed the torture.

"Promise me, when they find Blake, you'll tell him this little snuggle fest was all about saving your life. We wouldn't want to give him the wrong idea."

"Wh—why wouldn't you want to do th—that?"

"Let's just say I don't." Then he kissed her on the neck and squeezed her extra tight, like a big brother comforting his sister. He was trying to make light of the situation but she could tell by the sound of his voice he was terrified neither of them would ever see their friend again.

26

Daddy Dearest

AUDREY WATCHED FROM THE upper deck of the boat launch as Roy and his crew struggled to guide the waterlogged *Annabelle* into the travel lift's slings. Ryan was below talking to the captain of the tug boat that towed *Annabelle* back to Friday Harbor.

She wrapped the wool blanket tighter across her shoulders. Underneath she wore an old pair of sweats Roy had on his boat along with a pair of wool socks and black rubber boots two sizes too big. The chill from her near-fatal swim lingered in her bones.

Ryan rocketed up the ramp to join her.

"Where did they find her?" she asked.

"Stuart Island, grounded by the lighthouse." His eyes darted nervously and he was breathing hard from adrenaline. She felt it too, that feeling of helplessness that make your insides quiver and your fingers mindlessly pick at things.

"Did they find—"

His face sagged. "Nothing, yet."

It had been nearly eight hours since the orca's attack on *Annabelle*. Daylight was quickly fading and an early autumn storm was expected to make landfall shortly after dark. Search-and-rescue volunteers were returning, chased by high winds already blowing in from the southwest. Blake's chance of survival dwindled with each passing breath.

Roy yelled up to the travel lift operator, "Bring her up, slow!"

The lift's winch roared to life. *Annabelle*'s hull groaned when the slings tightened around her bottom. Slowly she rose, the winch squealing as her water-laden hull was lifted from the water. The hull groaned from the strain then jerked to a stop once clear of the upper deck. The travel lift slowly rolled forward until it was parked over solid ground where her hull could be fully examined. Salt water gushed from cockpit scuppers and a crack in her port side along the waterline.

Audrey gasped. In addition to the crack, there was an indentation the size of an orca's head punched into the side beneath the waterline. A wad of kelp clung, along with their shredded life jackets, to the splintered fiberglass where the transom was missing.

A knot cinched in her throat. Ryan grabbed her hand. Neither of them said anything.

Their moment of horrific realization of what happened was interrupted when a black de Havilland Turbine Beaver flew over. It wavered violently in the gusts, went into a steep dive, and landed on its floats with a shudder in the choppy waters building in the harbor. Audrey recognized it immediately.

She swung on Ryan with narrowed eyes. "Did you call my father?"

He held up his hands defensively. "Not me! Probably Roy or the sheriff's office."

The plane glided to the end of the dock, prop roaring and spray flying. The pilot cut the engine, jumped out, and tied the plane to the dock.

Her father's head emerged from the doorway, hair ruffling from the brisk wind. The silver at his temples flashed in the fading sunlight. He unfolded his lanky frame from the narrow doorway and gracefully leaped to the dock. He pulled up the collar of his pea coat and scanned the shoreline.

Their eyes locked.

He said something to the pilot and headed up the dock toward shore, pant legs snapping from the wind and the fury of his gait. He stopped when he reached the top of the ramp, a six-foot-four, one-ninety-five-pound ticking time bomb; a self-trained human weapon, powered by honed muscle and sharp wit. The lines etched on his face cut deeper than before, as if he had aged ten years in the two weeks since she had left Seattle.

Her breath hitched; his glacial gaze had that effect. For a brief instant his eyes warmed, then his nostrils flared. A cloud burst from his nose like an enraged bull seeing red.

She had no idea what she had done or not done to piss him off. She had hoped he was genuinely relieved that she was alive, that he would run to her and lift her in his arms and tell her how proud she made him feel, that he loved her—to be that father he once was before her mother died.

He came to her in two swift steps. "My God, Audrey." He chopped out the words like a woodsman felling a tree. Then he hugged her without warning, trapping her arms against her sides. "My baby girl, I thought I had lost you."

She tugged an arm free and patted him on the back. He shuddered and squeezed her until she could no longer breathe. She was shocked and a bit relieved when he let go. She stepped back, blinking. That was a first. A display of true affection.

Ryan stepped forward and held out his hand. "Mr. Grey, I'm Ryan, Audrey's friend. We met a few months ago at the U-Dub graduation, remember?"

Her father clasped Ryan's hand and gave it a firm shake, then he smiled, revealing his perfectly capped teeth. "Of course, please call me Robert. Audrey speaks very highly of you, and as I understand, you helped save her life, and for that, I am eternally grateful."

Audrey rolled her eyes. Her father could charm any man, woman, or child, young or old, shy or suspicious with his beaming smile and his lilting English accent. It amazed her how he could instantly project a warm and friendly persona by adding a twinkle to his eye. He was pouring it on. Ryan looked absolutely gaga.

When her father turned to her his smile faded and the twinkle in his eye was gone. All too often the case. She wasn't worth the effort to woo.

"I'm taking you home."

Audrey stepped back. "Are you kidding? My friend is still out there."

"There is nothing you can do to help."

"What if they find him? He'll need me. I'd also like to remind you that I live here and have important research to complete, lab work to oversee, reports to write." She elbowed Ryan in the ribs. "Right, Ry?"

Ryan's head swiveled between her and her father, unsure whose side to take.

"You're not safe."

"What are you talking about?" The blanket fell to her feet when she crossed her arms. "I'm perfectly fine."

Her father's gaze was drawn to the wind-whipped waves in the far channel. His jaw clenched, his nostrils flared. "When I found out you were attacked by those sea creatures I—"

Ryan cleared his throat. "Uh, Robert, I'm sure she'll be fine. Those orcas and their bizarre behavior—that was an isolated incident, possibly provoked by unannounced sonar tests by the military. Roy told us the sheriff is in communication with the officials at Bangor and the Canadian government. They have been most responsive."

Her father glared at Ryan. "How can *you* promise her safety?"

Audrey snapped, "Leave Ryan out of this. You know how hard I worked to get into the program at the Labs. I'm *not* leaving!"

He said nothing, which only infuriated her more.

She narrowed her eyes. "We made an agreement."

"Are you sure it was a two-way agreement? I don't recall that."

They glared at each other, neither willing to give, both stubborn to a fault.

His gaze softened, and he said in a voice she could barely hear, "I can't lose you."

"Then stop telling me what to do!" The words slipped out before she could catch herself. She sighed, that ever-persistent guilt that hung over her whenever they disagreed, questioning who was truly in the right. "Look, I'll check in every day. I can take care of myself—you taught me that much, *remember*?"

Her father looked up at *Annabelle*'s cracked hull. "Your confidence defies reality."

"How dare you! I'm alive, aren't I?"

"Did you think for one moment that you got lucky?"

"I did everything you taught me. I *survived*. I'm not that helpless little girl anymore. When are you going to figure that out?"

He stared back, his face a mask, thoughts grinding. Finally, he said, "You can stay under one condition. Promise me you will stay away from the water."

She won! Rare! She bit her lip to keep from smiling. "Agreed."

His attention suddenly shifted to the docks. Audrey followed his gaze to a sleek black boat about forty feet in length tied to the dock next to his float plane. It must have slipped into the harbor while she was distracted. It looked fast and expensive—like something out of a James Bond movie—a stark contrast to the weathered sailboats and scruffy fishing boats anchored throughout the harbor.

Roy was in the cockpit talking to a man with shoulders as wide as a refrigerator and dressed in all black. Roy climbed over the gunwale. The man followed, leaping with the grace of a cat. Very Bond-like.

The man slipped past Roy and jogged up the ramp. Roy struggled to keep up.

The man approached her father, extended his hand. "Mr. Grey."

"Captain Stokes."

Audrey watched the exchange with curiosity. She guessed the captain to be in his early thirties. His dark hair was cut short with sharp angled lines defining his modest sideburns and forming a V at the back of his neck. His brows cut equally impressive lines, dark and arched, neatly trimmed and plucked. His skin was golden-brown and his face held a hint of Polynesian origin. He had intense dark eyes that cut right through you. He wore black wool pants and a windproof coat trimmed with a wool collar, pulled up to protect his neck from the biting wind. Stamped on his coat above his left pectoral was a small white symbol. An oval-shaped circle set above a sideways "X". The same symbol was painted on the side of his boat. Nothing else. No name or point of origin.

Roy finally joined them, short of breath. "I hope you don't mind; I told the captain you'd answer his questions."

"Sure." Audrey crossed her arms.

The captain fixed her with his dark gaze. "The young man you were—"

"Blake."

"Was he injured before he fell overboard? Was he conscious?"

"Everything happened so suddenly. I'm not sure."

"Was he wearing a Personal Floating Device?"

Audrey's eyes swung to the tattered life jackets pinched in *Annabelle*'s shattered transom. They all saw her look. She bit her lip. Not wearing a life jacket was a big, bad no-no. Roy required everyone to wear life jackets when they borrowed one of his boats. She had always adhered to this rule, except this once.

Ryan gave her a dirty look.

Her father snapped. "I think not."

"We had them on, but then—" She winced.

The captain gave her a sympathetic nod. "That's all I need for now." His eyes shot to her father, before looking back at her. "Thanks to your sound judgment to trigger the Man Overboard feature we were able to retrieve the GPS location and time of the attack from the boat's electronics. Now if you'll excuse me."

"Wait," she grabbed the captain's arm, "I'm going with you."

Her father yanked her back. "No, you're not."

The captain nodded to her father before sprinting down the dock to his boat. He hopped effortlessly into the cockpit. The engines rumbled to life. A second man, wearing the same uniform as the captain, released the dock lines with equal speed and ease. From behind the darkly tinted windows, the captain maneuvered the boat away from the dock and set a course through the narrow channel at the south end of Brown Island sheltering the harbor.

Her father snapped, "You made me a promise. Did you forget?"

"I can't just leave him."

"If he can be found, I assure you, Captain Stokes and his crew will."

"How can you be so sure?"

"Because he works for me." Then he turned to Roy, lifted his chin toward *Annabelle* and pulled a slim billfold from his inside pocket. "Audrey mentioned you loan your boats to the students for their field studies. In light of this most unfortunate accident, may I help you, financially?"

Roy shook his head and patted *Annabelle*'s battered hull. "I don't need your charity. There's more sentimental value invested in her, not money. I'm just terribly sorry about what happened." His mouth bunched and voice caught. "I sure hope they find Blake, such a nice young man." It took him a moment to compose himself. He looked up at the travel lift operator with watery eyes. He pointed toward the boatyard behind his offices. "Put her in back, in the graveyard."

The graveyard was where sailors' dreams died after their boats' hulls were ripped open on a submerged reef, or in the case of *Annabelle*, mauled by an orca.

Roy patted Audrey on the shoulder, then scuffled across the parking lot to his office, looking like a man aged well beyond his sixty-five years.

Audrey turned to her father and spoke through clenched teeth. "Roy is one of the most successful businessmen on this island, only he chooses not to flaunt it." Her eyes cut to the float plane sitting at the end of the dock. "You didn't need to insult him."

Her father stuffed his billfold back into his pocket. His nostrils flared. The raging bull was back. She held her breath, regretting the debacle with the life jackets. She had won that last round but he had been known to pull a reversal, more often than not. Her fate hung in his icy glare.

He dug something from his pocket and handed it to her. A phone. "Stay off the water or you're coming home. Permanently." His voice was sharp as a razor. Message received loud and clear.

Audrey waved the phone, breaking the awkward silence that followed. "I'll check in every day." His eyes narrowed. "I know, texts don't count—a real phone call, I promise."

His eyes warmed and he smiled, genuine and endearing. He kissed her on the check. "I love you, baby."

Audrey gaped. He hadn't said those words or displayed warm emotion toward her in what felt like years. Not the reversal she was expecting.

She watched him hustle down the dock. The lines were cast and the float plane positioned for takeoff. Acrid and nauseating fumes of burnt kerosene swept across the water. The turbine prop screamed as the plane bounced across wind-whipped waves building in the heart of the harbor. The float plane climbed sharply and became a dark speck that quickly disappeared against the backdrop of angry clouds.

27

Ultimatum

RYAN WHISTLED. "YOU NEVER told me you were *that* rich."

Audrey gazed south at the angry dark clouds that gobbled up her father's prized de Havilland Beaver float plane. "Not me. Him. I don't care about his money."

"You're kidding, right? I was raised by my mom, bouncing around to different communes. I never met my real father and we were always broke. Maybe yours would adopt me."

Audrey laughed. "Careful what you wish for! All he cares about is making money and protecting his assets—one of which, at the moment, is me. Before that it was my mom. Drove her crazy until she—"

Her mouth snapped shut. It hurt too much to say it.

Ryan said, "Hey... I'm sorry."

"Sorry for what?"

"Your mom. You never told me what happened."

She rolled her eyes. "What's there to say? It was my tenth birthday. She drowned. End of story."

"End of story? Ouch."

"I'm sorry, it's just…" She sighed. "There's a reason I never told you the whole story. If I did, you might run away and never come back."

"Try me."

She closed her eyes. She had opened up to Blake about her past, but not with Ryan, even though he'd been there whenever she needed his help, like the big brother she never had, patient and supportive, and critical when he needed to be. Especially when she considered doing something reckless or stupid. Ryan deserved to know the truth of her past, especially now.

She released a shaky breath. "After my mom died I was lost, we both were." She gazed up at *Annabelle*'s broken hull. Broken and irreparable like her. She bent and picked up the blanket at her feet, wrapped it around her shoulders, sifting through the wreckage of her childhood memories. "My father told me there were bad people who wanted to hurt me, like they hurt my mother, that I wasn't safe, would *never* be safe. I was just a kid, confused and susceptible. Naturally I believed everything he told me."

She drew a deep breath. "We moved to Seattle, to his sprawling estate north of the city. He erected a wall around the entire property, hired a full-time staff of guards—guys like that captain we just met—and whenever I left the grounds, it was with a bodyguard, shadowing me everywhere. You probably never noticed, they were good at hiding in plain sight. But to me…" She ground her teeth. "It meant he didn't trust me to take care of myself.

"Shortly after mom died, the training started, six days a week, three hours a day—self-defense using martial arts, situational awareness, weapon improvisation. He made me look at the human body as a vulnerable thing easily broken if you struck in just the right spot with just the right force." She shuddered at the nauseating fear she felt when he first demonstrated each and every place on her young tiny body. "When I woke in the night screaming, he would make me get up for drills in the dark, 'While the monsters are fresh in your head,' he told me. It was his way of making me face my fear.

"Years passed and nothing bad ever happened. I grew suspicious of his intentions, especially after I learned the officials filed my mother's death as a drowning accident. They had found no evidence of foul play. I despised him for lying, for justifying the abuse I endured, for emotionally abandoning me—"

She gazed at the gravel at her feet. "I never knew what it was like to have someone care, truly care for me without pretense or demands, like you and Blake." She hugged herself. "But today, when he said..."

She lost her voice, thoughts racing back to the magic words he spoke right before he left. Did he truly mean them? For the first time in years, it seemed he did—that they came from his heart and wasn't just something a father was expected to say to his daughter.

I love you, baby.

The travel lift with *Annabelle*'s broken hull crawled by, the operator taking her to the graveyard, the whine of its engine roaring. It had grown dark. The halogen lights surrounding Roy's offices and the parking lot switched on with a flicker and a low buzz, warming up and growing brighter.

Ryan squeezed her shoulder. "Hey, you okay?"

She blinked, unaware she had stopped talking. "Yeah, where was I?"

"Something he said."

I love you, baby.

She huffed, deciding that he had spit them out like all the other times, empty of meaning and merely meant to impress. "The point is, when I turned eighteen I gave my father an ultimatum: Let me go or I'd find another way out." She held out her left arm and pulled up the sleeve, showing Ryan the white six-inch scar between wrist and elbow. It tingled just thinking about it, how close she had come to killing herself. "Self-inflicted, during one of his knife-fighting sessions. It wasn't lost on him what I meant when I stabbed myself instead of him."

Ryan paled as the truth sunk in.

"Obviously, he agreed, but on one stipulation, that he must know where I am at all times." She raised the phone her father handed her before he left. "My leash. I'm sure it has some sort of high-tech tracking device. Like the one I lost today."

She buried her hands in her armpits. "Years of brainwashing and bruises, yet still…" Her body began to shake. She suddenly couldn't breathe, triggered by the image of her mother lying in her father's arms, salt-crusted lashes, eyes gazing at nothingness in the sky, water leaking through a smile frozen on her blue lips. A smile! As if she had welcomed her fate with glee. That smile still haunted Audrey after all these years.

"I didn't help him, Ry." Tears of anger welled in her eyes. Ryan reached for her. She pushed him away. "Did you hear me? Blake fell into the water and I—I didn't help him!"

"Aud, it's not your fault."

She felt sick to her stomach. "Yes, it is, I panicked—I—" She choked, struggled to find her voice. "I didn't throw him the life ring, and before that we took off our life jackets because he—" She itched all over. "We—"

She threw up. Nothing came out but sour bile. Ryan held her by the shoulders, braid coiled in his hand, to keep her from falling forward.

She stood and wiped her mouth with the sleeve of her sweatshirt.

She drew a shuddering breath then held up her wrist. "He gave me this." She pointed at the colorful friendship bracelet and the knot Blake neatly tied. "After he asked me to be his girlfriend. I think that was his wish, you know, associated with the bracelet, that I'd say 'yes'. That was right before—"

Tears welled in Ryan's eyes. "He was crazy about you and asked me to stay behind this morning. Now I know why."

She rolled her lips inside her mouth and bit down for fear that if her lips ever parted she would start screaming and never be able to stop. "I guess it doesn't matter anymore."

Ryan cupped her shoulders, forced her to look at him. "It was a freak accident, like what happened to your mom."

Her vision blurred. "Like my mom? But his life jacket..."

"You saw *Annabelle*, it wouldn't have made any difference."

Her chest knotted. "Nothing I could do?"

"Nothing."

A tear slipped down her cheek. "You believe that?"

"That's what friends do, they believe in each other."

"I wouldn't know. I never had a friend, before you and Blake."

He hugged her and they clung to each other, chests shuddering, gulping down sobs. It grew darker. Rain fell from the sky. Wind whipped their hair. Finally, Ryan wrapped his arm around her shoulder and led her to Blake's Pathfinder, parked where he had left it that morning in Roy's parking lot. He helped her into the passenger seat, went around to the driver's side, and scrubbed his face with his hands before getting inside.

He drew a sharp breath, grabbed the keys hidden beneath the floor mat, jabbed them into the ignition. "I'm not giving up on him. Not until I see him again with my own eyes." He swallowed hard. "Dead or alive."

No matter how many times Ryan told her it wasn't her fault, she knew better. She had been there. She failed to act. All her training was a smelly pile of wasteful shit. Blake disappeared beneath the waves with no life jacket, no life ring to cling to. Blake was most likely gone. Never to be seen again. Dead or alive. What was, was.

She looked over to Ryan. "Not giving up?"

He shook his head, holding on to that tiny seed of hope. A seed that maybe she was wrong.

She squeezed his hand. Who was she to spoil hope. "Me neither—together till the end."

28

Vacancy Filled

Sinto returned home exhausted and wound up. He had successfully completed the task his mother had assigned him but regretted having to return Audrey to her rightful world. The light gravity of his underwater home felt foreign to his step, the oxywater overly rich. Had he been away that long?

The Merahvu city, Tallamure, was located on Earth in the icy waters of the North Pacific. A large colony one-hundred-thousand strong, where the Merahvu had peacefully resided for hundreds of years, far from the nearest Sapien settlements. Sapien fisherman made their living far above the dome of the city unaware of what lay in the darkest depths: a thriving metropolis of humanity, a city filled with light and color and vast resources to sustain those who chose to live there.

He slipped into the private residence he shared with his younger sister, Naiada, to bathe before calling on his mother. He cast aside his animal skins in favor of a skareef, a common covering worn by the Seakai when venturing out into the city. He chose one in a rich forest green laced with browns and golds; traditional colors representative of his father's tribe, the Terrakai.

He wrapped the woven fabric across his right shoulder, between his legs, and twice around his waist before securing it in place at his left hip. It fell just above his knees, pliable but heavy against his skin, tied in such a manner as to allow him to tuck his tail along his spine or leave it hanging freely, as he chose to do so now.

He combed his fingers through his damp hair, gathering the golden waves into a short ponytail, secured it with several wraps of a beaded copper chain. The chain represented his Terrakai heritage and was given to him by his father on his thirteenth birthday.

As Sinto had explained to Audrey, he was of dual-tribe, born from the union of a Terrakai father and a Seakai mother. At first glance he appeared Seakai, like his mother, with flowing golden hair, naturally fair-colored skin, and fluked tail, but his upwardly-slanted green eyes capped with dark bronze-colored brows, strong jawline, and coppery-bronze streaks spreading through his hair with each passing year came from his Terrakai father.

He was proud of his lineage and though he appeared mostly Seakai, he always felt the tug of the land over the sea, acutely, as would a purebred Terrakai.

He passed through lush mature gardens growing throughout the sprawling compound at the base of the Great Tower, stopping only to pluck a ripe strawberry to pop into his mouth.

The tower was set upon a rocky outcropping at the far edge of the city, towering over all other structures. The highest of the trio of mountains cradling the city's protective dome was a looming and dark backdrop. The tower's curved walls were interlaced with swirled patterns of embedded gold, silver, and copper, glinting under the mock sun hovering at the pinnacle of the dome's sky. Each metal represented each tribe, symbolizing their independence but intertwined as one collective: the Merahvu. The Great Tower was where the Circle of Representatives busied themselves with Merahvu business. Business the rest of the

Merahvu were free to observe and comment on when prompted, if one so wanted.

The compound of residences, like the one Sinto occupied, were designated for the queen and the representatives of the Circle and their families, and for hosting visiting leaders and dignitaries or special guests from other colonies.

He ran up a steep stairway and entered the tunnel that cut through the tower's rocky base to the Great Chamber. He wandered confidently through the dark and twisty turns where he had played hide and seek with his sister when they were younglings after tiring of running through the gardens. He knew every turn and corridor, every crack and hole in the floor, including secret openings to the hidden chambers carved deep into the ocean floor.

Voices echoed and light bled around the last bend of carved stone as he neared the entry to the Great Chamber where the Circle met.

He rounded the corner and paused in the alcove, out of sight of the chamber.

He pictured the five representatives of the Circle. The twin Healers from the Arctakai colony located in the Southern Ocean: Sliver and Lucee, the gleam of their albino skin covered by long white skareefs, eyes a shock of blue, and uncut hair braided into fine silver strands and looped around their necks like glittering necklaces. The Seakai male and female duo from Tallamure: Beech and Surah, with vivid gemstone eyes, gleaming golden hair, and a splash of colorful cloth wound around their mostly bare bodies. Lastly, Jabal, the lone Terrakai representing the City of Green located in the fresh waters of Lake Superior. A giant of a man proudly adorned in fur and leather with dark-bronzed skin, gleaming copper-colored hair, and the green-flecked amber gaze of a stalking lion.

Sinto paused before entering, not wanting to interrupt their heated discussion, and quietly listened.

"We must seal the North Pacific portal," Beech said.

Jabal responded, his deep voice rumbling. "We cannot afford to lose our most direct access from the city to Merluma."

"What about the Salish portal?" Beech pressed.

Jabal growled. "And risk discovery? No one has used that portal for years."

A throat was cleared, followed by a great deal of whispering. Lucee said, "We must take no chances of Orange spreading to Merluma."

Another throat clearing. "I concur," said Sliver.

"And what will it be next? Seal them all? The consequences of such action are far too great." Jabal sounded irritated.

"Jabal, what do you suggest?" The voice cut through all the rest with an air of utmost confidence. One Sinto was intimately familiar with: Ianthe. The queen. *His mother*.

The Circle fell silent.

"I will lead a team to evaluate the risk and return with a proposal," Jabal replied.

His mother said, "Request granted. We are left with only hard choices at this point. Merluma is far too important for the future of our people. It must not be compromised. Would you all agree?"

There was a brief outburst of more than one conversation and it was difficult to decipher what was being said, but eventually the conversations died down and each of the representatives murmured their assent.

"Jabal, if you may, see to it immediately. Time, here, is not on our side."

"Consider it done."

Sinto thought he heard Beech grumble an objection.

There was the rustling of movement and it seemed a good moment for Sinto to enter. His mother was already on her feet, arms outstretched to greet him. She smiled, confirming what he suspected: that she knew he had been listening from around the corner.

Balls of electrical fire hovered above the stone table where the Circle was seated. The vast chamber was otherwise dark and the observation balconies empty. The Circle had erected a translucent seal separating the upper and lower chamber for privacy. Normally, the people were free to attend discussions between the Circle. Not today. It was late in the afternoon, a time when the people gathered for celebration of day's end, a much-preferred activity to observing the boring and mundane discussions of governing. A good time for the Circle to cover sensitive topics.

His mother came to him, her feet barely skimming the stone floor, propelled forward by the gentle swoosh of her fluked tail and the limited gravity of oxywater. She was dressed in her finest skareef, floor length and woven through with strands of twenty-four carat gold scavenged from sunken ships scattered throughout Earth's oceans over the past millennium. One of many gold skareefs passed down from previous queens.

Draped across her forehead and woven through her golden, upswept hair was a copper chain beaded with sacred stones collected from the Great Mountains on Merluma. A token of commitment Sinto's father gave her on the day they were Joined.

Sinto noticed the nervous quiver in her smile when her gaze, a tempest of lavender fire, reached for his mind, anxious to learn of his recent adventures. He surrendered freely, feelings and images mingled in rushed greeting. Then he offered his succinct and thorough summary, snippets of memories peppered with a commentary of his thoughts, from orchestrating the orcas' attack to the abduction of the brown-eyed girl.

Details were what she wanted so she delved deeper, sifting through private thoughts she had no business uncovering. His breath faltered when she relived his bumbling attempts to introduce himself and how his carelessness nearly cost Audrey her life, how it felt when he slipped into her mind and he shared his body while he healed her. She skimmed over his emotional struggle when the time came to leave her, a struggle he feared she would find a distraction to his assignment. He was surprised by her disinterest in his emotional attachment to Audrey, one that grew stronger after their recent reunion.

He struggled to reflect calm as she relived the memories fresh in his mind in the presence of the Circle. She smiled at him now, expressing her approval, not of his method, but of his achievement; gaining an important ally in the Sapien world.

The entire exchange was over in a matter of seconds, though it felt as if he had scaled a mountain. His heart beat heavily in his chest.

"*What next?*" he asked in mind-speak. A question only she would hear.

"Not *now*," she replied sharply. Then kissed him on the forehead, the tip of his nose, each cheek, and lastly his lips. Dry kisses of respect, not passion: a mother greeting her child.

"Welcome home, my son," she said for benefit of the Circle to hear, although it was unnecessary; they were perched on the edge of their seats, observing every gesture between Sinto and his mother. The air was electrically charged with anticipation, for something. Sinto wondered what.

"Forgive me, I'm interrupting." Sinto turned to leave but his mother grabbed his hand.

"Of course not." She arched a brow toward the Circle. "We were just starting." The five members seated around the stone table stood.

"Perhaps Sinto should join us," Jabal suggested.

Sinto looked from the five members of the Circle to his mother.

She smiled. "I agree, wholeheartedly."

Sinto's chest swelled. This was what his mother promised, that one day soon he would fill his father's vacant seat in the Circle as second representative of the Terrakai. Wantemo recently said that Sinto had completed all his lessons, and all that was left was his final test to prove he was ready. Was this a primer for that test?

Sinto followed his mother to the stone table where the five members had taken their respective seats.

"Malavee," Sinto said, bowing his head in greeting. *My pleasure.*

"Sayla," they replied together. *Equally.*

The transparent privacy seal he noted earlier had been removed. Rays from the mock sun now cut through the large opening several stories up at the top of the great chamber and highlighted the empty seat between Jabal and his mother. His mother nodded for him to take it. Sinto gazed once more around the Circle, their eyes pert and aglow. No one objected.

The seat had remained vacant since Sinto's father had gone missing the year before. His father's sash lay as he had last left it, draped casually across the seat. Sinto picked it up, rubbed the fabric between his fingers; coarse green silk woven with copper thread.

Each member of the Circle wore a sash across their shoulder, dyed and woven with the color and metal representing their tribe.

"It is yours, put it on," his mother said.

Did it mean that she had given up on finding his father, Ramasis? *Or...*

Sinto laid the sash across the skareef covering his shoulder, accepting his invitation to the gathering of the Circle. There had been no interview or tests as Wantemo indicated there would be, and the members seemed anxious for him to join them.

Did this mean the invitation was official, or merely temporary? Was *this* his final test?

Did they waive the requirements because they had grown desperate by Ramasis' absence?

Sinto and his sister were offspring of the queen—whose bloodline traced back to the original ancestral prophets of the Seakai—and Ramasis, the son of a highly respected Terrakai leader, since deceased. It was believed that Naiada, once she came of age, would bridge the deep-rooted divide between the Seakai and the Terrakai as a dual-tribe queen. *Sea vs. land.* Sinto had always been told that his duty was to nurture and support his sister. And that part of that duty meant taking over his father's seat in the Circle. Once Naiada reached adulthood and was trained to take over their mother's responsibilities, she was expected to be declared the new queen, though that was still several years off.

Already rumors swirled among the Merahvu, questioning his mother's motives and the integrity of the Circle. The murmuring of unrest. A whiff of rebellion. Some believed it was time to take a stand against the Sapiens and their disruption of the natural world. Others felt the sudden explosion of Orange in areas of the Pacific Ocean should be left alone; that nature should be free to run it's course. Heated disagreements that threatened to sever the tenuous relations established between the Seakai and Terrakai at the end of the Forever War over three hundred years ago. A long-fought peace agreement was at stake.

While fealty to his sister and filling his father's seat was an honor and a privilege, Sinto and his sister would be responsible for resolving this growing conflict simmering between the tribes and ensuring a viable and peaceful future for all. An honor he once coveted but had begun to question in recent days.

Sinto sat down in his father's vacant seat with mixed emotion.

29

Stirrings Among Us

NOTHING OF MUCH INTEREST was discussed after Sinto joined the Circle. No one raised concern about the accelerating increase of populations occurring on Merluma, the alarming number of younglings falling ill in the city, or the growing shortage of sucuvita to stave off premature illness and death. The whole affair was disappointing and quite boring. He didn't care what color the new amphitheater should be, or how next spring's fields should be planted, or which direction or pattern of planting would be the most aesthetically pleasing.

Exhaustion blurred his vision as deeply as denial blurred the Circle's.

His mother gave him a sharp look when she caught him in a yawn and thankfully suggested they adjourn before his lids slid shut and his chin fell to his chest. It suddenly dawned on him that he had not had a full night's rest for days. So much for first impressions.

Once the Circle parted, his mother insisted he join her in the gardens. Disillusioned and bone weary, he followed her through the dark and winding tunnel to the gardens surrounding the Great Tower.

The mock sun was setting in its fixed location at the top of the city's dome. Vivid streaks of coral and crimson painted the firmament that served as a false sky with a glorious sunset. Soon simulated clouds would bloom like fresh bruises and spill nutrient-rich rain to feed the plants adapted for the city's environment. And once the simulated clouds evaporated the fixed sphere that mimicked the sun would mimic the true moon state, shining down on the surface of the ocean far above. A million tiny lights would follow, twinkling in the false sky. Sinto liked nighttime best in the city. Without the glare of faux sunlight, the nighttime false sky felt remotely real.

He already missed the messy feel of dirt and leaves between his toes, the electrical charge of a sudden and unexpected thunderstorm, the sweet smell of forest decay, the chill of the morning frost, the snap and crackle of a fire, and the scent of wood smoke clinging to his hair. The city's temperature varied between eighteen and twenty-four degrees Celsius. Never more, never less. Every day perfect. Every day predictable. Sunshine, rain, moon, and stars. Shine, rinse, repeat. Home less than a day and the Terrakai in his blood screamed to escape the confines of the sea. A feeling becoming more and more pronounced with each passing year.

His mother paused once they reached the pond. "Naiada is craving strawberries," she said, point-of-fact, and Sinto knew it was true. Their mother always knew what Sinto and his sister needed, how they felt, if they were morose or ill, happy or troubled. Every unguarded thought was free for her taking.

They rounded a small pond covered with lily pads and croaking frogs, weaving among wildflowers, herbs, and edible greenery to a trio of cone-shaped terraces. Sinto had genetically modified wild strawberries to flourish in the watery atmosphere, allowing them to grow in the salt-laden dirt churned up from the seabed and the artificial sunlight cast from the mock sun. Wantemo had taught him, of course, but it was Sinto who perfected the color, texture, and flavor. A gift for his mother bestowed to her on his thirteenth birthday. A token of appreciation and respect for the life she gave him, as was custom among the Merahvu. Sinto's delicious creation was celebrated by all in the city.

Together they climbed the terraces and picked the lush berries, exchanging smiles and stealing bites. Sinto tucked those they collected into the folds of his skareef to take to Naiada later. They reminisced of happier times when they were together as a family, before his father went missing and Naiada fell ill.

Sinto opened his mouth to change the subject, but his mother's voice interrupted, threading through his mind as if a sudden worrisome thought. *"Be careful what you say, someone is spying on us."*

Sinto casually gazed across the pond. *"Where?"*

"In the trees, toward the Terrakai dwellings. Act normal. Give no reason for suspicion." She popped a strawberry into her mouth, eyes rolling in ecstasy. "Per-fec-tion. I must remember to thank Wantemo. He taught you well."

"Were they spying on the Circle?"

"Most likely, always. The privacy dome is all too easy to penetrate. I really ought to say something to Beech about that..."

She stood up, pointed to the strawberries Sinto held gathered in his skareef. "More than enough. If Naiada eats all of those she'll burst!"

Sinto laughed, playing along. "That I'd like to see." They casually strolled around the edge of the pond, stopping to pick flowers, debating color combinations and comparing scents, choosing ones that complimented each other. They spoke of these meaningless things in normal voices while they discussed more urgent matters, secretly, in mind-speak.

"Some among the Terrakai are spreading rumors about me. They claim I was responsible for Ramasis' disappearance among other outlandish accusations. At the moment, these outspoken rebels are powerless, spinning conspiracies and lies. They must not learn what

you are up to. I trust no one but you, your sister, and Wantemo. No one else, not even members of the Circle."

Sinto shifted the strawberries in his skareef, made another fold to hold the gathered flowers. His mother hummed a mindless tune. To anyone observing it would appear that they were gathering flowers in silence.

"What accusations?"

"That I have lost my powers of foresight and that Naiada is too weak to take my place."

"But she's getting stronger."

"Understand, they don't care. To them her illness is timely, a sign for change. It's merely an excuse. They seek a new leader, a leader willing to do the unthinkable, to confront the Sapiens directly. They blame me for misleading the people—making them believe the Merahvu are safe on Earth—and for doing nothing to stop changes here that impact Merluma."

Sinto stopped picking and captured his mother's eye, forgetting about the spy. *"But what they say is true. Something must be done, something bold, and soon! I confess, I overheard your discussion regarding Orange and the possibility of it migrating to Merluma. We know little of its true threat, only that it is growing and killing all within its reach."*

She touched the side of his head where some of his hair was still missing. She continued her merry hum. *"I agree! It is their methods I question. They seek to overthrow the Circle, a system of leadership refined and time-proven to work for the people for hundreds of years, even during times of disruption. They believe the only solution to solving our problems is with violence, such as fomenting an uprising against the Sapiens. They underestimate what the Sapiens are capable of, the weapons and technologies that they possess, their sheer numbers. What they propose will destroy us."*

"You have seen this, in a vision?"

She stopped humming and gazed at him unseeing. It happened in an instant. Him sparking the thought, her driving forth to confirm it.

Her eyes darkened and lavender irises swirled into a fiery tempest. The moist air crackled. A hissing mist swirled around her, snagging him in its electrical web, wrapping him into the violent vortex of the Timeless Dimension that she suddenly spun. Too late to escape. His eyes failed to blink, lungs to draw breath, heart to beat. For his sake he hoped she would find the answer she sought, and rather quickly.

No one but his mother knew how to enter the Timeless Dimension. She was the first queen who had discovered how to break into this mysterious and unexplained plane where she could travel forward or backward in time and to other Earth worlds. Through the virtual folding and expansion of space and time, she could predict fragments of the future by creating different events and observing their outcome. Billions of calculations in a matter of seconds. This, coupled with history—both memories and wisdom buried in her DNA from the ancestors and past events gleaned from the Sapien world—she was able to predict the future with surprising accuracy, for both worlds, Earth and Merluma.

While she gleaned much knowledge of the future from her journeys into the Timeless Dimension, she faced limitations. Truths did not seek her. She had to ferret out possibilities from many, like zeroing in the focus of a high-powered telescope on an unsuspecting target; like seeking a speck of dust in outer space.

Because of this, his mother had been the most powerful queen in the long history of the Merahvu and before that, the Seakai. Her mother before her, and on and on across the bloodline, drew power from employing a secret network of spies and using what they had learned from those spies to declare prophesies. Some more reliable than others.

She told no one how she discovered the Timeless Dimension, but many believed she had been chosen by the Wise Ones—fabled gods the ancestors once worshiped—to bring peace, prosperity, and unity to the warring tribes. From what Sinto knew, her discovery coincided with his parent's Joining and signing of a peace agreement between the tribes at the end of the Forever War. Until recently, peace had reigned for three hundred years. It was the people's ongoing belief in his mother's unique and uncanny ability that gave her great power, but that belief was waning.

He doubled over and gasped when she finally released him. It felt as if he had been punched inside out.

She seemed not to notice his distress. Her eyes cleared and she began humming once again, finally giving her answer: "*In one possible future.*"

He tensed, readying to flee if necessary. "*What possible future did you see?*"

"*One that involves the girl. Every time I replay it, she is there. That is why I sent you to find her. We need her on our side. That I am certain. Tell me, how did she react when you told her who you were, of the existence of Merluma. Was she frightened?*"

"*She was brave.*" The raised markings along his spine tingled at the memory of her fingers tracing the swirls. "*And curious. She asked lots of questions. And she is strong-minded. While there were challenges, she survived the brutal healing. Most would have died.*"

"*Brave is good, strong-minded might prove—*" She pursed her lips. "*Challenging.*"

"*But I don't understand why you wanted me to return her to the Salish Sea. She became upset when I told her. Why not simply bring her here? Is that not what you want?*"

She knelt next to a bed of tanzen, plucked one of the tender leaves, handed it to him. He took a bite. It tasted bitter, not sweet as it should—like the unsettling turn of their conversation.

"*We must not raise suspicions. More are joining the rebellion and suspicions are swirling like wildfire throughout the Terrakai. Nor should we raise suspicions among the Sapiens. Time must pass before we proceed. The Sapiens will conclude the attack wasn't an attack at all, just an accident. And the girl will eventually accept what happened to her friend, and what you have shown her—when it fully manifests in her subconscious—will override all other concerns. Her curiosity will work in our favor."*

"She was quite upset about her friend."

"Her friend is safe. Wantemo is seeing to his daily needs. If she cooperates, he will be returned, unharmed. Wantemo will stage a believable explanation for his prolonged absence. Struck with amnesia. He will remember nothing."

The strawberries in his stomach pitched and rolled. Sinto had eagerly accepted his role, trusting his mother's encouragement without thinking through the consequences. Audrey was smart and tenacious. One way or another she would learn the truth, explicitly through his mother or by tearing apart his lies. A cloud of guilt hung over him for his role in the ruse. He never considered that he would be the one to crack open her world, revealing secrets hidden inside. When his mother initially presented her plan he merely mused at the thought of rekindling a friendship cut short. He berated his naivety and short-sightedness.

"By the way, Wantemo shared the experience with me. You orchestrated the attack perfectly; there was no evidence of foul play. I trust you wiped the incident from the orcas' memories as I suggested. We would not want anyone to accidentally stumble upon the fact it was you who encouraged them."

He opened his mouth to answer, snapped it shut, and glued his eyes to the snapdragons he held in his hand, concentrating on not crushing the delicate stems pinched between his fingers. They slipped and floated to the ground. In all the excitement of the moment, he honestly couldn't remember whether he had dealt with the orcas' memories or not.

What other critical details had he forgotten? And what were the consequences? Blood rushed from his head. He squatted, pretending to gather the dropped flowers. He rolled forward on his knuckles until the dizziness passed.

Sinto asked, "What if the Circle learns what I have done? I have broken two sacred rules! One as you asked, and the second—it was the only way I could save her. Surely they will insist on the severest of punishments!"

His mother squatted beside him and shoved an entire leaf of tanzen into her mouth, grinding her teeth as she chewed. A warning. "Sinto. Calm. No one will find out if we are very careful. If they do, I will protect you. They think I am weak. They are wrong. Focus on the girl."

"What is it you would have me do? She is gone!"

"Did you not give her a token?"

"Yes, but..."

"Then stop worrying. She will seek you, and when she does, tell her everything. Endear her to the way of our people, make her sympathetic to our plight. Once she understands what is at stake, bring her to me. And I will tell her the truth about her father. Then we will learn whose side she is on."

"And after, what will happen to her?" And, selfishly, he wondered, What will happen to me?

His mother stood, drew a deep breath and released it. She picked up the flowers Sinto had dropped and handed them to him, avoiding his eyes.

"Naiada's calling for you. Go, now. Hurry."

~~~~~~~~~~~~~~~~~~~~~~~~~~

PART TWO

~~~~~~~~~~~~~~~~~~~~~~~~~~

30

Message

Lectures, research, lab work—and so Audrey's life resumed but not quite like before.

Every day brought strange and interesting curiosities and vivid lifelike dreams. She became obsessed with the color green and all things that looped and swirled, and oddest of all, polka dots, especially trios that formed triangles. She stared into the forest surrounding the campus expecting foliage and shadows to shift and reorganize into shapes of people. She watched for birds to beckon and guide her on a journey. Late at night she would sneak down to the docks to gaze into the water, looking for something, but for what, she didn't know. She had suddenly lost her fear of the water, not hesitating once to step onto the dock or feeling the need to recite the mantra.

She wondered if she was going crazy as she wandered aimlessly in the rain between classes; that maybe something triggered a gap in her memory, a traumatic experience she could not remember, a truth too painful to recall. But one thing she knew for certain; something was *off*. She kept to herself when possible and spoke nothing of these strange thoughts and obsessions. Not even to Ryan.

Two weeks had passed since "the incident" with the orcas. Neither Blake nor his body had been found, and he was officially declared deceased. An accidental circumstance. Chapter closed. Strangely, like everything else, Audrey felt nothing. No shuddering physical reactions, no mind-numbing shock, grief, or anger. She had already accepted this sad reality, but when, she didn't know.

Blake was gone. *Nothing to see here folks, move along please...*

This too felt *off.* She should have been riddled with guilt and grief.

At the end of every day she called her father as she had promised, and like every other day, the conversation went something like this:

"Hello Father, I haven't gone near the water." *Liar liar pants on fire.*

"I'm fine." *Except for the hallucinations and weird obsessions.*

"School's fine." *Did I mention I'm falling horribly behind?*

"I miss you too." *Miss? Not!*

"Until tomorrow." *Dreadfully yours...*

Then Ryan would find her in her room and offer to walk with her to the dining hall for dinner, giving her an excuse to end the call. Every night at dinner, she would push around her food, choke down a couple bites, and scrap the rest into the garbage.

This facade she had erected felt as off as everything else: with her life, with her closest friend, even with her father.

But no matter how much she tried she could not accept anything was actually wrong with her. She wasn't suicidal, and surprisingly, found joy in her new discoveries and obsessions. She felt an inner peace knowing the truth of Blake's fate. Yet she knew, *knew,* the wrongness of it all. Blake was gone and she should have felt anything but peace under the circumstances. It was as if she was merely a splintered piece of her before-the-incident self. A truly confounding conundrum.

"You know you can't keep that up," Ryan said at dinner one night.

"What?"

"Starving yourself."

"I'm not starving, I'm just not hungry."

"You never talk about him."

"Why? He's dead. What is there to talk about?"

"He was our friend!"

Her heart pounded and guilt tugged. He was right, chipping away at cracks in her facade. Why hadn't she felt the need to talk about it?

She took a bite then pushed the rest around on her plate to make it look like she'd eaten more than she had.

Ryan pointed at her plate. "You know loss of appetite is a symptom of depression."

"I am not depressed," she hissed, looking around the dining hall, embarrassed.

She got up, slung her backpack across her shoulder, and left her unfinished meal. Ryan followed her outside. It was dark. The sky wept. Gutters gurgled.

"Audrey, wait! I'm dying here. He was our friend. I can't lose you too. You know you can talk to me. So talk to me."

She gazed deep into his eyes, locking onto the irises—another new obsession. Eyes. She focused on the flickers of amber and green. Green? *Green!*

She touched Ryan's brow. "Your eyes, they're *green.*"

"They're hazel. You know that," he snapped. "You have been acting weird. People are talking. Are you high on something? Is there something you should be telling me?"

Audrey blinked and pulled her hand back. "Talking about me?" Her stomach growled. Maybe she was hungry after all. "I promise, I'm not high. Straight as a pin."

"You haven't been the same since... you know." He sighed. "I was thinking, um, maybe you should talk to someone." He dug a business card out of his front pocket. "There's a therapist, here in Friday Harbor, I've been seeing. Roy's helping me out with the fees and has been super supportive. She diagnosed me with a form of

PTSD. Not unusual after losing someone you care about in a tragic accident. PTSD can make people act or feel strange."

She stared at the card he held out in his hand. Her stomach churned. Could this thing that was *off* simply be a common psychological reaction to a traumatic event?

She sighed. "Okay, I'll consider it." She took the card. Shoved it in her pocket. "You're right. Something is weird, ever since that day." She drew a deep calming breath. "Promise to hear me out."

"I'm all ears."

"You won't freak out or jump to conclusions?"

"You know you can trust me. What is it?"

She looked around to make sure no one else was near. She felt vulnerable standing outside under a pool of light.

"I can't sleep—and—I'm having weird dreams but not while sleeping. More like reoccurring visions triggered by something I smell or see. The same ones over and over as if they're memories, not dreams—things I have actually experienced. And I'm obsessing over things, like the color green, and—shapes, like swirls and polka dots."

She dug her notebook out of the backpack slung across her shoulder and flipped to a page of notes she took in their last class. She held it out to him.

The page was covered in swirling lines threading through triangles of polka dots. "I thought I was writing notes, *words*, but when I looked down, this is what I saw. I don't remember drawing these."

Ryan took the notebook, thumbed to the previous day's notes. More swirls and dots. "This isn't normal." Ryan's face was etched with worry.

She nibbled her lip.

Dare I say more?

"There's more." She stepped closer and whispered in his ear, "I think someone is watching me. I can't see them, but I *feel* them, like eyes burning into my skin like laser beams."

"Maybe you shouldn't be alone. I can crash on your floor tonight."

She stepped back, looked around. "I don't think that's necessary. The thing is, I'm not scared and I don't feel threatened. I think whoever it is, is there to watch over me, to protect me."

A long silence passed between them.

Ryan broke it. "I still don't think you should be alone. I don't care if it's the middle of the night, call me if you change your mind. Promise me?"

She nodded.

"Come on, I'll walk you to your room. Maybe you just need a good night's rest." He didn't look like he believed it.

"I'll think about calling your therapist."

"I hope you do."

They walked in silence. Audrey buried her hands in her sweatshirt pockets, tipped her head back, and lapped up raindrops falling from the treetops. Even rain tasted different than before.

Ryan snapped his fingers. "Wait. I almost forgot. I have something for you."

They detoured off the path and stopped by his room. Audrey waited outside while Ryan ducked inside. He stepped out with a black plastic bag in hand.

"What's that?"

"Your clothes. Roy dropped them by earlier, but you were in class. I hung them up to air out. Warning, they stink."

She opened the bag and peered inside. "Ew, smells like the labs that time the recirc system failed."

"My whole room smells like that." He closed the door. "Want me to walk you to your room?"

"I'll be okay."

He cocked a brow. "You *sure*?"

She play-punched him in the arm. "Stop worrying. I'll try to get some sleep."

Once she left, she pulled her hood over her head, secretly wishing everything would be normal again.

She considered the value of talking to Ryan's therapist. It wouldn't be the first time in her twenty-odd years. She was fully aware of the drill. She talks, they listen, some wise words are shared. Talk, rinse, repeat. After several sessions she would prop herself up and declare herself good as new, until the next traumatic thing her father put her through.

The rain came down harder and she picked up her pace. The air bloomed with the scent of freshly tilled earth and sap. A gust of wind whipped through the trees. Fir needles rained down on her head.

It started off slowly, triggered by the woodsy smell, that same waking nightmare that haunted her every day, each time becoming more and more real...

~ ~ ~

A tiger chases her through a forest of giant evergreens; streaks of lightning and clapping thunder fill the sky. The ground quakes from the cacophony. Her heart pounds, a stitch pierces her side, but she dares not stop running. The tiger gains.

A giant tree, a low branch; she leaps, pedaling her legs. Rough bark tears at her hands. Ignoring the pain she climbs higher.

The tiger paces below, flashing its fangs and snarling. Its silky blue fur ripples and a bold dark stripe runs along its spine—a magnificent and deadly creature.

It claws up a nearby tree and crosses to a branch hanging above her. A terror fills her as never before. The tiger roars and jumps.

She's blinded by an explosion of green fire.

The branch snaps. Together they fall, tiger and girl, a tangle of claws and legs.

Then—

~ ~ ~

Audrey came to gasping on all fours, in a puddle, with sharp gravel digging into her palms and knees.

Not all of her visions were frightening, but all were just as real. Her favorite was surfing inside of a wave, fearless and exhilarated, with dolphins nipping at her toes.

She didn't have the nerve to share the details of these strange visions with Ryan, not wanting to raise further concern.

She stood.

There it was again. That feeling of being watched. Coming from shadows in the trees.

She sprinted to her room. By the time she reached the door her heart thundered and she was gasping for air. She fumbled the key into the lock, slipped inside.

Pitch black.

Am I alone?

Back pressed against the door she shakily reached for the light switch.

Click.

Her room was exactly as she had left it.

She exhaled in relief as she dropped her backpack and the bag with her clothes on the floor.

Notes, partially outlined reports, and books covered her desk; dirty clothes littered the floor. But she didn't care. She flopped onto the bed, staring at the ceiling. The ripeness of unwashed sheets wafted up.

It was happening all over again, the paranoia and fear. Only this time it was different. Before, it was her *father's* fear, spilling over and ruling her life after her mother died. This was something else. This was fear born within herself, triggered by "the incident."

She dug the card Ryan gave her from her pocket, ran her finger across the phone number. She held it for a beat, then tossed it on her desk.

She lay in silence, listening to the rain drumming on the roof, considering Ryan's suggestion. She believed her visions held an important clue, as did the doodles in her notebook. She envisioned the pattern of dots and swirls filling the lined pages. What would a therapist think of that?

And what was it about the color green?

Before the incident she always said her favorite color was blue, like the clear turquoise waters that surrounded the island where she was born. But after the incident, it was clearly green that captured her attention and gave her joy whenever she saw it. All shades, like the teal-green of the Salish Sea, or the moss growing in the woods round her room, or the muted green of a Douglas fir.

Or a pair of eyes, green like emeralds—eyes of green fire.

A distant memory sparked. She sat up suddenly and scanned the shelves above her desk. Tucked away on the top shelf was her collection of glass figurines, gifts from her mother. She wasn't sure why she suddenly remembered they were there, but felt a strange urge to see them.

She climbed onto her desk to get a closer look.

There were ten in all, covered in dust and laced with cobwebs. Each one represented a birthday she had shared with her mother. Her father had showered her with every toy, doll, or electronic device imaginable, but her mother's gifts were those she treasured most. She had forgotten about them. *Girlie things*, Ryan called them when she showed him her collection on the day she moved into her room. She had felt a little embarrassed about packing around these childhood treasures and had hidden them out of sight after he left.

One of the figurines stood out from the others, the one she had to see. Her hand trembled when she picked it up. It was the one her mother gave her on the night before she died. Her mother's last gift to her. All the others were mermaids, but this one was different; a merman with golden hair and—

She gasped. "Green eyes!"

She wiped accumulated dust from its surface with her thumb and held it up to the light, admiring the way it glittered, especially its eyes.

Eyes of green fire.

She sat down in the chair at her desk, remembering what her mother said when she gave it to her: *One day you'll meet a young prince meant only for you, like your father is meant for me.*

Audrey set the crystal merman on the desktop, proud and strong though standing a mere three inches tall. She rested her chin on the back of her hands, her nose inches from his magnificent fluked tail. She stroked the top of his head, wondering why his green eyes intrigued her.

She must have fallen asleep. When she opened her eyes, her cheek was lying in a puddle of drool and the green-eyed merman was lying on his side, staring back.

She wiped her cheek and checked the time on her phone: 1:35 AM

She yawned and stretched, wide awake and refreshed. It was the first time she had slept without dreaming of turtles or a massive shark or blue-striped tigers.

She wrinkled her nose when she caught a whiff seeping from the bag she had left by the door. Ryan hadn't been kidding. Her room stunk like low tide.

She picked up the merman figurine and put him back with the others. She slipped on shoes and a coat, grabbed the bag, and stepped out the door. She waited a moment for her eyes to adjust to the darkness. The rain had stopped and clouds had parted; the ground lit by faint moonlight. She started down the path, dotted with mushroom-shaped lights, toward the garbage dumpster.

A dark shadow fell from the trees and landed on the gravel path. A huge black bird whose head stood well above her knees, blocking the path.

She flicked her hand. "Shoo!"

But the bird stood firm. It squawked, loud and forceful, setting off alarm bells in her chest. She tried to walk around it, but it stepped in her way. She tried passing on the other side but the bird spread its massive wings. Its beak was sharply pointed and its talons were equally threatening.

She stepped back. It stepped forward, fixing her with a fierce gaze. Its pale eyes captured the faint glow of the moon and appeared to glow on their own. She considered turning and running for her room. But the way the bird was looking at her made it clear that too would be futile.

The bird cocked its head and leaned forward. She stood still as a rock. It took another step forward and shifted its gaze to the bag she held in her hand. Then with a quick and forceful peck, it took a bite from the bag.

A shred of black plastic fell at her feet.

"What the hell," she whispered.

When the bird looked up its eyes flickered, white to blue and back again. It fixed its gaze back on the bag and squawked.

She dropped it.

The bird attacked it. Shredded bits of plastic flew, littering the path. It made quite a ruckus, screeching and tearing and beating its wings. A light clicked on in a nearby cabin.

"Shh. I get it!"

The bird quieted, tucked its wings and fixed her with its moonstone-like eyes, as if waiting for something.

She opened the bag.

The bird moved forward and buried its beak inside. It rummaged for a while, popped its head out, and started stomping its feet.

She dumped the bag's contents on the ground. "Warning, it stinks."

The bird picked through the pile with purpose, poking at her jeans, casting the tattered bra aside. When it found her coat, it clasped the collar in its sharp beak and hopped from one foot to the other, flapping its wings, pushing it toward her.

"You want me to have this?"

The bird dropped it at her feet and chirped in reply.

She noticed her coat felt heavier than normal. She shook it. Something jingled in the pocket like a set of keys. She unzipped it and reached inside. Whatever it was shocked her, enough to rattle her teeth and render her fingers numb. She dropped the coat and cradled her hand.

"What the frick!"

The bird jumped up and down. "Hak. Hak. Hak."

Audrey glared. "Think it's funny, huh?"

But curiosity overcame humiliation. She picked up the coat and peeked inside the pocket. She saw a flash of silver and the glow of something white. She knelt and shook whatever it was out of the pocket. It fell to the ground. She shifted her stance until the pathway light better illuminated the thing lying at her feet.

It was a necklace. Its main feature was a large, razor-sharp claw with sections of looped silver, pounded flat. Pearls and other small stones dangled from silver links like polka dots. Attached in the center of one of the swirled loops was a green stone, the color of the Salish Sea.

A tiger's claw, swirls and dots, the color green. All of my obsessions!

Audrey picked up the necklace, only this time it didn't shock her, but vibrated and warmed in her hand. Then a mild ripple of electricity raced up her arm, raising every hair, triggering buried memories that came rushing back in a crush of sights, sounds, and smells—Merluma and the golden-haired boy with electric-green eyes, the one she had met long ago and had long forgotten, a memory she had buried under grief and sorrow. That same boy, no longer a boy but grown up, like her—now a merman with eyes of green fire.

She gasped, remembering his name. "Sinto!"

She cupped the bird's head in her hands. "And I remember you too! Moonstone."

Moonstone squawked excitedly.

Audrey ran back to her room, burst through the door, and grabbed the merman figurine from the top shelf. Was he smiling like that before?

She rolled the necklace in one hand and the figurine in the other.

Sinto. Not a merman but a Merahvu, born on Earth but with ancestry on Merluma.

Her heart pounded so furiously she had to sit down.

The visions are real. He is real. I'm not crazy!

She laid the necklace on the scratched surface of her desk, carefully splaying the links and each stone. The pearls reflected the light, their luminous surfaces clear and perfect, like Sinto's unique skin. The soft green stone matched the color of his eyes when he was calm, without fire.

She pictured him perfectly in her mind's eye when he offered her the gift; the way the sun reflected off the copper-colored streaks sprinkled through his golden hair, the necklace lying in the palm of his hand, the translucent webbing between his fingers.

She startled when she heard his voice threading though her mind, so close and real she stood up and spun around, convinced he was standing behind her, whispering in her ear...

I've much more I must show you; the way of the Merahvu, our secrets, our plight. Wear this necklace and think of me; a token to summon me from the waters near the island where I left you. Come soon, and at dawn's first light. Moonstone will help guide you. I wait, patiently yet expectantly, to see you again. Salamora, Sinto.

She clasped her hand over her mouth. Her heart rattled. That off-ness that had plagued her over the past weeks unraveled, and the pieces of her lost memories found their way back to their rightful place. Her confidence was bolstered by what she now knew was real and true. Sinto. Earth and Merluma, connected sisters with portals linking them together. Real. The visions. *Real.*

She picked up the necklace. So much more than a piece of jewelry; a special token he had given her to call him. It quivered and sparked, warming her fingers. She fingered the sharp tip of the claw and gazed in wonder at the pearls and silver. She held it to her heart, closed her eyes, and imagined him holding her in his arms as they crested a giant wave.

And something else unexpected happened. Not a memory set back in its rightful place, but something new for her to digest, a confirmation. She felt a deep sense of calm and closure; Blake had not suffered, was not suffering; whatever had happened to him, wherever he may be, Blake was whole and at peace.

She pondered what that meant, along with the meaning of Sinto's message, both mysterious and convoluted—*our secrets, our plight... Blake, whole and at peace.*

Nothing would stop her now. She would find a way back to Andrews Island, and soon, as Sinto requested. Her mind reeled with the promise of answers to her questions; about that new world, ripe for her to discover, and the truth about Blake's ultimate fate.

31

Favor

AUDREY SLEPT SOUNDLY FOR the first time in weeks. Dawn was yet to break but she snapped awake at 6 AM sharp, mind calm and body rejuvenated.

She slipped on her sweats and running shoes, then ran from the Labs to the heart of Friday Harbor, past the ferry landing, and on to Roy's marina at the south end of the harbor. The sun crested the treetops on neighboring Brown Island.

Moonstone flew above, merrily squawking.

The natural world came alive—the tree, the beetle, the chickadee—scenting the air and singing their unique songs. They had much to teach, she had much to learn! All she had to do was open her mind, observe and listen, as her mother had taught her—and Sinto too, in his quiet and otherworldly way. Lessons disguised as stories. Those lessons made sense, following the flood of memories about the splintered-off world of Merluma.

She felt newly born, running swift as a deer, toes gently tapping down to propel her forward. She could run for miles and never tire!

Along a low-lying beach, beams of sunlight kissed the sand, lifting a blanket of fog from the water lapping along the shore. A gentle breeze brushed her cheeks. Seagulls screeched and frolicked in the waves, stirring up an intoxicating perfume of the sea, like the scent that clung to Sinto's hair.

She floated through the rest of the day in a daze. She attended lectures, taking all the right notes—actual words, not doodles—but she wasn't fully present. In the corners of her mind and the sidebar of her notebook, she was formulating a plan. She wanted to squeal with delight and tell the world of her discovery, but gnawed her lip instead.

It was Wednesday. She planned to skip class on Friday, sneak off to Andrews Island, and use the necklace to call Sinto from the Salish Sea.

But how would she get there? And more pressing, could she wait two days?

Audrey ate lunch alone at a picnic table under a large maple tree. Her stomach was a knot of nerves and she found it difficult to eat, even though she knew she must. She had already choked down a sandwich and was working her way through an apple when Ryan sneaked up behind her and poked her in the ribs.

"Hey stranger, want to grab lunch?"

"Already am." She showed him the apple and took another bite.

He sat down across from her and gave her a quizzical look. "What's up with you today?"

"Nothing, just thinking." She grinned, apple bits in her teeth.

"Care to share? Based on that grin it must be something spectacular."

She was curious if he'd believe her if she told him the truth—all of it.

She looked around to make sure no one was near, then leaned forward and lowered her voice. "What if I told you everything around us was merely a fraction of reality? That there's an Earth world, splintered off from our own, that spawned an evolved version of Homo-Sapiens, secretly living among us, who can live on the land or in the sea, possessing powers beyond our imagination?"

Ryan sat back, arms crossed. "Special powers like in X-Men?"

She shook her head. "No! Humans, like us, with a few extra body parts, not fictional comic book characters that have weird quirks."

"Yesterday you were paranoid about being watched and drawing strange symbols instead of writing notes, and today you believe in a new species of humans from a splintered-off version of Earth?"

Heat rose in her cheeks. "I guess that does sound ridiculous."

He fanned his palms on the smooth gray wood of the table. "Seriously, have you considered contacting the therapist I told you about?"

She sat back. "I considered it, but haven't made the call. Really, I think I'm much better today."

He looked doubtful. "Right."

She smiled. "I'm serious! I kinda had a breakthrough—I thought about what you said and did a little soul searching and it—it just kinda hit me, and now everything makes sense."

He crinkled his brow studying her. "Well, I still think you should consider getting help."

She said nothing.

He sighed, thought for a bit, and she braced herself for another lecture. "How about a change of scenery? Let's get off this rock and cut loose. Couple of people are talking about going to Vancouver this weekend. You're old enough to get into the clubs there. Let's join 'em."

Ryan's offer was tempting but she had something else planned, like meeting up with Sinto and learning more about his mysterious world.

"Can't," she replied a little too quickly. "I've got to—you know, my father, he wants me home this weekend." She was surprised at how easily the lie slipped past her lips. She tossed her unfinished apple into the bushes and tapped her phone.

"Oh no! Looks like we're late for lab." She jumped up and slung her backpack over her shoulder.

Ryan didn't move.

"*Late*, come on!" Her voice quivered, afraid Ryan would see through her bullshit and the lie lingering bitterly on her tongue.

Reluctantly, he stood and followed.

Lab dragged on forever. At three o'clock sharp, she grabbed her backpack and raced to the parking lot, avoiding Ryan's suspicious gaze. Blake's Pathfinder was still parked where they left it after returning on that fateful day, the keys still tucked under the floor mat. All through lab she sensed that Ryan knew she had lied about this weekend, so she wasn't going to give him a chance to press for the truth. Now she was officially stealing their dead friend's car. She hoped Ryan wouldn't notice it missing.

Ten minutes later, she sat in Blake's car at Roy's marina mustering courage. She grabbed the sweats and boots Roy had loaned her the day she was rescued. By the time she knocked on his office door, her heart pounded and her palms were slick with sweat.

"Audrey! What a nice surprise. Come in, have a seat."

"I laundered these." She set the sweats on his desk and boots on the floor, and sat in the chair facing his desk. "I also wanted to thank you for saving me, and to apologize for my father's... audacity."

He shook his head, waved a hand, and sat across from her. "No apology necessary."

Roy gazed back, warm and receptive, waiting for her to say something else.

She nibbled her lip. She needed a boat. All she had to do was ask.

But what if he says no? What if he asks too many questions? She was a terrible liar. Ryan usually called her out every time. Why hadn't she practiced her pitch?

She scanned the photos of happy customers lined up across his credenza, standing by their shiny new boats. She crossed and uncrossed her ankles and twined her braid in her fingers, trying to find the right words.

Roy watched her fidget, pursing his lips, wrinkling his nose, and tugging on his ears. Roy's face and fingers were always in motion, a twitchy habit he had. A guy who liked to stay busy. He puffed his cheeks and asked, "What's the real reason you came to see me?"

Her fingers knotted in her lap. "I've been thinking. It might be good for me to get out on the water again. You know, face my fear."

"I'd be happy to take you out."

"I was thinking—um, that I should go alone."

His brow dipped and stayed there. "Winter's coming, and so are the storms. You know these waters can be dangerous. You might want to rethink boating right now. It's not safe."

She rolled her eyes. "You sound like my father."

"Well, he's right." He leaned forward. "Look, I'm not trying to lecture you, it's just," his lips pursed a couple of times, "I care about you, cared about Blake too, and some people are pretty shook up around here, not knowing exactly why those orcas attacked *Annabelle*."

"I would use utmost caution. No whale watching."

Roy sat back, chin in hand, fingers scratching rough whiskers.

"It's just—I need some time to think, to be alone. I haven't had the chance to truly grieve. Everyone's talking about it—I haven't even shed a tear." She looked up, at least that last part wasn't a lie. "Maybe a weekend in the outer islands would give me a chance to accept that Blake's gone, to mourn, with no one around to judge me. I was thinking Reid Harbor. There's a dock and it's protected from weather."

He stared out the window deep in thought, bushy brows twitching like caterpillars doing the hokey-pokey. She began to sweat again. This wasn't going as expected. She opened her mouth to argue more, but Roy interrupted.

"Have you ever operated a boat?"

Audrey's heart leaped with hope. "Blake usually captained *Annabelle*, but I know how to work the electronics, to navigate and read radar. I frequently plotted the course on each of our trips. My father taught me how to sail, steer the boat, how to read the water. It was long ago, but I remember the basics."

Roy's hands slid back and forth along the edge of his desk.

Audrey held her breath.

Pleasepleaseplease.

"I suppose I could loan you my power boat, teach you to drive. It's smaller than *Annabelle*, easier to maneuver by yourself, and it's safe and reliable."

"How about now?"

He looked at his watch and puffed out his cheeks. Then he grinned. "Why not? Afternoon's shot anyway."

32

Reunion

Roy's boat was fast and nimble, powered by twin diesels. Over the course of two days, he taught Audrey how to maneuver and to find the rhythm of the water, adjusting the speed for a more comfortable ride. The part about reading the water she already understood from outings with Blake and Ryan and sailing with her father when she was a child. Last summer she had earned her Boater Education Card. She recited standard navigation rules, types of markers and what they meant, how to properly pass another vessel, and how to call for help.

On Thursday, after her final lesson—which she readily recognized as a test—Roy offered her the use of his boat whenever she needed.

Friday morning, at the crack of dawn, she waved goodbye to Roy with a promise to be careful and to call if anything went wrong. Once she cleared Friday Harbor, she veered north and set a course for Andrews Island. She had thought about leaving her phone in her room knowing her father used it to track her comings and goings, but thought it best to keep it. Just in case. She shut it down and wrapped it in layers of foil hoping the foil would cause interference and make it impossible to track.

She felt like a caged bird set free—giddy and untethered, and she basked in defiance. It was the first time she had ignored her father's unreasonable demands. If he knew what she was doing, he would most certainly fulfill his threat and lock her away in his sprawling Seattle compound forever.

She felt at ease on the water. Gone was her need to repeat the mantra. It was a silly thing that now felt contrived and unnecessary. She was fairly certain it was Sinto who had given her this newfound courage for venturing on the water.

Evergreens pierced the fog hovering atop the islands. Gauzy fingers of mist stretched beyond their rocky shorelines, laying a blanket of calm across the water. As dawn broke, the misty sky behind Mount Constitution glowed a soft pink. No other boats were on the water as far as she could see.

A perfect day for a secret rendezvous.

Visibility quickly degraded when she cleared the narrow passage between Stuart and Johns Islands. Andrews Island was just beyond on the southern edge of Haro Strait. The island emerged on the radar screen, masked by a curtain of fog. She pulled back on the throttles to half speed, eyes glued to the radar screen.

Andrews Island was an enigma. She had spent the previous night researching everything she could find about it. She had learned it was owned by a private corporation, and *very* private at that. She found the board was made up of, well, made-up people. The surrounding waters had been deemed environmentally protected many decades ago, before environmental protection was a thing in the islands; no fishing, anchoring, or snooping around allowed.

The staff at the Labs said it was off limits, except the buoys and the reef on the southeastern shore, and those were accessible by strict permit only. Only it was unclear exactly how one requested a permit. The staff at the Labs were just as baffled about the island as she was. Who owned it and why was it so secretive?

She was hoping she wouldn't find out. She had every intention of violating whatever restrictions had been imposed, either by the state or those made-up corporate people.

She tried to memorize every square inch using Google Earth and an old paper chart she found on Roy's boat. Like military locations, she found the Google images were blurred, and the chart was just as vague, providing only a rough outline of the land and depths of the surrounding waters. From what she could tell, it was uninhabited. She saw no obvious color changes indicting structures, just the color of thick trees and rock. But one little detail they had not blurred enough, maybe by mistake since it was on the far western side of the island. There appeared to be a small uncharted cove hidden by a rocky outcropping, visible on the satellite image only to the most discerning eye. The cove seemed to have a dock and offered a well-protected place to moor Roy's boat, undetectable from others passing by.

As she blindly neared her final destination, she wondered if Sinto knew about the risk she was taking and why he had chosen this particular island. Maybe it was because of its secrecy and isolation.

The island emerged from the fog. She slowed the boat to a crawl and cruised along the rocky outcropping where the entrance to the cove should be. It was camouflaged with overgrown bushes and trees and she almost missed the turn. She thrust the starboard engine into reverse and tapped the bow thruster. Roy's boat spun around, lining up with the entrance to the passage. The GPS rang in warning as she slowly punched her way through a tunnel of foliage and into the narrow channel. The boat's navigational chart registered the channel as land.

The channel was more like a narrow fjord formed of solid rock cleaved by geological force. Sixty feet high, roughly thirty feet wide, with forty-two feet of water below the boat's keel, according to the depth sounder. Evergreens gnarled by wind and time hung over the gap like gargoyles guarding the gates to a forgotten kingdom. The sky darkened and the sound of the engines reverberated loudly as she passed through a tunnel of wood and stone.

The channel spilled into a mirrored cove, large enough to hold a couple of small boats at anchor. Douglas fir, Garry oak, and bigleaf maple grew to the water's edge. The tide was high and their foliage kissed the mirrored surface, making it impossible to distinguish real from reflection. Her presence rippled across the surface disturbing the calm image. On the far side was the dock with a ramp to shore, the only man-made structure visible in the cove.

Without wind or current to contend with, Audrey easily docked the boat.

Silence fell heavy when she shut down the engines, and she stood in the cockpit, marveling at the wildness and isolation. It felt like she had traveled hundreds of years back in time.

A dark shadow passed over. She looked up. Moonstone swooped and playfully dove for her head. He hovered for a heartbeat before flying away and landing at the top of the ramp. She now knew Sinto had sent his bird to help her find the necklace and to guide her, just like his message promised.

My secret guardian.

She snatched her backpack and a flashlight from the cabin and hopped over the gunwale to the dock. It looked new and well-maintained, the decking fabricated from modern-day resin materials that don't rot. The posts that secured the dock in place were steel, not creosote, as was the ramp connecting it to shore, built extra-long to minimize the changing angle based on the state of the tide.

She scurried up the ramp to where Moonstone waited. He took flight when she reached the top and flew above a recently graveled trail that cut through the forest. The sun had begun to light the sky but the forest floor was still quite dark. She clicked on her flashlight and followed Moonstone.

The air was sweetened by a carpet of golden leaves. Birds twittered in the treetops. Moonstone flew ahead, swooping from side to side. Audrey ran after, laughing and leaping for his tail.

The trail cut through a meadow with tall grass and overgrown apple trees where a six-point black-tail buck blocked her path. Audrey skidded to a halt. The does and fawns by his side startled and fled, but the buck stood its ground and sniffed the air around her. He fixed her with a hard gaze before slowly sauntering away, tail flicking, his pungent musky scent hanging heavily in his wake.

Moonstone squawked from the far side of the meadow where the trail continued through a thick dark forest.

Giant evergreens towered, rotten tree trunks nursed huckleberries, and multi-generational families of seedlings encircled mother trees. Patches of ground along the trail were stomped and munched clear of tender flora by the local deer. A tangle of fallen branches made passage anywhere but on the trail impossible. Wildly textured moss carpeted glacially deposited rock and the forest floor, dotted with red-capped amanita. Unseen rodents rustled through the waxy-leaved salal as she passed by.

The forest abruptly ended at a beach covered by a blanket of fog rolling off the water. The same beach she tried to swim to from the buoy, but failed to reach. Agate pebbles and gray sand crunched beneath her feet. The air was crisp with brine.

Moonstone disappeared in the mist. She followed the sound of his soft chirps, stepping over tangled heaps of kelp and eel grass brought on shore by a high tide, full of feasting bugs. His silhouette emerged near the shore, perched on a large rock facing the water.

Audrey shoved the flashlight into her backpack and carefully pulled out the necklace from an inside pocket. She clasped it around her neck.

The silver links came alive, radiating heat where they touched her skin. She shivered with excitement, uncertain what to do next. His message was clear; come to the beach at first light, and soon. Check, and check.

A minute passed. Gentle waves lapped near her feet.

She whispered Sinto's name several times.

Five minutes passed, nothing.

She yelled, "Sinto!" Silence. "Hello?"

Still, nothing.

She looked at Moonstone. "Now what?"

Moonstone twitched his wings.

"You're no help."

She grabbed her backpack and wandered to the top of the beach to a pile of logs. Moonstone followed on foot, talons clicking on rock, stopping once or twice to steal glances toward the water or pick something from the sand. She sat on a log, disappointed. Moonstone plopped down in the sand beside her and fluffed his feathers. He gazed at the water also looking disappointed.

Sinto's message clearly said dawn's first light, but Audrey feared that moment had passed. It would have meant navigating the boat in full dark and stumbling through the dark forest to the beach. Did he mean early morning in general or exactly as the sun crested the horizon?

Rays of sunlight burned through the fog, setting the sea aglitter. She shaded her eyes against the rising sun and waited some more. It was certainly well past dawn's first light; it was outright daytime.

She whiled away the time, picking through the colorful agates at her feet. The necklace lay cool and still against her chest. She drew a sharp breath when it began to snap and spark.

She stood. Moonstone hopped to his feet. Both intently gazed at the water, anticipating Sinto's arrival.

He emerged, silhouetted by the sun and sea glitter. He wore a dark-green wrap slung across one shoulder and around his hips and through his legs. Lorica rolled off his skin like beads of water from a duck's feathered back. His eyes were aglow and his tail lazily trailed behind him, scratching a trail in pebble and sand.

He took her hand and pressed her palm to his lips.

"Hey," she said.

He smiled and breathed deep from her hand. "Hey."

"You're real."

He chuckled. "I hope so."

She debated—confront or not—but she was itching to know. "Why didn't I remember meeting you or anything about Merluma?"

He smiled. "I was expecting 'Hello' or 'How are you?' Isn't that customary in your world?"

A nervous laugh escaped her lips. "Yes, it is—but you didn't answer my question."

He glanced down at his feet, looked up. "What would have happened if you did—I mean, remember everything right away?"

She was caught up short. "I suppose I would have—"

He quirked a brow, encouraging her to finish.

"I would have told everyone what happened to me, about you—about Merluma." She sighed. "I guess it makes sense now that you mention it. But my memories were completely lost, except snippets. How did you do that?"

"They weren't lost, merely delayed, though I did add a new one. My message, that is all. A gentle coax to your mind. No harm was done."

"What about how I feel about Blake?"

A pause. "Blake? What do you mean?"

"I mean, after my memories returned, I had this deep and profound settling about his fate, that he didn't suffer and was whole and at peace."

"Perhaps the passage of time helped you to accept what happened to him. Does believing he is whole and at peace rid you of sadness, of guilt or anger?"

"I suppose, but—" She shook her head. "Probably nothing, sorry I brought it up."

"No reason to be sorry. I'm sorry about your friend, truly."

She nibbled the inside of her cheek, debating whether she could forgive him for giving her mind a coaxing nudge even if his intent was for her own best interest. She decided to let it go, resigning herself to be more aware in the future, to be a little more guarded. She smiled. "So, here we are, now what?"

He grew somber. "There's something happening." He pointed toward the water. "In the ocean."

His tone caught her by surprise. "What's happening?"

"I need to show you."

She took a step back, wondering if there was truth to her father's warning.

"There's nothing to fear, merely to observe."

Audrey stole a glance down at Moonstone who was standing at their feet, head swiveling between them, listening to their brief exchange.

Sinto waved his hand. "Off with you, Rave. Your chores are done, you are free to go."

Moonstone squawked and sat down.

Sinto knelt and brushed Moonstone's neck with his finger, clicking his tongue. Man and bird stared at each other in silence, then Moonstone twitched and Sinto's brows shot up in surprise. Sinto looked up at her. "Moonstone?"

"Because of his eyes."

Sinto stood. "He says he likes it. I guess he's Rave no more."

"What else did Moonstone say?"

"That you should trust me."

33

Orange

Sinto led her to the sea's edge. Once his toes touched water, thick liquid seeped from tiny pores in his skin. "You remember this part?"

She nodded and stepped into the gelatinous substance pooling at his feet. It stretched around their bodies like a film of flexible thick plastic.

"Oh, one other thing: did you have anything to do with the fact I no longer fear the water?"

He didn't answer right away.

"Be truthful," she prodded.

"I may have seeded a suggestion about that."

"Hmm." She pondered, *may have... a bit vague.* It was a thoughtful suggestion but she wondered what other less desirable suggestions he may decide to plant. "Maybe we should discuss any and all suggestions you may have in the future, before and *verbally.*"

He nodded. "Of course. It was a bold assumption and one I should not have taken without your consent." His eyes reflected genuine sincerity but she decided it best to keep her guard in place. There was so much she didn't know about Sinto, or the Merahvu, and what was acceptable or not within their culture.

"Good, please don't forget."

They waded deeper until they were fully encased by his lorica and surrounded by liquid green. He pulled her back to his chest and they dove into the depths of the Salish Sea. His pliable lorica hugged their bodies. It cast a soft green glow, lighting the surrounding water.

Audrey held out a hand. Sinto's lorica stretched between her fingers. She spread her arms. His lorica stretched from her sides like translucent wings. "It feels like flying!"

He stopped swimming and they bobbed weightlessly far below the surface. His heart drummed against her back. "Are you ready to learn what it's truly like to fly?"

"Fly through water?"

"Like flying across the universe."

"Tell me what to do."

"Nothing, just hold on."

She wound her arms tighter around the one he had wrapped around her waist.

His merlux came to life with a rumble, vibrating against her back. He flicked his wrist. A sparkling green thread burst from his fingertips and cut through his lorica. The thread curled into a tight spiral, stirring the water into a swirling whirlpool. It bored a waterless hole into the darkness, a spinning vortex large enough to fit the two of them. Green sparks flew from its yawning mouth, setting the sea aglow. Its centrifugal force tugged at their bodies.

She gasped when Sinto dove inside.

Air was momentarily sucked from her lungs as they were launched at incalculable speed into the tunnel of the vortex, a void with no resistance—like a wormhole cut in the sea.

"How is this possible?"

"Mind over matter." Sinto relaxed his grip. "I hope you're not afraid of the dark."

"It's already dark."

"I mean truly dark. The deeper we go, the faster we go, the darker it will be." His eyes clouded and brow set, deep in concentration. Their trajectory steepened downward and she sensed their speed increase.

The dark Sinto spoke of was nothing like the dark she had once feared as a child. This was a darkness from which nothing escaped, sucking up every bit of light surrounding it, like a black hole in outer space.

She willed her mind to be calm, to trick it into believing she was tucked in her bed with her eyes squeezed shut, not racing inside a vortex cutting through the deep ocean.

Every so often they would veer past the bioluminescent glow of some undersea obstacle. Was it another Merahvu? An undiscovered creature of the deep? At one point, they swerved back and forth in wide swooping turns as if flying blindly through a series of canyons. She wanted to ask how he knew where they were but feared that if she distracted him, he might falter and they would crash into the side of an underwater mountain or into another Merahvu crossing their path.

She had learned of sonar and magnetoception in school—innate senses whales and birds possessed to aid in migration using sound and Earth's geomagnetic field. Had the Merahvu mastered those skills?

Mind over matter. What did he possibly mean?

Time passed quickly.

The darkness receded as they began to ascend. She sensed a change in speed, slower than before. Bright light filled the vortex, then they were spit out into a murky sea, and quite suddenly. Sinto's body spooned around hers as he held her tight in his arms. It felt like they had fallen from the sky, then landed in a soft, muddy swamp. The vortex shrank to a thread and snapped back to his fingers with a loud zap. He fisted his hand as if strained from a vigorous workout.

They bobbed several feet below the surface. She opened her mouth to ask where they were but all she had to do was look. Colorful bits of plastic floated all around as well as other discarded plastic things; a partial bucket, half a toothbrush, a crumpled water bottle, and a rusty razor blade encased in plastic. Larger pieces were covered with varying degrees of algae, shellfish, and barnacles. Those encrusted with more organic matter were slowly sinking to the bottom.

She had learned about these plastic time capsules in the sea, swirling in gyres formed by ocean currents. The largest was northeast of the Hawaiian Islands and halfway to California. The Great Pacific Garbage Patch in the central North Pacific Ocean.

"Is this what I think it is?"

He nodded. "Sad, isn't it?"

"Beyond sad—it's reckless." In the distance, a fishnet, green and made of plastic, just like the one that ensnared her mother, held the rotting carcass of a dolphin. She closed her eyes, wishing the awful image away. "There are people dedicated to cleaning this up."

"A noble and daunting task but it keeps coming and in greater numbers. The source is the problem."

"You mean Sapiens."

"I mean the creation of it."

Silence fell between them. Plastic was essential to Earth's modern world and her world was built upon it. Plastic was in everything and everywhere. Audrey wondered how humanity functioned before it was invented, long before she was born.

When Audrey first learned of these garbage patches in the ocean, she imagined it accumulating as floating islands that could easily be scooped up and collected. But the reality wasn't that simple. Plastic didn't naturally decompose. It could take decades or upwards of five hundred years to break down completely, depending on the type. It came from rivers and beaches, ships and commercial fishing. Plastic netting was one of the worst offenders.

Once in the ocean, plastics broke down into tiny pieces that would linger twenty or more feet below the surface, like the pieces floating around them; a toxic soup. Birds and other sea creatures mistook it as food and die from ingesting it.

Audrey never considered the implications of endless plastic while growing up, and she imagined that neither did most other people. Floating in it was eye-opening, a sickening gut punch. Sinto was kind not to say it, but she felt guilty knowing she was part of the problem. Things that were part of her everyday life and she took for granted, like the phone tucked inside the backpack she had hidden on the beach, as well as the polyester fabric the pack was made of, and the hairband securing her braid.

"As awful as this is, I didn't bring you here to see this. This you know of." He pointed at their feet. "But what's happening down there is where the true horror lies."

He cut a hole at their feet. It yawned like an elevator shaft. They hovered for a second then dropped in free fall. Her stomach balled up in her throat and stuck there. They dropped into a void of black ink.

A pinprick of orange light emerged from the bottom like the flame of a candle, then a campfire, then a wildfire, orange and fiery, spreading as far as the eye could see. Whatever it was, it was alive with movement.

Sinto swished his tail and legs to slow their descent. They landed with a soft bounce on the squishy ocean floor well clear of a glowing reef of orange that stretched into the distance.

Tentacles reached up from the vibrant reef and snared encrusted chunks of plastic as they dropped from the surface. The chunks hovered for a beat like lumpy balloons, then more tentacles burst from the reef and slithered across their surfaces, prying off barnacles and seashells and spitting out clouds of algae, until all that was left was the scoured man-made thing it once was. Then the scoured thing would sink into the blanket of orange, followed by a pulse of light, a gurgle, and a pop—consumed completely in a matter of seconds. The reef swelled and it inched a little closer to their feet.

Audrey took a step back. "What is it?"

"We call it *Orange*, a new strain of waterborne fungus. We discovered it six months ago but believe it's been festering here for quite some time. Where it came from or how it came to be, we're uncertain. Possibly from radiation leaking into the sea from the Far East, but we have found no conclusive evidence that was a factor."

"It's so prolific."

"It favors pretty much anything petroleum-based." Orange light danced across his face like the flames of a fire. "We were ecstatic when we first discovered it—an organic way to clean up waste in the Pacific. But the more we observed, the more concerned we became. It mutated and became less discriminating, growing at an alarming rate, heating the surrounding water well beyond normal, and smothering anything that got in its path."

The reef inched a little closer.

"Your message. You said something about your plight. Is this what you mean?"

Sinto gave her a pained look. "Oh, there is more that troubles us, but this," he gestured toward the orange reef, "affects us all. Sapien and Merahvu alike, Earth and Merluma."

She could feel the heat radiating through Sinto's lorica.

"Is this the only place you found it?"

"So far. It seems placated by the abundant supply of plastics trickling down from above."

"How do we stop it?"

"How do you stop anything from surviving? Starve it of what it needs."

"Without plastic—and other petroleum-based products—you believe it will die?"

"That's what we hope."

"So the solution is to rid Earth of petroleum-based *anything*? Impossible."

Sinto's eyes cut to the reef; the gills on the side of his neck flexed.

"That's what we're afraid of," he said. "That impossibility, and the consequence of not doing anything at all."

"There's nothing else that will stop it?"

"Not that we have discovered."

Audrey gazed at the blanket of Orange spreading across the Pacific seabed, feeling unsettled. "And this was what you wanted to show me?"

"Not all." He grinned and cut a new tunnel.

34

What Lies Beneath

SINTO EMBRACED HER AND together they dove inside the dark tunnel cut through the sea. The orange reef slipped away like waking from a bad dream. Audrey could feel his powerful heartbeat and electrical power vibrating in his chest, soothing and hypnotizing to the weary. He told her the next part of their journey would take longer. With nothing to see but blackness she closed her eyes and tried to think of more pleasant things and rid her mind of the nightmare unfolding in the Pacific.

She was startled from deep thought when they came upon a bright blue light. They slowed and the vortex disintegrated. Sinto circled the source of light: a giant translucent dome, nestled in a valley between a trio of underwater mountains. Two of the mountains were perfectly peaked, while the third was missing its top and had a pile of rubble at its base, as if a giant sea creature had taken a bite and spit it out. Inside the dome was a vividly-colored city, bustling with activity.

"Where are we?" Audrey gasped.

"Tallamure. This is where I live, my home."

"*Tal-la-mure...*" she repeated, the pleasant sound rolling off her tongue.

"The name is derived from our ancestors' original language. It means 'cradle of peace.' The city was built after peace was established at the end of the Forever War over three hundred years ago as a symbol of our unification: three tribes, one people, living in peace under a single governing body representing the interests of each tribe."

A school of squid cut across their path, mesmerized by the light. Sinto muscled his way through and landed in a narrow gap between the dome and the steep side of one of the mountains. He took her hand and they stepped through the dome's wall like stepping through a waterfall, Sinto's lorica rolling off their bodies and evaporating into the dome with a quiver and a soft pop.

Audrey blinked in disbelief and drew a deep breath of fizzy oxywater, cool and refreshing to her lungs.

They stood in a meadow smelling of lavender. Clover and chicory grew at her feet. Beyond the meadow, the city spread before them like a giant coral reef perched atop rocky outcroppings. Structures mimicked various types of coral; round, pillared, tall, and some flat and stacked atop one another like pancakes. They came in a rainbow of color and textures; smooth, pocked, or stamped with intricate patterns. Windows and doors were artistically cut in their sides; the movement of life visible within. Wispy branched trees and vibrantly colored plants filled the spaces between. In the distance an evergreen forest pierced the sky.

"This is impossible! Coral, plants, trees—" She bent to pick a purple chicory flower. "And flowers?"

He grinned. "It's all very possible."

"And all that's keeping the sea from crushing us is this?" She poked the dome wall, a thin gelatinous membrane no thicker than the one Sinto formed from the pores of his skin. To the eye it appeared quite fragile, but the resilience she felt against her finger was quite the opposite. The wall rippled like molten steel and blue sparks flickered at the spot where she touched it. A hot, tingling sensation rippled up her arm; electrified, like Sinto's lorica.

"How deep are we?"

"Do you really want to know?"

She thought for a moment. Did she? Some things were best ignored, especially things that might induce a severe case of needless panic. She shook her head and looked up to the ball of light hovering at the top of the dome. "Sunshine?"

"Simulated," Sinto added. He led her to a path where wild strawberries grew.

"Strawberries too?"

"Genetically adapted to grow in oxywater." He bent, plucked one, held it out to her. "Try it."

Sweetness exploded in her mouth. The berry was deep red all the way through and seeds got stuck in her teeth like real strawberries. "Delicious!"

She took a few steps. She twirled. She waved her arms. It felt as if she was underwater yet her skin and hair felt dry to the touch, as did her clothes. It felt the same as being cocooned inside Sinto's lorica but she was free to move on her own. Gravity was much weaker than she was used to, and coupled with the increased density of oxywater, walking took effort. But when she leaped, she floated down gracefully until her feet were firmly planted on the seabed.

"Swimming is more efficient than walking." Sinto flicked his tail and swam above her in a lazy circle with his legs and tail pressed together as a single appendage. His body rippled as if made of liquefied muscle and cartilage. He moved with the grace of a dolphin. Silhouetted by the simulated sun he resembled a merman as depicted in the myths: a human with no legs and a sleek fluked tail. He spun and flipped, twisting sideways and backwards before gracefully landing on his finned feet.

"Show-off." She tried to sound sarcastic, but it came out as a breathless gasp.

He held out his hand. She took it, then they were soaring above the city, her mouth agape in wonder.

The Merahvu had grasped the true meaning of living in harmony with nature and gave it life in the dark depths of the brutal sea. Plants bloomed between coral dwellings, a riot of texture and color in every crack and crevice, free to take root and flourish.

Children played in a leafy forested park, swinging from vines and leaping from tree branches, their fins fluttering like wings. Squeals of laughter drifted on currents sweeping through the city like a gentle breeze.

Merahvu gathered in courtyards, hovered in the sky, bartered in marketplaces. The city was filled with a song of foreign lyrics, high-pitched squeals, and rapid clicks.

Merahvu swam in coordinated groups like schools of fish, darting around Sinto and Audrey with grace and ease as they busily moved from place to place. Sinto pointed out those belonging to each of the three tribes that made up the whole of the Merahvu—Seakai, Arctakai, and Terrakai.

Sinto explained that the majority of the Merahvu who lived in the city were Seakai, who normally preferred warm tropical waters and found the mild and even temperature of the city pleasant and hospitable. Sinto shared their same physical characteristics: fluted tail, fair-colored skin, golden wavy hair. They flitted about with their whale-like tails and were adorned in a simple wisp of fabric wrapped around their bodies, like the one Sinto wore, which reminded Audrey of a pā'ū or sarong favored in Sapien Polynesian culture. He said the Merahvu call it a *skareef*. Some of the passing Seakai wore them loosely, revealing much of their bodies and unique markings.

Arctakai they passed less frequently. Arctakai lacked much color, having skin pale as snow, eyes of pale blue, and silver hair. Their hair was extraordinarily long, braided and twined atop their heads or wound around their necks like multiple necklaces. Sinto said the Arctakai preferred icy waters and frozen lands, and most of the Arctakai resided in another colony located in the Southern Ocean. They wore a version of skareef, long and white, draped like a toga, with a narrow slit in the back so their sharply pointed, fluked tails could sway freely.

"The Arctakai primarily practice healing and maintain a vast library of knowledge passed down from our ancestors. They keep mostly to themselves. While they can be fierce, they are the most contented and peaceful of the three tribes."

They passed even fewer Terrakai.

"The Terrakai are the most unique among the Merahvu," Sinto said. "They prefer land and freshwaters over the sea. Those who live here reside in the simulated forests on the far edge of the city."

The Terrakai's dark hair and skin matched closely to her own, and they presented themselves more like the indigenous people that once populated North America than descendants of a people evolved to live in the sea. They wore animal skins like those that Sinto had worn on Merluma and that he made for her from the fur of the bluestripe tiger. Many were ornately decorated with colorful beads of stone. Sinto told her that the Terrakai never wasted anything, and the skins they wore came from animals they hunted both on Earth and Merluma. But the greatest difference between the Terrakai and the other tribes were their fluke-less tails, with multiple wispy fins like that of a goldfish, sheer and translucent.

Sinto explained the Merahvu had no concept of currency or social classes. Earth and Merluma gave and the Merahvu reaped their gifts equally and with respect, knowing that to survive, so must Earth and Merluma and all living things. To take meant to give. A system of continuous balancing. Like nature itself. Adapting and evolving to surrounding changes.

"The city was designed for sustainability, and as the population grew, the impact of such growth was calculated and resources adjusted, as it is to this day. Those who live here share equally in that responsibility, understanding that when one helps another it benefits all. Just as we learned from our own war, we also have Sapiens to thank, watching your societies thrive and collapse over the millennia. We study to understand why success can lead to a tragic end. We have learned greatly from these mistakes and our goal is not to forget those painful lessons of the past."

Audrey patiently listened to Sinto's tale of how peace was established and maintained, of the nobleness of every citizen. She struggled to understand how the Merahvu successfully overcame deeply rooted biases and animosity between three uniquely different tribes in such a short period of time. Sinto claimed the Merahvu were human, but humans were greatly flawed, easily falling victim to greed and power and those who understood how to manipulate the masses. Yet, here she was, witness to the Utopian world Sinto described and in which he lived.

Maybe the Merahvu had evolved to something beyond human. Something Sapiens could learn from.

"Show me more," she asked.

35

Crack In The Dome

Sinto swam to a large wasteland at the edge of the city. The stark white seabed stretched before them like the crackled salt flats of a desert playa. He dropped down where the dome sank into the seabed.

On the other side was a second, much smaller dome glowing brightly like the simulated sun above their heads. Hovering above the mini-dome was a trio of giant jellyfish tethered like hot air balloons. Each one a different color; yellow, blue, and red. Transparent tentacles extended from the mini-dome into their bellies, filling their gelatinous skins with a matching colored liquid. Bubbles rose from the top of the mini-dome and disappeared into the inky void above. A shoal of giant squid swam around it, mesmerized by the light.

Sinto cocked a brow. "Care to guess what it's for?"

"Is this a test?"

He nodded.

"A processing plant?"

"Yes, but for what?"

She shrugged. "Oxywater? Heat?"

He nodded. "Any thoughts on how?"

Audrey chewed on her lip. "I study biology, not chemistry. How about a clue?"

"What process produces liquid oxygen and hydrogen gas from seawater?"

Audrey perked up. "I know this, um—" She snapped her fingers. "Electrolysis?"

"Correct!" He pointed at the jellyfish. "Yellow, oxygen. Red, hydrogen. Blue, fresh water. And those rising bubbles are chlorine gas." He wrinkled his nose. "Nasty stuff we've no use for."

She recalled the lesson, one she learned from an online chemistry class several years ago that she found quite challenging. The concept of electrolysis had intrigued her as a potential source of clean energy from seawater.

She was surprised she remembered the details, and dug deeper, reciting the complete story. "Electrolysis: the decomposition of ionic compounds by applying an electrical current, from saltwater in this case. The result: hydrogen gas and liquid oxygen."

She gazed up at the simulated sun burning brightly above. "Burn hydrogen for heat and light." She drew a deep moist breath. "Formulate oxywater from liquid oxygen. And a by-product from burning hydrogen... fresh water, for the plants. Brilliant!"

Sinto nodded, then cocked a brow. Signaling the test was far from over.

"But," she said.

"Yes, but," he said.

She crossed her arms. "Something else is required in great supply: Electricity, and lots of it. Where does it come from?" She poked him in the solar plexus. "I would find it hard to believe it would come from combined merluxes."

"True. But there is a single source capable of producing far more than we could ever use, in many lifetimes. The sun."

She looked up to the vast darkness. "How do you capture solar energy from here?"

"Through a microorganism that rises to the surface of the ocean during the day—*solarites*—skittish little things barely visible to the eye and linked by a transparent network of fibers much like a spider's webbing. They convert solar rays into small electrical pulses to aid in their digestion, thereby generating an endless supply of electricity." He pointed to the darkness above. "You can see them if you look carefully, billions and billions of them like so many other living organisms spread throughout the ocean, some so small we can't see them with our limited range of sight."

Audrey scanned the sea above the smaller dome. If she squinted just right she could see fragmented flashes, like tiny shooting stars in a midnight sky. Minuscule filaments crisscrossing and connected. Invisible except by brief flashes of light scurrying along their gossamer surfaces. "Barely, but yes!"

"We organize them to gather solar light from the surface wherever the sun is shining. There's a thick blanket of webbing surrounding the dome. You just can't see it because of the light."

"How do you organize them?"

He pointed to his head.

"Mind over matter? Like how you formed that crazy tunnel we traveled in? I don't suppose you'll share how you do that."

"I could try but you wouldn't be capable of understanding."

Audrey bit her tongue. His words were condescending but considering the way he was looking at her, that was not his intent. She reminded herself there were many things about Sinto she truly did not understand, nor did she want to come across as arrogant or whiny by confronting him. She trod carefully. "Another special adaptation I suppose."

"An advanced form of sharing."

Audrey studied the pattern and movement of the tiny lights with fresh eyes, intrigued that there was so much about life in the ocean that Sapiens didn't know. Her studies at the Labs were just a tiny scratch on the surface. Sinto could probably teach her more in a month than earning a PhD or a lifetime of research could reveal. She wished she had a way to take notes.

A bright flash followed by a distant rumble drew her gaze to the dome outside. Squid scattered in all directions and fell limp, momentarily stunned. Then they resumed their melodic march, swimming in the opposite direction.

Sinto smirked. "The tenders get a little over-zealous when stoking the fire. It is a bit of a trick to get hydrogen gas to ignite in oxywater. Sometimes they over-compensate. It's quite volatile."

"And corrosive. How can something as delicate as a jellyfish contain it?"

"Those jellyfish were gently evolved for that purpose, one of many adaptations that have enabled us to build this city and help vegetation prosper in its environment."

"*Gently* evolved?"

"You aren't the only ones tinkering with Mother Nature, though our methods vary."

Audrey studied him. It was her turn to ask questions. Questions that had nothing to do with biology and chemistry. "Why did the Merahvu build this city, here on Earth? What drove you away from Merluma, a place so abundant and clean."

"Merluma is much more limited than you may believe. Simply put, we outgrew it and there are some organic resources it lacks that we have found here. Remember that it's covered in water. We may be capable of travel and building a pseudo world in the ocean, but we need what thrives on land to survive."

"How many of you are there?"

"Five million, maybe more."

"Here in the city?"

"No, this city is much too small to support more than a tiny segment of our population. We have tried but found we can't support much more in this type of environment."

"How many live on Earth?"

"Currently, most of us."

"Where?"

"Here and two other underwater colonies." His voice trailed off like he had more to say.

"Where else?"

"Here, there, everywhere."

"In the sea?"

His gaze wandered. "No."

"Are you saying there are possibly millions of Merahvu living among Sapiens?"

He didn't answer right away. "There are many places we've carved out an existence far from your heavily populated areas. Some have fully integrated into your society. You may be unaware because we tend to keep to ourselves and live here on Earth under strict rules."

"What kind of rules?"

"Never reveal who we are and where we came from. Rules necessary to avoid the consequences of exploitation, of us or Merluma. There are many riches on Merluma we have no interest in, but Sapiens may find irresistible."

"Oil?"

"Oil not so much, but Merluma is rich with rare metals that you seek for your technologies."

"If this is a big secret, why are you telling *me* this?"

He didn't answer.

"Sinto..."

"I trust you. Can we leave it at that?"

"But I hardly know you. How do you know you can trust me?"

He didn't answer.

A seed of unease took root in her belly. "So this life you have described, the way of this city, is it accepted by *all* Merahvu?"

"Many agree and accept the mandates set down by our governing Circle."

"Sinto, you've not fully answered my question. Do *all* agree?"

His eyes dimmed a little and she sensed he was calculating how to answer. What was he afraid of telling her? Did she want to know?

Silence stretched.

He sighed. "Not all agree."

"Ah, so therein lies the rub."

"What's that mean?"

"A figure of speech. The kernel of the problem. A friction point—our human flaw, or asset, depending on who you ask. We can't seem to agree to something even if it is for the betterment of all, especially if someone believes that someone else will personally gain from it."

His gaze shifted to his feet.

She felt a little guilty for pushing the conversation to this point. It had shifted from a lighthearted game of "test your knowledge" toward her tearing apart his Utopian story. Remembering his message, she couldn't shake her building unease. Yet she had learned from many interactions with her father that answers did not come easily—if at all—if forced. Answers often revealed themselves through nonthreatening conversation and keeping the one who held fast to them unaware of a cleverly crafted interrogation.

She backpedaled. "I don't mean to be critical." She laughed. "Understanding that being critical is yet another human flaw, I mean at least, a *Sapien* flaw... What you have created with this city is difficult to grasp. I—I mean, it's amazing! You've helped open my eyes to believe the impossible." She brushed a lock of hair from his brow. "But I sense something's wrong. Something bad. You said so in your message. You wanted to share your plight, which I take to mean a difficult and challenging situation. You ask me to trust you, so I ask you the same."

His brow furrowed. "You're right. The truth is things are much worse than most know." His eyes glazed with moisture. "Merluma is dying, we are dying, our population is stagnant—dwindling even. We initially came to Earth out of curiosity, to study and learn from you, to gather resources unavailable in our world, but then changes happening on Earth began affecting Merluma. Some came here to better understand the problem and propose solutions, but those proposals have caused great disagreement between the tribes. We found influences from your world have affected some of our people. Old conflicts and grievances are reemerging. The concept of political gaming and division have bloomed within our vernacular. We're finding it harder to agree, to find common cause."

"Does this have something to do with Orange?"

"That is merely a symptom of the problems we face."

"We, as in the Merahvu, or do you mean all of us?"

"All of us."

"And what do the Merahvu believe is the problem?"

"Many obvious things: infinite consumption of finite resources, shifting climate, accidental leaks, and burning things that should never have been extracted from the bowels of Earth in the first place. We call it the Great Imbalance. Put too many rats in a cage, what happens? Put them on the run, what happens? Poison the air and the water they consume, what happens? Starvation, territorial conflict, illness... This triggers nature to reset the balance. Nature always wins in the end. The way of nature is neither compassionate nor empathetic to you or me or any species. It just *is*, however it needs to be, to destroy, create, or adapt. One day the Earth and Merluma will outlive their purpose and the sun will run out of energy and explode, sucking up everything we know to be reabsorbed by the universe and repurposed. Nature is the ultimate law. One we cannot change."

"We're well aware of these problems."

"We know that—we have read your writings, current and historical. Yet you do nothing about it."

"That's not true! There are many impassioned people working on solutions, scientists like myself. Reducing carbon emissions, spreading awareness, organizing toxic cleanup, protecting endangered species."

"Yes, but are they making a difference?"

"Of course!"

"And you believe this?"

She swallowed. "Why shouldn't I?"

"Because it's not enough. Some think it's too late. Do you remember what you observed on Merluma?"

"Life was abundant, not dwindling. The air was fresh, the oceans pure. A perfect Eden!"

"That is not what was happening."

"What do you mean?"

"There may be a reason those turtles and other species are reproducing rapidly. It's as if they are preparing for something. With each new generation come potential evolutionary changes—adaptation. A pre-cursor of what is to come, like our ancestors experienced. Before, they had this Eden you speak of; plenty of food and fresh water, a mild climate. But something upset the delicate balance between Earth and Merluma, perhaps a partial decoupling. It was after that when things took a turn for the worst on Merluma, like what happened during the Great Upheaval. Something like that may be happening again."

"A decoupling?"

"Perhaps I misspoke. That's merely an unproven theory..." He sighed. "But something else more troubling is happening—nothing to do with nature, but human behavior. Rumors are swirling among the Merahvu, generating fear and uncertainty among the tribes. Rumors that the Sapiens are to blame and the only way to stop the changes affecting Merluma is to—" He took a breath and looked away as if debating whether or not to tell her the truth.

"To what, Sinto?"

"Eliminate the source of the problem."

"You mean humans?"

His gaze wandered to the dark sea just beyond the dome.

Her stomach chilled. "You mean *Sapiens*."

"Just rumors, really, I—I've told you too much. I'm sorry."

"Finish this. *What* is going on?"

"The truth is, not all of us shun your kind, or believe the rumors. Some believe that drawing the attention of the Sapiens will only make it worse, that you should be left in the dark whilst our leaders address these challenges, like stopping the spread of Orange and squelching the rumors among the Merahvu. Others believe it is time we reveal our presence in your world, that Sapiens can be educated, that if you were made aware of how dire—"

"Is that what these tests have been about? Testing my level of intelligence? Is that why you brought me here—as some sort of *experiment?*"

"No! I've merely asked you those questions because—"

She jabbed her finger in his chest. "Because of *what?*"

"Because you intrigue me."

She extracted her finger. It took a moment for the thick layer of skin to bounce back. "Oh."

His brow softened. "And because you're different from other Sapiens."

"In what way?"

"You respect Earth and understand it is not yours to own and control."

"I'm not the only one who believes that; many, if not most of us, do, actually."

He sighed. "We know that, but unfortunately, people like you don't possess the power to do anything about it."

She rubbed her temples, trying to ease the sudden ache spreading across her brow. "Where are we going with this conversation?"

"You tell me."

She knew the answer. Plant seeds of uncertainty. Sever trust and isolate. Foster conflict, rule with violence; innocents killed as an accepted and inevitable part of the outcome. There are those who dedicate their lives to burning it all down, waiting to see what rises from the ashes. Not a hopeful situation, and one that was a frequent topic of discussion late at night between her, Blake, and Ryan—one which they went around and around, trying to solve, until they were utterly discouraged. Ryan would offer another round of beers and the topic would veer toward music or Ryan's latest sexual conquest. Maybe the Merahvu were the missing piece to solving the problem, or maybe they *were* the problem. Regardless of who was to blame, if the rumors Sinto alluded to were true and could be stopped in their tracks then maybe...

"Shake things up. Expose yourselves. Show us what we fail to see, just as you have for me."

"Ah, therein lies the rub—did I say that right? There are those who will use the situation to their advantage and do everything in their power to control it. We're all human, Sapien and Merahvu, with the same stubborn flaws. Adding a tail or merlux to the mix doesn't change who we are, at the root."

A school of angler fish hovered outside the dome, chomping their crystalline needle-like teeth as if anticipating the taste of her flesh. She said, "It has nothing to do with tails or merluxes. It has everything to do with character; empathy, determination, optimism. These are but a few of the positive qualities we possess. Look at what you've done here, creating the impossible at the bottom of the sea. Look at what Sapiens have achieved in the last hundred years—global communication, medical advancements, high-speed transportation—"

"Weapons of mass destruction."

"We—we put men on the moon!"

"So, what are you saying? Build an elevator to the moon? Colonize Mars once Earth and Merluma are no longer habitable?"

"No, that's not what I meant. We'll find a solution before it's too late."

He palmed the dome wall, drawing the attention of the fish outside. "Those fish are starving. Their food web is nearly depleted and what is left is tainted with toxins bleeding from your shores, feeding new organisms, like Orange. Organisms we fear will overwhelm Earth's shores and bleed into Merluma. Many of these advancements you speak of are literally killing us, here and now."

"How do you know? You just told me no one knows what's happening between Earth and Merluma. Orange is super scary and a mystery, so bring us into the conversation. Let us help with solutions. Show the world what you've shown me."

"And risk everything we've fought to protect?"

"But we've learned—"

His eyebrows shot up. "To play nice?"

"Many of us are compassionate about the earth. Not all of us are driven by greed. You need to give us a chance." Audrey tried to swallow but her mouth had suddenly gone dry.

"Do you truly believe your kind could change?"

"Can yours? From what you're telling me, we're both at fault."

He stepped forward. "What do you suggest?"

Her breath caught. "I don't know—become our teachers?"

His gaze drew distant, and suddenly, she felt that tingly feeling of unease. She was pinned against the dome wall, a mere inch of oxywater separated them. Even though she'd become accustomed to physically touching him every time they ventured into the sea, something felt different about the electrical charge building between them.

"Sinto," she whispered. "What do *you* believe?"

He didn't answer right away. He stepped back, breaking the tension growing between them.

She should have asked herself that question: What did *she* believe? Truly believe. How deeply had she thought about the problems facing her world, other than parroting things she had read or assumed, believing someone else would step up and fix them. Her head pounded. All she wanted was to crawl into a corner and hide. The same way she felt when similar conversations veered to the hopeless; like crawling under her bed on her tenth birthday, believing as long as she stayed there that her mother's death had never happened. Maybe that was the problem. Avoidance.

Sinto looked up, deeply troubled. "I honestly am not sure anymore." He gave her a weak smile. "I think we've said enough to ponder, don't you think?"

She sucked a sharp breath, and nodded.

He took her hand. "There's someone I want you to meet."

36

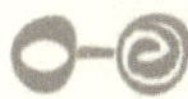

Naiada

SINTO TOOK HER HAND and swam a short distance across the stark white seabed and landed where it ended and reedy wetlands and a thickly treed forest began.

An Arctakai man wrapped in a long white skareef stood with his back to them, arms crossed, staring intently at the pale ground at his feet. He was tall, and as lean and lithe as Sinto. The length of his braided silvery hair loosely coiled around his neck was extraordinarily long, dipping as low as his knees and around his neck several times. The twisted ends snaked down his back beside his sleek tail.

Sinto laid his hand on the man's shoulder. The man turned and fixed Audrey with his icy blue eyes. His face was weathered and an old scar cut through a silvery brow. It was impossible to tell how old he was but his face told the story of a long and adventuresome life. He portrayed an aura of agelessness. Fathomless wisdom oozed from his steady gaze. She sensed kindness too, though her heart beat in warning.

She slipped behind Sinto as Sinto and the man faced off, shoulders squared, hands loosely fisted at their sides. They stood like that for well over a minute, eyes locked and glowing bright.

Audrey sensed a conversation passing between their fixed gaze. The moment passed and each respectfully bowed their heads, keeping their eyes locked.

"Wantemo," Sinto said. "I would like you to meet someone."

The man craned his neck to see Audrey standing in Sinto's shadow.

Sinto drew her forward. "Wantemo is a friend I have known all my life. You can trust him."

Her curiosity about the man deepened.

Wantemo waved his fingers and smiled at her like a parent greeting a child. "Hellooo!"

She laughed. "Hello! I'm Audrey." She held out her hand.

He took it, pressing her hand flat between both of his palms. His palms were warm and smooth and alive with electricity. He smiled. "Sinto has spoken highly of you. My pleasure to finally meet you."

He slipped his hands from hers. Her skin tingled where he touched it.

"I would love to visit longer but I've fallen behind and have much to do." Then he excused himself and turned back around. Audrey wondered exactly what he meant by "much to do". All he was doing was staring at the pale, cracked seabed.

The answer came quickly.

The ground swelled at his feet and hundreds of large worms rose from the barren sea floor and began expelling steaming piles of excrement. The oxywater filled with a stink that made her reach for her nose, but that wasn't much help. The smell clung to the moisture-laden air and she could taste it with each breath. Wantemo and Sinto seemed not to notice the smell at all.

Beyond the growing mound of excrement, the sea floor came alive with movement as an army of giant white ants seemingly came from nowhere, their bodies perfectly camouflaged against the pale ground. They meandered in circles, their backs coming to her knees.

Wantemo flicked a finger. They lined up like troops preparing for battle. His cheek twitched. The first line ran forward and began scooping up piles of the foul-smelling excrement with shovel-shaped mandibles. A click of his tongue and they broke into groups, dumping them into several piles. He raised a finger. A second line of ants with paddle-shaped feet scurried forward and began stomping and patting the piles into walls. Wantemo rewarded their fine work with a nod and a smile.

On this went—poop, scoop, stomp, nod, smile—until several dome-shaped structures were formed.

"What are they building?" she asked.

"Homes for a new community." Sinto replied. "Healers we've recently summoned from the Arctakai's colony in the Southern Ocean. Once they finish the shelters, the worms will till the soil. New crops will be planted to support the increase in population."

"You seem to know him well."

"Wantemo is my mentor. He has taught me everything I know."

She addressed Wantemo, "And now you orchestrate the building of new homes?"

Wantemo wagged his finger at an ant that got out of line. "Oh, I've still got plenty to teach, but I find that tackling simple tasks, such as this, is the best way to calm the mind when you have something great to ponder."

Sinto patted Wantemo on the shoulder. "Then we shall leave you to it."

After bidding Wantemo farewell, Audrey and Sinto swam across the flat wasteland to a circular, windowless mound emerging from the dreary seabed. It lay as pale and lifeless as the grounds surrounding it.

"Where are we?"

"The House of Healing. What you might call a hospital in your world."

Hospital. Healers summoned. It could only mean one thing.

"Please, you don't need to show me this—tell me instead."

Sinto ignored her plea, took her hand, and led her inside. As one might expect when entering a hospital there was a waiting area. Merahvu milled about listlessly. No art adorned the pale walls. The sparse furniture sprinkled throughout the small waiting area was purely functional. No fluffy pillows, no flowers, no pastel colors or photos of soothing landscapes to soften the reality of what this place represented.

A strange smell seeped from long hallways that radiated outward like spokes on a wheel. The smell was like no other she recognized, metallic and musky.

Sinto approached a silver-haired woman who appeared to be in charge. She smiled when she saw Sinto, although it never reached her weary eyes. She pointed to one of the hallways, indistinguishable from the others, stretching in opposite directions.

Sinto noticed Audrey's distress. "Try to see past the pallor. The Healers prefer muted environments—less distraction from their important tasks."

They walked in silence down the tubular-shaped hallway as pale as the face of a Healer who nodded as they passed. The murmur of many voices drifted from ahead, followed by a wave of heat. The metallic-musky smell grew stronger. They rounded a bend and stopped to peer down at a vast open space carved deep into the seabed, dropping down a couple of stories.

It was filled with hundreds of softly glowing bubbles, and inside each one was a body with grayish-mottled skin stretched over a skeletal frame. Audrey wasn't able to easily decipher men from women, young from old, Seakai from Terrakai from Arctakai. They all looked the same: pale, shriveled, and weak, with little or no hair growing from their heads.

Silver-haired Healers tended the sick and infirmed tucked inside the bubbles. A Healer would press their hands to the bubble's surface. Their eyes would cloud over and the bubble would spark and glow. The occupant inside would twitch and liven with vitality.

Their bodies would straighten, skin flush with a healthy glow, and eyes brighten. Reassuring words, a smile and a soft touch would be exchanged. Then the Healer would reach out to a neighboring occupant and the process would start all over again.

One of the occupants was a young boy on the cusp of puberty, fighting for life. His eyes were dim and skin pale but he managed to sit up and greet a Healer, who poured a shell filled with something red. He readily sucked it down, the syrupy liquid dribbling down his chin.

"Sucuvita, the same elixir I shared with you to help you heal on Merluma," Sinto said.

The boy wiped his chin with the back of his hand, a smile gracing his youthful face. He said something that made the Healer laugh.

"It started with our livers and kidneys, and progressed to our immune and nervous systems. Infertility followed. Our younglings are hit the hardest."

Audrey looked back at the boy. Once the Healer left him his color quickly faded, along with his joyful smile. The surface of his bubble sparked and dimmed until the glow extinguished completely. The Healer rushed back to save him, waving another over to help. No matter what they did, his skin withered, eyes paled, and he rolled into a ball. The boy's body disintegrated, then the bubble. Ash rained, joining the growing pile below. That strong metallic-musky scent followed.

Audrey closed her eyes. When she opened them, another body disintegrated, another assault of that sickening scent. She turned away, no longer able to watch. Feelings of despair and helplessness consumed her, like that moment she realized her mother was dead.

Sinto gave her a solemn smile. "Our minds—we're self-programmed to do that when we die, so there's nothing left but ash to mark our existence."

Audrey felt sick to her stomach. "Please, take me away from here."

He wound an arm around her shoulder and she buried her face into his chest, tears soaking his skareef.

"Death is an essential part of life."

"Not when it is taken away from you, like those in that room."

"True, but there is hope."

He led her further down the hall. It curved, so she could no longer see the carved-out chamber where death feasted on the sick and the weak. Arched doors lined the walls, covered with a gelatinous seal; organic, like the dome protecting the city. He stopped at one of them and pulled her inside. The seal rolled across their bodies.

Balls of fire hovered over a lone bed where a girl on the verge of womanhood lay, her golden hair spread across the pillow like a halo. She opened her eyes, captivating and smoldering with lavender fire, and filled with the fierce will to survive. Her skin was sallow but naturally dark, like a Terrakai. Deep pockmarks marred her cheeks, like scars from a severe acne breakout. She was clearly dual-tribe like Sinto, and while her facial features differed from his, the way she quirked her brow made it abundantly clear she was Sinto's sister.

She gave Sinto a weak smile.

He brushed his fingers across her brow. "How are you feeling today?"

She sighed. "Not as good as yesterday. I think I need another treatment."

"Soon, I promise." Sinto shifted on his feet and turned to Audrey. "This is Naiada, my sister. Naiada, this is Audrey."

Naiada gazed back, first at Audrey, then at Sinto. Silence stretched. His brow dipped. Her lip twitched, broke into a slight smile. She shifted her gaze to Audrey. Audrey's neck prickled. A secret exchange that was over in a matter of seconds.

Naiada held out a hand. "Sinto told me all about you and your adventures on Merluma. Malavee! My pleasure to meet you." She stuck Sinto with a fiery gaze. "Finally."

Audrey took her hand. Naiada squeezed back a little harder than expected. She may have appeared weak but from the way she held Audrey's hand and her eyes crackled with fire it was clear she was a fighter.

Sinto took Audrey's hand and released it from Naiada's firm grip. "Naiada nearly died, but she's getting stronger."

Naiada rolled her eyes and huffed. "Not fast enough. I hate this place."

"Patience, Sister."

"What happened?"

"She was exposed to a toxin that attacked her nervous system." He brushed her scarred cheek as if his touch could erase a bad memory. "It started with a bad rash then settled in her blood. She has responded well to transfusions." He leaned down and kissed her scarred cheek. "I will bring you home soon, promise."

"What kind of toxin?" Audrey asked.

"One administered to cause harm," Naiada said bitterly.

"From one of... us?"

The accusing look in Naiada's eyes confirmed her fear.

"I'm sorry."

"I'm sorry too."

Audrey sensed a deep-seated anger in the girl lying in the bed. Anger toward whoever had poisoned her, and maybe something else. It didn't help that her facial scars were a daily reminder. Innocence lost at a tender age. Audrey knew what it felt like to be victim to a traumatic event. A cut by an invisible knife called fate. She wondered how deeply Naiada's cut went—where the tip of the knife pierced the deepest. A wound slow to heal if at all. No amount of rest or medical intervention or mental counseling may ever eliminate the deep-seated emotions that stemmed from her trauma, no matter how much anyone who cared about her tried, even her brother. Time may dampen the festering ache or the need to strike out at something, to seek revenge, or maybe strike out against one's own self-interest. Was Naiada strong enough to tamp down that festering rage? How many others in this underwater city felt the same way?

The nausea she felt earlier returned. "I need fresh air—I mean—excuse me. I'm sorry."

She backed away from the bed and slipped out of the room before Sinto could stop her.

In the hallway, she slid down the wall and hugged her knees. A couple swam by, clinging to each other. She recognized the empty look in their eyes. That same emptiness she felt long after her mother had died. That place where the tip of the knife had festered, eating a hole, filling it with nothing but darkness.

After a short while, Sinto stepped out of the room. "I need a break."

"Me too."

37

Shame

AUDREY HAD REACHED TOTAL saturation. The city became a blur of color, emitting a dull hum. Sinto murmured something about taking her somewhere she could rest.

He swam along the dome wall and over the Terrakai forest that butted up to the wasteland and the outside mountains. He swooped up toward the top of a grand tower on the outskirts of the city that soared higher than any other structure. Its exterior was covered with twined loops of silver, gold, and copper. The top was open to the sky with a balcony circling the lip. Within were rows of balconies ringed around the inside walls. Audrey guessed it could seat many—hundreds, maybe thousands. At the bottom was an open chamber. In the center was a large round table with seven seats, one of which shimmered like pure gold.

Mushroom-like structures surrounded the tower's base. Lush gardens and ponds grew in between and sprawled toward the evergreen forests of the Terrakai on one side and to the edge of the city on the other. The largest of the three mountains soared just outside the dome. The one with the bite out of it.

"This is something special," Audrey commented, as they circled the tower.

"It is. The Great Tower represents the unification of Merahvu. It's where our governing Circle conducts its business, open to any and all who wish to observe. Each tribe chooses two members to represent their interest; every tribe has equal say in all matters. It appears there's not much business happening today."

The tower and surrounding compound were anchored to a rocky outcropping stretching from the mountain and the massive pile of rubble just outside the dome's wall. Paths meandered up and around rocky rises, around the tower, and throughout the garden and mushroom-like homes that randomly dotted the landscape as if nature chose where they would grow rather than following an architectural plan.

Sinto landed at the base of the tower.

Audrey gazed up, marveling at the swirling and intertwined patterns. "You live here?"

He pointed to one of the mushroom-like dwellings wedged between the tower and the dome wall. "That's where I live." He turned. "These others are provided for Circle members and their families, and for hosting visitors with Merahvu business."

"So this is where everything important happens, like Washington DC, in America."

He pondered for a moment, then smiled. "The seat of your government... Yes, something like that."

She waited for him to say more. She wanted to ask: if this was where dignitaries and those who governed the people lived, what was *he* doing there? She decided to let it go, deciding to let him share that part of his story when he was ready. Besides, she'd heard enough for now, and quite frankly, wasn't interested in veering anywhere near political topics, especially after their recent conversation.

They wove through the gardens filled with delightfully fragrant things. He stooped and plucked a triangular-shaped leaf from a bunch of greens. "Tanzen, try it."

She took a bite. It was thicker than lettuce yet tore easily in her teeth. Sweet with a spicy finish that made her tongue tingle.

"What do you think?"

"Different." She picked another leaf and wolfed it down with a playful snap of her teeth.

She hadn't realized how hungry she was. Sinto must have been hungry too. He grabbed her hand and detoured deeper into the garden. They grazed on persimmon and pear and nuts that Sinto cracked open with a rock. It was a much-needed distraction after visiting his sister and watching that little boy die.

After the snack, they continued along the path toward Sinto's home.

The entrance was filled with a reflective, lively, gelatinous barrier that rolled around their bodies as they passed through. Typical homes had a living room off of the entry; Sinto's had a library. Book-lined shelves were carved into the walls and spiraled floor to ceiling. There was a large hole in the high ceiling to access other spaces above. It made sense. Why have a bulky stairway hogging space when you could easily flick your tail and reach the top?

She turned her attention back to the shelves, bursting with hardbound books, and the floor where paperbacks, magazines, and old black-and-white print newspapers were stacked into neat piles. It would take a lifetime and more to read everything Sinto had collected.

"You've read all these books?"

"Many, not all; a few more than once."

Audrey circled the room, tracing their spines with her finger. Many were educational textbooks from the Sapien world that covered every known topic. There were classic and modern fictional stories, children's books, a few graphic novels. "I know some of these."

She knelt and flipped through a pile of magazines specializing in motorcycles, cars, airplanes and jets, and the most recent reports and news articles on rocket launches to space. The pages were heavily used and dog-eared from being studied repeatedly.

Sinto said, "I find your mechanical technology fascinating. The ability to travel rapidly across land and through the sky, and all the way to the stars. The possibilities are endless, if only—" He shook his head. He didn't need to finish his thought. She knew what he wanted to say. It was the advent of technology that dirtied the air and profoundly changed the surface of Earth, for better or worse.

She said, "Technology is a double-edged sword; a tool to solve challenging problems, but it creates them too."

He nodded in agreement.

Sinto had collected an impressive library, but one book in particular drew her eye. Her hands shook when she pulled it from the shelf. It was the book she gave him a decade ago and had long forgotten. It must have gotten wet at some point. The cardboard cover was warped and the dust jacket was torn. She opened it. The ink had run, but just inside the cover and clear as the day she had written it was her name, scrawled in her ten-year-old handwriting. She closed the book and traced the title with her finger—*Stellaluna*—one of her favorites, where a bat learns what it's like to live in a bird's world. Sinto had been intrigued by the story, so she loaned it to him. She now realized why it must have intrigued him at the time. Him being the bat in her world.

"Sorry, it got wet. Do you want it back?"

The book held too many painful memories. Her mother read it to her before bed until she could read it herself, which she frequently did until she gave it to Sinto. The last time she held it in her hands, her mother was still alive and Audrey was unbroken.

"No, keep it." She slipped it back on the shelf.

Sinto sorted through a pile of worn paperbacks stacked to his knees. "Your world is intriguing and confusing at the same time. There are many things I struggle to understand, especially some of the topics in your fictional stories. Quite educating."

Audrey knelt and was picking her way through another pile. "How do you keep the paper from rotting?"

"We seal the pages in a protective coating similar to beeswax, translucent and flexible."

She took the book from his hands. The pages felt slick. Then she noticed the cover; a bare-chested, golden-haired man holding a dark-haired maiden. Her green velvet corset barely contained her breasts. A romance novel. "You read this, for *education?*"

When he saw the cover, his eyes darted across the room and the slits on the side of his neck bloomed red. He muttered, "I may have—maybe to better understand how Sapien males and females, um, interact."

She was amused at the thought of Sinto reading a romance novel to better understand Sapien relationships, curious as to how they might differ from theirs. "I would imagine they're the same."

"Pretty much."

He grabbed her hand and with a flick of his tail, they rose and passed through the hole cut into the ceiling. The paperback slipped from her fingers and fluttered to the floor below.

He landed in a circular foyer with two doors. One seal was purple, the other was green. Their sealed surfaces were alive with movement like the one they entered below, where purple and green danced like clouds reflected on a lively sea. Opposite the doors was an arched hallway. At the end of the hallway was a third door, its seal alive and swirling like a pot of molten gold.

Sinto gestured toward the purple door. "Naiada's room. Take your time to refresh and rest. I think you'll easily find everything you need."

Entering Naiada's room was like stepping back in time to a place she knew well. Audrey felt dizzy at first, as if she had donned a virtual-reality headset and dove into the metaverse. The entire room was painted—floor, wall, ceiling—to represent a stunningly realistic scene of the Salish Sea and the lands surrounding it, not as it was today but as it must have been in the past, long before it was inundated by opportunists. Hundreds of islands sprinkled throughout the Salish Sea were furred with giant evergreens and vine maples at the height of autumn splendor. The mountains of Vancouver Island were silhouetted by a setting sun and the golden sky was streaked with soothing purple and fiery magenta. In the distance, a snow-capped Mount Baker and Cascade foothills were tinged pink.

Pods of orca and dolphin frolicked in a teal-green sea. Seals captured the last of the day's sunlight on exposed shoals. A frothing river ran from the distant mountains, thick with spawning salmon. Bear and raccoon fished along the shoreline, dragging their catch to nosh under the trees. Deer grazed in open meadows and cougars stalked from the shadows.

Gazing up one wall was like gazing at the underside of an old-growth evergreen, so perfectly rendered that she imagined the smell of sap oozing from the tree's ripened cones. Beneath the tree, Merahvu and indigenous Sapiens gathered around a fire, feasting on berries and salmon.

Here Naiada's painting came to an abrupt stop, enough to jolt Audrey from her reverie. A partial brush stroke cut short. A faceless woman. A moment in time, interrupted and left unfinished. Audrey imagined the frustration Naiada must feel, stuck in a sterile and colorless place, smelling metallic-musty with death, while this thing of beauty sat unfinished.

She looked past the images to the rest of the room, which was modestly furnished with things that naturally blended into the encompassing scene. A round bed with a patterned quilt of fallen leaves and a pair of chairs, scooped out of large tree trunks, cut and polished to a smooth oiled surface. Between them lay a large rock, honed flat and smooth.

The sound of trickling water came from an arched doorway to another small space, vividly painted like the main room. A trio of oval windows overlooked the gardens and fresh oxywater flowed from outside.

Audrey stood under Naiada's unfinished painting, feeling like a stranger in a foreign land. While the painting was of the place Audrey lived, she hardly recognized it. The march of civilization had made its mark, especially with the wildlife. Accusing eyes stared back; the orca, the bear, the cougar. She was ashamed to have played a part in what ravaged their world.

The weight of the day bore down as did her hope about her future. She didn't know what she expected when she set out to find Sinto, but hadn't expected the day to unfold quite like this—learning of a deadly fungus and the troubling turmoil brewing among the Merahvu, to witness sickness and death...

She thought of her mother, Blake and Naiada, and that boy she watched die, cheated of the life they deserved. The taste of death lingered in her mouth.

She thought of her father's warning. While the city was hospitable and Sinto accommodating, it didn't change the fact that she was trapped at the bottom of the ocean with no means of escape. The exact situation he trained her to avoid. She had freely given Sinto her trust without fully realizing the potential consequences. How well did she know Sinto? She cringed at the thought her father might be right, and of how disappointed he would be if he knew where she was and how vulnerable. She was surprised by how much she suddenly missed him.

She lay on Naiada's bed mentally exhausted but physically jacked on adrenaline. She tossed and turned, stuck in a vivid and very real nightmare of being trapped in a watery world, inside a painting that tricked her into feeling she was at home.

38

Date Night

A MUFFLED VOICE STARTLED her.

Audrey opened her eyes, confused and groggy. It took a moment to remember where she was. The lifelike images stretched across the room.

Tallamure. Naiada's room.

"Audrey?" Sinto's voice snapped her fully awake.

She sat up. It was much darker outside the windows. She had no watch and no idea how much time had passed. Her heart pounded, ready to fight or flee, a state she found herself slipping into frighteningly often since venturing here. She willed herself to calm down as she gazed at Naiada's realistic painting and filled her lungs with sweet oxywater.

"Audrey, are you there?" Sinto's voice drifted from outside the door.

Her gaze cut to the door. "I'm here."

"I have a question for you."

She drew a sharp breath. "Please, no more tests."

A pause. "No... a request." She thought she heard a sharp intake of air, muffled by the door. "Will you go out with me?"

She perked up. "Out, like on a date?"

"A date…" Another pause. "Yes, something like that." She could hear the smile in his voice and found herself smiling too, remembering the day he revealed what he was and took her for a wild ride in the sea.

She rolled off the bed, landing gently on her feet, and half-swam to the door. She placed her hands on the reflective surface, her palms sinking into the soft gel. Sinto's hands pressed against hers on the other side.

They lingered like that in silence, as if time was a thing you could stop and rewind, back to when things were less complicated; as kids digging in the sand on the beach, playing hide and seek in the jungle, escaping together in a book. She felt every nuance of his touch—the heat radiating from his palms, the webbing between his fingers, a slight quiver when she ran a finger across his palm—and she wondered if his heart was pounding as hard as hers.

She looked up and imagined gazing into his strange and dazzling eyes, wondering if he was doing the same on the other side.

"No more tests, no more scary truths?"

"Only if you ask."

She felt a wave of electricity surge through the gelatinous door, that same tingling feeling she often felt drawing her to him. She couldn't have pulled her hands away if she tried.

"I have something for you, out here in the hall." A chill swept across the palms of her hands and the magnetic pull faded. "Take your time. I'll wait for you in the library."

When she stepped into the hall he was gone, and lying at her feet was a neatly folded emerald-green garment, like the color of his eyes when aglow. When she picked it up, the neat folds slipped through her fingers like fine silk. To her surprise, it was a dress, scented by roses. The kind of dress you read about in a fairytale, the kind you wore to a grand ball. Was there such a thing anymore?

Her hands were shaking when she slipped back into Naiada's room. She cast her clothes aside and slipped the dress over her head. It rippled across her skin like a cool and refreshing shower.

The dress had been designed for someone with a tail, open in the back with a halter-like top. Silky folds draped across her chest. The waist was tapered and the skirt fell all the way to her toes in a gentle A-line cut. Fine boning was sewn into the finished edges along her ribcage and the dip at her back, securing the whisper-thin silk snugly against her body. It flexed as she moved, as if it was a living thing embracing her.

She stared at her reflection in the door. Her skin was dewy and plump from the moist air. A tendril of hair had escaped her braid and corkscrewed perfectly down the length of her neck. She left it but knotted her braid into a bun atop her head, a messy bun like she'd observed other girls wear. Messy, but alluring. The looped-silver necklace lay against her chest, perfectly framed by the draped neckline. She hardly recognized herself.

She felt guilty for questioning Sinto's intentions and chalked it up to paranoia and fear pounded into her day after day by her father over the years.

The dress lifted her mood. She tingled with curiosity, hoping Sinto intended to show her the other thing he promised in his message; the way of the Merahvu. She certainly had had her fill of their plight.

She had never attended a prom, a wedding, or any type of event requiring a formal dress. She wracked her brain for the last time she had worn a dress at all. It was her mother who encouraged such things and her father who deemed such formalities as frivolous and unnecessary distractions.

A date... yes, something like that.

She stepped into the hall. The seal on his door was gone and his room dark. Sinto said to meet him in the library. She called his name, but he didn't answer. She knelt by the hole in the floor, debating the most graceful way for her to drop down in a dress. She leaned forward, seeking a place for a foothold, anything to help her climb down.

She slipped and rolled, falling like a leaf from a tree, folds of silk ruffling around her legs. She huffed when Sinto swooped in and caught her.

He set her on her feet. His gaze swept head to toe. "Wow. You're green—I mean, your dress, it's stunning with your dark features." His eyes flashed every time he blinked, which turned out to be with every word he said, as if looking at her caused his eyes to catch fire.

She laughed, noting the clothes he wore; navy slacks and matching silk shirt with silver buttons and an Asian-styled mandarin collar that stopped just below the slits in his neck. "And you're... dressed... in real clothes, I mean." Except for his tail—sticking out above the waistband of his pants—and his glowing eyes, he would easily pass as a Sapien.

"So what's with the clothes?"

"You'll soon see."

"Not even a clue?"

"I thought you said no tests."

39

Trust

THEY LEFT SINTO'S HOME and swam toward the Terrakai forest thick with cedar and fir, passing a meadow where Terrakai women gathered roots and vegetables, and then reedy wetlands where black-and-white striped snakes slithered among cattails.

Audrey shuddered at the sight of the snakes. Sinto laughed, saying she had nothing to fear. They were harmless and considered a delicacy when prepared properly.

The forest floor where Sinto landed was blanketed with a copper layer of fir needles and cedar flagging. Furry, domed mushrooms erupted from nearby moss-covered stumps. It smelled of earth.

A small Terrakai woman waited beside the trunk of a giant cedar. A shock of copper hair with dark bronze streaks was knotted at the base of her neck. The woman wore an animal-skin dress that covered her shoulders and fell below her knees. The neckline was embellished with stones and pearls like those Sinto incorporated into the necklace he made for her, now lying pleasantly warm against her chest.

Sinto greeted the woman as he had greeted Wantemo; in silence, eyes locked, a facial twitch here and there. Then he nudged Audrey forward.

The woman took Audrey's hands and gently stroked her palms. She felt electricity ripple up her arms as the woman's cat-like golden eyes intently studied every line and pore in her face.

Sinto whispered, "Her name is *Nawtuga*."

"I'm honored to meet you, Nawtuga. My name is Audrey."

Nawtuga's brow furrowed and her eyes cut to Sinto's.

"Nawtuga only communicates in our native language, as do some of the Terrakai who chose to settle here. The Terrakai are fiercely protective of their cultural ways."

"*Ahhh ta wee*," Nawtuga said, using her mouth, the click of her tongue, and an exaggerated stretch of her lips.

Audrey smiled at the refreshingly different pronunciation of her name.

Nawtuga beamed, literally, setting the space between them aglow with her bright amber eyes. She waved for Audrey to follow her through a narrow crack in the cedar's trunk.

She was confused when Sinto squeezed in behind her, not knowing where to go from there. They were all smashed together in the darkness of the hollowed-out tree husk. Pencil beams of light shot through the darkness from knotholes above.

Nawtuga snapped her fingers. A golden ball of light hovered in her palm and she held it out like a candle. At her feet was a steep stairway carved into the ocean floor. She descended. Sinto prompted Audrey to follow.

The steep stairway led to a dimly lit tubular network of tunnels carved deep into the ocean floor below the forest. The walls were unadorned and pale, like the hallways in the House of Healing. It was less humid and smelled of freshly tilled earth mixed with brine. Audrey found her feet more heavily grounded. The oxywater was less dense; it was more like breathing ordinary air.

Nawtuga moved fast. Audrey struggled to keep up with the silk twisting around her legs. She focused on memorizing every fork and turn, but Nawtuga was moving too fast and there were too many to remember. Her father taught her to always know the nearest exit for escape. She was hopelessly lost. The more she tried to relax the more anxious she became. Walls pressed down, palms grew slick, breath came fast and shallow.

She grabbed Sinto's hand and yanked him to a stop. "Where are we going?"

"Nawtuga has invited us for dinner. The Terrakai are accustomed to living underground. You have no need to be afraid."

Nawtuga stopped at a gelatinous, mirrored doorway and gestured for them to step inside.

Inside was like a rustic cabin, cozy and warm and modestly furnished. On one side was a rough-sawn wooden dining table with two three-legged stools. A patchwork of colorful woven rugs covered the stone floor. There was a pair of cushions on the floor; between was a chess board, a game still in play. Finely woven tapestries decorated the pine-paneled walls, showing scenes of Earth from long ago, like Naiada's paintings; an old-growth forest cloaked in mist, a field of grazing buffalo, a frozen lake surrounded by mountains and pine.

Audrey felt the wall. Stone, not wood, painted to replicate knotty pine. Like everything else in the city, Nawtuga's home reflected the natural world. Like the trees in the Terrakai forest and the coral forming the city and the giant mushrooms where Sinto lived. At first Audrey thought they were real—adapted, like the plants growing in the gardens—but Sinto confessed these structures and the forest were merely fabricated to *look* real; that many of the Merahvu who lived in Tallamure had been born here, had never ventured beyond the city, and had never visited Merluma or seen a real forest or a shallow reef on Earth. They were content to safely live in a world perfectly rendered.

Sinto didn't delve deeper into the reasons why, only saying that many were fearful of discovery by Sapiens or the struggles of living on Merluma and had become comfortable with the city's safe harbor and vibrant community. Audrey realized that in many ways the Merahvu were not much different from Sapiens—having a patch of ground to sow and call their own and a safe community to raise a family was all many humans needed and desired.

But complacency was a double-edged sword; expectations led to entitlement, and disruption to those entitlements lead to resentment, disagreement, blame of others, and in some cases, violent encounters. One only need to delve into Earth's daily news for evidence.

Sinto pulled out a stool and Audrey readily accepted it. Sinto and Nawtuga conversed using their mouths, tongues, and gills—a high pitched squeal, the click of a tongue, a guttural bark—a combination of sounds made by dolphins, seals, and birds interspersed with smiles and exaggerated facial expressions.

Nawtuga disappeared around the corner with a flick of her multi-finned lacy tail.

"What were you talking about?"

"The menu."

"Please, no snakes!"

He grinned. "That I cannot promise."

"So how long have you known Nawtuga?"

"She took care of Naiada and me when we were younglings."

"The shape of your eyes are like Nawtuga's."

"A Terrakai trait, like my father's. And the green as well, though green eyes are rare among the Terrakai."

Audrey leaned forward on her elbows. "Why haven't you told me about your parents?"

"Perhaps the same reason you haven't told me about yours."

She crossed her arms. "Perhaps we should change the subject."

"Perhaps you shouldn't have brought it up."

Audrey chewed her thumbnail. Sinto tugged at his collar. Nawtuga entered the room and broke the awkward silence with a squeal and a click when she presented the first course of their meal.

Audrey looked down and suddenly lost her appetite.

Lying inside a large pink shell was a white blob the size of her fist. Transparent tentacles were splayed from its center exposing a soft underbelly. The surface glistened as if covered in slime.

"What is that?"

"A fish of some sort." He picked up his knife and stabbed it. Dark-red liquid oozed from the cut. He sliced it up into several pieces until smaller white blobs floated in a soup of what looked like blood. Sinto scooped up a bite with a spoon. A drop of red liquid fell to the tabletop when he held it up to her mouth.

She wrinkled her nose.

"Trust me, it is delicious."

She closed her eyes and reluctantly opened her mouth.

The outside was chewy and tasteless and the tentacles tickled the roof of her mouth, but the inside was soft as butter and tasted alarmingly sweet. The red liquid was tart and made her tongue tingle. A strange and delectable treat.

"Oh, my, that is yummy—weird, but delicious."

"As I said, trust me."

She lingered on those last words. *Trust me.* What was trust and what did it mean to trust another? Believing that you were safe and protected? That someone or something would ensure no harm or pain, or in the case of a strange and exotic meal, that she would like it and it wouldn't poison her?

At what point did one give in wholly to trust?

Audrey's mother had been a strong swimmer, free diving with just the air in her lungs and a spear gun. She would disappear beneath the surface for many minutes and emerge giddy and joyful with a bounty from the sea. No one questioned her choice or asked her if she trusted the sea to pose no harm. After her death her father believed otherwise and often preached, *Trust no one but yourself. Not the sea, and certainly not a stranger. Your life may one day depend on it.*

And here she was dining with the boy she met long ago, locked inside a city at the bottom of the sea, with her heart giddily thumping. The anxiety she felt a few short hours ago quickly vaporized. She slid her fingers across the folds of her dress and blushed recalling how she looked.

He's kind and thoughtful with a fine sense of clothing choices.

Which made her all the more eager to prove her father wrong.

Sinto had been true to his word and had gone to great extremes to save her life. When he was by her side, she felt safe, more so than with anyone her father had hired to protect her when she was growing up. Those relationships were fleeting and she never felt a connection. She had made a connection with Sinto a decade ago and it was growing stronger every passing second.

"Another bite?"

"Yes, please!"

The rest of the meal was equally bizarre and delicious. Every time she thought to broach the potentially touchy subject of why Nawtuga was content to live in this false world, Sinto would tell her something that made her laugh or remind her of the precious days they spent together when they were younger. Then another course would be served.

She was quite sure one of the courses was snake, but never guessed which one, not wanting to ruin the moment. Their date was proceeding fabulously. She vowed not to screw it up.

40

Mind-Blowing Adventure

AUDREY AND SINTO BID Nawtuga farewell, grateful for the generous meal.

Night had fallen and thunder rumbled through the dome's sky. Lightning crackled from clouds, purple and blue. Rain fell from the sky, rolling off their bodies like silvery balls of mercury before slithering into the grass at their feet.

Audrey stuck out her tongue, licking up drops of rain.

Sinto warned, "Drink no more or your hair will turn green!"

And like the finale of a fireworks show, bolts of lightning struck in successive waves. The dome shuddered from their thunderous booms and electricity rippled through the moist air. It tickled to breathe. Then the clouds dissipated like puffs of steam, and so too did the other Merahvu who had stepped out for the show, melting back into the city, back to tasks set aside for a surreal moment of wonder and distraction.

The simulated sun became the moon, partially full and softly glowing. A thousand stars winked from the dome ceiling.

The city was aglow like the bioluminescent creatures of the deep. Audrey stared in wonder as they swam through the starlit sky over the reef-like city, glowing in every color of the rainbow.

Sinto gave her a mischievous grin, the same one he gave her on Merluma seconds before pretending to feed her to a megalodon.

"Where are you taking me?" she asked with concern.

"Dancing."

"Dinner then dancing? Sounds safe and a little unlike you," she said suspiciously.

He laughed. "Perhaps you should wait to hold judgment."

He veered toward a spherical structure shaped like a giant brain coral located in the heart of the city. The largest structure by far, set at the pinnacle of the reef, towering ten stories high. Its brain-like surface flashed in zigzagged patterns of neon blue and green before shifting to pink and orange.

A young man greeted them at the base of the round structure. He wore a pinstriped suit with a white fedora and sported dark bushy brows. He looked like a young Al Capone, except for his eyes, which flickered blue and green, pink and orange in sync with the club's flashy exterior.

Sinto fixed him with an equally lively gaze and bowed his head. As they gazed at each other in silence the back of her neck prickled, like when Sinto greeted Wantemo, his sister, and Nawtuga.

The young man raised a brow and turned to her, "Are you here for a mind-blowing adventure?"

She stole a sideways glance toward Sinto. He gave her nod of encouragement.

"Sure," she replied.

The young man smiled, gesturing toward the door. "Welcome to Club Ballo!"

Up until that moment, it had been silent; once they stepped across the threshold they were engulfed with thumping bass, tremor of guitar, screaming keyboards, and throaty vocals.

Sinto slipped his arms around her waist and swam up through an elevator-like shaft—minus the elevator. Halfway up he veered into a curved hallway that ran along the outer wall of the sphere.

The music grew louder.

A girl dressed in hot-pink leathers brushed by with a flip of her matching ponytail and snap of gum. She stopped and gave them a brilliant smile. She raised a fist, Sinto did the same. "Hiya, Sinto." They fist-bumped. She turned to Audrey, gave her a wink. "I'm Victoria, would love to chat but gotta go. Later!" She waved her fingers and disappeared down the shaft.

Sealed doors lined the inner side of the hallway. Sinto checked petroglyph-like symbols pulsing on the gelatinous surface of each door. He stopped in front of one and pulled Audrey inside.

Globes of light hovered along the ceiling. A red sofa sat facing a mirrored wall. Two frosted glasses and a pitcher of water sat on a glass table. Audrey gazed at Sinto's reflection, wondering what he had in mind.

She laughed nervously. "I thought you said *dancing.*"

Sinto smirked and led her to the mirrored wall that was gelatinous and pliable like the seals on the doors. It dissolved when he touched the surface. Her heart leaped and she stepped back from the rail-less edge, staring five stories down to a concave floor.

The club was roughly eight stories high and completely open. Hundreds of private balconies lined the outer walls, most occupied. Eager faces gazed back. There didn't appear to be a dance floor, just a wide-open space in the center of the club.

The music shifted with no obvious source of where it was coming from. It reverberated from everywhere. A mash-up of electronic dance music interwoven with whale song and the strong rhythmic beat of tribal drums.

Different holographic images from the Sapien world hovered in the vast open space, morphing to the music like a music video. Sapien faces morphed from different cultures and eras, lip-syncing to the lyrics in different languages. A fighter jet streaked across the ceiling, a motorcycle raced in circles around the concave floor, a rocket launched, and a nuclear submarine stealthily floated by. Then those faded and a brilliant sphere of fire rose from the floor, followed by colored orbs that varied in size, mimicking the planets in Earth's solar system orbiting the sun.

Merahvu gathered in groups, talking and laughing. Like the man who greeted them and Victoria who they passed in the hallway, they were dressed up in a variety of Sapien-styled fashions, from past to present to futuristic.

Their hair varied too—wild or subdued, short or long, straight, spiked, waved, corkscrewed or none at all—as well as the color of their skin—light to dark, pink to gold, patterned or smooth, some tattooed with moving images.

During dinner Sinto had explained that the Merahvu frequently change the aspects of their appearance as a form of expression, especially the younger generation. They favored dressing up to reflect styles and cultures observed both past and present in the Sapien world with an added touch of panache. It felt a little like Halloween.

"I never would have imagined this. I thought the Merahvu shunned my world, but this—it's like they want to be a part of it."

"They do."

"But you said—"

"I said not everyone shuns you. Many want to make contact." He gestured toward a group of girls casting flirtatious glances at a group of boys. "They want to live in your world, openly and freely. They believe there are things you could teach them."

"Are you trying to make me feel better?"

He smiled and nodded, began moving to the music, fingers drumming his thighs.

His uplifted mood was contagious. She grinned, bobbing her head in rhythm with his. "Well, it's working."

They watched the club fill with bodies gyrating to the music, jammed together on couches, perched on the edge of balconies, and hovering in groups on the fringes, tails swaying. Voices and faces were bright with excitement and anticipation.

"This is like a night club in my world."

"Ah, but with a vast difference."

She frowned. "Another test?"

"You set yourself up."

"Well, then, game on." She scanned the crowd with fresh eyes looking for clues to how it might be vastly different. One particular thing stood out. There were no speakers, no blinking electronics, no wires. No one seemed to be in charge of the music.

"Where's the music coming from?"

He pointed to a balcony across the way where a couple held hands, swaying to the beat in a trance-like state, their eyes glowing white. "Them. Scouts who frequent your world, to observe and learn. They come here to share their experiences, edited and mixed up in an entertaining way. Those two are quite popular. That's why the club is so crowded tonight."

She scanned the club again, taking in the holographic and very realistic images unfolding in the open space. Images of busy city streets, a rock concert, boarders at a skateboard park. "So how do they project those images and the music?"

"Nothing is being projected; what you see and hear is coming from within your mind, as they are from mine."

"What?"

"When you entered the club, you gave the Scouts permission to share, to inject their experiences into your mind."

Her jaw dropped, remembering exactly how the door man stated it.

Are you here for a mind-blowing adventure?

"Mind-blowing, for real?"

"No need to worry, perfectly harmless. Although…"

"Although, *what*?"

He tucked a loose strand of hair behind her ear. "Your lack of understanding leaves your mind open, and an exposed mind can be vulnerable."

Audrey narrowed her eyes. "You mean I can be easily tricked."

He looked away. "Not easily; stubborn minds can be challenging."

Stubborn? She studied his profile, recalling her obsession with swirls and dots, and the color green. Bits and pieces of the memories he tried to bury, temporarily. Had he intended those thoughts to slip through? Or was it because her mind was stubborn?

"So I pose a challenge, naturally, because I'm *stubborn*?"

He chuckled. "Stubborn or not, I must teach you how to guard your mind, to know the difference between your thought and the thought of another."

She gave him a tight smile. "Maybe we should start right now."

"It comes with risks."

"What, brain damage?"

He traced her hairline where it met her forehead. "I would never subject you to anything that would damage your mind."

"So this is another way we differ."

"Our brains are alike. The trick is to learn how to use all of it."

"Could you teach me?"

His eyes fell to her lips. "There are subtleties to mastering mind-speak and deeper forms of telepathic connection. There are moral implications and rules. For example, it is considered rude and inappropriate to invade one's mind without permission."

"Like you did with me."

He winced. "Yes, that was a violation, but one not taken lightly and only with good intention." He touched the claw hanging around her neck. "Those memories would have resurfaced, even without finding the token I gave you."

She reached up and laid her fingers over his. "Is that all I need to be concerned about?"

He withdrew his hand. "In a perfect world. But the world's not perfect, mine nor yours. I think we are both aware that words alone can cause great harm."

"True."

"And there are other subtleties to sharing. Like how to decipher what you wish to share. It's hard to explain, but mind-speak is much more than mere words. It's thoughts and images, feelings and concepts. The trick is how you bundle them up to make sense, and more importantly, how to filter what you want to share from that which you don't."

"So if, say, I want to share that I like ice cream—would I focus on the reasons why? Like how the flavor bursts as the creamy texture melts across my tongue, of the pleasant memories it invokes?"

"Something like that." He reached out for her hand and traced the lines crisscrossing her palm with his finger. "The tricky part is filtering your feelings. They're harder to control and easily slip through, especially when sharing more delicate topics. Feelings don't lie."

Her gaze fell to his fingers, stroking her palm. Heat rose to her cheeks. He twined his fingers through hers; the webbing between felt strange and wonderful. The way he was looking at her, she wondered if she had accidentally led him on, let a thought slip by without knowing it. Like what it would be like to kiss him.

Yikes, this conversation is getting... complicated.

She regretfully pulled her hand away and tucked it under her chin. Touching him made it hard to concentrate. "Why not teach us? I mean, think of the possibilities. To break down misunderstandings through clarified communication. Wouldn't that be beneficial?"

"That depends. Imagine if you could communicate with all living things. Not just humans."

"*Every* living thing?"

"Large or microscopic."

"Could you command these things to do as you ask?"

He paused before answering. "Yes. Though the concept of suggestion is a gentler way to describe it." He opened his mouth to say something but stopped.

She grew suspicious. "What else aren't you telling me?"

His fingers fidgeted with his pant leg. "Some of us, very few, have mastered a higher level of knowledge—we can... do more than just suggest."

"And..."

"An unsuspecting mind can be manipulated, thoughts planted that it believes are its own."

"Unsuspecting, like a bird or a shark."

He smirked. "Birds are more clever than you think, but yes..." His voice turned somber. "As well as humans."

"Like me."

His gaze fell to the floor, then he looked up, capturing her eyes.

"Obviously, *you* have mastered that higher level of knowledge."

"Yes, Wantemo taught me, but with this knowledge comes responsibility. It is taboo to manipulate the mind of the unsuspecting and susceptible. That is why very few are taught the subtleties of how."

"But you did with me."

"Yes, for the reason I explained."

"And you tamped down my fear of the water."

"I merely planted that suggestion. What happened after was how you interpreted it."

She stared at him a beat, gauging his sincerity, remembering their conversation on the beach. He had confessed to hiding her memories and planting his message. As far as she knew, all was right with her mind after her memories returned. She flashed back to that night he saved her life. The fear she saw in his eyes as she lay dying, and sharing a space in his mind as he healed her. She sensed no ill will on his part, then, nor did she now.

"Could a Sapien master this knowledge?"

"Theoretically."

Audrey's mind swirled with the possible implications of what Sinto was telling her. That an idea could be planted, maybe not just in one mind, but in many unsuspecting minds—and not just by the Merahvu, but possibly by Sapiens, if they learned how.

It took great effort to steady her voice. "Words alone have done immeasurable damage in my world in the past. Maybe it's not such a good idea to teach us everything you know."

"Now you understand."

I'm not sure I understand anything, except that I'm terrified—and growing dangerously attracted to you.

His eyes did that electric-spark-thing and his lips curled ever so slightly, deliciously so, taunting her to reach out and touch them. Did he know the effect he was having on her? Did he feel the same way about her? Or was this part of his lesson, how easy it was for him to manipulate her unguarded mind; to fill her with these feelings and watch her reaction? She tore her eyes from his.

"Have the Merahvu ever abused this power?"

"We have had no reason to."

"But you *could.*"

"No more than words can be twisted to instill fear and hate in others."

"Not words, but thoughts that someone might misinterpret as their own."

Sinto nodded slowly. "Anything is possible."

Her stomach slithered down the silky-green folds of her dress and nestled somewhere between her toes. Could one immoral Merahvu manipulate many unsuspecting Sapiens? Plant seeds of desperation and fear, turn neighbor against neighbor? Make them believe those were their own thoughts and theirs alone, not knowing someone else was behind it?

Propaganda on steroids!

Sinto reached out and pulled her hand from her mouth. She hadn't realized that she was chewing her thumbnail. He rolled her hand over and kissed her knuckles. Her heart raced; it was difficult to breathe. A storm of emotion warred.

His brow furrowed. "What's wrong? You look terrified."

"I—I don't know, maybe it's just everything we talked about today and seeing your sister, the possibility of unsavory mind manipulation. It's a bit overwhelming."

"It is and still will be, tomorrow. Can we agree there is little we can do about it tonight but have fun?"

Her gaze swept across his raised brow and questioning eyes. She nodded. "Tomorrow worry, tonight fun. Got it."

Sinto led her to the sofa, sat down. She sat beside him.

He poured a glass of water, held it out to her. "Maybe this will help."

She downed the entire glass in three gulps, then gave him a shaky smile.

Roll with it. Tomorrow I worry.

41

Ballorue

A DARK-SKINNED MAN ZIPPED through the back door. His short hair resembled a purple sea urchin perched atop his head. His pale blue eyes were lined in black, and a swirled silver earring looped through multiple holes in his ear. Chains clipped to his black leather pants jangled. He wore no shirt. The markings along his spine and tail were inked like tribal tattoos. Except for his sharply pointed fluked tail, she never would have guessed he was an Arctakai.

He set a small ornate bottle containing red liquid and two shot glasses on the table. He gave Sinto a flirtatious wink and left.

The lights lowered throughout the club and the pace of the music picked up, as did Audrey's pulse.

Sinto popped the cork off the bottle and poured two shots. The vapor rising from the glasses made her eyes water. She recognized it immediately.

Sucuvita.

Sinto handed her a glass.

"You drink this when you're well?"

"Especially so. This is our most precious resource, the elixir of life, the fountain of youth that heroes in your fictional stories seek.

For us it is real, a gift from nature." He raised his glass to hers. "To life."

The elixir exploded on her tongue wickedly sweet and peppery, and spread from her stomach straight to her bloodstream. The rush was instantaneous, just like before.

Heat rippled up her neck, inflaming her cheeks. She suddenly felt lightheaded. She drew a deep breath and when she exhaled she felt weightless as a feather, falling from the sky.

The muscles in her arms and legs hummed with power. Her skin tingled with heightened sensation. Her mind and senses sharpened.

She heard the quiet murmur of a couple nearby, tasted the first bite of dinner lingering on her tongue, felt a ghostly shadow of Sinto's lips brushing across her knuckles. Her gaze was drawn to Sinto's eyes, pools of green fire, roiling with vitality. She imagined diving inside and swimming toward the darkness of his pupils, slipping through his optic nerve to the sanctuary of his mind. From the darkness a holographic image of Sinto emerged, dressed like he was now, inviting her inside...

She tore her eyes from his hypnotic gaze. "Holy shit." She held up her empty glass, the bottom stained red from the elixir. "What exactly is this stuff?"

"A secret I am not allowed to share."

Like portals. The reason for which was obvious; sucuvita would be worth killing for. The answer to long life, miraculous healing, enhanced senses. Maybe sucuvita was what made it possible for one to poke around where one should not poke in another's mind. Disarm then attack.

He picked up the bottle and swirled the contents inside. "Its source is becoming more and more scarce, especially with so many falling ill. Without sucuvita many more will die and the longevity and quality of our lives will be greatly compromised."

"Why do the Merahvu believe it necessary to extend natural life?"

"Ah, sensible question. After the Forever War we were nearly decimated, on the brink of extinction. Sucuvita saved us. By strengthening our bodies, extending our lives, and encouraging procreation, our numbers have slowly grown to a level we believe give us a fighting chance to survive far into the future." He shrugged. "Though some think it is time to embrace our natural lifespans and only use it for healing. Illness has become our new foe."

Audrey put down her glass. "Is this the part where you tell me you're two hundred years old or something?"

He laughed. "No. I'm the same age as you, maybe aged a little beyond that because of the time I have spent on Merluma. But the man you met earlier, Wantemo, is well over three hundred years old. So is our queen."

"Queen? You said earlier representatives from each tribe governed the Merahvu."

"Along with our queen."

"So you're ruled by a monarchy? Isn't that a little archaic?"

"Quite the opposite. She merely provides wisdom and guidance. All members participate in every decision as does she. It's how we maintain balance amongst the tribes and work together to solve problems and settle disputes." He leaned forward and cradled her hands. "Which reminds me. I'm afraid there is one more important thing I must tell you."

As much as she hated to escape the warmth of his touch, she gathered her hands in her lap. "Now?"

"Would you like to know why I brought you here?"

She nibbled the inside of her cheek. Maybe ten minutes ago she would have, but the way he was looking at her set her heart aflame and stirred the need to forget all she had learned today and focus on kindling their relationship into something more than just friends. That shot of sucuvita might have extended her life by a month but she was feeling recklessly indulgent.

"I thought you said it could wait until tomorrow. Besides, a date's supposed to be fun, not depressing."

"That's assuming what I need to tell you is bad."

"Good or bad, I think I've heard enough."

"I can accept that, for now."

He poured a second round of sucuvita. Five seconds later it swirled in their bellies and raced through their bloodstream.

Audrey burst out laughing. "Did I just add ten years to my life?"

"Something like that." Then he pried the glass from her hand and twined his fingers through hers. They were hot and electrified.

The music notched up in pace and volume as did the ruckus coming from the mob of people filling the club.

He stood, pulled her to her feet, and led her to the edge of the balcony. "You want fun? Let's join them." He embraced her from behind and dove into the crowd of bodies before she could object. They swam their way into the center of the gathering crowd.

The music and images faded and the glowing balls of light dimmed. The light cast from glowing eyes cut through the darkness. The crowd stilled and voices fell silent, merluxes crackled and buzzed with anticipation. Tails wagged expectantly. Eyes grew brighter. A strong pungent smell filled her nostrils. Ozone, a warning that lightning was about to strike. The couple beside them felt like live wires pressed against her skin. The hair on her arms stood on end.

"Are you sure about this?"

He pulled her back against his chest and slipped his cheek alongside hers. "As long as we're touching, you won't get electrocuted. I am your ground. Whatever you do, don't let go." He looped his arms through hers, threaded her fingers through his. "It's best if you relax."

How could she relax? Her mind raced, heart pounded. It felt like she had swallowed a moth. Sucuvita raced through her bloodstream. Feeling mighty and invincible, she wanted to shout,

Look at me, I'm a Sapien. Together we can fix the world! She imagined the response, *Hurray!*

She closed her eyes. Strange feelings and thoughts filled her, terrifying and exhilarating and intensifying with each breath, revealing her true self, bound at the core of every cell, seeded in the marrow of her bones, entwined in her flesh and nourishing her mind—an ethereal and ageless being, free of physical matter, a thing that never begins or ends but just *is*, forever and ever, cycling through the universe like stardust—her *soul*. And within the darkest corners of her soul, ills festered and slowly ate away at the good. Ugly black things named Anger and Paranoia, born the day her mother died and in all the days after, a lonely and broken and scared little girl taught to fear everything in her world...

She opened her eyes with a gasp.

Was sucuvita some sort of hallucinogen?

Sinto gently shook her. "Are those tears in your eyes?"

She blinked them away. "That stuff you gave me is messing with my mind."

He laughed. "That is not just from the elixir. It's the crowd gathering, preparing for the dance of life. You will learn truths about yourself, see and feel things you may have never felt before. It's what happens with a co-mingling of minds, it's how we share what we have learned, and how we support those who need help with love and encouragement. We call it *Ballorue!*"

"*Ballorue?* How? What do I do?" He wrapped his legs around her ankles, sandwiching her between leg and tail. His heart hammered against her back.

"Open your mind. Open your *essence*."

"My essence?"

"The core of who you are. The good, the bad, the conflicted, the settled. Everything that uniquely encapsulates *you*. What you might call a soul, the Merahvu call your *essence*."

The music started. The crowd surged and they were swept up inside a swirling mass of humanity, twisting and turning and rolling in on itself, like a ball of herring fending off an attack by predators.

Sinto laced his fingers through hers and stretched their arms wide. They dove like a bird, darted in and around with the crowd quick as a herring, twisting seamlessly around one another, knowing when to dive or soar, or to dart left or right but magically never touching.

Threads of electricity sparked and snapped. Lightning arced, striking walls, ceiling, and floor. She closed her eyes, marveling at the waves of electricity flowing across her skin, raising every hair on her head, coursing through every cell in her body.

Her fear melted and her mind yawned acceptingly. Colorful flickers of light darted past her mind's eye, one for each person in the crowd. She too was a flicker of light—gold and burnished amber like the soft flame of a candle. Sinto was green and white like the froth of a crashing wave. *Auras.*

A torrent of emotions flowed through her; love and scorn, gratitude and frustration, compassion and fear. She heard mournful cries and joyful laughter, felt fiery hot and bitterly cold, the crush of something heavy upon her shoulders followed by a whispering lightness.

The sounds and images filling her mind were foreign and beautiful, exhilarating and disturbing.

Sensations and emotions not her own flowed through her body and bombarded that thing Sinto called her *essence.* Her mind became overwhelmed and fear rushed to fill the void, spiraling out of control. She fought the sensation by focusing on what was real to her, here and now—the smoothness of Sinto's cheek pressed to hers, the flutter of his hair across her shoulder—and blocked the thoughts and emotions of others needling her mind.

Tears streamed down her cheeks; her heart felt ready to explode. Unable to catch her breath, she pleaded for Sinto to stop.

They slipped from the crowd and dropped to the floor, clinging to each other, and before she could catch her breath Sinto kissed her.

Audrey was taken back to the day they first met and the dark days that followed, wondering if she would ever see him again, wishing that one day he would find her and put an end to her grief and sorrow.

But it wasn't just her own thoughts she was experiencing, but Sinto's too. He had thought of her often, secretly searching for her, driven to find her for some reason.

How did she know this?

She reluctantly broke the kiss.

"What?" he whispered.

"I don't know, but it scares me."

He touched her lower lip with his finger. "Me too."

Their lips touched, then fevered, and she felt a strange tug inside, like being turned inside out and yanked whole from her body. She watched as if from afar as they kissed, marveling at the colorful light dancing around their bodies.

And in that instant she *knew*, as deeply as a mother loves a child, that fate had brought them together. A Merahvu and a Sapien, a joining of foreign worlds, Earth and Merluma, land and sea, technology and nature—a new era of discovery and possibility.

Her heart swelled with love for the boy who had opened her eyes, and the man who offered hope for a brighter future: two souls destined for something greater.

Move in harmony with force of life, flow as water, like stream around rock.

The light engulfing their bodies began to swirl, faster and faster, until it became a blazing whirlpool that tugged her back into her physical body, cradled in Sinto's arms, tongue entwined with his.

Sinto broke the kiss with a gasp. His brows scrunched and he blinked, and with each blink his irises grew brighter, along with the swirling light, a whirlpool drawing them both inside. The oxywater surrounding them crackled and sparked. Her skin stung and eyes burned.

Gazes locked, they clutched one another and tumbled into—

42

Marked

—A SEA OF DARKNESS. The music, the club, the mob swirling above faded.

Audrey floated in what felt like outer space. Orbiting above her was a gigantic orb with a glowing amber center. Ghostly shapes, both light and dark, swirled inside.

She touched it. Soft and pliable. Ripples radiated outward from her fingers. The ghostly things moving inside skittered away from her touch.

Sinto whispered something undecipherable. She spun to face him.

Floating above him was a second orb with a green center, the same as the color of his eyes. It too glowed and was filled with the same ghostly shadows.

His gaze fell to an object floating between them. He blinked. Their eyes met.

The blood had drained from his face. His eyes were wide with confusion and fear.

She felt differently, excited and hopeful. She felt no fear, but anticipation.

"Where are we?" Her voice sounded flat and quickly faded as if this strange dark place fed on noise, sucking up the sound as soon as it was projected.

Suddenly, their feet were grounded and she was standing across from him, the glowing object floating between. His gaze fell to the object, a symbol of some sort, a swirl like the mouth of a whirlpool and a circle connected by a thick line. The object was the size of a large key, one that would fit perfectly in the palm of her hand. She felt the urge to touch it.

"This can't be," he murmured.

"*What* can't be?"

He gazed above their heads. The orbs were slowly moving towards each other. His eyes darted nervously between her and the glowing object floating between them. "How? How did you—I haven't told you about this—I barely understand it myself."

She stepped forward. Sinto did the same. The key-like object cast an upward shadow across his face.

"Where are we? Is this because we kissed?"

"No—maybe."

"Is this bad?"

He gave her a troubled look. "That would depend on who you asked."

"I'm asking you!"

His eyes sparked. "It's good." Then his brow furrowed deeply. "And it's bad."

She swallowed, even though her mouth was dry. Sinto had been so sure about everything; now he wasn't. He kept diverting his eyes from hers, as if looking at her caused great pain.

"What is that?" She pointed at the object hovering between them.

"A *Mark*, a unique symbol representing an eternal bond."

"A bond? Eternal? Between *us*?"

"If we choose to accept it, I think." His eyes were locked on the object between them. He looked up. When their eyes met, it was like magnets clicking together. The muscles in his face relaxed, his breath quickened, his tongue swept across his lips. He took another step forward, started to take another but something held him back. An internal struggle. She could read it in real-time on his face. He looked away, fighting the urge to look her in the eye.

"Is this—is this why I'm here?"

His eyes snapped to hers. "No!" He forced his gaze to his feet, clamped his hands behind his back.

"What are those?" She pointed to the orbs. They were rotating now, like synchronized planets.

"Us," he said. "The shadows moving inside are memories, thoughts, dreams, everything that makes us who we are, elements of our essence."

"Did you do something to me? Is this a mind trick?"

"Not a trick. Not me. You—I think you've *Marked* me."

"Marked as in what?"

"As your mate."

"Mate?" Her voice came out an octave higher than normal.

His eyes shifted to the glowing symbol, hovering between them. His hands were back at his sides, fidgeting with his pant legs. "And more, much more. Cannot have another—nor want another." He cast his eyes to hers briefly, before looking away. "Our essences bound and linked, eternally. Our *purpose* in this life bound and linked as one... so the myth says."

"What myth?"

"A very old one, about something rare and reserved for those deemed special..."

The symbol began to hum and quiver. Her body resonated like a tuning fork. Sinto's breath hitched. She knew he felt it too. Her gaze fell to the symbol, pulsing with light.

Mesmerized, she reached for it.

Sinto was on her in a flash, his hands clamped around her wrists, spinning her to press her back to his chest. "Don't touch it, don't look at it! It's not done yet." He turned to put the object he called the Mark to their backs. He crossed her arms over her chest with his on top and held tight.

"What's not done?"

"Our choice," he gulped. "Once accepted, what follows—the Joining... it's irrevocable."

The shadows in the orbs slammed against the inner walls, trying to break free. With each strike the orbs shuddered and rumbled and inched closer together.

The urge to grasp the Mark was unbearable, an unseen master controlling every impulse. It was what she had to do. A choice already made. She squirmed to escape from Sinto's grip, arching back, kicking her feet. "We mustn't resist! We must embrace it, together!" Why or how she knew this eluded her.

Sinto held fast, bared his teeth, screamed in frustration.

We both want this. I can feel his struggle as keenly as I feel mine. Why is he fighting it?

The Mark fed on their need and desire. It spun faster until it was a blur of light, pulsing in rhythm with their hearts. A high-pitched whine pierced her ears and numbed her mind. The orbs spun just as wildly as the Mark.

A surge of strength came from deep inside and seized her. Her hand broke free from Sinto's grip, then an arm. She arched back and grabbed the Mark. Light bled through her fingers. Sinto's hold loosened when he saw the Mark clasped in her hand. A sea of emotion rippled across his face; desire, guilt, fear. To accept or not. He looked her in the eye. She made her choice. No words were necessary, the gaze they shared said it all—he wanted it too.

He wrapped his hand atop hers.

The Mark broke into two duplicate copies and slithered beneath the skin of their palms, burrowed, then settled deep within their inner forearms, forging an eternal bond with flesh and bone, a trail of fire in its wake. They released their hands and screamed.

The Mark was seeded but not done. The orbs inched closer together, a spinning blur glowing like suns.

Sinto's eyes were on fire. He bound her in his arms, putting the orbs to their backs. "Don't look at them." He sucked a sharp breath. "Close your eyes."

She felt his control weakening, fighting to stop the orbs from crashing into one another. Something she realized would be bad by the urgency of his actions.

"Close your eyes." He said it again, voice frantic. "Think of the club—*hear* the music—*see* the others. We must do this, together. *Now!*"

Against every instinct and thought controlling her mind and body she yielded to Sinto's plea.

43

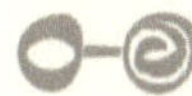

Date Interrupted

MUSIC ASSAULTED AUDREY'S EARS. She opened her eyes, gasped for air. The club. A ball of bodies swirling above their heads. Her forearm simmered from the Mark, recently born.

Sinto released his death grip. She rubbed that place where the Mark had settled.

Sinto's face was beet red, eyes bleached of color. A trickle of lorica snaked down his cheek like a bead of sweat.

"Are you going to tell me what just happened?" Her voice wavered.

Sinto was hunched over, hands on knees, gulping air. The redness in his face faded as he slowly caught his breath.

She looked around the club. "Were we here this entire time?"

"Physically, yes." He stood up. "Consciously, no. Our minds were—" He grasped her by the shoulders, pulled her close and gently rolled his forehead across hers. "We were in here, our minds momentarily conjoined."

She held out her arm; the skin was pink and puffy where the Mark had embedded itself. "This Mark, this is real?"

He held out his arm. That spot below his elbow was just as inflamed as hers. "Yes."

"This means, uh, you and I are destined to be mates forever?"

His brow furrowed with worry and doubt.

"Please, answer me."

He closed his eyes, drew a shaky breath. "I only know of the myth, so I'm not quite sure, but I believe what we started isn't finished."

"What's not finished?"

"Marked but not Joined." He diverted his gaze. "This changes everything. I'm sorry."

"Sorry for what? Can we make it go away?"

He gave her a pained smile. "I don't think so."

"So be it. You said this was good, and I—I want you! Why are you acting funny?" She coiled her fingers through his hair.

He extracted her fingers, stepped back. "Whether we want this or not, it can't be finished, not now. We mustn't encourage the Mark."

"Because I'm a Sapien and you're a Merahvu, is that it?"

He didn't answer.

"Talk to me!"

"That is certainly a complication, but not the only."

"Is it because of the reason I'm here?"

He didn't answer right away. "No one can know about this."

"I won't tell."

"It's not that easy, you'll—there's only one way to bury the truth."

"Make me forget?" A tear slipped down her cheek. "But I don't want to for—"

His lips cut off her words when they found hers.

She felt a sharp prick in her ear.

And then—

She was lying on the red sofa, staring at herself in the mirrored wall. She sat up. Dizzy and unbalanced, a bout of nausea swept through her. She closed her eyes, swallowed, and willed her stomach to calm. Sinto was slumped on the sofa beside her, eyes shielded by the crook of his arm. Muffled sounds of the wild romp unfolded on the other side of the mirrored wall. She looked between Sinto and her own bewildered reflection. The last she remembered was kissing Sinto beneath the swirling mob. And what a kiss!

How did we end up here? When did he raise the mirrored wall?

"Hey," she shook him. "Did I pass out?" He rolled his head in her direction. His eyes were sage green. They actually looked normal.

He didn't answer right away. "Passed out—yes. Perhaps I shouldn't have given you a second shot of sucuvita." His voice had changed too, somber and deflated, like someone had flipped off his power switch. He closed his eyes and took a deep breath.

Maybe the Ballorue wore him out.

It was a hell of a ride, like a roller coaster without the rails, ended by a fiery kiss. "Why so morose? This date's been amazing so far."

He gave her a weak smile that made her cheeks flame.

"You look like you could use another shot."

He sighed and scrubbed his face with his hands. "Yeah, I could."

Audrey picked up the bottle and filled his glass. He sat forward and took it from her fingers. She shivered when they touched. A distant spark ignited in his eyes.

He gulped it down, twiddled with the empty glass, then scrubbed his hands through his hair and across his face, as if trying to cleanse himself of something unpleasant.

Silence, a distant gaze. Then he stood and held out his hand.

"Time to tell you the real reason why I brought you here." He gazed around the room. "But not here, somewhere more private."

44

Bedtime Story

Sinto took Audrey back to his home.

He should have locked her in Naiada's room and escaped to the far side of Earth. But here they sat beside each other on Naiada's bed, shoulder to shoulder, stuck together.

Guilt and frustration riddled him. He had violated her mind without her permission and erased everything about the Mark, the hovering orbs, the fact that what was started remained unfinished. He had cast the memory aside like garbage. One she may not remember but he would.

Regardless of the moral wrongness of what he had done, he had no reasonable explanation for what had happened. How or why she was able to Mark him. What it meant. As the story goes, once the Mark was accepted, there could be no one else. He would never desire another, nor would she. Merahvu history had but one instance of a shared Mark between a Merahvu and a Sapien. A fact not widely shared; a secret fiercely protected by his mother for obvious reasons.

And that instance did not end well.

He rubbed the inside of his right forearm. Buried within the muscle was the gristle of the Mark, forged of his flesh and blood, hardening with each passing second. He could see the same hardening of flesh forming in Audrey's arm as well.

Marked!

The consequence of which was becoming shockingly apparent. The Mark left him vulnerable and weak, with every thought and action seemingly spurred by it, filling him with a single-minded purpose to take the next step. Exactly what that entailed he didn't know, but he believed the circling orbs were presented for a reason, and they had come dangerously close to Joining.

Thankfully, he ended it, unsure if it was the right thing to do or not.

But that didn't explain the depth of his carnal desire, strong and persistent.

Of this he was certain: he should leave, and now; lock Audrey in Naiada's room until the morning. He didn't have to tell her anything more about the reason she was here. That particular conversation he could leave to his mother. He had done his part to earn Audrey's trust, and with the Mark, she had unwittingly committed to being more than just an ally. She had declared Sinto, a Merahvu, as her lifelong mate.

She put her hand on his thigh. Fire shot through him like a bolt of lightning. His groin stirred and mind went blank. He could hear her heart pounding. His gaze drifted to her lips, tempting as a sweet strawberry, then to the swell of her breasts, rising and falling with her elevated breath, the skin flushed. His carefully crafted control was slipping.

Leave her!

With a twitch of his tail, he was on the far side of the room.

"What's wrong? You're acting funny."

"Nothing." He kept his back to her, summoning the strength to face her.

"Is it the reason why I'm here?"

How could he tell her the truth? *Especially now.* He turned, forced a smile.

"Is it bad?"

She looked so vulnerable perched on the edge of Naiada's bed. A crystal in her necklace caught the light and winked at him. His eyes fell to the soft curve of her neck where a swirled loop of silver drummed to her heartbeat. Silver that he once held in his hands, forging and polishing to perfection. He was jealous of it, free to caress a place he dared not.

He licked his lips.

Her eyes followed the traverse of his tongue and her cheeks bloomed red. She fingered the loop of silver that had captured his gaze and gasped when it shocked her. Her honey-sweet scent swept across the room, advertising carnal desires. He could hear her heart pounding faster, see the fevered pulse in her neck. These physical reactions must be because of the Mark. A door blasted open, for both of them.

His tail tensed, ready to bolt back across the room, to do the thing every cell in his body was screaming for him to do.

He did not.

He closed his eyes and shut out all sound, wrestling with that one troubling fact that changed everything, for both of them, from this moment forward.

The Mark. A revered gift. One that did not present itself to just anyone. Some believed it was divine intervention cast from somewhere far across the universe. Others believed it was merely a myth, used to prop up those in power. As the story went, one presented the Mark while the other was responsible for initiating the Joining. The Mark itself meant they had been chosen for a profound and noble shared purpose. One that may or may not entail great sacrifice. A purpose revealed only during the Joining.

Wantemo had been the one to tell Sinto of this myth, shortly before his eighteenth birthday, *Is it real? I cannot say for sure. You can only look to your parents for that answer, as I am unaware of any others who have been presented the Mark and Joined for as long as I can remember, and that is a very long time. Will it happen to you? Most unlikely, or never, I believe. I can only suggest you choose wisely to whom you offer yourself, for you never know if or when it might happen. But if it does, the tale claims you will only desire the one who Marks you—an insatiable want, so the story says, until death takes one of you.*

Want, want, want—oh, how he wanted her.

Wantemo had been wrong about the never part, but correct about insatiable want. Not such a myth after all. The Mark found them and was revealing itself to be horny and impatient.

"Are you doing that? My necklace it—" She shivered. "It tickles. Like the way it feels when you touch me." She held out her hand. "Come here. I don't bite."

The Mark in his arm gave him a little jolt.

Oh yes you do, deeper than you could possibly know.

She gave him a coy smile. "Please?"

The Mark flared in his arm; he had no choice but to succumb to her will. Another startling fact he was learning. He crossed the room and sat, carefully putting space between them.

The smell of her filled him and he struggled against the urge to smother her mouth with his lips and do so much more. He fisted his hand; fingernails cut into his flesh. Pain was a welcomed distraction. He made note and squeezed tighter, and gathered his thoughts.

"There's a Sapien man who seeks vengeance against our queen. She has tried to reason with him, but he refuses to listen. The last time she tried, he attacked her messengers: my father and Naiada. You saw her, learned what happened to her. My father has been missing ever since. We fear he is dead."

"So there are other Sapiens besides me, who know about the Merahvu?"

He paused for beat. "He's the only one—along with a handful of close associates—besides you, that are still living."

"How can this one man thwart your queen?"

"He has been searching for our city for years and with their technological advances, they will soon find us. The queen has been hiding this secret from the people for years. A truth about things that threaten us. She vowed never to lie to the people, to harbor no secrets. The queen has put the future of this city and our people in jeopardy."

"What does this have to do with me?"

"The queen believes you can stop this man."

"How can I stop a man that you can't?"

"She believes he will listen to a Sapien. To tell him she means him no harm, that what happened in the past was all a misunderstanding."

"You're kidding, *right*? This man sounds dangerous."

"If he finds the city, everything we have fought to protect will be for nothing. If the truth comes out, the people will lose trust in our queen and the governing Circle. Orange will continue its destructive march across the Pacific. Merluma will reel out of control. No one will care what becomes of us."

She touched his arm. "I care."

His gaze fell to her fingers resting on his arm, then up at his sister's painting. He focused on how close Naiada came to dying and the mystery of his father's disappearance; summoning painful distractions from the way his skin tingled from Audrey's touch.

"That's why you were chosen to help us. We knew you would care."

"*You* chose me?"

"The queen chose you. She asked me to find you."

"Me? Out of seven billion people?"

He chose his words carefully. He found lying to her, even innocent little lies meant to protect her, shredded his insides. Another consequence of the Mark. "Your compassion burns bright. It surrounds you, colors your aura. Even Moonstone noticed."

They both smiled when he referred to his bird companion, Rave, by the new name Audrey gave him.

"Why does this man seek your queen?"

"He was once a close friend."

She tucked her feet up on the bed and faced him. "Tell me more."

He took a moment to collect his thoughts and quell the fire simmering in his loins. Thankfully, she had removed her fingers from his arm.

"Long ago the Merahvu lived freely along the shores of the Salish Sea before it was discovered by traveling Sapiens—"

"As shown in this painting?" Audrey gestured to the walls.

"Yes, Naiada has painted these images from ancestral memories she acquired from Arctakai Keepers of Knowledge. At one point, the Merahvu comingled with the indigenous people who populated the shores around the Salish Sea long before it was discovered by seafaring Sapiens."

He paused to gaze at the wonder his sister had painted.

"Go on."

"The first ship of Sapien sailors that sailed into those waters struck a reef during a fierce storm. The captain was injured and thrown overboard. The queen found him near death. She healed him and saved his life. She had intended to return him to his crew, to make their chance meeting seem as merely a dream, but then she learned he was an outlaw, a pirate running from his past. She grew curious as to why he would risk his life, venturing so far from his kind. Their friendship deepened and over time the queen and the pirate captain shared valuable knowledge from their respective worlds."

"A pirate and a mermaid?" Her eyes sparkled with intrigue. "Has anyone written this tale before?"

"I doubt it. Very few know this story."

"So how did they become enemies?"

"The queen's daughter, Leela, learned of the queen's friendship, and secretly came to know one of the captain's crew. They fell in love and were married in Sapien tradition. When the queen found out, she felt betrayed by the captain who was the one who blessed the union."

"Couldn't the captain and the queen have agreed to annul the marriage?"

"It wasn't that simple. They had forged what the Merahvu believe is a sacred bond—a coveted union; joined in purpose, of single heart, essences stitched together. As the queen's firstborn female, Leela was destined to be the future queen, a duty she could never fulfill while bound to a Sapien. The queen panicked. The monarchical bloodline would be broken for the first time in our history, and she feared that if the people learned the truth it would shatter the fragile state of peace newly established, which was tenuous at the time, especially between the Seakai and the Terrakai.

"At that time the Terrakai were being uprooted by the influx of Sapiens where they had settled near the Great Waters in North America. The Terrakai wanted to strike back, but the queen's mother ordered them to return to Merluma. She prophesied war and disease would eventually take the Sapiens and the Terrakai would be able to return and claim the Earth lands for themselves.

"As an offering of goodwill, the queen's mother established a new tradition: that all future queens take a member of a different tribe as their mate to become an active member of the Circle, governing the people in tandem with the queen. So the future Seakai queen chose a popular and highly respected member of the Terrakai tribe as her mate.

"Leela was half-Terrakai bound to a Sapien. Something the Terrakai would never accept. Desperate to keep the peace, the queen severed the bond between Leela and her pirate lover, believing that once freed, no one would ever know and Leela could one day fulfill her obligation as queen representing both Seakai and Terrakai. Only the queen didn't know..." Sinto drew a deep breath. "Their sacred bond was *irrevocable.*"

"What does that mean?"

"Unfortunately, she learned the answer to that question that day. Once the connection between Joined mates is inadvertently severed, one of them dies."

She gasped. "Was it Leela?"

He nodded. "The queen inadvertently killed her own daughter, unaware of the consequences. She panicked, lied, and placed blame for her death on the pirate captain. Because of this, the queen, with agreement from the Circle, declared that all interaction between our species cease immediately. So we went into hiding. All contact with the indigenous Sapiens was broken."

"When did all of this happen?"

Sinto paused a beat. "Three hundred years ago."

Audrey gasped. "But this man—he should be dead..." Her voice trailed off and she gazed unseeingly, lost in thought, piecing together all the things he had taught her. Her aura flared and he felt the oxywater ripple between them when the realization struck. Her eyes locked on his. "Sucuvita."

He nodded. "Before the incident with Leela, the queen gave the captain the secret of the source of our elixir, which is found only here on Earth in a few places. She also gave him treasures gathered from the sea—precious metals, jewels. But most valuable of all, she shared visions of the future, significant events forthcoming in your world; the industrial era, world wars, the advent of computers, global communications, artificial intelligence, and more. That man is very much alive, and very rich and powerful because of the queen."

"But I don't understand. Why would he seek vengeance against the queen? It was the queen who suffered a loss, not him."

"After Leela's death, the captain and his men fled but were hunted down and attacked. Most of his crew was killed. He blamed the queen for his men's deaths."

"Did she order the attack?"

He shook his head. "She had no hand in the attack, nor has she revealed who may have, perhaps because she didn't know who was responsible. Regardless, that man has been hunting us ever since, and he is very close to finding this city. Her request is simple. She wants you to give him a message."

"What message?"

"She seeks a truce. That is all. A simple request."

Audrey pondered. "Is it really that simple?"

"What do you mean?"

She unfolded her legs and leaned forward. "I'm talking about us."

His heart skipped a beat. "Us?"

She put a hand on his knee, touched his cheek. "What constitutes *interaction* as defined by your queen and her Circle?"

He couldn't answer if he tried. Certainly, the way she touched him fit the description. Fire radiated from her fingertips, igniting the Mark buried in his arm, fueling that carnal need. She must have felt it too. She stole a glance at the puffy flesh below her right elbow, rubbing it mindlessly, unaware of the Mark that lay beneath the surface. Then she shifted, pressing her body dangerously close to his.

"If what you say is true, then the Merahvu are bound to be discovered, and soon. Won't that change everything?"

The answer weighed heavily on his mind, especially now. Even their Keepers of Knowledge had yet to solve the mystery of the Mark and the Joining, or confirm it was real, other than the fact his parents shared a Mark and had Joined, an event that had been celebrated by the people as a sign of a divine blessing for the newly established peace.

Sinto was stymied why the Mark choose him and Audrey. Before now, he thought of the Mark as just another of Wantemo's many fables. It was what happened after that things became concerning and, he feared, was far from simple. And what would possibly be their shared purpose?

If they gave in to the carnal desire the Mark stoked, would their fate be forever sealed? Wantemo failed to clarify that part of the myth, and Sinto had failed to ask.

She touched his chin. "Sinto, say something." Her eyes were fiery as a sunset, and unbeknownst to her, the door to her mind swung open, beckoning him to step inside.

Fire pumped through his bloodstream. He put her hand back in her lap. "We shouldn't be touching each other right now."

She crossed her arms. "Why not? You've been sending different signals all night, and that kiss, that wasn't nothing. Why can't I touch you?"

"Because of the potential consequences."

She blushed. "I have no intention to steal your—your *essence*! It's just, I like you—I like you a *lot*. Is it so bad to *like* someone?"

"No, but it could lead to…"

"To what?" She wagged a brow. "A forbidden tryst?" Her gaze swept across Naiada's room. "Who would know? It could be our little secret, just between me and you."

He gasped. "Please, let us not talk of such things."

"Really? After what I witnessed at the club, the intimacy of the *Ballorue*—the way you kissed me. You can't convince me that the thought hasn't crossed your mind at least once. Aren't you curious what it would be like, you and me?"

He laughed nervously. "More than you can imagine."

She gave him a sultry smile. "Try me."

He stood, ready to bolt. That thread of control slipping through his fingers. Before he could step away she took his hand and sucked one of his fingers into her mouth then playfully took a bite. His knees quivered.

Is this her or the Mark making her do and say these things?

He found it difficult to breath, his gaze slipping to the place where the folds of green silk swept across her breasts, the press of nipple hard and firm against the thin fabric. He gritted his teeth and fought to keep his feet planted and knees still and free hand from reaching out to touch her.

Her brow quirked, eyes blinking as if waking from a dream. She gazed down at the imprint of her teeth slowly bouncing back on his finger. "I'm sorry, that was a little uncharacteristic of me. I think that second shot of sucuvita went straight to my head!"

"No need to be sorry."

She looked around the room, smoothed the dress across her thighs. "You're right, we should take it slow, considering the risks."

He said nothing, afraid that whatever he said he wouldn't be able to stop himself from doing something they both may regret.

She looked up, eyes pleading. "But I'm worth *some* risk, aren't I?"

"Absolutely," he quipped.

She tugged at his arm. He sat back down beside her.

"Is it wrong to want someone?"

"No."

"Is it wrong to want to be with someone no matter where they're from, Earth or Merluma?"

Sinto grappled. What was right? An old edict declared hundreds of years ago or the presence of the Mark buried in his arm. He drew a shaky breath. "I don't think so."

"And we are both human, are we not?"

"Yesss…"

"Then what are you waiting for? Kiss me, like you did at the club."

He drew a breath but it failed to satisfy his lungs. What he needed was not air, but her, and she had affirmed her desire, given her consent. The tether that held him back disintegrated. He didn't hesitate or feel guilt. The Mark spoke and he acted. They fell on the bed in a tangle. He kissed that place where her neck curved and her heartbeat moved her silky flesh. He kissed the sweet nectar from her lips and when her dress fell apart in his fingers, his lips found her breasts, one then the other, her skin soft as peaches.

And in that fevered state he confessed that she had moved him the first time they met, that a day never passed when he hadn't thought of her, that he spent the last ten years trying to find her, at how disappointed he felt every time he returned to the beach to give back her book only to find she wasn't there, then of their reunion on Merluma and his delight that his feelings for her had not changed, how they had only grown stronger—frighteningly so. He stopped short of confessing the full new truth, that he could not live his life without her—literally—because of the Mark, until the day he died.

She would certainly feel the pull of the Mark, regardless of the fact that Sinto had snipped that all-important memory. She would feel as certain as he, that he was hers, and her his—connected in way that transcended the coupling of two humans for mere romantic reasons; a connection that twined their essences at the root of every cell, mind and body. Maybe not now, or tomorrow, but soon. He feared how her feelings might manifest, not knowing the truth of what happened, of the Mark and the power it wielded, of the unknown purpose they would soon share. A purpose Sinto couldn't possibly guess.

As they delighted in their current physical entanglement, the Mark tugged at Sinto's heart and mind, reminding him that he was the one to take the next step, the Joining—him not quite knowing what that entailed. Though he was quite certain it included what she wanted of him right now, at least part of it... maybe.

And while he struggled to control his own actions, Audrey could not. She ripped off his shirt, buttons flying. Then she tugged at his zippered pants, the only thing separating them from crossing that line into uncertainty. And once crossed, he was certain; there would be no going back.

So he stopped her. He grabbed her hands and bound her arms. Her eyes pleaded, her hot breath mingled with his. That thread of sanity and control stretched to the point of breaking. He had no choice. There was only one way to stop her.

More violation of mind.

Once it was over, she lay on his sister's bed gazing back, her body paralyzed from his mind manipulation. The full realization of what the morning would bring crashed down in an avalanche of dread. While her heart burned for him tonight, after tomorrow he was certain it would no longer. For he would be the one to rip it from her chest and hand it over to his mother.

And his mother would tell Audrey the parts of the story he so carefully omitted, crushing her dreams and her innocence, and condemning him to a living hell; for he was certain that once Audrey Grey learned the truth, regardless of the Mark they shared, she would never want to see him again.

45

Sorry

MORNING LIGHT STREAMED THROUGH the windows and prickled Audrey's skin. She yawned and stretched like a cat after a long and satisfying nap.

When she sat up, the top of her dress fell to her waist. She plucked at the torn straps, remembering how her belly had caught fire when Sinto tore it away. Her skin still tingled from his electrified kisses.

Lying next to her was Sinto's shirt. She picked it up and rolled the silky fabric through her hands. She held it to her nose, breathing deep his unique scent. She marveled at the way her body ignited just thinking of him.

While smothering her with his mouth Sinto had confessed how he felt that first time she touched him and made his eyes burst with green fire. How he had searched for her over the years, his shock and delight when they were recently reunited. While his confessions set her heart aflame, she felt he was holding back, wanting to tell her more. But then she remembered the story he told of potential consequences because she was Sapien and he Merahvu.

Her giddy mood wilted, ashamed of what had happened next.

Something had suddenly possessed her that she couldn't control. Her blood fevered, she clawed at his clothes, tore the shirt from his back, and when she grabbed for his pants he leaped from the bed and told her to stop. She had shamelessly begged for him to take her—wholly and completely—that she didn't care about the consequences.

He had cradled her head in his hands and the effect was immediate. She crumpled to the floor powerless, tamed by a mind trick. As if from afar, she watched as he picked her up and gently laid her on the bed. A tear stole from his eye when he covered her bare chest with the torn pieces of her dress and laid her arms across her stomach, like Snow White trapped in paralyzed slumber.

Then he stood by the bed in silence, gazing down at her, a deep sadness filling his eyes. She could only gaze back, her voice muted and body paralyzed. He stayed with her until her heart calmed, the fire in her blood waned, and her eyes fluttered shut.

Then he kissed her gently. He whispered, "I am sorry, truly and deeply, for what has and will soon come to pass." Then he left.

That was the last thing she remembered before waking up.

She pondered: what had possessed her? Was it the elixir or something else? What if he hadn't stopped her advances—would he be lying beside her now, nuzzling her neck with kisses? How would she feel, gazing into the eyes of the man to whom she gave herself so freely?

She smiled when the answer came to her.

I'd feel no regrets because—because I'm in love with him.

She sat up and swung her feet to the floor. Her stomach fluttered when she padded across the room to the bathroom. She had never felt love like this, not even for—

She gasped, stopped dead in her tracks.

Blake.

Guilt knifed her heart. How quickly she forgot.

She held up her hand. The friendship bracelet Blake had tied around her wrist was gone. She stole a glance back. It was lying on the floor next to the bed. She crossed the room and picked it up. The carefully tied knots were frayed and the bracelet had unraveled sometime in the night.

Tears welled in her eyes. She squeezed it in her fist. Blake was gone, she was most certain. His wish—and her promise—gone with him. Why did she suddenly feel guilty? She tamped down this newfound guilt and wiped away her tears.

She thought of Sinto's story. What his queen would ask of her. Was it really just a simple message? Delivered and done, a quick thanks and wave of hand to move along?

Last night she felt invincible. Now, without Sinto's calming presence, she wondered if she had the strength to go through with it. Doubt burrowed into a knot at her brow.

She shed the lovely dress torn beyond repair and found her original clothes. She slipped them on and tucked the unraveled bracelet in her jean's pocket.

She stepped into the hallway.

Sinto's door was sealed. She made a quick study of her reflection, smoothing skewed brows, taming the wavy strands of hair escaping her braid hanging loose, the knot of it having come undone during the night. She took a deep breath and pressed her palm to the door. It bowed inward, then snapped back, refusing her entry. She gazed at herself befuddled. Maybe she had missed something. Before they had freely passed through every mirrored door they encountered.

She tried again with more purpose.

She heard it before she felt it. A crackle then a zap. She cried out, cradling her hand. A deep reverberating ache, jarring every bone in her arm, raising every hair in its wake.

Sinto told her their doors were telepathically linked to their minds, the same as the city's dome and his protective lorica. He mentioned once that they were programmable, to decipher who could pass and who could not.

Sinto had locked her out.

"Hey," she said softly. "Why did you do that?"

Silence.

"I know you're there."

Silence.

"If this is about last night, I'm sorry—you had every right to stop me."

The door evaporated. Sinto stood before her; hair disheveled, chest bare, pants rumpled. He looked as if he hadn't slept.

Her heart leaped. He looked delicious.

How can I feel guilty and horny at the same time?

She held up his shirt. "You left this."

He snatched it and tossed it aside.

Her heart pounded, not from lust but the feeling something was horribly wrong. "What is it? Something I said?"

"It's complicated." His voice was different too. Deep. Troubled.

"After everything you've told me, I think I can handle it. Please, talk to me."

Something *was* dreadfully wrong. It rolled off him in icy-cold waves. She looked for a clue in his eyes, but got nothing in return.

"She is waiting for us." He pushed past her.

"Who's waiting for us?"

"The queen."

"Wait!" She gripped the braid lying across her shoulder like a life line. "I'm a mess and I'm starving."

"We'll tend to your needs. Come." Sinto marched through the arched hallway, toward the gold-sealed door.

Audrey followed, smoothing imaginary wrinkles from her sweater. The embers Sinto had ignited last night crawled to the pit of her stomach.

"Does she know—what we were..." she lowered her voice to a whisper, "doing last night? That wasn't *illegal*, was it? It's not like anything *happened.*"

He stopped walking. She ran into him. "No."

"Is that why you stopped me?"

He cast a wary smile over his shoulder. "I stopped you for other reasons—for your best interest."

"Who are you to decide what is in my best interest?"

The fire rose from her stomach to her heart when she looked into his eyes.

"Trust me, it was for the best."

There it was again, *trust me*. So far she hadn't considered that she had been set up. Her primal brain stirred not in fear but need. She desperately needed to trust him, to believe that he had not lied, that everything he told her was true. She balled her hands into fists at her sides so he would not see them trembling. As much as she wanted to believe, she got a sinking feeling that Sinto had not been entirely forthright. She suspected someone was about to get hurt, and that someone was her.

Sinto continued walking. "She waits."

She blindly followed, resolved to face whatever fate waited.

Sinto stepped through the golden door as if it wasn't there. It splintered into a million shards like glass, the sound jarring but peaceful at the same time, like glass chimes caught by a sudden gust. Beyond was a transparent bridge connecting Sinto's home to the base of a rocky outcropping supporting the Great Tower. The bridge was clear as glass, had no rails, and hovered a couple of stories above uneven rock. It was dizzying looking down. She stopped halfway across.

Maybe I should take my chances and jump, hide in the gardens, so I can think of a way to get home.

She stole a quick glance forward. Sinto stood in the shadow cast by the tower's high balcony. He must have known what she was thinking. His brow dipped and he shook his head.

Audrey kept walking.

When she reached the other side, Sinto took her elbow and led her through an opening in the rock at the base of the tower. Cold seeped through the soles of her shoes. Dripping water echoed from somewhere deep within the darkness. It smelled musty. He snapped his fingers and a green ball of fire sprang from the palm of his hand. Shadows slithered to dark corners.

Sinto flicked his finger and the ball of light took flight down a narrow passage. He prodded her forward. "Follow the light."

The tunnel meandered left and right, past other passages—cut in the walls, the ceiling, the floor—a labyrinth leading to a queen's lair.

Audrey dutifully followed the light. Sinto followed in silence.

She was utterly lost by the time they reached the end of the tunnel where a curved gold-, silver-, and copper-flaked wall rose from rock. Cut into the wall was an arched doorway with another gold mirrored door.

Audrey struggled to breathe and set her gaze on her untied shoelace. Sinto knelt and tied it, then stood, facing her. He tilted her chin up, capturing her gaze.

"I haven't told you everything, but what I have told you is true. Please know that I never intended to hurt you. Promise me, you will remember that."

"Alright, I promise, but wh—"

He pressed his finger to her lips, quieting her. "There's one more thing I should have told you last night but I was afraid of scaring you."

She drew a jittery breath. "What should you have told me?"

"I would rather die than live without you, and that is the complete and absolute truth." He cradled her face in his hands and kissed her tenderly on the forehead. "I am truly sorry for everything about to pass."

Then he pushed her though the door.

46

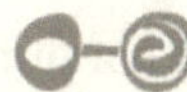

Queen Ianthe

AUDREY BLINKED IN SURPRISE. Stepping inside the Great Tower was nothing like she expected. The looming tower and outside walls shimmering with gold, silver, and copper screamed of opulence. But the circular room where she stood was small and modest and tastefully decorated. A private residence.

The walls were a pale gold and embossed with random patterns of dots hinting at various natural themes—a tree, swirling currents and waves, the sun, moon and stars, flowers and grasses, a frog, a fish, an eagle, and more—subtle images that leaped into being once your eye focused on it; hundreds of images spinning in different directions connected together with swirling patterns of dots. Otherwise, the effect was of a lightly textured surface.

Light streamed from a large opening in the ceiling with the hint of more spaces beyond.

In the center of the room, four clamshell-shaped chairs encircled a solid wood table carved from the trunk of a grand tree. An ageless woman sat in one of the chairs, twirling a long lock of golden hair. The woman said nothing, but a soft smile slowly curled on her pert, full lips. She watched as Sinto quietly slipped into the room.

A trio of purple balls of fire rotated and hovered above, casting lively shadows across the table set with a bouquet of purple flowers, a glass pitcher of water, and three place settings. A buffet of delectable dishes sat on a cabinet pressed against the wall, near the table. Above the cabinet was a large symbol—a triangle of three green dots entwined with a purple swirl and encrusted with faceted gemstones, emerald and purple sapphire. The only opulent thing in the room.

Audrey faltered on her feet when the woman rose to greet them; the mere movement surged through the modest space with the power of a shock wave.

The queen wore a full-length, gold skareef draped across one shoulder and wrapped round her hips. The fabric was lively and rippled like liquid gold. Half of her chest was revealed. A protective layer of skin covered her breasts, which were embellished with her markings in raised swirls thick and wild, like kelp strewn across a beach after a fierce winter storm. Her hair was pulled into a tight ponytail at the top of her head. From there it spilled in layers of golden waves across one shoulder to the long tapered fingers entwining it. A classic beauty of a by-gone era—heart-shaped face, high cheekbones, skin iridescent as a pearl—but it was her eyes that drew a gasp. Smoldering orbs of purple fire.

The queen reached out with both hands. "Welcome to my city, my home. Please, be my guest. No matter what Sinto has told you, you may address me as Ianthe."

Audrey accepted the queen's hands. "I'm Audrey Grey."

Ianthe's eyes sparked. "Oh, I know who you are and have been dying to meet you."

Audrey felt something race up her spine and crawl into her ear, like a spider zipping along a silk thread. She tried to bat it away, but nothing was there.

Ianthe flashed a warm smile. "Please come, sit!"

Something tickled the inside of her ear. She tugged on her earlobe, then it was gone.

"Something wrong?" Ianthe asked.

Sinto glared at the queen.

"It's nothing." Audrey sat in the chair Ianthe held out for her.

Ianthe turned to Sinto who hadn't moved since they stepped inside. She gently grasped his head and kissed him on the forehead, the tip of his nose, each cheek in turn. Then she kissed him on the lips. Not a lover's kiss, but the kind of kiss an adoring mother would give to a child.

It all made sense now; Sinto's odd behavior, the similar pattern of swirled markings, the triangle of dots on the wall. Audrey had seen a much younger version of Ianthe's face the day before, when she met Sinto's sister.

The swirls I inherited from my mother, the dots from my father.

Ianthe confirmed Audrey's suspicion when she patted Sinto's chest and whispered, "You have done well, my son."

Sinto sat in the chair beside Audrey, stone faced and avoiding her gaze.

Why hadn't he told her?

The queen's son—a prince!

Audrey must have looked as sick as she suddenly felt, for the queen gave her a sympathetic frown. "You must be famished!" She gestured toward the cabinet. "I've prepared refreshments."

Ianthe busied herself, transferring several platters from the cabinet to the table, a feast for many; fruit, dates, nuts, dried fish, caviar, crispy seaweed, and other strange unrecognizable things like the meal Nawtuga served them the night before.

Ianthe slipped into the seat beside Audrey. Close enough that Audrey could smell heat rising from her skin, sweet and seductively salty. She never really thought about how a mermaid queen might smell, but Ianthe definitely nailed the profile.

Ianthe poured Audrey a glass of water. "Don't let the moist air deceive you, my dear, you are quite dehydrated."

Audrey drank, irritated by how she knew she was thirsty.

"Did Sinto tell you why you are here?"

That last sip of water got stuck in her throat. She forced it down, set down the glass. "He said you want me to deliver a message."

"And?"

"He told me you fear a man who once was your friend."

Ianthe asked Sinto to pass Audrey a platter piled with round bite-sized things that looked honey-coated, the size of a walnut. Audrey took one of the proffered bites and popped it in her mouth.

"Spermazond," Sinto said, eating one himself, "giant squid sperm, quite nutritious, high in potassium among other things."

Before she could spit it out, it slid down her throat and landed in her stomach like a slimy dumpling. Sinto offered another bite. Audrey pushed the platter aside, trying not to heave.

Ianthe's gaze bored. "I do not *fear*, sweet girl."

Ianthe's eyes brightened and Audrey felt that pull to gaze past the fiery purple and plunge inside. She blinked and pointed to the platter of fruit. "That looks yummy, may I please?"

Sinto passed the platter.

Audrey felt that tickle again, deep inside her head, beyond her eardrum, like a feather sweeping across the bone inside her head. It abated, then she felt downy strands wrapping around the top of her spine; a gentle squeeze, a wash of calm.

"This man is causing me great distraction."

"So why me?"

Ianthe flashed Sinto a questioning glance, then leaned forward and touched Audrey's cheek. "So Sinto did not tell you everything." She ran her fingers along Audrey's jawline, gently grasped her chin and swiveled her head from one side to the next, studying every detail of her face. Ianthe slipped a finger into Audrey's mouth, ran it slowly across her front teeth.

Ianthe stood up and gestured for Audrey to do the same.

She stood. "What didn't Sinto tell me?"

Ianthe ignored her question and stood back, eying Audrey's stature, the size of her feet. Ianthe was equally as tall. She plucked a lock of Audrey's hair from her braid and rubbed it between her fingertips. "Lovely texture. I see you take good care of yourself."

Audrey wanted to scream. "What are you doing?" she asked as calmly as her heart would allow.

Ianthe dropped the lock of hair and flashed her teeth. "Just curious. Now be still."

Ianthe fixed her with a look of warning. Audrey took heed and froze. Ianthe leaned forward and burrowed her nose in the hollow of Audrey's neck, breathing deeply the scent of her. Audrey bristled. Then Ianthe licked her, starting from her shoulder up to her ear, a long slow travel of moist tongue leaving a cool and tingling wake.

Audrey recoiled in disgust.

Ianthe sucked her tongue, narrowing her eyes in concentration. "Hm, sweet and something else. You taste a little like—" Her brows shot up and she slipped a curious glance at her son. A look that said Sinto would have much to explain later.

Ianthe gave Audrey a final sweep with her eyes. "I must say, you don't look anything like him, except for your stature—tall and lean, and I bet you can bend like a pretzel. You taste like him too. But your vulnerable innocence..." Her eyes widened and she made a sweeping gesture with her arms. "The color of your aura! Except for the fact that she was a curvy petite thing, you look exactly like her, right down to that cute button of a nose."

"What are you talking about?"

Ianthe cocked her lips. "Have you not figured it out yet? I am surprised. Sinto told me how intuitive you were. Perhaps the moist atmosphere is dulling your senses. Shall I spell it out for you? *Your father* is this man you claim I fear. He was once my friend, a very *dear* friend."

"My *father*?" Her ears began to ring, dual tones clashing. His paranoia. His warning she stay away from the water.

"Sinto, is that true?"

He took a breath, nodded.

Audrey fell back in her chair. The room swirled, and the next thing she knew she was bent over at the waist, a puddle of water and a single spermazond at her feet. Her mind went blank. The only thing she knew for certain at that moment was that the wretched thing was much more horrible coming up than going down.

Ianthe slipped behind Audrey's chair and began to knead her shoulders. "Do not blame Sinto; his intent was to protect you from the truth."

Audrey wanted to rip Ianthe's hands from her shoulders, but fell victim to her calming touch and soothing voice.

"Is it true he has three scars running across his chest?"

Audrey nodded. Her father had always been self-conscious of his scars; she rarely saw him without a shirt, even at the beach.

"Your father's real name is Robert Culliford. I found him with half his ribs broken, his chest sliced open, nearly bled dry and drowning. I gave him *everything*; a second chance, good health and long life, wealth beyond imagination."

Audrey remembered Naiada, scarred and dying. She shook Ianthe's hands from her shoulders, turned to face her. "My father would never harm an innocent girl."

"You mean Naiada."

"Yes."

"How well do you know your father?"

Audrey pondered the queen's question. Sinto told her Naiada was poisoned. Was it an accident or a premeditated act? Was her father capable of murder? Of harming an innocent girl?

She flashed back to a recent memory. One before she left home for the Labs in Friday Harbor. Her father insisted on a final hand-to-hand defensive training session. He was relentless, slamming her to the mat, striking harder than called for, breaking the rules of controlled engagement. He wouldn't look her in the eye or acknowledge that she was his daughter, but treated her as a thing to maim and kill. He was a monster, filled with uncontrollable rage.

Afterward, he told her, "*Strike first, you won't get a second chance. Never forget that.*" He made her repeat it over and over, until she was breathless.

The bruises from that lesson never faded.

"Please, tell me," Ianthe gently prodded. "How well do you know your father?"

A million possible responses swirled, but none of them made sense.

Ianthe's gaze was magnetic and Audrey was drawn in. The feather's gentle grasp at the top of her spine let go and fluttered anxiously inside her skull like a trapped butterfly.

Ianthe's eyes grew bright—going from purple to white fire. Audrey felt a shift at her feet, like water sucking down a drain, like that thing Sinto called *essence* being extracted through the bottoms of her feet. Electricity crackled through the moist air. Sparks stung her face. Her lungs froze. She couldn't breathe.

Audrey watched her entire life pass before her eyes, like a movie running in fast forward. Ianthe controlled the images and the feelings, editing them down to a mere few seconds.

A promising start. Loving parents, deeply in love—Her mother's death. Her father's transformation and the grueling training. Impenetrable walls. Shadowy men, fake moms—Fitful nights of sleep. Her fear of the water—Her mother's death confirmed us an accident—Her fight for freedom. Her ultimatum. Daddy relenting—Moving to Friday Harbor. Blake tying the friendship bracelet around her wrist. A shared kiss. Orcas attacking...

The last image Audrey saw was Ianthe's eyes reflecting back from her own, like two mirrors facing each other, reflecting back and forth for infinity.

Ianthe closed her eyes, breaking the connection.

Sinto squatted beside her, clutching her hand, glaring at his mother.

Ianthe said, "I see there is more you still do not know."

Sinto sprang to life. "No! You said it was not nec—"

"Your father believes I killed your mother."

Audrey was momentarily stunned. It was an accident. Audrey replayed the event in her mind, exactly as she remembered. Her mother swam too far from the beach, got tangled in the fishnet. There was an investigation, no criminal intent found.

"What do you know about her death?"

"Nothing! I wasn't there. Your father is convinced I was. I tried to explain, but he will not listen. He has gone mad! Blaming me for something I had no part of."

"So this is why I'm here? So you can churn it all up again?"

"The reason you are here has not changed."

"And you asked Sinto to go through this whole charade to schedule a meeting? Can't you write a letter? Have one of your Scouts deliver it?"

"I tried that." Ianthe's eyes smoldered. "I sent my most trusted messengers. One is barely recovering. The other is still missing, presumed dead."

Sinto touched Audrey's shoulder. "It was not a charade. What I showed you, what we talked about, us, that is real."

Audrey shook off Sinto's hand and challenged the queen. "All you want is for me to deliver your message?"

"Convince him my intentions are pure. I wish to resolve our grievances, peacefully. I mean no harm, to you or him."

"How do I convince him he can trust you?"

"Have you not felt safe in my city under the care of my son?"

It was true, so much so that her heart yearned for him in a disturbingly deep way. Ianthe had been kind enough and Audrey believed there was an element of truth to her story. Yet Sinto himself had carefully pruned facts. Facts that mattered and twisted meanings into something else. What was she not telling Audrey? That was what she aimed to find out. That, along with her father's insistent warning and what it meant.

"What if I refuse to comply?"

Ianthe turned to Sinto and frowned. "I was afraid it would come to this."

47

Abduction

Ianthe stated, "So you want the unvarnished truth?"

"Yes, all of it," Audrey confirmed.

"So it shall be. Stand and give me your hands, both of you."

Audrey looked at Sinto, confused, and stood reluctantly. Sinto hopped to his feet as if prodded by a sharp stick.

Ianthe gestured for Audrey and Sinto to face each other, then placed Audrey's hands in his.

Sinto's face was pale as snow. That deeply troubled look from earlier filled his eyes. "Please, Mother, is this necessary?"

"She wants to know the truth, Sinto, all of it, and I am going to give it to her." Ianthe fixed Audrey with a fiery gaze. "Is that not what you want?"

Does she want to know the truth? Would she regret not knowing?

Ianthe said again, much more forcefully. "The truth? Is that not what you want?"

Sinto was breathing hard. What was he afraid of?

Her father's last lesson threaded. *Strike first, you won't get a second chance. Never forget that.* Fists weren't necessary. Truths bruised deep and lingered, sometimes forever. Ianthe was poised to make that first strike.

Sinto looked terrified. He said, "Don't fight her. You won't win." The fear she saw in his eyes fueled her determination to escape.

Ianthe smoothed Audrey's brow with her finger. "I know you crave the truth. I have not lied to you, not about your father nor my involvement in your mother's death. I sense your defiance. You are so much like him. Listen to Sinto. You cannot fight me. I too can play his game."

"Game—" Before Audrey could say another word, sharp pain shot through her skull, like being stabbed through the ear with an ice pick. Her knees buckled, Sinto caught her in his arms. She felt a deep tug, a sensation of slowly being turned inside out, a stinging rip, instant and fleeting like a Band-Aid ripped from an open wound. Then—

Darkness, weightless, deaf, dumb, blind, numb. Then—

A flash of light and a tingling sensation starting with her toes, a leg, then the other, her waist, chest, arms, warm and moist like slipping into an ill-fitting suit of human flesh. Her hips and shoulders nestled into all the wrong places.

She recognized the strange sensation, the sounds. The taste in her mouth.

Sinto.

She was inside his body again, like when he healed her on Merluma.

Everything that followed played out like a movie reel with her, as Sinto, the star of the show.

A vivid and recent memory...

~ ~ ~

The thunder of a pounding heart. Cool water rushes through slits in her neck, across her bare body. A spark and a jolt, vibration in her chest. Electricity courses through her blood. A rush of adrenaline, a flutter in her belly, a quiver of tongue, anticipating.

She hears the distant voices of orcas in a language she understands, not of words but images—thoughts, ideas, questions—that visually play out in her mind like a hologram.

They inquire, "When do we act?"

A shrill cry slips through her lips and quickly sweeps the distance between them. This too she understands, Sinto responding, "Soon, be patient."

A series of clicks sweep back acknowledging.

She turns her attention away from the orcas, opens her inner ears and listens. A propeller slicing through water, the deep rumble of an engine, the shrill sound of a sonar ping.

A boat approaching.

She swims toward the sound with the flip of her mighty tail.

A shadow passes overhead, the underside of a boat's hull—red bottom, single prop, skag keel...

Annabelle! The orca attack. Sinto was there!

The boat's engine quiets, the propeller stills, the pinging stops abruptly. Blessed silence.

She feels the excitement building in her chest as she waits; Sinto recalling how he felt when his mother tasked him to capture the girl he once met on an island in the Pacific, the one who was once his friend, the one he had sought for ten long years but could never find again.

As she waits she reminisces, replaying snippets of memories from Moonstone employed by Sinto to help find her. A mosaic of sights, sounds, and smells from a bird's eye view: The day before, her and Blake gathering lab samples from the docks at the Friday Harbor Labs, reviewing their plan to borrow a boat. That night, dark and raining, peeping through her dorm room window while she scribbles on her tablet and packs a backpack. The next morning, Blake hesitating to gather himself before knocking on her door. The sound of her breath catching when she opens it to greet him. Watching from

Roy's dock. She and Blake *walking toward Annabelle's slip, dawn barely cracking the sky. Her saying, "K Pod was last sighted in Haro Strait, north of Andrews Island." Blake responding, "Then Andrews Island it is."*

The flutter of black wings, rising up to the sky, a victorious squawk...

Sinto's memory is interrupted by a splash above her head, a hydrophone attached to a cord. She hears her remembered voice, muffled, "Try turning it up."

A string of clicks flow from her mouth. Sinto prompting the orcas to approach.

~ ~ ~

What happened next came fast and furious. Ianthe was in control of the show, playing it forward in fast motion:

~ ~ ~

The orcas circling the boat, their gleeful squeals as they spray its occupants with misty breath. Then—

Silence.

She drops deeper, her eyes trained on the boat above. Another shape crosses her vision, not black and white, not an orca. Another Merahvu. Pale body, braided hair, scar across silver brow; Wantemo. He settles by her, so far pleased with Sinto's work and the orcas' performance. Together they wait for the final act.

Sinto's chosen males attack the boat. Blake falls into the water. Wantemo snatches him and draws him deeper. Blake fights to break free. Wantemo is stronger, binding his arms and legs. Then he wraps them both in his gelatinous lorica.

Blake witnesses Sinto orchestrate the final act. Shock and disbelief register in his eyes. Wantemo cradles his head with his fingers. Blake's eyes roll back and he collapses into his arms. Wantemo launches a thread of bright blue light from his fingertips and a gaping hole opens in the water.

Blake and Wantemo disappear in a fizzy burst of bubbles.

48

Silent Confession

When Sinto opened his eyes, Audrey was on her knees, clutching her stomach. He looked away, afraid to look at her.

He was ashamed of what he had done. That he had suggested kidnapping her friend for leverage, that he had orchestrated the orca attack. How proud Wantemo was of him. That he planned to keep Audrey captive on Merluma as long as possible, so he could steal a glimpse into her mind, back to the day they first met, to learn if she had felt her essence quiver like he did when their fingers first touched—that moment, he now realized, which planted the seed for the Mark.

After Audrey summoned him on Andrews Island, he could have easily told Audrey who he was, then delivered her to his mother and secured his seat in the Circle. Because if Audrey had refused to do as his mother asked, he had devised a fail-safe alternative to the plan. And its name was Blake.

But it was Audrey who wielded the ultimate weapon: the Mark, sundering his life and destroying the future he had been promised.

With trust broken, how could she ever forgive him?

Sinto picked Audrey up from the floor. She felt fragile, like a delicate butterfly's wings pinched between his fingers. He set her in a chair, brushed loose strands of hair from her eyes and knelt at her feet.

He drew strength from the Mark and prepared to tell every truth, as a Marked man must confess to the woman who had Marked him; to tell her that he never intended to hurt her, that her friend was safe and would be returned unharmed, that all she needed to do was to deliver the message for his mother. And that afterward, everything would be all right, that they would be free to complete the Joining, that he could teach her everything she wanted to know about the natural world, to help her realize her dream, to take her places she never imagined existed, to love her from the very depths of his essence.

Her breath caught. She looked into his eyes, and in that fraction of a second, he saw she wanted that too. But the image was quickly drowned by a roiling sea of anger. Her gaze sharpened into daggers aimed straight for his heart. Her lips curled back over clenched teeth.

A butterfly no more, she shoved him with the full force of her body. He fell back on the table. Platters of food skittered and crashed to the floor in a din. He rolled off the edge and landed on his knees, fully prepared to grovel.

He reached for her hands. "Please let me explain."

She held up her palms. "Do. Not. Touch. Me."

He opened his mouth to beg but she pushed him aside, stood up, and faced his mother.

"If I agree to help you, will you tell me why?"

His mother gave Audrey *that* smile. Simply a smirk and nothing more, but one that screamed *victory*. But it was the firestorm swirling in his mother's eyes, daring Audrey to challenge her, that enraged him.

His hands fisted and breath labored. Never had he felt violence like this, coming in spurts and jabs of raw emotion. His heart raced, his face felt on fire. He wanted to rip that victory smirk from his mother's face.

But he stopped himself from acting and settled his gaze on the floor, confused by his sudden need to break something. Or hurt someone. He tried to calm his heart and mind—splaying fingers against his thighs, concentrating on the surge of oxywater rapidly passing in and out of his lungs.

Everything he tried to gain control of his emotions failed him. He grasped his forearm. The Mark buried in his flesh smoldered. That was when he realized these feelings were not his, but Audrey's, shared through the Mark that bound them.

It was her hands that were fisted, her lungs that were laboring, and her wish to strike his mother. To wipe the smirk off her face. Her emotions bled into his bloodstream rendering him weak and belittled—anger toward her father, humiliated for being played a fool, guilt for what happened to Blake because of her—and somewhere in the maelstrom, he felt her heart rip in two.

He cursed his stupidity. What had he expected? That she would never learn what had happened? That it was him who suggested the abduction of her friend? That he had lied to her about it? That she would understand why he did what he did, and simply forgive him? He told himself it wasn't over, that once she calmed, she would listen, possibly sympathize, and maybe, just maybe—

"Tell her, Sinto."

His mother's voice snapped him from his thoughts and he looked at her with dread. He had not heard a word spoken between them during his distraction. He could only guess that they were not amiable. Audrey glared accusingly. His mother was no longer smiling. Wildfire burned in her eyes. Bad, *bad* sign.

"Tell her what?"

"Why did you have to trick me?" Audrey asked.

"Not a trick, *incentive*," Ianthe answered for him. "Sinto suggested we kidnap your friend. I now understand his wisdom of reading so many of your books. Blackmail. Brilliant."

Sinto gritted his teeth. An inferno was eating its way through his arm.

Audrey growled. "This is between you and my father. Why are you punishing me? Why would you make Blake suffer?"

"Your friend, this *Blake*, is not suffering," Ianthe snapped. "We are the ones who have suffered. Because of your father and others like him, many of my people live in fear of exploitation, of extinction. We are one of the most intelligent species on Earth and because we are few in number, it is we who must hide, who are imprisoned at the bottom of the sea and in the withering world of Merluma."

Audrey's demeanor shifted, a new tactic. Her gaze softened, so did her brow.

"I'll do it, I'll tell my father anything you want. But." She fixed his mother with a steely gaze. "Only if you let Blake go. Now, with me."

Dark clouds swirled in his mother's eyes. She thrust out her chin and glared down her nose at the fierce young woman brave enough to challenge her.

Sinto's heart sang with pride.

"I've already made my decision," his mother said. "Blake will remain in my care until your assignment is complete."

Sinto leaped to Audrey's side. "Please, Mother, do as she asks, you can trust her."

His mother studied Audrey for a brief moment. "I think not. She is born of her father's seed, and she is broken. I have seen what he has done to her. Sad, but true."

Audrey stepped forward, tears bursting from her eyes. "I'm nothing like my father. I will do as you ask... more! Please, let Blake go!"

"You will need to be much stronger than that if you are to convince your father."

Audrey trembled, drew a jittery breath, held it, exhaled long and slow. She unclenched her jaw, wiped her cheeks with her shirtsleeve, laid her braid across her shoulder, smoothing it. The color of her aura shifted from red to peach to purple.

Sinto sensed the frustration that fueled her determination. One that gave Audrey an inner strength far beyond what his mother may realize.

Audrey looked his mother in the eye and said, "Prove to me he's alive."

His mother's fingers twined around a lock of her hair. It was a subtle gesture. Audrey did not know what it meant, but Sinto did—a flinch. After a beat of silence she said, "Certainly. Show her, Sinto."

49

Telling Kiss

Sinto lead Audrey through the winding tunnels carved in stone back the way they came before, before her heart was shattered to pieces. He detoured from the main tunnel and stopped at the lip of a bottomless shaft. From the darkness came the sound of rushing water and a musty scent.

He spread his arms. "Together, we go." Audrey reluctantly pressed her back to his chest and he embraced her. She felt his heart pound, heard his ragged breath, sensed his hesitation.

He jumped and together they fell, swift and blindly into the darkness, that musty scent growing stronger. Her heart gathered in her throat and she wondered if Sinto had planned this: young lovers caught in the cross-fire of a long and bitter dispute between families, suicide their only hope of escape. She closed her eyes and accepted it. Maybe Blake was dead and it was her turn to die.

But they didn't splat at the bottom. Sinto pumped his tail, slowing their descent, then made a sudden swerve. Her hip slammed against the wall, a sharp pain jolting her back to the moment. They traversed through another series of caves, into an entirely new world carved into the depths of Earth's ocean. Dim orbs of fire lit the way. The further they traversed, the thicker and more stale the oxywater became.

Her guilt turned to anger. How long had it been since that fateful day? *Weeks,* she fumed. She had been tricked, entertaining Blake's captor while he was left to rot beneath the bottom of the ocean. Sinto once warned her: *A weak mind can be easily manipulated.*

Not weak. A fool too blind to see.

The cave ended. Sinto released her in front of a crack in the wall sealed in green; the same color as his eyes. Sinto undoubtedly controlled the lock.

Oxywater sat heavy in her lungs. The weight of the ocean and rock pressed down. She feared what waited inside.

Sinto turned her to face him. She sensed he wanted to say something, but didn't give him a chance.

"Open it."

Obediently he pressed his palm against the seal.

Audrey stepped inside a large hollowed-out cavern. Cool, fresh oxywater filled her lungs. Tiny balls of fire hovered high above like stars in a night sky. The white stone floor curved outward from the cavern's center like the petals of a giant moon flower. Perched in its center was a transparent bubble, radiating heat and light. Blake lay inside.

She slid down the sloped floor to the bubble, placed her hands on its surface, and felt the pulse of life within. Her fear lifted. Blake was curled up like a fetus in a womb, sleeping peacefully, oblivious to his plight.

She gently slapped the bubble. "Blake, wake up," she whispered. "Show me you're okay. Wake up so I can promise to take you home where you belong."

Blake's face floated inches from hers, but he might as well have been a million miles away.

She sensed Sinto standing behind her. She glanced back. "Please, let him go."

"I can't."

"Let him go and—I'll forgive you."

His voice caught. "I'm sorry, but, I *can't*."

At first glance, she thought Blake was healthy; then she noted the pallor of his skin, the hollow of his cheeks and eyes. Despair overcame her. "Blake, wake up! Show me you're alive!" She pounded the walls of the bubble. Sparks flew; Blake's body jolted and rolled to the other side, still unconscious.

"Look at him! He's dying!"

"He's not dying, he's in a state of hyper-sleep. That's why he looks like that. All of his physical needs are attended to, and when he wakes up, he won't remember a thing. I give you my promise."

"How can I trust you? You took him from me. Tricked me. Made me fall in love with you!"

"Tricked you into falling in love with me?" His eyes suddenly glistened. "That's not possible—love is born of the heart, not by a trick to the mind."

"Please tell me this wasn't a game. Tell me that not once did you lie to me."

His face wadded up. "I never meant to hurt you."

She closed her eyes. He had lied. Lied about Blake that day back on Merluma, when she asked him if he had seen Blake when he found her in the Salish Sea. A lie that cut deep. She gathered strength from what her father had taught her; numb all emotion, focus on purpose, line up the target, and strike when they least expect it.

She breathed deep to quell the nausea in her stomach and knife burrowing in her heart. "Too late."

"No, it's not too late, we'll find a way."

"Find a way? Find a way for *what*? To turn back time? To manipulate my mind and make me forget?"

She felt his despair and her heart awakened. He was dying inside the same as she. She felt the urge to comfort and forgive. But—but how? How did she know what Sinto was feeling?

She ground her fists in her temples. The warmth of Blake's bubble pressed against her back, Blake blissfully asleep inside. Sinto lied, made her believe Blake was dead. That Sinto found her alone in the Salish Sea. All the while Blake lay in this deep dark place like an abandoned object. A part of his plan to fulfill his mother's bidding. A clever ruse, one she swallowed whole.

Yet...

Her very being quivered with a desire to forgive him from the depths of her soul.

It made no sense and she loathed her weakness.

Sinto looked equally confused, feverishly kneading his right arm. Watching him made her own arm twitch with a deep-rooted itch.

"What's happening to me? Is this another mind trick?"

Sinto shook his head. "What you feel... it's not a trick."

"How do I know you're not lying?"

"I lied to you before, yes, but not now. I can't explain why, at least not here or now. But believe me when I say I can no longer lie to you without incurring great angst and pain."

Her heart clenched at his honesty. She believed he spoke the truth.

How did she know that as certainly as she did?

She got an idea. A test. The idea of which made her heart drum and belly quiver expectantly.

"Vow to return him unharmed and seal it with a kiss. A kiss never lies."

"What?" He stepped back, eyes whipping around the vast cavern. "Now?"

At first he looked doubtful, scared even, then his face hardened with purpose. His gaze locked on Blake floating in the bubble. His eyes sparked with fire and crackled with victory as if he was an alpha claiming his mate.

"He will be returned unharmed. I promise."

Then he pulled her into his arms and did as she asked.

His kiss sparked an explosion in her heart. The deep-rooted itch in her arm turned to fire and spread to every cell in her body. A war raged; the urge to push him away, the urge to never let go. She feared losing him as certainly as the fear of running out of air. Of drowning in the dark ocean depths. That there was nothing he could do or say to change the way she felt. That she forgave him no matter what he had done...

How can I be so deeply and madly in love with him? I must stop this insanity!

Audrey pushed him away. He stumbled and fell to his knees. She looked away. She didn't trust herself. Blake lay in the bubble like a discarded rag doll and here she was wooing his captor and wanting more. All she desired in that moment was Sinto. Only Sinto. Forever and ever. A man who knowingly lied to her.

Yet...

She knew he was being sincere, an innocent victim like herself; she felt it acutely in her thrumming heart.

Damn Ianthe! Damn my father!

He was hers, and she his. How could she feel so certain?

She had to get away. She needed to think. To distance herself from him, or else regret doing the unthinkable. To run away with him and never look back.

She stiffened her spine and stifled a sob. "I want to go home. Please. Take me, now."

50

Another Way

A SHIVER STARTLED AUDREY back to consciousness. A gust of wind wrapped her in a biting cold embrace. A dark and ominous sky hovered. Andrews Island. The beach where she had called Sinto from the Salish Sea, giddy and naive to his true intentions.

She clenched a fist full of sandy pebbles in her hand. She screamed and threw it. Her head throbbed, stomach burned, heart felt ripped in two, and the incessant itch in her arm drove her crazy. She screamed again. Raindrops fell from the sky. Coin-sized and reluctant at first, then giving way to a deluge, soaking her to the bone. She felt a hundred years old but none the wiser.

She sat up. *Blake's alive!* The world spun, nausea surged, overwhelmed with this truth. She stood, knees weak, body shivering. *And my father, he's—he's—*

She threw up.

Moonstone swept down from the treetops and landed at her feet.

"Go away, Moonstone!"

He stared at her incredulous.

"You spy! Traitor! Never come back!"

He quirked his head, stepped aside. "Bah-ha-ha," he softly chirped when she stomped by.

"I'm not kidding! Go away! Shoo!"

She felt guilt for yelling at Moonstone. A pawn, like her, in a sick game between her father and Ianthe. As much as guilt tore at her, she couldn't bring herself to look back. Best to forget her new feathered friend. Moonstone reminded her of Sinto. Thinking of him hurt too much, like suffocating.

Stumbling through the forest back to the dock, she fumed about her father. Why did she have to pay for his mistakes? He made her life all about him. She hated the idea of running home and seeking his help, admitting that he was right; she wasn't safe. Because of him! And once she told him her tale, he would never let her out of his sight. He made that point quite clear.

Not happening. Ever again.

And Sinto. Damn him! She was too furious to untangle all the reasons why fate brought him into her life. Twice. Everything she loved stolen from her. Her mother, her budding relationship with Blake. Her future, her heart. Stolen. When would she ever get to claim her life as her own?

Damn fate! Damn them all!

When she reached the dock where Roy's boat waited, she took off the necklace Sinto made for her. A heavy chain wrapped around her heart. She held it over the water in her fist. All she had to do was open her fingers, let it drop. Break the connection. Good riddance. No going back. She shook to her core, fist hovering. Fire erupted in her arm. A knife pricked her heart. A gasp of frustration.

She couldn't do it!

She threw the necklace into the cockpit of Roy's boat and screamed, the remnants of it echoing across the water and bouncing back.

She hopped on the boat. Dug the key out of a storage locker. Unlocked the cabin door. Started to enter but stopped mid-step. She looked back at the necklace lying in the cockpit.

An idea sparked. One that made her smile.

There was another way. Always another way. A way to get Blake back without involving her father. She retrieved the necklace and stuck it in her pocket, then fired up the engines and set a course for Friday Harbor.

And I know just the person to help.

51

Schemer

AUDREY SPENT THE NEXT day plotting out her plan and gathering things she needed. It was Sunday; Ryan would be returning from his weekend in Vancouver that evening.

She impatiently waited in her dorm room for him to return, whiling away the time anxiously going over the details of her plan, sitting on her unmade bed, with the same unread books and unwritten papers piled high on her desk.

She munched down a turkey sandwich and a giant-sized bag of extra-greasy kettle chips she had picked up from a local deli. She did everything possible to avoid others. She was too distracted, fearing she'd run into someone she knew and say something stupid. What would she have to talk about anyway? That an ocean-dwelling merman stole her heart, and that Blake was alive and locked up at the bottom of the sea?

She checked the ferry schedule, guessing Ryan would be taking the six o'clock ferry to the island. The app on her phone confirmed it had been on time. She waited another fifteen minutes, then rushed to Ryan's room.

A blast of heat hit her face when he opened the door. He fixed her with bloodshot eyes and winced. It looked like his hair hadn't seen a brush since he left, sticking up in every direction.

"I see you're working hard on our research paper," she said.

He rubbed his forehead with the heel of his hand. "You missed a hell of a weekend." His voice was rough, lacking sleep. She pressed by, raking her fingers through his disheveled hair.

If only you knew.

She kicked off her shoes and leaped on his bed. "So spill. How was it? Did ya get lucky?"

Ryan plopped down at his desk opposite her. A sly grin crossed his lips. "Maybe it's good you didn't come."

"What? So I couldn't scold you for sharing your prized man-bits with just anyone?" His fair-skinned cheeks turned crimson. It was rumored Ryan was quite talented with the ladies. It wasn't that he was a hunk, quite the opposite; he was a little pudgy but cute and cuddly in a teddy bear sort of way. He claimed his reputation had to do with his intuitive grasp of female physiology, not his looks. "Blond or brunette?"

"Brunette, blue eyes. You know what a sucker I am for blue eyes."

"Of course." She smirked. "Don't know why I bother asking anymore."

"And you? How's *Daddy*?"

Audrey grabbed a pillow, rolled onto her back hugging it to her chest, and stared at the ceiling. Lying was a funny thing, the way your face burns and your armpits suddenly become clammy, maybe because the synapses in your brain fire hotter when you lie than when you tell the truth. "Daddy's *fine*."

"Uh oh, what'd he do this time?"

Audrey laughed. "I'm not sure you would believe me." She tossed the pillow aside and rolled onto her stomach. "Got anything to eat?"

Ryan rummaged in the mini-fridge under his desk. He held up two long-necked bottles. "Beer is food." He flipped the top off one and handed it to her.

She grinned. "My father wouldn't be very happy to learn how you've indulged me."

"Eh, whatcha got, a few more weeks till you turn twenty-one?"

"Something like that." Audrey gulped down some liquid courage. "Okay, so I lied. I didn't go to Seattle. I went somewhere I shouldn't have and met someone my father wouldn't approve of. He'd kill me if he found out."

He chuckled. "That's not a lie, that's a defense mechanism."

She blew out a nervous breath. "But it—it didn't end so well."

Ryan slammed down his beer. Bubbles burst from the top and beer overflowed on his desk. "Did this *someone* hurt you?" Her courage melted faster than the frost on her beer bottle. She sucked in her lower lip to stop it from quivering. He sat forward, elbows on knees. "Tell me what happened."

"It's not what you think."

"Who? Someone from school?"

She shook her head. "No one from around here."

"If he hurt you, if he touched you in a way he shouldn't have—I'll kill him myself."

"He didn't touch me, not like *that*." The inside of her arm suddenly felt like she'd been stung by a wasp, with the sting starting as a deep ache and slowly building to a prickly burn. She rubbed it with her opposite hand. "He sort of lied to me, and wasn't entirely truthful about some pretty important stuff."

She wanted to say, *Like the fact he kidnapped our friend and said nothing when I thought he was dead.*

Ryan sighed. "Get used to it, happens all the time."

"Duh! Not stupid! Just saying!"

He raised his hands in surrender. "Geez, Aud, chill. You came to me, remember?"

She pressed her beer against the inside of her arm. The coolness helped to ease the burn. "You're right, I'm sorry. I came to see you because... I need your help."

"You want me to rough him up?"

"Not exactly." She nibbled her lip. "We can't hurt him, I just want to—to keep him locked up for a while." A question mark etched itself between Ryan's bloodshot eyes. "We'll need to assemble the underwater cage, the one in the storage shed down on the docks, and lash it to the pilings where the water is deepest. No one else can know, only you and me."

He grabbed another beer from his fridge and popped it open, then sucked down half of it. "You want me to participate in a kidnapping *and* murder?"

"No! Absolutely not! No one's going to be harmed."

"Does this have something to do with that nonsense you were spouting the other day about super-beings that live in the sea?"

She closed her eyes and nodded.

"Did you even consider calling that therapist? I mean, if you want me to believe you, I'm going to need a little more convincing than crazy talk."

"Hear me out, Ry, it's true, and I'm going to prove it to you, and when you see this guy for yourself, it's going to blow your mind!"

"I'm not saying I agree yet, but say I do... How do you plan to get this guy to the cage?"

"I'm going to lure him to Roy's boat and bring him here. That's where you come in."

"What are you going to use to lure him?"

She wagged her eyebrows. "Me, of course."

Beer exploded from his mouth. "No way, not if he's dangerous."

"I said he lied. He wouldn't physically hurt me."

Ryan finished his beer in two gulps, tossed the empty bottle under his desk, and crossed his arms. "Then what? I get a good look and we let him go?"

"Um... not exactly, it's complicated."

"How complicated?"

She sucked a deep breath, let it go. "Blake's alive."

Ryan's eyes bugged. "What? You have proof?"

"I saw him, Ry, saw him with my own two eyes. Safe and alive. Please believe me. It's complicated… and it's tangled up with my father's past. You're going to have to trust me. It would be best if you don't know everything."

"This sounds like a very, very bad idea…" His voice trailed off, then his face paled. "Oh shit, this isn't a supernatural mafia-like thing, *is it?*"

She sat up. "Absolutely not. Look, all I need is for you to have the cage ready."

"Does Roy know about you planning to heist his boat?"

"Uh… not really, he loaned it to me for the weekend, and technically, he gave me the okay to borrow it anytime."

Ryan rubbed his temples with his thumbs, the indulgences from his weekend deeply etched across his brow. "Maybe I should come along."

Audrey flinched. "No!"

Ryan's eyes narrowed in suspicion.

"Look, this guy is incredibly perceptive. To pull this off my act will need to be genuine. He'll bolt if he suspects anything."

"I'll hide."

"He'll know you're there. Don't ask me how, but he'll *smell* you, or *hear* you. I have to do this alone. I can't screw this up. Blake's life depends on it."

"You're doing this for Blake and no other reason?"

The burning in her arm was driving her mad. *Was there another reason?*

She swallowed and said, "Absolutely. No other reason. Let me prove to you Blake is alive."

"When are you leaving?"

"Tomorrow, before dawn."

He glared at her for several moments, then said, "I'll have the cage ready, but only if you promise not to do anything stupid. And I want a running report—texts saying where you are, once you have him, when you're leaving, if you get into trouble. Promise?"

"Of course."

"And if what you say is true, then when this is all over you are going to the therapist, got it?"

"Of course."

"You better be telling the truth about Blake."

"I bet my life on it."

"Heaven help me," he muttered.

52

Thief

Nine hours later, Audrey drove to the marina with her stomach in a tangle of knots. It was dark and the streets of Friday Harbor were desolate.

After agreeing to help, Ryan had continued to grill her about her father and what he would do if he found out what she was up to. She reassured him her father would understand her reasons for doing what she was doing, a lie that felt flimsier and flimsier each time she told it. Eventually, he dropped it, much to her relief.

Guilt goaded her. Not just from sneaking around behind her father's back and lying, again, to Ryan, but because, officially, she was stealing Roy's boat.

She looked at the canvas bag lying next to her on the passenger seat. Stealing wasn't the only thing she was going to do; she would be desecrating Roy's boat too. She placated her guilt by placing blame where it lay and drove on.

This is Father's fault. He can compensate Roy for the damages.

She parked Blake's Pathfinder down the street from Roy's marina. Nothing stirred. The moon was a slip of a smile in the sky. A million stars winked over the harbor. The water reflected the sky like a mirror.

She gathered her things as quietly as possible. Slung a canvas bag across her shoulder, heavy with weapons of mass destruction she had gathered before her conversation with Ryan. A battery-powered drill, heavy-duty stainless-steel latch plus screws, and a Master padlock she'd stolen from a maintenance closet at school. She'd purchased a tube of marine-grade caulk the guy at West Marine claimed dried fast and held like welded steel. At the time she had laughed, claiming it would be more than she needed, but now she wondered if steel would be strong enough to contain Sinto.

She scurried down the dock to Roy's boat, dug the key from the outside locker, and slipped inside. She set down the bag with a loud *clunk.*

First step was to secure the forward hatch so the caulking would have time to set. She grabbed the caulk and the caulking gun from the bag and crawled into the forward cabin. She opened the hatch, poked her head out.

Nothing stirred but her clouded breath.

She sliced the tip off the tube of caulk with her pocket knife, slipped the tube into the gun, and pumped the trigger. She had never applied caulking before, but thankfully the guy at West Marine was real talkative and helpful. *Like decorating a cake,* he'd said. *Lay it on real thick.* She had laughed at that too, as if she had any idea how to decorate a cake.

She ran a liberal bead around the hatch opening. It was a messy application, with some places much thicker than others—just like she liked her frosting.

She dropped down, pulled the hatch closed, and twisted the handles, locking it securely. Caulk oozed around the seal.

Next, she mounted the latch on the forward cabin door, whispering a silent apology to Roy when she drilled one too many holes in the perfectly varnished wood. She tested closing the door several times, flipping the latch, and slipping the padlock through the loop, perfecting the sequence of movements, knowing she might only have a second or two to act. She hid the open padlock in a drink holder next to the driver's seat.

The boat was ready to go.

She checked her watch: 6:39 AM. Twenty-one minutes ahead of schedule. She stole a glance up the dock to Roy's apartment located on the second floor of his business. Audrey knew he was an early riser, but every window in his apartment was dark. Even though he was hard of hearing, she feared he would recognize the low rumble of his boat's engines firing.

She untied the dock lines, gently pushed the boat from the slip and hopped on, starting the engines at the last possible moment.

The rumble shattered the silence. A light clicked on in Roy's apartment.

For a second she considered going back, but the damage to Roy's boat was done. Ryan was busy assembling the cage. She had made a silent promise to Blake.

She pushed the throttles forward. Didn't look back.

She had planned for this. It wouldn't take long for Roy to figure out who the thief was, and he would call Ryan. Ryan would tell Roy she was upset the night before and had said something about coming back too soon, that she still needed to be alone. Ryan would placate Roy, convincing him to be patient and to wait for her return. It would be dark for another hour, with plenty of time to get to Andrews Island and set the trap for Sinto. Even if Ryan failed, she would be back with Sinto before Roy could organize a search party.

Easy peasy.

The lights from Friday Harbor slipped away. It felt like flying on the far side of the moon, and she was forced to navigate in the dark. Not being able to see played tricks on her mind and at first she spun the boat in circles. It went against all her instincts not to look beyond the windshield, but she glued her eyes to the electronics screen and navigated solely by GPS and radar.

Thirty minutes later, she reached her destination. Her eyes burned from staring intently at the bright screen, afraid to blink for fear she would miss a marker or strike one of the many submerged reefs sprinkled throughout the islands. As she neared Andrews Island she breathed a little easier, having avoided hitting a log or an island of tangled kelp that littered the water this time of year.

She idled down and used the spotlight to find the opening to the cove. She tied the boat to the dock, shut down the engines, and checked the time on her phone: 7:26 AM.

The eastern sky began to brighten. A ruckus of chirps and tweets filled the trees kissing the edges around the cove.

Audrey grabbed her backpack. Preparing the forward cabin to hold Sinto was her original plan, but Ryan had suggested another less aggressive tactic: sleeping pills.

She set out a thermos, mugs, spoons, tea bags, and several packets of sugar on the dinette table. She dug the pills from Ryan out of her pocket. He suggested giving Sinto a double dose, enough to knock him out for several hours but not enough to harm him. She dropped them into one of the mugs and picked up the spoon to crush them to powder, but stopped. While Sinto claimed to be human there were profound differences in his anatomy.

The spoon wavered over the mug.

What if the drug causes adverse effects? What if he has an allergic reaction? What if the pills put him in a coma? What if the pills don't work at all? What if the lock to the forward cabin can't hold him? What if the guy from West Marine was wrong about the strength of the caulk?

Her well-laid plan was unraveling fast.

She broke out in a sweat and dropped the spoon, exasperated.

Stick with the plan!

Before she could change her mind, she grabbed the spoon and crushed the pills to powder.

She patted her chest, confirming the necklace was safely tucked beneath her sweater. Her hands were shaking by the time she slipped on her coat. She was so worked up about the pills, she almost forgot to grab a flashlight and a blanket.

By the time she reached the beach, her stomach was a writhing mess.

She set her things on a log and walked to the water's edge, where waves gently tumbled the colorful stones that made up the beach. The soft clacking soothed her nerves.

She tugged the necklace from under her sweater and rubbed the claw between her fingers. But something was different from before. The claw was stone cold and the silver lacked spark. In contrast, her arm was on fire, a maddening sensation that ebbed and flowed, intensifying as time passed, spreading from her arm to her heart and back, like a looping band of hellfire.

She looked down at the spot where it burned the hottest. She rubbed her arm, alarmed. It felt like a hardened knot of muscle or an inflamed tendon. Otherwise, the skin was flawless. The tender redness she had noted the day before was gone. She decided it was nothing of importance and turned her focus back to the claw pinched between her fingers.

Sinto, where are you?

She wrapped the blanket around her shoulders and sat against a log, watching for a glint of golden hair or flash of green emerging from the water.

She even searched the sky for Moonstone.

Nothing.

She suddenly felt like an idiot. She had trashed a nice man's boat. Dragged her best friend into a potentially dangerous situation. Wasted precious time while Blake continued to languish. Maybe she should have come clean to her father, full stop.

Sinto wasn't coming. Why would he? He was a prince in an underwater kingdom! Girls were probably fighting over him at this very moment, begging him to take them home after a night of *Ballorue*, sucking down sucuvita, and twining their tails in a knot.

Why would he want a stupid Sapien girl like me?

But her mind refused to believe. She relived every detail of their parting kiss; the way his breath came in a rush, his hesitation, his questioning. And when he finally succumbed, the way he trembled and his lips fevered.

A kiss *never lies...*

Or so she thought.

An exasperated breath. She was exhausted. Her eyelids felt like steel curtains. She cast the blanket aside and yanked off her coat. Cool air prickled her skin. She glued her gaze at the water, determined to stay awake.

He will come, she told herself, *if I wait long enough, he will come...*

53

Playing With Fire

AUDREY WAS TANGLED IN a blanket fast asleep on a bed of pebbles and sand. Ribbons of pink velvet swept across the eastern sky, coloring the tips of her lashes and washing her lips a rosy glow. Her eyes danced behind their lids, dreaming.

She whispered Sinto's name.

The sound of her voice brought him to his knees.

The Mark screamed, *"Take her!"*

His mind screamed, *"Flee!"*

The Mark smoldered while his heart hammered and loins prickled.

He jumped to his feet and stumbled to the edge of the forest, far from the web of her aura and intoxicating scent.

It was a mistake to come, but a single purpose moved him. One did the Marking, while the other completed the Joining. It was impossible for him to ignore her. He had fought the urge to initiate the Joining that night at Club Ballo when Audrey first presented the Mark, and later when she begged him to take her in Naiada's room. If she offered again, he wondered if he would have the strength to stop it.

The myth of the Mark stipulated that if he failed to complete the Joining he would go mad. Though the details were scarce on that aspect. Wantemo had told him nothing beyond the superficial and Sinto suspected that was because he didn't know what the Joining entailed, how long after the Mark was presented it was to be initiated, or how long he had before he went mad. So it nearly killed him to leave her on this same beach when she asked him to bring her back, believing she would never want to see him again. But here she lay, having summoned him through the Mark and calling him from her dreams.

Audrey flinched and cried out.

He crossed the sand in a flash and knelt beside her, afraid something was wrong. But she was still asleep, living out a dream. Her feet kicked, her body writhed, and her hand feverishly kneaded the Mark buried in her arm.

She whimpered, "Sinto, help me—it burns—please, make it stop."

Fire rushed through his veins. The Mark beckoned, driving him to satisfy her wish. Ready to accept wholeheartedly. He pulled her into his arms and kissed her.

Audrey responded hungrily, but when she opened her eyes, her brow scrunched in confusion.

She pushed him away. "What are you doing?"

Reluctantly, he yielded. It was a curse of the Mark he was quickly becoming aware of; he had to obey her requests and be keen to her wants and needs. It was a lopsided partnership, in which the one who was Marked was slightly disadvantaged from the one who presented. He suspected that once they completed the Joining, then they would be balanced as equals, like two halves making a whole.

"I'm sorry—I thought you wanted—you called my name."

She sat up, brushed sand from her fingers, and smoothed her braided hair. "I—I guess I did." She briefly looked bewildered, then she cast a smoldering gaze. "I had to see you."

Sinto's chest swelled with relief. "I never intended to hurt you or your—"

She put a finger to his lips. "Shh." She smiled. "I forgive you."

Something about her smile was odd but her words were magic. He grabbed her hand and kissed her fingers. "You have done something to me. I have never felt like this before."

She extracted her hand from his lips and tucked a lock of hair behind his ear. "Oh, Sinto, what happened between us happens every day, friends become *more* than friends. They become *beyond* friends."

"We have become more than beyond friends."

"What do you mean?"

Blood roared in his ears; his body was not preparing to *talk* about it.

She said, "Enemies, perhaps?"

"No! That's not what I meant." Sinto tore his eyes from her face and stared at the sea. "Not everyone is destined to find a true mate, but when they do, they can never rest until they accept the truth."

"Are you saying that's what's happening to us? Oh, no, no. No! Maybe you go that fast in your world, but let's rewind a bit." She gave him a suggestive smile. "You do mess around, don't you? I mean, running around mostly naked, pressing flesh late into the night, doing that thing you call *Ballorue*. Those people at the club weren't cruising for a *true mate*. They were clearly seeking something of a more physical nature."

"Of course we seek comfort with others. Like you, we have desires, physical needs to fulfill."

"You mean, sex?"

His heart pounded its way up his throat. "Yes."

She touched his shoulder and teasingly circled her finger down his arm, stirring things she had best not stir. "Well, I have needs of a sexual nature too."

She pulled off her sweater, exposing an undershirt with thin straps and tiny satin bows sewn across a dipping neckline. His gaze fell to her pert nipples encircled by dark orbs which he could clearly see through the whisper-thin fabric.

"Audrey, no..."

"We started something we never had the chance to finish."

His breath came in short gasps, his control fleeting. If he lost control and let his desires take over, would he, in essence, seal their fate without her knowledge? Were these physical desires tied to the Joining or was it something different all together? He didn't know for certain, which infuriated him. Was the Mark driving her actions? She was playing with fire with no knowledge of why. He cursed his weakness and ignorance on the topic. Both were acting blind.

Why did I make her forget?

He knew the answer, as clearly as he could see the curve of her breasts and pert nipples.

Because it seemed like the right idea at the time.

But now...

She pressed closer, engulfing him with her delicious scent and swirling aura. "Do you agree?"

It took every ounce of strength to jump to his feet. "No, not like this."

"Why not?" She rose to face him. "No witnesses, a beautiful sunrise, on a beach," she glanced down at the blanket splayed on the sand. "How much more perfect could it be?"

"You don't understand." He cupped his hands on her shoulders and held her back. The fire in his arm and chest was unbearable. He ground his teeth and fought the urge to let go, to let her take him, her way, any way.

"Run away with me, Sinto."

He gasped. He wanted everything she offered and more. To be free of his obligations, to be free of the fire in his heart and the thirst on his tongue. To have her now and everyday forward.

His hands slipped from her shoulders. He cradled her face and pressed closer.

Before their lips locked she placed her hand on his chest, pushed him back. Then she gave him that queer smile. "Want me?"

"Forever."

She pinched his cheeks. "Cute, how about we make a deal?"

He leaned in again with his lips but she dodged them.

"I need an itty bitty favor..."

"Anything." It was the Mark talking, not his common sense. She could ask him to eat all the sand on the beach, and he would, without hesitation.

"Right answer." She pulled him to the ground and rolled atop him. When her lips found his they stayed there, kneading desperately. He found peace in that moment, knowing she forgave him, lying with her atop him. The fire in his arm quelled, the Mark temporarily satisfied—a reprieve to collect his thoughts and gather inner strength.

And it was in that moment of distraction that Audrey did the one thing that would unravel his carefully crafted control...

Her lips trailed from his lips to the slits on his neck. That place he warned her of that day on Merluma when he revealed what he was and she marveled at his unique features. A very sensitive place that, once caressed, as she was doing now, triggered an overwhelming carnal response.

Adrenaline roared through his veins. The Mark awoke with fevered impatience and fire erupted in his chest. He rolled her over and kissed her with a desperation that surprised him. Teeth cut flesh. Their mixed blood swirled in his mouth. Their entwined auras flared red. The Mark summoned him to act. It was time. He was ready for her to open her mind and invite him in. This time there would be no hesitation, no stopping.

He probed for the usual opening, but her mind was closed. Stubbornly guarded.

He grew desperate, launching an arsenal of mind probes. Invisible tentacles slithered through her hair, slipped inside her ears, up her nose, even past the corners of her eyes.

"Ow, ow, my 'ead, my 'ead—'op, *stop!*" she screamed past their locked lips.

His tentacles snapped back from where they came. He leaned back. What he saw shocked him.

Fear filled her eyes. Her lips were smeared with blood. He lay between her legs, the tips of his fluke pinning her feet.

He rolled off her, horrified. He didn't remember pinning her that way beneath his body or hurting her, only trying to connect with her mind and failing, miserably. He was too ashamed to even look at her.

He scrubbed his face with his hands and buried his head between his knees.

Leave her, forget her. Accept the madness.

Those thoughts infuriated the Mark. It launched an inferno incinerating everything inside. Its primal forces overwhelmed reason, controlling the physical. Not unlike when his mother wielded her full power, controlling his thoughts. A force not to be reckoned with. The thing controlling him now was the Mark, wielding a power that grew stronger every day. It would never stop until he bowed to its demands or died.

Did she feel the same way too? Sinto debated. He should tell her the truth, let her decide.

Audrey kneaded her temples. "My head—it feels like—being jabbed by a thousand tiny needles—were you..." Her eyes narrowed suspiciously.

"I—" Sinto winced and silence fell between them as he struggled to find the right words. No matter how clearly he stated the facts, the truth would scare her. It scared him. He had become a monster of her creation, one that would hunt her down to the ends of Earth, until she accepted him wholly and irrevocably. He would be asking her to risk everything for him.

Was that what he was afraid of, that she would reject him and he would be doomed to a life of madness?

"I never told you this, but Blake is—he's kind of..." she sighed heavily, "He's my boyfriend. You do know what a boyfriend is, don't you?"

"It means you're beyond friends. I gleaned that much from your books."

And by the way you looked at him when I showed you he was alive.

"I can't believe I betrayed him like that! You must think I'm..." She sucked on her lower lip where his teeth had cut her. "I'm so confused. When I thought he was dead, I buried him, then I met you, and just now... it was like he was gone again and all I wanted was—" She rolled her eyes. "I lost my head, like that night in Naiada's room."

Sinto gave her a sad smile. *It's because of the Mark,* he wanted to say, but instead he replied, "My mistake. I kissed you first." Then he tilted his head and pointed at the slits in his neck. "I thought I warned you. Next time stay away from my neck. My instinctual urges can be difficult to control, especially..."

The Mark writhed in his arm.

Tell her!

She stared back innocently, inviting him to say more, but the words got struck in his throat.

She shivered and scrubbed her hands across her arms, then reached for her sweater.

"I sure could use a hot cup of tea. Do you like tea?"

54

More Sugar

Audrey asked, "Ever been on a boat before?"

"No," Sinto quickly replied.

After their encounter on the beach, Sinto had grown quiet and pensive. He said nothing as they strode through the forest back to the boat. Audrey feared he'd grown suspicious.

Did he steal a peek into my thoughts? Did he discover my intent?

She decided to soldier on with her plan, so she hopped into the cockpit and opened the cabin door.

The wind had picked up, whipping treetops and rippling the surface of the cove.

Sinto fidgeted on the dock, tail twitching, and looking disheveled. His green skareef hung low around his waist, with the part that had been slung across his shoulder hanging to his knees. His eyes darted between the boat and the water. She held out her hand. He ignored it and hopped over the gunwale with ease. When he landed, the boat rocked and his fluke slapped the deck. He lost his balance along with his grace.

"Careful. It's different floating on top of the water."

He replied with a nervous grunt.

She gestured for him to enter the boat's main cabin. "Guests first."

He drew a deep breath, tucked his tail up along his spine, and took one step inside but no further. She squeezed past, closed the cabin door, and slipped into the forward seat of the dinette opposite the steering station. "I think you'll be more comfortable sitting."

He eased into the seat closest to the door. His eyes had that wild look about them, glowing like bright-green lightbulbs.

Her armpits grew clammy. A squirrel ran circles in her belly. She tried to act natural and smiled.

She tore open two tea bags and opened the thermos. A puff of steam escaped and bounced off the ceiling. She poured two packets of sugar into each mug, then the water. She stirred the mug with the crushed up sleeping pills with extra vigor, placed the tea bag in the water, then handed it to him.

"I like mine with lots of sugar."

"Of course, sugar, sweet." He took a sip, made a face.

"How is it?"

"Bitter."

"More sugar will make it taste better." She added two more packets of sugar, swirled it with the spoon.

He took another sip and smiled. "Better."

She knew he was lying by the way his lips flattened across his teeth and his tongue rolled up inside his mouth.

He took another sip, feigning enthusiasm. "Good. Hot. Sweet."

They anxiously sipped their tea, exchanging glances through swirls of steam filled with the essence of bergamot. The sound of lapping water reverberated through the hull.

Sinto smiled, she smiled back, then they both spoke at once.

"There's something I—" he said. "I didn't mean to—" she said.

Sinto laughed nervously. Audrey bit her lip.

He set down his mug. "You first." Audrey noted it was empty. He had calmed, too; his eyes were a soft velvety green and he relaxed back in the seat.

She set her own mug aside, ready to kill time until the sleeping pills did their trick. "I'm sorry I accused you of kidnapping Blake. I, of all people, should understand what it's like to be used by a parent."

He leaned on an elbow and propped his chin in the palm of his hand. She noted the slight waver in the movement and continued, buying time, "You want to know what my father is really like? He's obsessed! Always telling me what I can do, who I can hang out with, where I can go. He told me to stay away from the water, that it wasn't safe. Can you believe that?" She rolled her eyes. "I mean, I'm studying marine biology! And I'm sick and tired of doing what he tells me. Makes me want to do the opposite, just out of spite! What about you? Does your mother boss you around too?"

He nodded slowly.

"And did I ever tell you about my friend Ryan?" She rambled on about Ryan—how they met, what he looked like, that he grew up in hippie communes—until Sinto's eyes were stuck at half-mast.

She touched his hand. "Are you okay?"

He blinked, lids straining on the upswing.

"You look like you could use a bite to eat. I know a place in Friday Harbor that makes killer hash." Her eyes fell to his bare chest. She hopped up, started rummaging through drawers. "I think I have a pair of sweats that you could borrow..." She found the ones she had borrowed from Roy previously, held them up. "With these on, no one will know that you're a..."

He blinked. "Suure."

"You don't need to do a thing, just stay put and enjoy the ride." She started the engines. They rumbled and she had to shout over the roar. "It might not be as thrilling as tunneling through the sea, but I think you'll be amused."

She jumped down into the forward cabin to grab a couple of life jackets. Sinto watched with glassy eyes. She held up one of the life jackets and laughed.

"Guess you don't need one of these."

His head fell onto the mug sitting on the table and stayed propped like that for a beat. Then his head jerked up. "Ha. Ha." His face melted into the palm of his hand and his eyes slid shut.

The pills worked. Ryan was a genius.

Her phone vibrated. She dug it out from her back pocket. A text from Ryan.

Where the hell are you?

She nibbled her lip. *Got behind schedule, on my way now.*

She looked over at Sinto, face down on the table. *Pills worked great! He's out cold. Oh, I forgot to mention, bring rubber gloves.*

There was a short delay, then: ???

She chuckled, imagining what was going through his mind. *Will explain later. Rubber gloves. Don't forget, super important! See you soon!*

Her phone pinged one last time. *BTW Roy's roy-ally pissed. Hate to be you! Slave boy signing out.*

She cringed. Roy would be more than royally pissed when he saw what she had done to his boat.

She stuck her phone back in her pack.

Deal. With. It. Later.

She snapped the clips on her life jacket and cinched it tight. She wasn't going to take any chances in case things went sideways. She released the boat from the dock and slipped into the driver's seat.

Sinto was splayed across the dinette table, quietly snoring as she guided the boat out of the cove. She pushed the throttles forward, driving into oncoming waves whipped up by a stiff southeastern wind.

55

Hoodwinked

SINTO'S HEAD HIT SOMETHING flat and hard. His eyes felt glued shut. When he forced them open, his vision blurred. It felt like his head was pounding against a tree. His eyes focused. He blinked. He saw the distinct pattern of wood grain.

I am *pounding my head against a tree.*

He looked up. *Where am I?*

He was suddenly weightless, then his head slammed down with a crack.

The sound of rushing water alarmed him. He caught a glimpse out a window, then he remembered.

Audrey. A boat.

He leaned back, gripping the table with his hands, trying to focus on the white object rolling back and forth on its surface. It took a couple tries to grab it.

A cup. Tea.

After drinking it he felt strange and sleepy.

Audrey sat across from him. She gripped a metal spoke wheel, gaze forward with her brows set in a determined slash.

The boat fought the rough seas, bucking over the cresting waves, racing down the backside, and crashing into the trough in between, jarring him to the bone.

What an insane way to travel the sea!

They hit a monster wave. Audrey rolled the wheel back and forth and nearly fell from her seat. Sinto clung to the table. She exhaled a nervous breath once the boat cleared the wave.

She stole a glance in his direction and startled. She suddenly sat up straight, her eyes darting, her hands nervously clutching the wheel.

He rolled the cup in his hand, remembering.

"How is it?"

"Bitter"

"More sugar will make it taste better."

Bitter. Naiada said she tasted something bitter right before she got sick. Poison? But why would Audrey want to kill him? He struggled to think of other possibilities.

When Naiada had teetered on the brink of death he had asked the Scouts to dig up what they could find about Sapien drugs; chemicals to make them feel happy when sad, numb when in pain, sleepy when not tired.

His stomach clenched tight as a rock. The seductive act on the beach, an invitation for a cup of tea, the funny way she smiled. He remembered his mother's warning not to trust her, that she sensed she was like her father in many ways.

Sinto looked at the girl he thought he knew, watching the waves whipping by.

She's taking me somewhere.

The bitter taste of chemicals crawled from the depths of his throat. The world smeared; up felt like down. He slid to the edge of the seat and tried to stand. The boat lurched; he lost his balance and fell back on the table. His arms and legs didn't move right. He tried to think, but his mind was numb and his heart beat slowly in his chest. Even the Mark was tamed.

He felt rising panic. The drug coursed thickly through his bloodstream. It was a mighty struggle to keep his eyes open. All he wanted was to sleep. She must have slipped him something to knock him out. A depressant. That would certainly explain the reason she startled when she saw him staring at her. He knew time was needed for depressants to run their course. Time he did not have. Maybe he could burn it from his bloodstream. Speed up his internal clock.

But his merlux sputtered weakly in his chest. He tried revving it up, but it only sparked and fizzled. Like the Mark, tamed by the drug.

He fixed his gaze on the back door, his only means of escape. He gripped the table and stood up. Cramps stole his legs out from under him. He grabbed Audrey's arm for support.

"What did you give me?" His voice sounded distant and gruff.

"A taste of your own medicine." Her voice quivered and her eyes filled with fear as she grappled for a pair of silver handles on her far side.

She slammed them backwards.

The bow of the boat burrowed into the face of a wave and shuddered to a sudden stop. Things crashed to the floor. He was launched through a narrow doorway and into the pointy end of the boat.

Audrey jumped from her seat and slammed the door shut, trapping him inside. He heard the scrape of metal and a resonating click. A lock on the door.

Anger radiated through the Mark. His and hers. Both were angry for different reasons. His for being so stupid, hers at him for tricking her. He felt the urge to beat down the door as acutely as she felt the need to keep it locked. But he couldn't muster the energy, weakened by the drug she had slipped into his tea. He lay suffering, with the Mark's fury poisoning his essence.

So it begins... Madness.

The drug coaxed him to fall into the depths of slumber and he sank deeper into despair. She had rejected him, not knowing the consequences. If that was her final decision, so be it. Death would be his only hope for peace, and once he was gone, the Mark in her arm would shrivel and die, along with the yearning and the truth of it.

What better gift could I leave her, but my body to dissect? I could stop my heart and still my lungs and smother that part of my brain that makes me turn to ash upon dying. She could cut me up and ogle over every piece of me, put me on display for the scientific world to see. Is that not what she wants? To be a scientist of the sea? And what better discovery than being the one to expose me for what I am?

And long after she tires of poking my shriveling parts, she will be free to embrace her dark-haired lover, the one I foolishly tried to steal her from.

Sinto thought of those who might miss him: childhood friends, a distant cousin, his faithful bird Rave who Audrey so easily won over and renamed Moonstone. Sinto knew Wantemo would miss him and probably be a little disappointed. Sinto had failed to apply his wise lessons and fell for a Sapien girl named Audrey—daughter of their nemesis, Robert Culliford—which led to his ultimate demise.

He thought of his mother and father. Mother would also be disappointed and Father... well, who knew how he would feel, if he could feel at all. But it was Naiada he feared would miss him the most, and at such a tender age. He pictured her lying in her bed, calling his name, reminding him it was time for her treatment...

He drew a sharp intake of air. His eyes popped open.

Naiada will die without me!

He sat up, bracing himself with his hands on the low cabin ceiling, and berated himself for his selfishness. And for having blindly fallen victim to Audrey's trick without a thought to the consequences.

I must find a way to escape!

He shook off the dizziness as best he could and tried to fired up his merlux. It sparked to life, but barely. Electrical current slowly trickled through his veins. He worked his muscles and joints, starting with his fingers and toes. His mind cleared a little and his eyes began to glow, filling the small cabin with green light. Adrenaline flowed alongside the electrical current that swirled through his bloodstream. He felt his strength slowly return. He slid from the bunk to his feet, landing solidly on the floor.

The engines continued to rumble and water gurgled past the speeding hull. He still had time to escape. He pressed his shoulder against the door. It was solid and unforgiving.

He looked for another way out. Hope kindled when he saw the glass hatch in the ceiling directly above the V-shaped bunk. He climbed up, stood on his knees, and turned the hatch handles. He pushed but met solid resistance. He rolled to his feet with bent knees, placed his back to the glass, and drove up. The hatch refused to budge.

He noticed white globs of something that oozed from the seal, hardened but still sticky as if recently applied. He had seen this stuff before on sunken boats, a glue-like sealer the Sapiens used to plug holes and seal windows. *Clever girl*, he thought. She had anticipated he would try to escape. But there was one important thing she failed to consider. Heat.

The hatch was made of glass with a metal ring. He lay on his back with his feet pressed to the glass and stirred the current running through his bloodstream, collecting it. If he could heat the glass, it might soften the seal just enough to make it pliable and weak.

He funneled the current to the bottoms of his feet. The glass heated and the metal ring began to spark. He coiled, focusing every ounce of his energy into it. He popped up his hips and kicked the hatch like a snake, striking its prey.

The hatch tore free of its hinges and became a speck in the sky.

56

Miscalculation

AUDREY GASPED WHEN THE hatch cover exploded off the forward deck. Sinto jumped from the hole and landed in a crouch with his hands splayed against the windshield, glaring back at her. She could feel the heat radiating from the glass where he touched it. His eyes were bright as the sun.

"Stop the boat!" he screamed.

Her throat constricted. Her hands froze on the wheel.

He pounded the windshield with his fists. "Stop the boat!"

Terrified, she whipped the wheel hard to port.

Sinto lost his footing and smashed into the stainless-steel rail. His feet slipped out from under him. He grabbed the rail to keep from falling overboard.

She whipped the wheel back and forth, trying to loosen him. He held tight by the crook of his elbow. His body slipped beneath the rail and he thrashed, trying to swing a leg up. His tail unfurled and slapped the side of the hull. Plumes of salt spray exploded from wave tops, clipped by his mighty fluke. He managed to wriggle back onto the deck and wedged himself on the narrow deck, between the rail and the side window, inches from her face.

Her heart pounded. He could easily escape. Why didn't he?

She set the autopilot, jumped up, locked the aft cabin door, doubled checked the padlock to the forward cabin, and slipped back behind the wheel. She set her gaze forward, trying to ignore the fire burning in her arm, his fiery gaze and thundering fists, the bitter taste of guilt rising from the pit of her stomach.

"Audrey, don't end it like this, stop the boat." His voice was raw and muffled by the screaming wind, the roar of the engines, the hull crashing against waves.

A bruise bloomed on his cheek and blood leaked from his nose.

Her chest knotted. Who was the monster now?

She gripped the throttles, debating what to do.

A large dark shadow passed overhead. Not a bird. Something much bigger.

Sinto whipped his face toward the sky. When he looked back, his eyes were wide and full of fear. He frantically pounded on the window. "Stop, before it's too late!"

The boat jolted from a sudden displacement of air. Then she heard it, the *whamp-whamp-whamp* of whipping rotors, pounding her ears. A black helicopter dropped into view, racing alongside, close to the surface of the water.

The helicopter popped up, out of her view. Its dark shadow loomed directly above. Four-inch metal darts rained, struck the windshield, and peppered the deck with a sharp *tink*-ing sound.

Sinto was gone in a flash.

Sea spray coated the windows, whipped up by the helicopter's rotors. She fumbled for the wiper switch but they did little to help. The rotor's wind skewed the wipers, sucking them from the glass. Salt spray and froth coated the windows. She was driving blind.

She scanned the decks for Sinto, turned, and saw him cowering in the cockpit, yanking on a dart stuck in his shoulder.

A second wave of darts rained, striking the inflatable dingy lashed to the top of the cabin and tearing away most of the lashing. Deflated and loosened from its ties, it slapped violently from the force of the wind—from the helicopter, from the speed she was traveling, from weather blowing in.

She looked back again. Sinto was still on the boat, back pinned to the aft cabin door, seeking what little protection he could find from the menace above beneath the overhanging lip of the cabin's roof. A third wave of darts rained. He danced as darts struck the deck at his feet.

The vibration and noise suddenly faded when the helicopter veered away.

Sinto rattled the doorknob. "Open the door!" he screamed.

The helicopter looped around, lining up for another assault from behind.

She slammed the throttles to their forward stops. The engines screamed. *Faster, faster, FASTER*, she willed the boat to go.

The helicopter filled the horizon as it drew up close behind. The assailants inside were obscured by dark windows. A side door slid open and a man in black leaned out and aimed a crossbow at Sinto, with deadly intent.

She swerved hard to starboard, then to port. Sinto was tossed like a rag doll, smashing into the cockpit gunwales, until he landed in a heap. He looked up. She could see him through the door's full-length window. Their eyes locked.

She opened her mouth to scream—for help, mercy, forgiveness—but all that came out was a feeble wisp of air. She didn't know who to trust anymore—the animal she had awoken in Sinto or the dark menace in the sky.

So she ran, as fast as Roy's little boat would take her to the nearest populated shore, oblivious to the high-pitched shrill and warning flashing on the GPS screen.

At thirty-five knots, the boat struck a rocky reef submerged just beneath the surface. Audrey slammed into the windshield. The hull peeled back like a sardine can, rolling open. The engines rang out before gurgling to silence.

57

Irrevocable Fate

Sinto was knocked senseless. The boat slid off the end of the reef and began to sink. His tail was tangled in a rope attached to the boat and it took him with it. Audrey was trapped inside, held buoyant by her life jacket, face up in a pocket of air. He freed himself from the rope and swam to the back door. It was still stubbornly locked. He swam around the cabin, pushing against windows, testing locks. One budged. He slid it open and squeezed inside.

Audrey's blood stained the water.

Sinto swam to her. A knot protruded from her forehead and her nose was skewed and bleeding profusely. He slipped into her mind and scanned her brain for signs of trauma or swelling. He pressed his hands across her body, testing for broken bones, bruised or torn organs.

He found nothing fatal.

He pinched her nose between his fingers, wriggled the bone and cartilage back to where it belonged, then stuck his smallest finger up each nostril, cauterizing broken vessels with electrical fire. Had she not been unconscious, her screams of pain would surely have undone him. He cradled her in silence as the boat settled on the marshy bottom, thankful she was alive.

The helicopter hovered; its mighty rotors flattened wind waves on the surface, sixty-feet above. Audrey jerked awake from the ruckus, dazed and glassy eyed. Her mouth worked failingly, until she found words, "What? Where... am I?"

Sinto had no time to explain. He had no doubt the men above would take her away after finishing him off with their deadly weapons. The dart that had found his flesh was filled with a powerful drug—one that tugged at his consciousness much more strongly than the one Audrey had slipped into his tea.

His vision doubled and heart beat erratically. Vertigo threatened to overcome him. Flueox from his merlux coursed through his blood and helped to counteract the worst of its effects. He fought to cling onto consciousness.

He dragged Audrey to the back door, flipped the lock, swung it open. The last of the air escaped. He pinched her nose, clasped his hand over her mouth, and dragged her out the door to open water.

She suddenly came to life, kicking and fighting. When they popped to the surface, she drew a rattled breath.

The helicopter quickly descended. Rotors churned the sea and sucked the breath from their lungs.

A man jumped and landed in the water beside them, eyes flashing, teeth gritted with determination. Sinto swam from his reach, Audrey held tight against his chest. He rolled, coiled his tail, and smacked the man in the head.

The man rolled to his back momentarily dazed. Sinto cupped his hand over Audrey's mouth and dove for the bottom.

Lorica bled from his pores. In his weakened state, he barely produced enough to wrap them both in a protective cocoon. Once filled with fresh oxywater, he pulled his hand from her mouth. She spit out a mouthful of water and gasped for air.

Three men circled in the water above like sharks catching a whiff of blood. Flashlights and spear guns probed the depths.

The drug soldiered through his body, striking him with waves of nausea and chills, eating away at his strength and his lorica.

Audrey squirmed in his arms. He coaxed her to be still but she ignored his pleas and fought to break free of his grip, back arching against his chest and kicking him in the shins. He drew every ounce of strength to still her, afraid his lorica would fail if stretched too thin. He grabbed her by the wrists and crossed his arms around her chest, pulling her tight against him. He wrapped his legs around hers in an effort to still her. Darkness winked from the strain.

"I have to tell you something."

She arched back, twisted left and right, grunting with frustration.

"Stop fighting me," he wheezed. "My lorica, it will fail."

Wisely, she stilled.

Sinto spun her around to face him, wrapped his tail around her back and pinned her to his chest, their noses nearly touching. His lorica flickered. He blinked to stay conscious, determined to tell her the irrevocable truth.

"I lied to you."

"Really?"

"Give me a chance to explain."

"What, that Mommy forced you, threatened to shred your brains if you didn't comply?"

"She didn't force me. I readily accepted her assignment, did what I thought was best for my people, and selfishly for me. I didn't fully consider the consequences, how much it would hurt you."

She drew a ragged breath. "Or my friend." A tear slipped from her eye. "You deceived me... How can I ever forgive you?"

The truth cut deep. And the forgiveness she spoke of on the beach was a lie, a trick so she could lure him to her boat and drug him. His grip slipped. She broke free and pulled back, stretching the walls surrounding them, dangerously thin. His lorica flickered and sparked.

He reached for her.

She pulled back. "Don't touch me."

His hand fell to his side, heavy as a brick. "Then hear my words. You *Marked* me, chose me to be your mate. All I feel and think about is you. All I am is *you*. I am weak and incomplete without you by my side."

He held out his right arm where the Mark bulged. "It waits here, the Mark, a coil of steely flesh shaped into a unique symbol representing us, united as one." He traced it with his finger. "A swirl, a circle, a connecting line. My world, your world, *connected*. You, me, bound forever."

Audrey grasped her arm, looked up. Her brow quirked.

"I know you feel it too. What I feel, you feel, physically and emotionally. We are connected, but not completely. I stopped us from finishing it, from *Joining*. That is why you may feel... conflicted."

Tears welled in her eyes. "That's what this is? You did this to me?"

"Not me, *we*. We did this, together, we chose each other. You took the first step by rendering the Mark and I accepted it. But it is up to me to initiate the final step. To fuse our essences together. On the beach... that was what I was trying to do, I didn't want to but—your advances—push me beyond control."

She hugged herself, her fingers mindlessly tugging at the fabric of her sweater, lower lip quivering.

Sinto ached to tell her it didn't need to be this way. They could run away as she had suggested. He knew places they could hide and carve out their own little world, far from the troubles in his city and the feud festering between their parents.

"When did this happen?"

"That night at Club Ballo."

He could no longer feel his shoulder where the dart had entered. His vision faltered and his lorica flickered, casting them into darkness for a brief moment. Time was running out; soon he would be too weak to support both of them and his lorica would disintegrate.

"Why don't I remember?"

"Because I…" He shivered. The drug from the dart had reached his heart and was slowly passing through his bloodstream, numbing every cell in his body.

"Because you made me forget." Her face wadded. "You told me that was taboo. I trusted you!"

He cringed. "I panicked. I didn't understand how you were able to Mark me. I don't fully know what it means; the how or why or what happens to us from this point forward." He clasped her gently by the shoulders, wagged his tail, began a slow ascent. The men still searched from above. Their beams of light pierced the depths.

"Why?"

"I was afraid."

"That your mother might kill one of us, like she did your sister?"

"I would never let her do that."

"Then why?"

"Because of something else—I'm running out of time—that dart—my lorica is—" A wave of darkness rolled over him, not from his failing eyes, but from his failing lorica. It sparked, but held, barely, glowing dimmer.

"What if I want this—this *Mark* to go away?"

"There's only one way."

"Death?"

"One of us."

A tear slipped down her cheek. He brushed it away with his finger.

"Neither of us have to suffer. Come with me, run away from all this."

"I can't…" She looked away. "I don't trust you anymore."

It felt like a knife pierced his heart. His vision faltered. He sucked a deep breath. The oxywater mix was off, lacking oxygen that he desperately needed.

His lorica contracted, wrapping its paper-thin skin around them.

Audrey's eyes grew wild with fear. "What's happening?"

Before he could answer his lorica disintegrated. The sea crushed in, casting them into darkness.

The gills in his neck flared. The sudden infusion of oxygen rejuvenated him enough to stave off unconsciousness.

He adjusted the lenses in his eyes to see clearly underwater. Audrey floated, eyes wild. He grabbed her and swam for the surface. Bubbles erupted from her mouth. She gaped, fingers clawing at his chest. He was too weak to form a new lorica. His only choice was to deliver her to the surface and into the hands of the waiting men.

But he didn't reach them in time. She heaved. Then her body stilled and gaze settled on nothingness. There was only one choice. He shoved her upward with a mighty swish of his tail, to the men above, believing they could save her. It destroyed him to let go.

He watched from below, his empty fingers reaching. The silhouette of her body slowly ascending, arms and legs splayed, buoyed by the air in her life jacket.

The helicopter descended, rotors thumping. Audrey broke the surface. The men grabbed her, shoved her into a basket, and drew her into the belly of their mechanical bird.

The helicopter lifted and retreated. The noise waned and the sea calmed.

The Mark's fire faded and grew cold. He could no longer feel her.

He sank to the bottom, knees settling into muck, hands cradling his head.

The Mark lay dead in his arm. He had no doubt what it meant.

He had been wrong. It was too late. The men couldn't save her.

Audrey was gone.

PART THREE

58

Stardust

AUDREY ORBITS A FIERY sun in a star-studded sky. She feels no pain or fear or the persistent ache from a heart torn in two. She is without memory of who she was or how she came to be in the orbit of this glorious sun. She feels no want, no need to find a new world and a body to fill.

But as suddenly as she settles into this calm place, she feels the quiver of disruption, the shadow of a fleeting thought, a distant memory of something unfinished buried deep within her vapored core.

And being ethereal without means to resist, she surrenders to this unfinished thing.

The fiery sun falters and flickers, its surface buckles and cracks, and when it implodes, it takes Audrey and everything around it with it. She becomes one with the stars and sun and unseen connective matter in between, a solid ball of the Everything folding in on itself in an endless crush of destruction, forming a dense black thing with no center.

It grows tinier and tinier and tinier until it turns inside out.

The Everything readies to spill and reanimate into something else.

But something is missing. Something vitally important.

So it is that destiny pierces this tiny, twisted, black thing before it can become something else.

The essence of Audrey Grey is spit out and sucked back to her previous life—to a future of uncertainty with a deep yearning unfulfilled and a purpose yet to reveal itself. Back to the world where a boy with exploding green eyes waits, to whom she is irrevocably bound, heart and soul, forever.

59

Back From The Dead

A THOUSAND NEEDLES PIERCED Audrey's chest.

Water exploded from her mouth.

Someone yelled, "She's alive!"

Her eyes cracked open, blurry at first, then her vision sharpened, filled with the face of a brown-skinned man with neatly trimmed brows and intense dark eyes.

"Breathe!" he screamed.

She tried but nothing happened. He stuck his fingers in her mouth, flattened her tongue and pressed his mouth to hers. Her lungs rose with his breath, then with her own. His eyes swelled with relief.

Before she could speak, another man with a pale face and round glasses pressed something over her nose and mouth. Pain radiated from the center of her face and shot through her temples. She tried to scream but the thing covering her face prevented her voice from escaping.

Cool air filled her lungs. Her vision sharpened once again, as did the pain wracking her body. The choppy pulse of a helicopter's rotors battered her ears.

A sea of men's faces hung over her. Her gaze locked on one in particular. The first man she saw, the one with perfectly groomed brows and brown skin like hers. A muscular man who moved graceful as a cat. The man she met on the dock in Friday Harbor. The one her father hired to find Blake.

Captain something...

The captain released the oxygen mask from her nose. The air was heavy with salt and sour sweat. He breathed a sigh of relief.

"Welcome back," he said. "You're one lucky lady."

She tried to sit up, but the man with the round glasses pressed her down.

"Lie still." He shined a light in her eyes.

She recognized his kind voice and the pale eyes behind his glasses. The man who had found her the night her mother died, scared and alone in her room, hiding under her bed. He was the one, not her father, who had comforted her in the days and years that followed.

"Dr. Wickman?" she whispered.

"You're safe now, Audrey." He drew a dose of clear liquid into a syringe. "But you must rest."

A prick and a sting. Coolness swam up her arm. The face of the kind doctor from her past blurred. The beat of rotors faded. Darkness greeted.

She succumbed to the peaceful calm she felt before opening her eyes, reaching for that strange place with a million stars and a fiery sun and that teeny tiny black thing that spit her soul out for some sudden and unknown reason.

60

Old Friend

THE NEXT TIME AUDREY opened her eyes, she was lying in a sterile white room that smelled of disinfectant and a pleasant cologne. A machine next to the bed softly beeped in rhythm with her heart. A bag of saline hung from a metal stand above her head. A clear tube snaked down and was plugged into a port inserted into her left wrist and secured by white tape. A nasal cannula stuck in her nose fed her lungs fresh cool oxygen.

Breathing hurt. Everywhere hurt from the slightest hint of movement, as if she had tumbled down a flight of stairs more than once.

She peeked under the sheets. Someone had dressed her in a pair of men's black pajamas. The buttoned top was splayed open. Her chest was stamped with two patches of reddened skin glistening with ointment, one above her right breast, the other below her left armpit. A bruise bloomed above her heart. Other bruises riddled her abdomen.

Dr. Wickman sat at a desk, watching. "We had to restart your heart; the burns are from the defibrillator." He stole a quick glance at his watch, made a note, then stood and came to her side.

He wore a black sweater, black slacks, and black leather shoes. It was the first time she had ever seen him wear black and was taken aback at how unnatural it looked with his pale skin that burned easily. Otherwise, he looked the same as he did the first time she met him, ten years old and grieving. His fine sand-colored hair was clipped neat and shorter, but his trim runner's body was the same. She had guessed him to be in his late thirties, back then and even now. Ageless. Maybe he had aged well or maybe he too imbibed in sucuvita, like her father. Living proof it was truly the elixir of life.

She remembered him as a patient man with a kind heart, sensible wisdom, and a deep understanding of biology, science, and the human psyche; a doctor of multiple practices with a curiosity about the natural world that matched her own.

He carefully pulled the nasal cannula from her nose with deft fingers, the nails neatly manicured. He gazed into her eyes. His glasses were round and spotlessly clean, perched on a narrow nose. Behind the glass, his pale blue eyes glowed with a warmth she had grown to trust. "How do you feel?"

"I hurt all over."

"You took quite a beating."

She touched the tip of her nose and winced. "What happened to my nose?"

"You broke it."

"Can I see?"

He frowned. "Are you sure?"

She nodded.

He retrieved a hand mirror from his desk and reluctantly handed it to her.

She gasped when she saw her reflection. There was a bulging welt on her forehead, a mask of bruises around her eyes. And her nose... *Holy shit.* White tape held the bridge in place and dried blood ringed her nostrils. The tip was angry purple and looked ready to explode.

"Funny, the cartilage and bone were perfectly set when we found you." He studied her reaction, continued when she didn't give one. "Once the swelling goes down and the bruises fade, your nose should look good as new."

She noted his careful use of the word *should* not *will*.

Dr. Wickman handed her a moistened washcloth. "Here, so you can clean yourself up. Your nose will be tender for quite a while. I didn't want to hurt you."

She dabbed at the blood dried around her nostrils. Tender was an understatement. She handed back the mirror. "Maybe you should hide this." It hurt to talk too.

"You hit your head pretty hard. You're lucky you didn't get a concussion. Do you remember what happened?"

"I remember being chased by a black helicopter, the boat hitting something in the water." It took a moment to put all the pieces together. Ones to share and ones not. She stole a glance at her arm, the Mark burning within. Sinto telling her what it meant, and after that, something too horrible to remember.

"Did I drown?"

"Not exactly. The muscles surrounding your larynx contracted, a reaction known as *laryngospasm*. Technically, you suffocated. Not from water in the lungs but from lack of oxygen, and certainly not long enough to cause any brain damage." He rolled a table from behind the bed. Sitting on top was a box of tissues and a stainless-steel cup with a straw. "You swallowed a lot of sea water. Ice water will help soothe your throat."

Dr. Wickman held the cup while Audrey took a sip.

"So I *died* momentarily?"

The corner of his lips curled, which was enough to confirm her question. "What matters now is that you're alive." He set down the cup. "Better?"

She nodded.

He regarded her with his pale eyes. "Do you remember what I taught you?"

"Of course." It was Dr. Wickman who helped her get over her mother's death. Not completely, but as much as anyone possibly could have. "Accept what I cannot change."

"And?"

"Focus on what I can, and to know the difference." She sighed. "I'm not a child anymore, Dr. Wickman. Everyone knows that."

"Sometimes the simplest notions are the hardest to live by. By the way, the captain wants to talk to you. I'll let him know you're awake." He turned to leave.

"Captain?" Audrey realized there was something abnormal about the room. One wall was gently curved and the ceiling was lower than normal. A low rumble and gentle vibration emanated from the walls. "Where am I?"

"You're on a ship owned by your father."

"My father owns a ship?"

"Ships," he said, emphasizing the plural.

He walked back to his desk and opened the drawer to retrieve something.

"I almost forgot. You were wearing this." He held up the necklace Sinto gave her.

Her hand instinctively reached for her neck and she felt her heart quicken. The machine next to her bed beeped faster.

He fingered the claw, then handed it to her. "Exquisite."

His brow raised in question.

"A gift. From a friend."

He set it on the table. "Hmm, I see." His eyes narrowed and he studied her face looking for a clue. She tried to look indifferent. It must have worked. His gaze fell to his hands and he tidied up her blankets.

"Now rest, doctor's orders." Then he left, quietly shutting the door behind him.

61

Jolly Roger

Audrey wallowed in self-pity. How could she have been so stupid?

The bump on her nose throbbed like a big bass drum. Blood still seeped from both nostrils. She grabbed a tissue from the side table, rolled it into a thick coil, and stuck the ends up both holes in her nose.

She hooked the necklace around her neck and buttoned up her pajama top to keep the necklace out of sight. She lay there trying not to panic. Whatever she told the captain she was certain would be relayed to her father, word for word. She struggled at first to formulate a believable explanation for being on the water and stealing Roy's boat, a carefully edited version that kept Ryan out of it. She decided to keep her story simple, say nothing about Sinto. Fewer lies to trip her up under intense scrutiny. Maybe she could claim she didn't remember anything at all.

She took a sip of water and lay back, convincing herself none of this was her fault. If it hadn't been for her father none of this would have happened; she would be Blake's girlfriend, researching feverishly, anticipating earning a master's degree.

No Sinto, no Mark, no complications.

Dream on.

The stark white walls of the infirmary pressed in. She could feel it now, the slight wallow and pitch of the sea. Trapped on a ship owned by her father. The smell of disinfectant and the sea's motion were tempting her stomach to revolt.

Captain Stokes entered. The one who brought her back to life and stuck his fingers in her mouth, pressed his lips to hers, and fed her air. The one with tidy brows and intense dark eyes. He seemed younger than she remembered, or maybe it was because she felt older.

He wore black wool sailor pants, the kind with two vertical rows of buttons and another row linking them together along the top of a high waistline. His shirt was fitted and tucked in, accentuating his flat stomach and narrow hips. His shoulders were muscular and broad.

Embroidered on his shirt was the small white symbol she remembered from his coat and painted on the side of his boat—an oval-shape atop a sideways X—its meaning now clear after learning of her father's long and colorful past. A clever and subtle modern-day, interpretation of the Jolly Roger—like the oval shape of a white skull sitting atop a pair of crossed femur bones that eighteenth-century pirates sewed on black flags they raised whenever they attacked.

His eyes narrowed and he raised a perfectly groomed brow when his gaze fell to her nose. She yanked the tissue from her nostrils and tossed it aside. It landed on the floor with a bloody splat.

"We met previously," he said.

"I remember. My father hired you to search for Blake."

"A most unfortunate accident." His eyes softened. "You're bleeding."

He plucked a tissue from the box on the table by her bed. She reached to take it but knocked over her water instead. They both reached for the cup but the captain's fingers got tangled in her IV tubing. They bumbled around, both trying to untangle them, but only made it worse. Audrey cried out when the captain yanked back his hand and the IV popped out of the port buried in her wrist.

The captain cursed and tried to stick it back in. Audrey pulled her hand to her chest and burst out laughing. It hurt to laugh, but she didn't care. It was a relief to vent her pent-up anxiety. The captain gazed back in shock at first, but soon was laughing too. He was disarmingly handsome when he smiled.

Audrey tossed the IV cord aside. "I owe you my life."

"It isn't every day we pluck a damsel from the sea. You've got the crew buzzing." He grabbed the chair from the desk, rolled it next to the bed, and straddled it, his arms resting on the back.

Once his smile faded there was something foreboding in his dark gaze. "I was hoping you could tell me about that man attacking your boat. Your father's expecting a full report."

The mention of Sinto and her father in the same breath smothered the light mood and shot a huge hole in her carefully crafted story. She had planned to gloss over that part, striking the fact that Sinto was an active participant in the chase. Stupid! Of course the captain knew about Sinto. He was on the helicopter with the other men. They were the people firing darts at him.

She was reluctant to answer and debated how much she should tell the captain. Did he know about the Merahvu or the true identity of her father?

"Maybe I should talk to my father first."

"Very well," he stood up, checked his watch. "He'll be here within the hour."

"Wait." Audrey grabbed his hand. "How well do you know my father? I mean, how long have you worked for him?"

A wave of uncertainty crossed his face. "Maybe you should ask your father once he arrives." He shook his hand from her grip. "I'll ask Dr. Wickman to bring you something to eat. You're going to need your strength."

Peachy. So I'll have the strength to walk the gangplank on my own two feet.

62

Man Behind The Mask

AN HOUR LATER, AUDREY'S father walked through the infirmary door. He laid a wool pea coat, crew hat, socks, and a pair of leather sneakers on the bed. All black, no surprise. He looked haggard, but managed to slip her a smile.

"Feel up for a walk?"

"Sure."

She pushed aside the stainless-steel table with her unfinished sandwich and slipped off the bed. The floor was freezing against her bare feet. She grabbed the socks and bent over to pull them on. The sudden jolt to her ribs drew a gasp and the drumming in her head picked up tempo. She slipped her father a pained smile as she stepped into the shoes and fumbled with the laces. She felt five years old again, tying her shoes under his scrutinizing gaze.

Her father held out the coat so she could slip her arms inside. He must have been wearing it before he entered the room. The warmth from his body and the scent of his cologne lingered in the folds. It was a kind gesture and reassuringly comforting. Coupled with his earlier smile, her spirits lifted a little.

She followed him out the door and into a stark white corridor. The rumble from the ship's engines was louder here and her new sneakers squeaked on the diamond-patterned steel floor. Exposed pipes ran along the low ceiling.

They passed a second infirmary, a supply room, and a steel door with a massive spinning wheel and a dead bolt of such mass that a kraken could be locked inside.

At the end of the hall was an open doorway. A plaque on the wall indicated they were on level zero. She cringed at the irony.

Rock bottom. Only way to go from here is up.

A second sign said, "Keep Doorway Clear. In the event of an emergency, doors will automatically close." On the wall beside it, someone had scrawled with a black Sharpee pen, "Get your ass topside and pronto, else kiss it goodbye!" Her father didn't bat an eye at the blatant desecration of the pristine white wall.

Tucked discretely into the door frame was a thick, sliding steel door like the one they just passed. Beyond the doorway was a circular stairway, winding around a giant oval cylinder.

"After you," he said.

She started up the stairs, pausing briefly to peek inside a porthole cut into the side of the cylinder. Moisture clung to a second layer of something dark and metallic inside. By the time they reached the fourth level, she had to pause to catch her breath.

"When was the last time you trained?" He asked.

Audrey's gaze cut to her feet.

"That's what I thought." He stopped at the top of the stairs. Another sliding steel door was tucked within the door frame with the same warning sign mounted beside it. He waited for her to pass by and into a wide corridor. It was wood-paneled with a rich teak floor, gleaming brass sconces, and handrails stretching fore and aft. The stairway was located somewhere mid-ship. How big of a ship she was uncertain, but from what she had seen, it was significant.

Her father opened a pair of mahogany doors located directly across from the stairway.

She followed him into a warmly lit, carpeted library with a dozen or more chestnut-brown leather chairs placed about. On one wall was a large built-in digital screen. Another wall held bookshelves filled with an assortment of hardback books, with storage cabinets below. On the same wall was a bar with a sink, ice-maker, and beverage cooler. Above the bar were wooden shelves with elaborately carved rails to secure an assortment of bar glasses; cut-crystal, she guessed, by the way they reflected the light. On a third wall were floor-to-ceiling glass-faced cabinets packed with electronic devices, illuminated with the glow and blink of some important purpose. The far wall was a bank of oval-shaped windows facing the darkened sea.

It followed the cliché of what she imagined a man-cave to be, smelling of warm leather and freshly rolled cigars.

Bronze poles were placed throughout, worn to a sheen at the height of her hands. She pressed her weight against one of the chairs. Bolted to the floor. At that moment the ship's motion was slight. Based on the strategically placed poles and secured furniture, Audrey feared that wasn't the norm.

Captain Stokes sat in one of the chairs, writing in a leather-bound journal.

The captain stood and slipped the journal under his arm. "Ready sir?"

"Give us a minute."

The captain nodded and left.

She strolled across the room to the bank of darkened windows, feeling things along the way; soft leather, cool bronze, Berber beneath her feet.

She cupped her hands, pressed them to the glass, and gazed outside. The sun had recently set; the snow-capped peaks on Vancouver Island were tipped in pink, quickly fading. Steely cold water stretched as far as she could see.

"Where are we going?"

"Venture to guess?"

She turned and stepped back from the window. "Out to sea?"

"The North Pacific, a hundred miles south of Kodiak Island. Stokes estimates we will arrive in three days, provided the weather cooperates."

"What's a hundred miles south of Kodiak Island?"

"We will get to that soon enough." He pulled a worn leather case from one of the cabinets below the bookshelves and set it on a table.

The case was very old. Cracked leather straps and brass buckles held it shut. When he flipped it open, she caught a musty whiff. Set inside a worn red-velvet encasement was a wedge-shaped bronze metal object. He handed it to her.

"A sextant?" she asked.

Her father smiled. "We have a break in the clouds. We should be able to get a good read." He stole a peek at his watch. "Perfect timing." He grabbed a coat hanging on a hook by the double doors. "This way."

They were back in the wood-paneled corridor heading toward a distant oval-shaped door. Mounted along the wood-paneled walls were framed drawings of sailing vessels rendered with meticulous detail. She stopped to view each one and scrutinized the dates recorded on the plaques. The first dated back to 1700; the others later during the same century. All were named "*Sea Lark*" —the original through number five.

She recognized the drawings as her father's—a favorite pastime of his—each signed with his initials. She zeroed in on the G, missing its tail. She had always believed it was merely part of his signature stylization. All along he had signed his work with his true initials: RC for Robert Culliford, not RG for Robert Grey.

There was a gap on the wall between this first set of five drawings and the next two. Maybe it was a time he was without a ship or maybe it was a time in his life he chose to forget.

But it was the last pair of drawings that piqued her curiosity. Two modern-day ships with the same black hull and sleek lines:

one with three wing-shaped sails and a finned keel weighted at the bottom with a missile-shaped bulb, the other without.

She recognized the ship with no sails as the ship that had launched wild speculation among residents of the San Juan Islands and the professors at the the Labs. It carried no identifying flags or point of origin; in fact, its decks were clear of any distinguishing features other than the three large domes atop a multi-windowed bridge. It dwarfed the Washington State ferries that serviced the islands. Ryan had guessed the mysterious ship to be over four hundred feet in length.

Based on the tags mounted in their frames, both ships were put into service five years after her mother's death, and both were named *Requiem Sea.*

She pondered the name, wondering what it meant. A mass for the dead, taken by the sea? Or was it a form of Purgatory? A place where he'd been stuck since the death of her mother?

Her father waited patiently by the oval-shaped door. She pointed at the drawing of the motorized ship. "This is that ship?"

He nodded.

"Impressive," she said, swallowing the knot that formed in her throat whenever she thought of her mother.

He spun the steel wheel mounted in the center of the oval door and pushed. It swung outward with a *whoosh*, breaking the airtight seal.

The onslaught of cool sea air made her eyes water and nose run. Stars blanketed the sky to the north; an ominous dark line of clouds gathered in the south. Steely water rushed past the hull. A trail of churned-up sea disappeared off the stern.

The black helicopter that chased her earlier sat on the ship's helipad one deck below on the aft-most part of the ship. Two men were in the process of securing the rotors, bantering about a UFC fight they had watched the night before. Their voices faded as they rolled it off the pad into a garage located below the deck where Audrey and her father stood. The light washing the helipad disappeared when a door rumbled shut.

Audrey knew her father was rich, but this was obscene.

"When did you get a ship?"

"You know I build ships."

"I thought you built ships for the military."

"That was true, in the past, but the focus of Grey Industries shifted once your mother died. Building ships for the private sector freed me to pursue more personal endeavors."

She wanted to say, *like hunting down Merahvu*, but bit her tongue instead.

"Stokes and I have a little wager going. May I?" He pointed to the sextant she held in her hand. She handed it over. "I like to keep my navigational skills honed. You never know when you might find yourself stuck in the middle of the ocean with just your wits and one of these." His eyes sparkled in the starlight. "Give me the sun and the stars and I will point you in the right direction. Give me a chart and a forward-moving ship and I will tell you exactly when we'll get there. If I predict correctly, I win."

"What's the prize?"

"A bottle of rum, winner's choice."

"Teach me how to win."

He grinned. "That's my girl."

He led her up a metal stairway to the top-most deck where they had an unencumbered view of the night sky. Only the bridge and the massive domes mounted above blocked their view of the surrounding water. He positioned himself against the rail on the side of the ship. He brought the sextant to his eye and leveled its sights on the fading horizon. "First, we locate our position. You see Polaris?"

"The North Star? Barely, but yes."

He handed her the sextant, pointed to a notched strip of polished brass along the outer curve. "The numbers along the frame are degrees; the ones on the index arm are minutes. When you spin the knob the index arm moves the mirror toward your target—Polaris, in this case. Line it up on the horizon and you're done. Give it a try."

She raised the sextant to her eye. "I see Polaris in the upper corner."

"Good." He shifted the angle of her shoulders. "Now slowly turn the knob until it is centered on the true lowest point on the horizon."

She turned the knob as he instructed. "It's centered."

"Let me look." She handed him the sextant and he confirmed her sighting. "Excellent. Now we record the minutes and degrees." He pulled a pad of paper, a small flashlight, and a pen from his pocket. He stuck the flashlight between his teeth and jotted down the reading.

Audrey was reeled back to a time before her mother died when her father taught her things of the world that did not include three swift movements sure to maim or kill. Like the ways of a sailboat, sailing in the warm blue waters off the shores of their island home located within a day's sail west of the Hawaiian island of Kauai. She remembered his sailboat at the time as modest in size, but sleek and fast, with a small cabin where she could shelter out of a sudden rain shower or sleep in the afternoon, her father commanding the helm, racing for home, tuning the sails for optimal speed and direction, his eyes alive and smile easy.

She beamed at the memory and his wager with Captain Stokes. Her father had taught her several useful knots, but her favorite was the bowline, linked to the story of a rabbit and its hole. They had competed over that, too—who could tie the bowline the fastest. She learned quickly and always won, maybe because of her small and nimble fingers. Maybe because he let her. She now suspected it is was the latter. The reward was ice cream after coming ashore.

Her throat constricted. She missed those days of her youth. The days they spent together, father and daughter, plotting how together they could make the world better. Those days were few and numbered, stolen by tragic fate. The death of her mother and the downward spiral of a broken man.

A tear ripped from her eye. She missed that man who was once her father. A man dead and buried behind the mask of what he became, angry and suspicious. Grief and vengeance consumed the joy and desire for life and the love her mother had once brought him and, Audrey hoped, that maybe she had too.

Was it too late to rip off his mask, a shell of his former self, and free the man behind it?

A gust rippled across the deck. She crossed her arms and shivered. "That's it?"

"Not quite, we need two more readings to give us our line of positioning." He repeated the process on two other stars—Capella and Vega. He glanced at his watch and jotted down the time. "Now we do the math. It's critical to take into account every factor. One miscalculation and we could end up in the Kuril Islands."

"A miscalculation. Like my little stunt today?"

He stared at her in silence, his eyes masked in shadow.

"Why haven't you said anything? You must be angry."

The flashlight quivered in his hand. "Livid."

And with that he turned his back to her and they lingered in dark silence, neither daring to saying anything else.

63

Daddy Gonna Fix It

AUDREY CURSED HERSELF. THEIR little reunion had been going so well until she brought up her miscalculation.

A gust of wind from the south cut deep. Mist from a rogue wave striking the ship swirled from the surface of the sea. The stern rose and dipped. She braced her legs, adjusting to the sudden motion.

She pulled the collar of her father's coat around her ears and tried to bury her face inside.

Her father pressed his phone to his ear. "Stokes, resume course." The phone quivered in his hand. "And give us some goddamn light out here!"

An instant later the deck was awash in light and the bow of the ship swiftly rounded up to the north. The moon slipped behind the wall of clouds advancing from the south. Another icy gust cut through her coat and ruffled her father's hair. He said into the phone, "Storm's on us. Time to raise sail."

Audrey thought she had heard him wrong. How could Captain Stokes raise sails when there were no masts?

She felt a slight shift in speed as if something big had fallen off the ship and was being dragged behind. That was when it dawned on her; the oval-shaped cylinder in the stairway, the second drawing of the ship with winged sails and a finned keel with a missile-shaped bulb.

Two ships, one name...

Her father nodded toward her feet. "I suggest you step aside."

She was standing on a rectangle painted with bright yellow hash marks about seventy-feet long and twelve-feet wide. In the center of the rectangle was a circle nearly six feet in diameter. Cuts in the decking made clear it was a hatch of some kind. Around the periphery of the hatch was a warning, painted in the same color yellow: "Keep clear at all times." There were two more hatches like this one, mid and fore deck.

The deck quivered beneath her feet and she promptly jumped aside. The round hatches popped up from the deck about a foot and slid to the side, exposing three gaping holes in the ship's deck. The main hatches swung up vertically, circles cut in their centers, and locked into place with a loud *thunk*.

Silence stretched for several seconds.

Then—

From the depths of the ship came a growling rumble and a sharp hiss. Red sails rose from the deck, solid and pointed like the tip of a knife. After ten feet, a second section rose up and snapped into place below the first section. Then another and another, telescoping into place, each seam barely visible and evenly spaced, each section larger than the one before. Eighteen sections total. The last section rose an additional eight feet off the deck revealing a large mast-like core running through each section. The rumbling stopped. The hatch doors swung shut with a *swoosh*, the round cutouts sealing around the mast-like cores.

The trio of red, wing-like sails pivoted a quarter turn in tandem and caught the wind. The ship heeled gently and rapidly picked up speed, and the sleek hull sliced through the rough sea like a knife through butter. The transformation from power to sail took less than a minute. Boldly displayed on the mid-ship sail was the white symbol she came to know as her father's favored logo, an oval atop an X.

Her father encouraged her to join him as he ventured beneath the aft sail, flying eight feet above deck. He pressed his back to the mast and crossed his arms, beaming proudly.

Audrey gazed up in awe. "Telescoping sails?"

"Wings," he corrected. "Made of carbon fiber and polymer resin. Exceptionally light and strong. Hydraulics lift the sections into place. The rigging's inside, frames connected together by high-tech rope-like wire that give it flexibility and strength. Computers fine tune each wing's arc." He gazed up. "It used to take a dozen men to handle one sail, but now Stokes can manage all three with the tip of his finger."

Audrey looked at her father with fresh eyes. "The sea... this ship, this is your home."

"The sea has always been my home, nothing will ever change that."

"Are you over three hundred years old, for real?"

"How did you learn this truth?"

"Ianthe told me."

"Ah, of course she did." He sighed. "I was born in Cornwall, England, in sixteen-sixty-six."

Audrey shook her head in disbelief. "You freely admit this, after all these years?"

"I was planning to tell you once you turned twenty-one."

"Did Mom know?"

He drew a sharp breath. "I never got the chance to tell her."

"Did she know about the Merahvu?"

His eyes darkened. "No, which I regret every day. If she had known, maybe she would have been more careful."

The Mark smoldered in her arm. "Maybe you should have told *me* sooner."

"I told you to stay away from the water."

"Geez, get a clue! Don't you know that's like feeding gasoline to a fire? Demanding someone to do something isn't part of the art of persuasion." She hugged her arm to her chest. "Now it's too late."

"What's too late?"

Her heart clenched. "Nothing."

His gaze fell from her eyes to her cradled arm, then back. He regarded her with a cold, hard gaze. Her stomach churned. A gust of wind stirred the silence between them and a bolt of lightning lit up the distant sky. He looked up, momentarily distracted.

"We had best get inside."

She regretted adding that last comment as they padded down the exterior metal stairway and through the aft door. They walked in tense silence past his drawings, past the library doors, toward the bow of the ship. The pitching motion grew more pronounced. They strolled past several doors; individual cabins from what she could tell.

"Officer's quarters," he told her.

Then he zipped up a flight of stairs. At the top was a darkly tinted glass door. Her father slid it open. They stepped onto the ship's bridge, bathed in red light.

It took a moment for her eyes to adjust to the darkness. Windows circled the entire bridge, offering a three-hundred-sixty-degree view of the darkening sea and working wings.

Captain Stokes was bent over a dimly lit screen with a computerized image of the ship under sail, making fine adjustments with his finger. She noted a highly-polished giant brass steering wheel set in the middle of the bridge. She wondered if it was there strictly for decoration.

She joined her father at the navigation station. He thumbed through a stack of well-worn paper charts from one of many extra-wide drawers. He pulled one out and slipped it underneath a hinged Lucite cover mounted atop the set of drawers. He pulled out protractors, a parallel plotter, a black grease pencil, and a nautical slide rule from the top drawer. He dug for his notes in his pants pocket.

He switched on a dim lamp, lighting the chart. He scribbled out numbers with the grease pencil on the Lucite overlaying the paper chart. "You asked me earlier where we were going."

She tipped her head to read the equation he was solving. "Yes."

"Your finned friend conveniently led us to his underwater city." He stopped scribbling, fixed her with his icy gaze. "Imagine my delight."

Audrey suddenly felt sick to her stomach. "How did you know he was a friend?"

"We have been tracking the Merahvu for months now. I suspected they were searching for you, and after those whales attacked your boat, I asked Stokes to keep an eye on you."

Her nose throbbed. Something moist trickled down her upper lip. "You've been spying on me?"

Her father set down the grease pencil, opened the top drawer, and pulled out a tissue. His nostrils flared when he handed it to her. "I warned you, which you blithely ignored. Look what happened. You nearly got yourself killed."

Audrey wiped her lip and pointed accusingly at Captain Stokes. "He was chasing me! How was I supposed to know it was your helicopter?"

His face softened but his eyes simmered with fury. "It was clever of you to slip out in the cover of darkness. We didn't know until Roy called me. Stokes was trying to save you from *that boy*." He tsked. "And stealing a boat?"

"I didn't steal it, Roy loaned it to me. I was going to give it back."

"Oh really? And how do you plan to do that? His boat is lying at the bottom of Spieden Channel. He was quite upset when he learned of the accident."

She winced at her stupidity. She would be dead if Sinto hadn't dragged her from the wreckage.

"Once Roy called me, we had a pretty good idea where to find you. You see, we happen to own Andrews Island, and have for hundreds of years. It's ironic that you chose that particular island for a secret rendezvous." His eyes glazed over for a beat as if drifting back to a distant memory, then they cut back to hers, glacial and unforgiving. "There's a hidden compound located in the heart of the island. Cameras monitor the shores for trespassers, including the hidden cove and the beach. Just so happened Stokes checked the feeds this morning." He raised his brow. "Care to explain what you were doing on the beach with that boy?"

Audrey gaped.

"Cat got your tongue?"

She snapped her mouth shut and swallowed. "I needed to distract him, gain his trust, so I could drug him." She jutted out her jaw. "It worked, too. I slipped a couple of sleeping pills in his tea."

"Why would you do that?"

"I needed leverage, enough to get Queen Ianthe's attention—a trade, for Blake."

He straightened. Shot a glance over to Stokes. "Ianthe has Blake?"

"Yes. The orca attack was planned to capture Blake and enlist me for her secret assignment. Blake's alive, I saw him myself. She's had him all along. She claims he's safe but I worry that his life may be in danger. Because of you, I might add."

He set down his grease pencil, clearly agitated, and paced a few steps, stopped, and asked, "Why because of me?"

"Queen Ianthe wants to negotiate a truce. She's threatened to keep Blake locked up until I convince you to meet with her, so the two of you can come to some sort of agreement. But truthfully? I want nothing to do with it. I only want him returned. Blake didn't do anything to deserve this."

"How much do you know about the Merahvu?"

"That they understand the natural world far more than we do. There's much we could learn from them."

"I was naive once, just like you."

Her cheeks flamed. "Why do you still treat me like a child?"

"I'm trying to knock some sense into that brilliant brain of yours. Your mother was murdered."

"I saw the net, and the reports confirmed it was an *accident.*"

He drew a noisy breath and held it. His nostrils flared when he let it go. "Tell me again the name of this finned boy who nearly killed you?"

She swallowed. "Sinto, and he didn't nearly kill me, by the way." She pointed at Stokes. "He did."

He ignored her jab at the captain. "Sinto," he said thoughtfully. "You knew this Sinto from before, didn't you?"

Her stomach constricted. "How did you know?"

"Your mother told me."

Audrey gasped. "She knew?" Audrey thought she had been so clever, hiding her friend whenever her mother was present.

"Did you ever notice your mother would disappear whenever he came around? She watched from afar, curious about where he came from. How long did your secret play dates go on?"

"I—I don't know, a couple weeks maybe."

"More like a month. When your mother told me about the strange boy I was curious. So I followed you and your mother one day. I hid in the jungle and watched. When your mother went for her swim, I saw him emerge from the sea. I watched the two of you, playing in the sand. I saw the way he gazed adoringly when you weren't looking, the way his eyes sparked every time you spoke, how he reached out to touch you, but drew back before you noticed. I nearly died when you begged him to come back.

"It was like my own first encounters with Ianthe. I was intrigued and enamored with her beauty and wisdom. It wasn't until later I learned of her true power and intent. They feign an innocent mystique to seduce you, to get close enough to manipulate your mind and use you as they see fit.

"I scared off your little friend. I wanted you to think he deserted you so you would forget about him. When he didn't return, I thought it was over, until I saw him by the outer reef, drowning your mother. He murdered her for his queen."

That tingling sensation of doubt sprouted in her chest. "No." She shook her head. "He couldn't, not the Sinto I know."

"Didn't you almost drown today?"

"It wasn't his fault!"

"Long ago, I vowed to do anything to keep you safe."

A knot gathered in her throat. "You don't understand. He could never kill me, not now, not ever. It would be suicide."

Her father glared. "What did you say?"

"N—nothing important."

The color drained from his cheeks. He reached for her. "Show me your arm."

Every drop of moisture evaporated from her mouth. "Why?" She hid her arm behind her back. The Mark felt like a red-hot brand pressed to her flesh.

He reached around, grabbed her hand, and yanked up her sleeve. His fingers shook when he pressed down on the knotted coils beneath the skin, tracing the symbol with his finger; the swirl, the circle, the line connecting them. A strange curdling sound came from his throat. "Do—do you know what this is? What this means?"

Tears filled her eyes, blurring her vision.

"Do you?"

"He said I Marked him, but..." The tears she had held back now ran down her cheeks.

His eyes widened. "You didn't complete the Joining?"

"He stopped it—he stopped me."

Her father suddenly embraced her, so tightly she could barely breathe. "He will never have you. We're going to fix this baby, don't you worry."

Every cell in her body felt on fire.

Maybe I don't want you to fix it!

A painful thought made her shudder. "What about Blake?" The words slipped out, a question not aimed at her father, but herself. What would she say to Blake once she saw him again?

Sorry, must break my promise, while you were sleeping I fell in love with another...

Her father released her. His eyes cut to Captain Stokes and he drew a deep breath. "We're going to fix that too. Blake is going to be fine. We'll get him back. I promise you that."

Trepidation danced in her chest. "So you agree to meet with Queen Ianthe, *peacefully*?"

"That will depend on her."

"And you promise you won't harm him?"

"Him who?"

"Sinto."

He froze her with his gaze. "That will depend on him too."

64

Sister Knows Best

Sinto sat with Naiada in her room, administering her treatment. She lay on her bed with her arm in his lap. His hand cupped her elbow, holding it firmly in place. Tubes of his flesh extended from his arm into hers, one feeding his blood to her system, the other drawing blood from hers.

He had jetted back to the city once the Mark he shared with Audrey sparked to life after several agonizing minutes. The only consolation from the near-fatal encounter with Culliford's men was that they reached her in time and brought her back to life.

Naiada nibbled on a thumbnail, scrutinizing her elaborate painting of the Salish Sea covering the walls and ceiling. She spit out a piece; it floated to the floor. "I will never get to finish it."

"You will."

She nibbled some more, rolled her eyes. "You seem real talkative today."

He exhaled and pinched his eyes shut. "I have nothing to talk about."

"Your aura is flickering. I can't get a fix on you."

"Just anxious, that's all."

"Perhaps your merlux is misfiring. It has been known to fire erratically when your hormones fluctuate."

He felt the whispery brush of her mind slipping gently through his eardrums, niggling under his skull, around and around his brain, seeking a weakness in the fortress he had built around his mind from the nosy women in his life; her and their mother.

He glowered at her, she glowered back. He didn't want Naiada in his head right now. *He* didn't want to be in his head right now.

He felt a swift smack inside his skull and the snap of a whip inside his ear as she hastily withdrew her mind's tentacle. Her body may be weak, but not her mind. Nor her keen instincts.

"You should have it checked out by one of the Healers. You wouldn't want to accidentally shock the wrong person." She cast her eyes toward the tubes of Sinto's flesh sticking in her arm.

"I've been spending a lot of time on Merluma. You know how vital it can make you feel. Perhaps that's what you are sensing."

She smirked. "Hanging out on Merluma is not what's firing you up, dear brother."

He chose to ignore her remark and retreated deeper into his troubled thoughts.

"No need to fight it, Sinto."

"Fight what?"

"Your feelings; they're strong, consuming you."

He ground his teeth. "What are you talking about?"

She stroked his wrist gently with her free hand. "What troubles you is about Audrey, is it not?"

He opened his mouth to deny it but stopped.

Nothing was a secret to Naiada. She had the uncanny ability to gain a sense of things. All she had to do was breathe deeply and inhale it. She had told him once that the secret was in one's aura. That the aura was the venting of essence, whether human, animal, or plant; that the land and the sea had essence, even the stars in the sky; that essence spanned all of eternity. That the essence of all things was connected by an energy threading throughout the universe, whose source was a mystery. And from these pinpricks of essence she could sift out what happened in the past and how the past, coupled with the realities of the present, might reveal one possible future.

Their mother required entering the Timeless Dimension to gain knowledge of such things, but Naiada... she seemed to glean bits of this knowledge organically and with little effort at all. Along with her ability to sniff out venting auras, and once their mother trained her how to leverage the Timeless Dimension, she would potentially be more powerful and influential than any queen who came before. That training would commence one day soon, when she grew strong enough.

Her brows arched. "Well?"

This charade could go on for hours, and with his vitality pumping through her veins, she would have the stamina to hound him until he had confessed every detail and she could sniff out the ones yet to be.

"Promise not to tell Mother?"

"Tease a shark with my blood, smack a grizzly with a stick."

Sinto smirked at their childhood dare. "My chest burns, my heart races, I have trouble concentrating when she's near." He closed his eyes. "All I think about is her and..." *The sound of her laugh, the way her brow bunches deep in thought, the feel of her breast in my hand...*

Naiada flicked his knuckles. "Go on."

He blinked back to the moment and Naiada's prying gaze. He leaned closer and whispered. "How does one know when they have found their chosen mate?"

"Have you melded minds? Seen the Mark?"

Again he was confounded. *How much do I tell her?* Something about the way she looked at him, she already knew the answer.

He frowned. "Yes."

Her face brightened. "I knew it! That is fantastic!"

"I'm not sure I share your enthusiasm. I mean, not because of her... she's incredible. But—" He took a deep breath, his heart hammering just thinking of her. "She's a Sapien. How did she know how to Mark me?"

"How does one fall in love? I guess it could be the same, only... Wait, where did this happen? What were you doing at the time?"

"I took her to Club Ballo."

"Did you give her sucuvita?"

"Yes."

"Was she receptive to all aspects of the club's experience?"

"Yes. Her mind was unguarded, and so vulnerable."

"That is *most* interesting." Naiada's eyes narrowed in thought. "Although I would expect there to be another reason she was able to Mark you. You know, some don't believe in the myth of the Mark and the concept of Joining. There's very little known about the subject. I know because I queried a Keeper of Knowledge while I was stuck in that horrible place, the House of Healing." She rolled her eyes. "She saved me from going full-on crazy, bored out of my mind... anyway, we talked about many things, and the topic sort of came up. She was a bit uncertain, though she stressed it must be real and that I was the result of such a union. So are you. But she didn't have anything to add credence otherwise. She said it was so rare that what was documented was based on word of mouth—myths and stories. Secretly, I pegged her as a non-believer." She shrugged. "I honestly can't blame her."

Her eyes cut to Sinto's arm. "Can I see it?"

He held it out. She touched it where the skin was smooth and flawless, but when she pressed deeper, her finger rolled over the tight coils beneath. Her mouth gaped. "The Mark! It's real. Did you attempt the Joining?"

"Naiada, you know the Joining is a private thing."

"So they say... You're the one who started this conversation, so finish it," she said, firmly.

"I didn't start it, you pried!"

"You know I will ferret out the truth. This is historic! Tell me."

Sinto suddenly regretted giving in to this conversation, but he needed to talk to someone, and Naiada was his safest bet. She could be trusted to keep a secret, and she did declare the dare after all.

He shook his head. "To be honest, I'm uncertain what I'm supposed to do, what Joining entails. I seemed close to doing it, twice, but again, how am I supposed to know for sure? It's much more complicated than the story would have you believe. Is it linked to the physical desires I feel for her? I can say that those are much stronger and difficult to control since she Marked me, not that it's bad, just..." A rush of heat spread through his loins. Just thinking about it had that sudden effect on him. He crossed his legs, hoping Naiada wouldn't notice. "But that doesn't matter now. She knows about the orca attack, that I kidnapped her friend. She hates me for it."

"She can't truly hate you; the Mark will not allow her."

"She told me she no longer trusts me."

Naiada laughed. "Sounds like an invitation for you to try harder."

"What?"

"Sinto, you are so naive! Stop moping around and go after her! Prove to her you're a worthy mate."

"What about Blake? She begged and pleaded for me to set him free. Perhaps he has already proven he's worthy. I certainly have not. It would be best to forget about her."

"As long as your heart beats in your chest, you will pine for her."

"And you believe the same is true for her?"

Naiada grasped his hand. "Absolutely. She may be upset, but remember, she *chose* you. *She* Marked *you*."

"My first assignment and I have ruined everything. So much is at risk. How can I justify pursuing Audrey for my own selfish reasons?"

"They are not selfish. Besides, she's worth the risk. Risk you must take now that the Mark has been cast. It's your fate. There is nothing you can do to reverse it."

"You believe that?" His heart raced, but only briefly. A sudden wave of weakness passed through him, like always near the end of Naiada's treatments, once her weakened blood filled him.

"The Mark chose you both for a reason. It's unwise not to accept it. You must see this through, Sinto. Find her, seize the Mark, seal the bond. A Joining is meant to be, and not by choice. Only then will your true purpose be revealed. A mutual purpose you both must fulfill, together. Otherwise..."

"Otherwise what?"

She didn't reply. By the way she looked at him, she shouldn't need to. The answer was of unfavorable consequence.

"But mother decreed that it's forbidden... with a Sapien."

"What we were told is a lie. There is no reason for it to be forbidden. It happened before but was interrupted. There are some paths that never fork and must be followed as presented. Sometimes I wonder what other lies we have been told, and why."

"What lies?"

She wrinkled her nose, shook her head. "Nothing specific I can pin down. Just a weird feeling."

Another complication made his heart sink. "What about Mother? My future in the Circle. What if they learn of the Mark? That I took Audrey to Merluma? Because of the rebels' attempt to prove them weak, they will surely demand the severest of all punishments... What if they deem my punishment to be the Undoing?"

Just thinking of it terrified him: a dreadful ceremony in which the mind was ripped from the physical body whilst still alive, and forced to watch the dissection of the physical self until there was nothing left to occupy. Without the physical to nurture and feed, the mind withered. No hope of redemption or a second chance at life.

"Last death, Naiada, *me* snuffed out, forever!"

Naiada squeezed his hand. "Calm down, your secrets are safe with me. Mother cannot pry into my thoughts, and you need not fear the Circle. Besides, because of the Mark, you may want to question your role in the Circle, if you even belong there at all."

They settled into silence. Sinto drifted into his own thoughts, more unsure of his future, influenced by his sister's honest and forthright wisdom.

Naiada's eyes had returned to their natural lavender color and glittered with youthful hope. He extracted his fleshy tubes and cauterized the insertion points in her arm. As he helped Naiada sit up, a wave of dizziness made him swoon and she stopped him from slipping off the bed. She helped him lie down, his head in her lap, her hand caressing his brow, their roles reversed.

"Sinto, I have a secret too."

He cocked a brow. Naiada never shared her secrets.

"I have been having visions."

"Visions? Like the sort mother sees in the Timeless Dimension?"

She nodded.

"Since when?"

She cast her eyes to the ceiling. "Since I was eight."

Sinto blinked. *Before puberty?* "Have you told mother?"

"No!" She swallowed hard. "And I think it would be best that she not know. Some of the things I have seen... They involve her, and I—I think her power of foresight is waning, or soon to wane."

"Did you foresee me with Audrey—the Mark we now share?"

"Yes," she whispered, then giggled. "Both, actually—her and it."

"What else have you seen?"

She shrugged. "Just brief flashes, nothing of significance. Too many things are shifting right now. Some of them make no sense, some of them are... *unsettling*. My clearest vision is of the rebels. Their numbers are growing and they are mostly Terrakai."

"Maybe your vision is linked to the changes on Merluma." His tongue felt heavy. "Things evolving much too fast." His eyes winked. "And those tigers challenged my commands." He took a deep breath. "Anyone visiting Merluma should use caution."

"Do you think that is what happened to Father?"

"Wantemo and I searched Merluma, and the Scouts searched the City of Green and scoured other places Merahvu were known to have settled on Earth. We found no sign of him."

"I can no longer sense him." Tears filled her eyes. "It was my fault we got in trouble. I sensed the trap, but said nothing. Not wanting to reveal my secret."

"It was not your fault." He reached for her but fell short. She caught his hand and hugged it against her cheek. He brushed his fingers across the deep pockmarks. "I'm sorry about the scars."

Her face hardened, briefly. "I am too." Then she tickled him in the ribs. "But I am alive thanks to you."

He was too weak to laugh. "And I need rest." He rose to his feet, crossed the room.

"Sinto, one more thing…"

He gripped the door frame, turned to face her.

"You must promise me."

"Promise you what?"

"When the time comes, lean left."

"What time?"

Her eyes widened. "You'll know."

65

All The Captain's Men

THE STORM RAGED THROUGH the night, growing more violent as dawn broke. The ship was heeled hard to starboard and the small porthole in Audrey's cabin dipped above and below sea level, awash with the frothing sea racing by. The ship pitched through mountainous swells. The groan of working wood and metal reverberated throughout the hull.

Audrey lay in her small bunk, her stomach a half pitch behind the motion of the ship. Saliva flooded her mouth, a warning of what was sure to follow. She hung her head over the side. There was a bucket. She grabbed it and retched.

She felt like she had been fed to the sharks then unmercifully regurgitated to live another day. Dr. Wickman warned her she would feel the full effects of the previous day's trauma twenty-four hours later. She had not imagined she would feel like this.

Aside from the nausea, every breath was a fight, her nose throbbed, and the coiled flesh of the Mark felt like molten lava in her arm. But worst of all was the indescribable feeling of unease that something terrible was brewing on the horizon.

She pressed her forehead to the porthole next to her bunk. The ship rolled. The porthole popped up above sea level, offering a glimpse of the angry Pacific. A slash of crimson light cut through clouds to the east and painted the sea as if it were blood not water.

Red sky in morning, sailor take warning.

A harbinger.

We're going to fix this, baby, don't you worry.

She buried her face in her hands. Her life was so utterly out of control and broken that her father felt compelled to fix it. Violently, she feared.

From the corridor beyond her door came the sound of muffled voices, slamming doors, and the fall of many passing feet. Then silence, followed by a light tap on the door.

She sat up and swung her legs to the floor. Another wave of nausea swept through her when she caught a whiff of the bucket. She swallowed hard and stood, grabbing a handrail running along the ceiling, and slowly crossed the canted floor. She braced herself against the wood-paneled bulkhead and turned the knob. Gravity swung the door open.

Captain Stokes filled the door frame. Shock filled his eyes when he saw her. She cringed and shielded her face with her hand.

The captain was alert and impeccable, dressed in his usual black uniform. He smelled like peppermint soap. "Time for breakfast."

An order, not an invitation.

"May I have a moment to freshen up?"

"Make it quick—we're waiting for you in the cafeteria. Level three, turn left. Can't miss it."

She stuck her head into the hallway. He pointed to the far end. She was currently on level one, among the crew's quarters. One level up from the infirmary.

She had heard the crew's comings and goings like a regular changing tide, but had yet to see anyone other than the captain, her father, and Dr. Wickman.

Audrey closed the door and frowned, wondering what had happened to Dr. Wickman's orders to rest and recuperate.

She grappled across the cabin, grabbed the bucket, and slipped through the door of the adjoining head. There was a single sink and a toilet. Regretfully, no shower. A second door on the other side led to another cabin whose occupant she had heard relieve themselves sometime in the middle of the night. The toilet yellowed with evidence.

She emptied the bucket into the toilet and flushed before facing herself in the mirror. She groaned when she saw her reflection. No wonder Captain Stokes recoiled. Raccoon eyes, dried blood smeared on her left cheek, disheveled hair.

She rummaged through the drawers. One drawer contained partially used toiletries, the other contained unopened items she assumed were left for her; deodorant, toothpaste, toothbrush, dental floss, and a hairbrush.

She would have done anything for a paper bag to pull over her head and pair of scissors to cut out eye holes.

She whipped off her pajama top, splashed water under her arms, and carefully washed her face with a washcloth, then she brushed her teeth and applied a generous swipe of deodorant. She struggled to brush the many knots from her wavy hair, then braided it as best as she could. She moistened her hands and tried to tame loose ends that sprang free.

Her reflection was pretty much the same as when she started. She rolled her eyes and slipped back into her cabin.

On the dresser next to her bunk was a note from the captain, indicating he had left her a selection of clothing choices. She wedged herself and opened the drawers with curiosity. Inside were several pairs of black socks, black fitted boxers, black undershirts, black knitted shirts, black lightweight sweaters, and an assortment of sizes of black wool pants like the pair the captain wore.

Seriously, choices? She chuckled at his choice of words.

She pulled on a pair of boxers and tried on different-sized pants until she found a pair that fit her waist but stopped short of her ankles. She cursed her height.

Lacking a bra, she doubled up on undershirts, then pulled on a sweater. The buttons on the pants were decorative only. Zippers secured them for quick and easy on/off access.

She winced from bruised ribs when she bent to slip on her socks and shoes.

She stole one last glance in the mirror above the dresser. Her gaze fell to the white symbol embroidered on her sweater. Did this mean she was part of Captain Stokes's crew?

She had a feeling she was about to find out.

The corridor on level one was wood-paneled like the others, only narrower. Bronze handrails ran along the walls and the ceiling, and brass sconces provided golden light.

It was challenging climbing the circular stairway with the way the ship was heeling, like climbing a steep mountain in one direction and slipping down its slopes in the other. A true test of grit in her current physical condition.

The cylinder was empty. The handrail attached to the cylinder wall vibrated from the sharp-edged keel and missile-shaped bulb cutting a swath through the sea, balancing the force of wind against the wings above deck. The way the ship moved under sail felt different than when it ran under power. She marveled at the technical wonder her father's company had designed and built; one ship, power or sail.

The smell of fresh brewed coffee and fried bacon grew stronger once she reached level three.

Her stomach heaved at the thought of eating, tender and on the verge of emptying itself with the subtlest of encouragement. But it wasn't only her stomach that felt uneasy. Deep boisterous voices drifted down the hall from the cafeteria. Men, lots of them.

She stopped just outside the cafeteria door to muster her courage to step inside. She truly regretted looking at herself in the mirror earlier knowing she was a fright to behold. She drew a deep breath, wound her braid across her shoulder, straightened the bandage on her nose, then took a step around the corner to the—

A man smacked into her, knocking her to the floor. She landed on her ass, legs splayed, mouth gaped in shock. The hit to her tail bone reverberated up her spine to her tender ribs. Pain seized her ribcage; she blinked away a wave of darkness.

The man bent over, scrutinizing her face. "So *you're* the new guy. Nice shiner." His eyes continued to wander all the way to her toes, then snapped back to hers. "Fly's undone."

She instinctively looked at her crotch, which was perfectly zipped up.

He didn't apologize or offer her a hand. Instead he leaped over her sprawled legs and disappeared down the stairwell, howling in laughter. All she could do was blink away the crippling pain radiating around her ribcage. The guy must have been six-four, was deft as a ninja, and looked like he should be in the movies, not a modern-day pirate.

Asshole, she thought to herself.

She stood. What little confidence she had mustered while climbing the stairs wilted. She double-checked the zippers holding her pants shut, scowling once again at the sight of her bare ankles. She gritted her teeth, then stepped around the corner and through the door of the cafeteria.

Faces turned and voices faded, a sudden hush. Dozens of men and not one woman. Her father seriously needed to come to grips with the modern world. Some of the men were young and clean-cut like the one who had knocked her over. Others were grizzled with age and silver-streaked. Many were covered with tattoos and scars. Several ethnic groups were represented. The truth of their pasts was written in their hardened gaze. A loss of innocence only a hard life would bring. She wondered where her father found the men who crewed his ship.

The wind howled beyond the windows and the floor bucked bow to stern. A dish fell to the floor, shattering the silence. No one flinched. They were waiting for her to make the first move.

Last night before parting, her father told her the crew hadn't been off the ship for months, a subtle warning she heedlessly dismissed. A warning she now heeded quite seriously. It didn't matter that she was Robert Culliford's daughter. She was a member of the opposite sex—the only one from what she could tell. She sensed their curious eyes.

She scanned the room for her father and felt a rush of relief when she found him, sitting at a table on the far side. She smiled and waved. He merely returned a cool gaze. The one he usually gave, right before one of his tests.

She willed her feet forward, but willing was far easier than doing. The floor was steeply angled and she was on the leeward side, her father in the farthest upper corner. Like in the library, floor-to-ceiling poles were scattered about the room.

She set out like a newly birthed fawn with shaky legs and unsure footing, grappling her way through a wolf's lair. She felt the prickle of hungry eyes.

She stole a quick glance at a man to her right. He winced when he saw her face. Her face flushed and she willed her nose not to spring a sudden leak.

Halfway to her father's table a rogue wave struck the ship. She grabbed a pole and wound her arms and legs around it, like a snake slithering up a tree. A collective gasp rose in the room when the ship crashed down with a shudder.

She lost her grip and fell against a man with a puckered scar running from ear to mouth. She reached for the pole; the ship lurched; she slipped and landed in his lap, spilling the cup of hot coffee he held gimbaled in his hand.

"I'm so sorry!"

He wrapped an arm around her waist. "I'm not," he quipped in a thick Australian accent. "Why don't ya settle that tight little ass 'ere in my lap and stay awhile."

Across the room, the others howled in approval.

The man with the scar clicked his tongue. Others joined in until the sound of the howling wind and the clatter of dishes was drowned out by the snapping of their tongues.

They patted their laps and made rude gestures with their fingers.

Run swift as the wind!

She leapt from the Aussie's lap and aimed for a pole but misjudged her timing; the ship wallowed port when she wallowed starboard, and she fell against another man. He shoved her across the aisle to a set of outstretched hands. Back and forth they pitched her, like a game of hot potato, clicking their tongues and howling like wolves, hands pushing and grappling.

She swung her fists in defense, but they bounced off hardened muscle and only served to provoke. They were tossing her across the room toward her father as an odd sort of initiation. She resigned herself to the humiliation, knowing it would soon end.

"Enough!" Her father's voice rang out.

The hands wrapped round her hips released her. Silence filled the room. Audrey bolted to her father's table and sat down with her back to the wolves filling the room.

He glared. "I see you've already forgotten how to handle yourself. I *told* you—train every day, no matter what."

She stared back in disbelief. Of course she had quit the first chance she got—she hated it. Mortal combat sessions six days a week, three hours a day, until he finally let her go and she moved from Seattle to San Juan Island. A whole decade of it. At first it had been a struggle for her to focus, being ten years old and having just witnessed the death of her mother. She knew firsthand how death destroyed the people left behind. The thought of killing another living being made her physically sick, yet her father insisted she learn how.

It all made sense now, knowing of his past and his fear of the Merahvu. Although he was a fool if he believed a swift kick to the nuts, a finger to the eye, or a slam to the kidneys would take down a Merahvu. You'd be toast before you could land the first hit.

She spied the men in his crew. They had resumed eating and talking, ignoring her now, as if their little stunt was all in a normal day's work.

She sat back, arms crossed. "I didn't think I needed to defend myself from your crew,"

"Never underestimate your foe."

She sat forward, gripping the table. "You told them to do that?"

"I was curious how you would handle yourself. You never should have allowed them to treat you that way."

She rolled her eyes. "I feel like crap, Dad—can't you lighten up, just this once?"

He smiled. "So it's *Dad* now?"

"I thought we made some progress yesterday."

"We did. Some. And I'm pleased." He dug for something in his pants pocket and produced a pair of black elastic wristbands. "I almost forgot, put these on. The round knob goes about three fingers down on the inside of your wrist."

She pulled them on. He reached over and adjusted them. "Acupressure. Should quell the nausea. Leave them on in rough seas. If they don't help, we've got scopolamine patches."

His gaze was drawn to the far side of the room. "Ah, here comes Stokes and an old friend I'd like you to meet."

Audrey spun around. Captain Stokes, Dr. Wickman, and a small wiry man were weaving though the cafeteria like monkeys, swinging from vines. The captain and Dr. Wickman sat down across from her.

The smaller man hesitated at the empty seat beside her. His dark hair hung in tight corkscrews and bounced with each jolt of the ship. His wire-framed glasses slipped down his over-sized beaked nose. He pushed them up with a thin pale finger and gave her father a curt smile. His teeth were worn to short stubs and yellowed like aged ivory.

Her father spoke up. "This is Salvo Alvarez."

His gaze fell to her outstretched hand. He reluctantly took it, as if the thought of touching her repelled him. His hand was cold and clammy.

"Call me Alvarez."

"Alvarez," she said, then turned to Captain Stokes. "Captain Stokes, good to see you again so soon."

Stokes' eyes swung toward her father. "I'm not the only captain on this ship... and you can simply call me Stokes if you like."

"Uh, I'm—" She was befuddled as to how to respond. Yesterday she noted her father addressed the captain simply as Stokes and the doctor as Wickman, and they in turn called him Culliford.

Am I a Grey or a Culliford?

Before she could decide, a man approached with a silver tray perched on his shoulder. He looked like a true pirate of lore with scraggly gray hair, a bushy white beard, crinkly eyes, and a nose that had been broken many times. A red bandanna topped his head. He set the tray on the table and doled out steaming plates of food.

Hers contained two hard-boiled eggs, a banana, and a freshly baked croissant.

Her father knew croissants were her absolute favorite. A thoughtful gesture especially after his crew's cruel stunt. She gave him a sheepish smile. He winked back.

The pirate man poured a round of coffees, then set two large pills next to her plate. "These'll set yer stomach right real quick. Ginger. Ye may thank me later. Me name's Leonard by the way." When he grinned, his cheeks bunched up in bright rosy buds. His teeth were white and perfect, like they were brand new.

"Is Leonard your first name?"

"Aye, me only name."

"I'm Audrey. Not sure what my true surname is, at this point."

He grasped her outstretched hand and planted a wet kiss across her knuckles. He was missing a couple of fingers. "Yer a Culliford through and through, and it's me pleasure to finally meet the fine Captain Culliford's daughter." He pointed to his nose. "And don't ye fret, ye won't end up lookin' like me. The doctor's a miracle worker, offered ter fix mine, but I like it the way it is." Then he turned to her father. "Anything else?"

"Just your company."

"Aye, let me get rid of this." Leonard deftly hoisted the tray under his arm and left.

Audrey leaned over the table and whispered to her father. "Is he... like you?"

"I met Leonard in Gujarati prison in India before we acquired our first ship, the *Sea Lark*. He knew how to catch and fillet a rat. If it hadn't been for him, I would have starved to death. Three years we ate like that. Helped him escape then recruited him to join my crew. Best chef on the seven seas."

Audrey's head reeled. How many men on this ship were from her father's past?

Her father must have read her thoughts. "Along with Leonard, Wickman and Alvarez are also from my original crew, along with two others, currently unable to join us. Only six of us are left out of an original crew of twenty-five. But that was a long time ago."

She looked around the table, trying to picture her father, Dr. Wickman, and Alvarez sailing the seven seas as eighteenth-century, plundering pirates. She turned to Stokes. "What's your story?"

"I was recruited by Alvarez when I was sixteen, living off the streets of Los Angeles. Would have been dead by now if it wasn't for your father."

Audrey paled. "Is that where you found all these men, living on the streets?"

"Some, but not all." Her father chuckled. "Not to worry, my dear. They aren't thugs—in fact, they're quite well educated, and they would never harm you. You would be surprised at how many talented and eager young men are overlooked in this world and misguided for more nefarious purposes. I offer the dangerous and disenfranchised a better path."

"Indeed," Stokes chimed in.

"Alvarez filters each through a stringent recruiting process and Wickman helps them overcome their demons. We educate and train them, and they are well compensated for their service. Every one of them earned the right to be a Larkian. These men are like family to me. They're your family now, too."

She flashed back to her father's drawings hanging in the corridor. The one of his first ship, *Sea Lark*. She imaged her father, Alvarez, Dr. Wickman, Leonard, and the shadowy figures of two others she had yet to meet, standing on the ship's deck. "Larkian, as in *Sea Lark*?"

His gaze swept across the others, sitting around the table. "We've been Larkians ever since our earliest seafaring days together."

She glanced around the room at the men filling the cafeteria. It was going to take a lot more than her father's encouragement for her to consider all of them as family.

"You've always been one of us, you just didn't know it. Now eat, you look pale."

She watched Alvarez as she nibbled on her banana. He had pushed aside his breakfast and was reading something on his laptop. She jumped when his fingers attacked the keyboard.

She cleared her throat. "So, what is it you do besides wandering the streets for potential recruits?"

"I am the strategist," he said. His fingers didn't miss a beat.

She leaned over, trying to steal a peek. "What are you strategizing?"

"How to rescue your friend."

She reached over and tipped the screen so she could see.

He slapped her hand.

Her cheeks flamed and fingers curled into a fist.

Her father shook his head, warning her to back off. "Alvarez doesn't like people touching his things; in fact, Alvarez doesn't like to be touched at all."

She glared. "But I have insider information."

Alvarez's glared at her over the rim of his glasses "A romp through their city and you think you know everything?"

She gaped. Brutes she could deal with, but this guy was an arrogant son-of-a-bitch. "I know they watch us and learn from us, and they could easily destroy us if they wanted to, but they haven't."

"They're cunning monsters who would not think twice about killing you."

"You're wrong." She looked to her father for support, but got nothing in return. She steadied her voice and addressed Alvarez. "What qualifies you as an expert on the Merahvu?"

Alvarez stood up. "Experience." He tugged his shirt from his trousers and raised it.

Her hand flew to her mouth. The skin on his torso looked like it had been torched by a flamethrower. Some of the skin sagged like melted wax and some was stretched so thin she could see the ribs underneath. One of his nipples was missing.

"This is what one of your finned friends did to me. I wasn't threatening him. He found pleasure in torturing me. I begged him to kill me. He laughed and promised that one day he would, but not to put me out of my misery. He said he would, one day, just because he could."

"When did this happen?"

"At a time we considered them our friends." He dropped his shirt, but the image remained seared in her mind. What Sinto had told her was true. Her father and Ianthe, and—by extension of their relationship—his remaining crew were once allies.

Her father said, "They can't be trusted."

Her mind and heart floundered. Setting her up, stealing Blake. What Sinto had done proved that too.

"Now do you believe me?"

Sadly, reluctantly, and regretfully, she nodded.

66

Key

TWO DAYS LATER, AUDREY was roused from her bunk by Stokes shortly after dawn. Sometime during the night, they had arrived where it was believed Sinto's city was located in the North Pacific.

She and her father stood on the aft deck above the cargo chamber and the sloping transom, bundled up against a North Pacific chill, sipping from steaming mugs of coffee. To the southeast, the morning sun winked farewell behind the next round of approaching weather. The brief reprieve from fierce seas would soon to be over. The ship gracefully rose and dipped on gentle swells.

The ship's transom swung down with a high-pitched whine until it hovered over the water like a dock. It locked into place a few feet above the surface of the water with a resounding clunk. A pair of rails slid out from the opening and extended into the water past the end of the transom door. A deep rumbling came from below their feet, and next came a forty-foot tender, sliding down the rails assisted by a hydraulic tender arm. It was the same slick black boat Stokes piloted into Friday Harbor on the day of the orcas' attack. It rolled down the rails and slipped into the sea with a gentle splash. The thruster arm withdrew back into the belly of the ship. A man aboard the tender fired up the engines and drove it clear of the ship.

Stokes barked orders.

A second access door dropped opened and locked into place along the port side where two more crewmen were preparing to launch remote submersibles, six total.

"I asked Alvarez to join us on the bridge," her father said.

"Has he figured out how to pass through the dome?"

"No, but he asked if I thought you might have any ideas."

"Really?"

"Feel lucky—it usually takes a lot longer for him to trust someone new. Shall we?" He gestured for her to lead the way up the stairs to the upper deck, through the aft door, and down the main corridor to the bridge.

"What if we don't find the city?"

"We'll find it."

"How can you be so sure?"

He grinned. "We have you, don't we?"

They were met on the bridge by Alvarez and the Aussie who had boldly grabbed her that first day. The guy with the scar running ear to mouth.

Her father said, "This is Tucker, our technical engineer. He specifically requested your assistance."

Why am I not surprised? she thought. "At last, a formal greeting," she snarked.

He held out a fist. She bumped it.

"Pleasures 'ol mine." The tautness of the scar on his cheek distorted his upper lip when he smiled.

She followed Tucker down a tight spiraled stairway cut into the floor of the bridge. It felt like dropping down into a stifling hot cave. Racks of electronics filled one side of the narrow windowless room. Keyboards, joysticks, and pointing devices littered a desktop on the other side; multiple flat screens hung on the wall above. The dark narrow space doubled as Tucker's cabin. A pull-up bar spanned the narrow space beyond the electronics, and along the far wall was his unmade bunk, nightstand, and dresser.

Tucker stripped off his long-sleeved shirt and grabbed an undershirt from the top drawer of his dresser. Audrey tried not to gape, but the guy was wiry and all muscle. The type of guy who moved with deadly grace and could probably scale the Empire State Building, on the *outside*. He smiled that distorted smile when he caught her looking.

"Gets hot in 'ere, but I like it." He pulled on an undershirt and ruffled his short blond hair. "Reminds me of 'ome."

He slipped into a high-backed leather chair positioned at the wraparound workstation. He pulled a second chair next to his and patted it. She sat down.

Between rows of joysticks and mini-keypads were empty Red Bull cans and a half-eaten sandwich. He muttered an apology as he scooped it all into a trash bin beneath the desk.

He flipped several switches and the walls came alive with blue screens. Curious, she reached for a bulb-headed joystick covered with several buttons that sat in front of her.

"Don't touch that," he snapped.

He typed something on his keyboard. Images of brightly lit plankton suspended in the sea filled six of the screens. One for each of the six submersibles descending to the sea floor.

Tucker opened a topographical chart of the North Pacific on the screen directly in front of him. He typed something and a large red circle popped up on the chart. He zoomed in until the circle filled the entire screen. Inside the circle were topographical lines and clusters of sea mounts.

"I lost track of the bugger before I'd hoped. Fish city is somewhere within that circle. The ship's parked smack dab in the center above. The submersibles start in the middle and work outward in concentric circles. That could take days. You and I need to narrow down the search."

"How do you suggest we do that?"

"You're the expert, you tell me."

"Uh…"

He laughed. "Tell me what you saw. Significant landmarks, valleys in the ocean floor, shape of mountain peaks… anything unique we can look for."

"Three sea mounts, big as mountains, evenly spaced, in the shape of a triangle." A detail sparked that might help. "One of the mounts had a crescent-shaped peak." She scanned the small dark room, looking for something that remotely resembled what she saw. Her eyes fell to the sandwich lying in the trash can. Tucker had taken a large bite before discarding it. She picked it up and tipped it sideways. "Offset like this."

Tucker nodded. "Interestin'." He started typing. "What else?"

"The city's nestled in between the three mountains, and sprawls over several outcroppings." "Except in one place…" Her voice trailed off, remembering the wastelands where the House of Healing was located. "There the seabed's flat and mostly unoccupied." She banished the sudden and disturbing image of the dying boy she'd witnessed from her mind, focused on finishing her answer. "A dome of organic matter covers the entire city."

"Geographic size of the city?"

"Um…"

His fingers hovered over the keyboard, wound up and ready to go. He bounced the balls of his feet. "Compare it to somewhere you know. Seattle? Washington State?"

"San Juan Island, maybe a little bigger."

He ran a quick Internet search for the size of San Juan Island. Then he scratched the scar on his cheek, mumbling to himself, converting square miles to meters, then cubic feet, then he added another ten percent. His fingers attacked the keyboard, writing a custom program in terse language. He compiled it, an error was flagged. He swore, fixed it, and compiled it again. He swiveled to face her, wagged a brow and made a grand show of pressing the Enter key.

Red flags began popping up within the circle on the screen.

"Those are clusters of sea mounts matching whatcha described." He pushed a mouse in front of her. "Your turn. Tell me if you find anything that looks familiar. Standard interface, zoom in, zoom out, scroll around." He sat back with his hands behind his head, watching as she clicked and zoomed. "Is it true yer trained to kill?"

She never thought of her martial arts training that way, but nodded.

"Did he teach you the clinch 'n guillotine?

"The what?"

"Ya know..." He locked his hands around an imaginary head, pulled it down to his chest, wrapped one arm under the pseudo neck, the other above, clasped his hands in a gable grip and yanked up. A move that would snap a victim's neck instantly. A kill move, one that made her nauseous each time her father made her practice it.

She rolled her eyes. "Oh yeah. That and the head roll and neck snap."

He whistled. "Sweet! You and I should tumble later."

"Uh, maybe, later." *Like waaay later, or better yet, never,* she wanted to say. Instead she pointed toward the screen. "Work, remember?"

He stabbed himself in the chest with an imaginary knife, jerked as if in a final death throw, then stilled, body splayed back in his chair.

She stifled a chuckle. The guy was scary but smart and quirky and starting to grow on her. She scrolled to the top of the chart, determined to stay focused on the task at hand. She started in the uppermost left corner and zoomed in. "These images are amazing. Did you get these from NOAA?"

"Nope, ours, surveyed last year."

"Have you run thermal scans?"

"Yep."

She zoomed in on another grouping. "And?"

"Nothing, nada, zip, cold as a witch's tit."

Audrey studied the chart while Tucker worked a hacky sack with his fingers. After forty-five minutes she was ready for a break. She sat back and rubbed her eyes.

Tucker tossed the sack in the air, caught it. "What's yer friend like?"

She gazed up at the screens on the wall, wondering which one displayed her encounter with Sinto on the beach. She felt the blood rise in her cheeks and the tip of her still-healing nose throbbed. "Are you the one who figured out how to track them?"

"Yep." The hacky sack fell to the floor with a dull thud. He rummaged in a drawer, pulled out a tubular metal object about the size of his forearm. "Ever seen one of these?"

It looked like some sort of pipe bomb. He handed it to her. It was much heavier than she expected.

"It's a sonobuoy," he said. "Listening sticks. Electronic spies of the sea. Navy's been using these for decades. I reengineered it to be smaller and lighter, with a longer range. Remote drones drop 'em in the sea in overlapping circles and a satellite reads their signal. At first, we didn't hear anything but the usual biologic ruckus, but once I figured out what to listen for, it was a snap. They pass through the water with hardly any cavitation. Those suckers are fast and quiet. Like a mouse."

"You peppered the entire Pacific with these things?"

"Oy! That'd be impossible! I found they mostly traveled north. Makes sense. Nobody would be sniffing around in these waters." He shrugged. "I got lucky, after Stokes picked you up, ya know when ya—" He made a face that mimicked someone drowning. "I had a feeling he might jet, so I tracked him. He was moving slower than usual which helped."

She set the sonobuoy on the desktop. Sinto was moving slower most likely because of the drugged dart that found his shoulder.

She wasn't sure she wanted to find Sinto's city. Last night she couldn't sleep. The Mark was restless and adrenaline coursed through her veins; the nightmares and paranoia her father had instilled had returned. She felt anxious, like something horrible was about to happen.

She gazed at the remaining red dots she had yet to zoom in on. She shoved her unease aside, remembering Blake, stuck in a nightmare of his own. She had promised to bring him home. She grabbed the mouse and continued searching, torn but with renewed vigor.

Alvarez descended the stairs. "Submersibles have reached the bottom. Stokes is standing by." He stepped up behind her. "Any luck?"

Audrey shook her head, selected the next grouping of red dots, and zoomed in. She sat forward with a start. "Wait. I think I found something." She zoomed in on three peaks, set in a perfect triangle; one was crescent-shaped. Nestled between their peaks was a blurred white image, lighter than the surrounding sea floor, perfectly round like the city's dome.

Tucker grabbed a headset and pulled it over his head. "Stokes, Audrey found something. Give me the controls to—hold on," his eyes shifted between the screens displaying the submersible's images, "number five."

He switched the submersible camera to his main screen, grabbed the bulb-headed joystick, and worked the buttons. Submersible number five burst into action, bounding across the colorless landscape.

Audrey's heart hammered when the back side of the crescent-peaked mountain appeared on the screen. Tucker guided the submersible into a vertical climb. The mountainside slipped away and they were staring up into the black abyss, then he tipped it forward. The screen was awash in blinding light. Tucker made quick adjustments to the feed.

Sinto's city spread before them in living color.

Tucker nearly fell out of his chair. "Fuck me! How the hell did I miss *that*?"

Alvarez shouted up the stairwell. "Culliford, you've got to see this!"

Tucker guided the submersible along the top of the dome, recording the movement of thousands of Merahvu going about their daily business. A child, playing in a tree, saw the submersible and pointed. Dozens of small faces looked up, then disappeared into the leaves like a school of startled fish.

Like the frightened children, the city seemed incredibly vulnerable through the thin veil of the organic dome. They passed over the center of the city where Club Ballo stood at its peak; in the distance was the Terrakai forest, surrounded by fields and wetlands, vividly green from a fresh rainfall. Beyond that was the pale seabed and the House of Healing where Sinto took Audrey to meet his sister.

Audrey's father stepped up behind her. The Great Tower and sprawling compound where Sinto lived winked in the bright mock sun on the far side of the city where it butted up against the largest mountain. Audrey pointed. "There. That's where she's keeping Blake. Beneath that tower."

"Take us closer," her father said.

The submersible rounded the top of the dome and slid down the other side. The lands surrounding the tower looked exactly as she remembered: The mushroom-like houses, lush gardens, transparent bridge, and the cave opening, cut into rock at the base of the tower, where Blake was imprisoned.

The submersible slowed as it drew closer to the Great Tower. Her father sucked a sudden breath. Ianthe stood on the balcony at the top of the tower with Sinto by her side, expectantly waiting to greet them.

Tucker zoomed in, framing their bodies on the screen. The queen tipped her chin and smiled, acknowledging their presence, *welcoming* them.

Sinto gazed directly into the camera. His eyes locked with Audrey's. The Mark in her arm quivered like a tuning fork. Sinto's arm twitched. He reached over and touched it. Her heart quickened. He nodded and smiled. Goose bumps rippled across her body like a fast-running tide.

The connection between them was foreign and exhilarating, pleasant and terrifying; a connection that held no bounds of distance or substance in between. She struggled to breathe evenly.

Her father was breathing faster too, a storm of emotion brewing in his eyes. "This is going to be interesting," he said evenly.

Audrey took a closer look at the queen. The clarity of the image was astounding. She could see a faint glimmer of moisture pooling in her eyes, the slight quiver of her lip, fingers madly twirling a lock of hair. Audrey looked at her father. He diverted his eyes from the screen.

The queen wanted him to find her!

"Get a full survey of the city," he snapped.

Tucker tipped the joystick and the submersible continued its trek toward the smaller dome and the jellyfish with glowing bellies located on the opposite side of the city, beyond the wastelands.

Her father said, "What's that?"

"Their atmospheric processing plant. They burn hydrogen to heat the city. The blue jellyfish is filled with fresh water, a byproduct."

"Which one's filled with hydrogen?"

"The red one."

Her father slipped Alvarez a sideways glance before turning to her. "Any ideas on how we get inside?"

The Mark still hummed in perfect pitch with Sinto's. She swallowed down her growing unease. The seed of truth planted firmly in her mind as if Sinto was there to whisper it in her ear.

"With me. I'm the key you'll need to get inside."

67

Infidelity

Sinto gazed into the lens of the mechanical spy hovering outside the dome. He sensed Audrey's heart quicken and his leapt in response.

His mother twirled a lock of her hair. Anxiousness stirred her aura. "Have you taken care of Naiada?" she asked.

"She is safe."

He had personally overseen her departure to the Arctakai's colony in the Southern Ocean, along with the Keepers of Knowledge. He chuckled to himself as he recalled her parting shot, after they said their formal goodbyes. She had zapped him in his buttocks with a bolt of electricity fired from her eyes.

"She's back to her mischievous self. I gave her a final treatment, though it was unnecessary. Her blood is pure and body is strong. Except for the scars, she's fully recovered."

"She's alive because of you," she said, wistfully.

A long moment of silence passed as they watched the remote submarine turn toward the atmospheric plant, glowing in the distance.

"Have the Healers moved the weak ones?"

He frowned. "The Healers let them pass." He closed his eyes and tried to bury the memory; their frustration over the meaningless waste as they watched the weak ones die. Too weak to save. Too weak to relocate. They had no choice.

"We were merely prolonging their suffering. How many survived with their help?"

"None."

She sighed. "It was the right decision. Difficult, but humane. We need to conserve what sucuvita we have left for what may come next."

"Regretfully, I agree."

After a long silence she faced Sinto. "My son, there are some hard truths we must discuss. Now. I fear my chance is slipping away." Her eyes darted toward the remote submarine, buzzing around the atmospheric plant. "The rumors among the people, the whispers among the Circle, they are all true. I have grown complacent. Time has come for that to change."

"What are you implying?"

"We need Culliford's help."

"I thought your plan was to convince him to leave us alone."

"Yes, for now, but..." She sighed. "Eventually, to survive, we will need him, all of them, the Larkians." She closed her eyes and he noticed for the first time signs of her true age emerging: the fine wrinkles around her eyes and across her upper lip, the slight sag of jowls, the looseness of skin down her neckline.

She seemed to hold her head higher and jutted her chin more than usual in an attempt to hide these signs of aging skin. Perhaps to hide the fact that the years were catching up and her strength was indeed waning. The same strength she drew upon for her visions. Changes that he had ignored until now. Changes that began in earnest when his father disappeared.

It was believed that Joined mates draw strength and power from each other, but once separated by emotional detachment or death, the benefit of their combined strength fades, slowly and surely, leaving one weaker than before.

Without Ramasis and her visions, his mother would be no different from anyone else. Once the people learned that she no longer possessed her gifts, she would be asked to step down. And with Naiada behind on her training and unproven to lead, the people would be left adrift. With so much dissent brewing, division and the threat of anarchy was real. As Naiada revealed to Sinto before she left, she sensed the rebels were growing in numbers. It was only a matter of time before they became emboldened.

Ianthe looked toward the center of the city where families with younglings were preparing to leave the city. "They are angry."

"You warned them this day would come."

"A warning made too late."

She reached for his hand and raised it to her lips. The Mark writhed. All she had to do was look down and she would clearly see it, dancing within the flesh.

Why had she not warned me? Did she not foresee this happening?

She kissed his palm and balled his hand inside both of hers; they were warm and comforting. "Son of my blood, what have I gotten you mixed up in?"

Sinto felt a tug in the pit of his stomach. Somehow he found his voice. "We'll get through this and once it's over, we will move on. We always have." He nodded toward the others, preparing in the distance. "And so will they."

Her eyes snapped to his. He swallowed nervously. She must know of the Mark. Was she seeking a confession?

The fire in her eyes retreated, replaced with uncertainty and fear. They darted nervously. "There's something you and I must discuss."

"It was my doing, please just let me—"

She pressed her finger hard against his lips. "Shh." Then she drew a deep breath. "I made an awful mistake."

He inhaled briskly. "Yes, it was a mistake sending me to—"

"No," she interrupted. "It is not that." She cast her eyes to his chest where his heart beat erratically. After a beat she looked up, and whispered, "Robert Culliford was my lover."

At first Sinto thought he had heard wrong, but saw the truth in her eyes. "When?"

"Before I became queen, and—" She drew a swift breath. "And after."

"After? More than once?"

She didn't answer right away and cast her gaze to the activity unfolding across the city. "I was young, like you, and Culliford was quite *intriguing.* I considered running away with him." She drew a breath and held it. "The—the truth is, I *planned* to run away with him. You see, your father and I..." She sighed. "Our Joining, it—it never happened. The Mark we supposedly share, the story of our chosen pairing, it was a lie. During my training, my mother convinced me it was necessary to gain favor from the people. It was more a threat than an ask. She told me what to do, how to convince Ramasis we were intended. Oh, the joy it brought to Ramasis' father, who was a powerful man among the Terrakai, and to the people, believing the Seakai and Terrakai were meant to be unified, that peace would reign at last. My mother was right, our fake Joining was confirmation of that fact. But it was a lie. Then, as it is today."

Sinto reached out and pulled her arm forward, exposing the raised Mark on the inside of her forearm, the swirl and trio of dots. The same symbol that represented unification. The same core symbol boldly stamped across the inner walls of the Great Tower; a golden swirl twined with a trio of three copper dots and linked together with chains of silver that represent the Arctakai.

The symbol representing unification and the Merahvu as one people, the very foundation of peace, based on a lie. The truth of it cut deep. Everything Sinto was taught to believe, based on a lie. Everything the people had been told, based on a lie. If this truth was revealed, the rebellion would certainly gain teeth.

He ran his fingers across the hardened ridges of the Mark buried in her arm. "How do you explain this? How did you convince our father into going along with this ruse?"

She gave him a sad smile. "I didn't have to. I never told him the truth. I tricked Ramasis as my mother instructed, presented the Mark and then forged the Marks embedded within our forearms once he accepted it. A sway of mind to trick the heart. The Joining was easy to fake, during which I planted the seed of our intended purpose: to lead the people and maintain the peace recently established, he as Terrakai representative in the Circle and I as overseeing consultant.

"Poor Ramasis had no more say than I in the matter. Once I Marked him, he believed he loved me, truly and deeply; that we were destined to be Joined, a fate sealed the day we were born. For as long as he believed it true, I could feed on his power. I needed his support and strength. Though it has been a constant challenge for me to feign the same depth of love for him."

Secrets and lies, then and now. So it was true: his parents' Joining was merely a myth. A fiction to prop them up as "chosen" to lead the people by some divine intervention no one could explain. Yet still, it didn't explain the Mark he and Audrey clearly shared and why...

Sinto dropped her arm. "You still love Culliford."

"I never stopped."

"How long, Mother—how long were you lovers?"

"I went to him for several years before I became queen. It ended when Leela died. Everything changed that day."

Sinto pondered these new facts. Her affair with Culliford must have spanned nearly two decades, both before *and* after she faked her Joining with his father. A lifetime of deceit to her mate, to the people. To her family. What other secrets did she hide? He thought back to his conversation with Naiada and her suspicions.

"Tell me about Leela. Was she," his voice caught, "*Culliford's?*"

"Ramasis was her father. I made sure of that. Please, Sinto, understand, I love your father, I always have, I just love him... *differently.*"

"Did he know?"

"No! I made sure of that too, nor did he ever suspect. I rifled his mind often to be certain." She winced, ashamed. "You know how skilled I am at uncovering secrets. I am even better at hiding my own. I have told no one this truth, only you. With Naiada fast becoming a woman, her strengths will soon fully manifest. I fear she will discover my secret soon after."

Sinto thought, *She may have already.*

He sat and buried his head in his hands. A wave of anger swept through him. He should be clearing his mind, focusing on facing Audrey and her father. And now? How could he stand firm by his mother's side, knowing she lied all these years? How could he look her in the eye without judging? How could he trust her?

"Father did not deserve this. Naiada and I do not deserve this. This family is a lie."

Ianthe sat down beside him, hugging her knees. "This family is not a lie. Your father and I love you and Naiada with all our hearts. It was our duty to bring forth both of you to fulfill your duties to our people. Their survival comes first. That is the way it has always been and shall continue to be. I know your father did not deserve this, but the heart is fickle. I should have had the strength to walk away from Culliford, and for that I am ashamed. I am not as strong as I have made everyone believe. Your father has been my strength and without him..." She looked away, fighting back tears. "This mess is my fault. I must put an end to this, whatever it takes."

"Leela died because of you."

A sob escaped her lips. "She followed me when I left on one of my indiscretions with Culliford, and met that boy, Thomas. She was only a few years older than Naiada is now, stretching the bounds of her strength and newfound powers. I thought she was merely playing with him and tricked him into falling in love, until I saw the Mark. I was utterly confounded because of what I was told; the Mark, the Joining, was a myth! How was I to know it was real? I only tried to break their love for one another, but something went horribly wrong. It was after that I realized their Mark was real, and their bond through it, real."

"You could have consulted your visions, you could have asked her."

She shook her head. "I acted out of arrogance, never considering the consequences. I never wanted to be the queen. I wanted to relinquish my duties once Leela was trained. I wanted to be free! Free from your father so I could run away with Culliford. Leela was my salvation, that is why I severed the love-bond she shared with the Sapien Thomas. She was not supposed to die!" She closed her eyes, fighting back waves of past emotions. "I lied to your father and told him Culliford's men killed her. What else could I do? If he had learned the truth, if the Circle had learned the truth, then I would have been banished, and you and Naiada would never have been born. The bloodline would have been broken for the first time in our history.

"Once I learned Culliford's crew had been hunted down, tortured, and murdered, I figured out it was your father. My visions confirmed Culliford had survived, and Ramasis' rage continued to fester. I feared he would eventually find Culliford and kill him. I could not let that happen.

"So I told Ramasis the truth—not of my affair with Culliford, but the reason for Leela's death. My discovery of the Mark and my fear she had Joined with a Sapien, that it was my decision to sever their bond, that it was I who was responsible for her death. It took many years for your father to forgive me, but we agreed to put the needs of the people before our own and continued our work, unifying the Terrakai into the fold of the Merahvu as equals with Seakai and Arctakai. Just as my mother and the Circle had intended at the end of the Forever War. He spent most of those years living in the City of Green while I oversaw the growth of Tallamure.

"Then one day he came back, confessing his undying love and that he forgave me. Shortly after, you and Naiada were born, and your father and I forged an agreement: that raising you both was of utmost priority, especially Naiada, our future queen. It was in the best interest of the Merahvu for us to forget the past and live together as the family we were meant to be. I swallowed my selfish pride that day."

"We must do everything to protect Naiada," Sinto said.

"She is the only one who can maintain the peace. The Circle is growing suspicious of me. I hear their thoughts demanding it. *Naiada.* I must complete her training once this mess with Culliford is put to rest."

"All the more reason to protect *you*. Perhaps you should leave before Culliford arrives."

"I am not afraid of him," she said, but he saw the fear in her eyes.

"Why are you telling me this, now?"

"Today may not end well. What that may mean, I'm unsure—it's just a feeling."

A *feeling*, Sinto thought. Naiada told him she had an uncertain feeling too, right before she gave him the vague warning about leaning left.

Ianthe shivered and wrapped her arms across her chest. "I feel so alone. I miss Ramasis terribly."

"You have Naiada and me." He wrapped his arm around her shoulder.

"And Ramasis." She touched the Mark on her forearm. "I know he's still alive, somewhere. He may be weak or dying, but he lives. Naiada will need him to gain the Terrakai's favor."

"Then I will find him when this is over. I promise." He stood and held out his hand. She took it and stood, then she kissed him in the traditional way of mother to child; on the forehead, nose, cheeks, and lastly his lips.

"I am sorry, Sinto, truly sorry for the things I have put you through. For what you have left to do."

His stomach roiled in warning, but he tamped down his unease. There was still much to prepare.

"Is there anything else you require of me?"

"Have you prepared our prisoner?"

"He is ready to deliver. Just say when."

68

Purpose

Sinto left his mother's side and wandered the gardens winding around the Great Tower, deeply troubled. After learning of his mother's infidelity with Culliford, so many things became crystal clear.

This mess stemmed from Leela's death, culminating on the day Audrey's mother died. A day he remembered vividly. He had returned with the book Audrey had loaned to him, only she was not on the beach. There was just a man, waiting. Sinto had no idea the man was Robert Culliford. When the man approached him, he panicked and fled back into the sea where he was confronted by dolphins. They were frantic, screaming and pushing him toward the outer reefs.

A woman was bound in a fishnet snagged in the coral below the surface. He had no idea how she could have become so fully ensnared in the net. Forbidden to be seen by a Sapien in his natural form, he hid, unsure what to do. But the dolphins nipped at him and screamed for him to act.

He swam to her aid, melted layers of netting with electrical fire from his fingertips. In his haste, he had accidentally shocked her over and over. Each time she flinched and air bubbles slipped past her lips. By the time he reached the last layer, her eyes were wild with fear and she sucked a watery breath. He had tried to suck the water from her lungs, but he had no air to replenish them, not while breathing through his gills. His lorica, at his young age, would not have been enough to support the two of them.

Believing the man on the beach could help the woman, he rushed her to the surface and created a commotion, slapping his tail and screaming for help as he struggled to drag her toward shore.

That was when his father, Ramasis, grabbed him, pulled him under, and reprimanded him for revealing himself to the woman and the man on the beach. When Sinto looked back, the woman was floating face down in the water. Eyes open, the light of her aura extinguished, as was her essence.

Afterward, his father announced his month-long errands in the islands were complete. He made Sinto promise to never tell anyone what happened to the woman or of encountering the man on the beach. Sinto was forbidden to ever return to the island.

Sinto never broke his promise. He hid this secret deep in his mind, where his mother and his sister would never find it. It wasn't until his mother gave Sinto the assignment to kindle a relationship with Audrey that he realized who Audrey's father was and the historical significance as it related to the death of his older sister, Leela.

After his mother's recent confession, he now understood the magnitude of what was at stake should anyone learn the whole truth.

It was his father who had suggested Sinto befriend the girl on the beach.

I'm going to take from him what he stole from me, his father told Sinto that day. When Sinto asked who and what, he merely replied, *Someday when you are a man you will understand who and what. Now off with you, do as I ask. I will call you when it is time to go.*

Despite his mother's assurances, Sinto now believed that his father had learned of her affair with Culliford. Jealousy rotted his essence. He used Sinto to distract Audrey while he waited for the opportune moment to murder Culliford's wife, and when the net presented itself like a gift, his father staged the perfect accident—until Sinto messed it up.

And years later, Culliford must have set the trap for Naiada and his father and poisoned them out of malice, believing it was Ianthe who ordered the murder of his beautiful new wife.

And so it began, a vicious cycle of murder and revenge, a flash-point for the rebellion simmering among the Terrakai. The peace agreement that unified all three tribes under a single sovereignty was teetering on the brink of collapse.

All because of a selfish mistake and a fickle heart.

Sinto sat beneath the coconut tree where patches of tanzen grew and he had watched with wonder as Audrey tasted it for the first time, at her playful snap of teeth when she gobbled down more. Would he ever have the joy of hearing her laugh or savor the tenderness of her lips again?

Despair and anger filled him. The truth must be buried. Their mother must be spared. Naiada needed to complete her training. After, and with the guidance of the Circle, the rebellion must be crushed, their poisonous ideals abolished, along with the truth of his mother's lies and deception.

Protect Naiada and his mother. Whatever the cost. That was Sinto's purpose, here and now.

He gazed at the small mechanical spy, crisscrossing the dome, with an uneasy feeling.

What is Culliford planning?

69

Hold It

THE NEXT MORNING, AUDREY stood beside Stokes and her father in the cargo chamber. The coat she wore did little to fend off the icy wind funneling through the open transom door. They watched several crewmen prepare the ship's submarine for the dive to Tallamure.

Last night, they hammered out details of the mission to rescue Blake. Since the submarine only seated four, it was decided that she, her father, and Stokes would go, leaving the fourth seat for Blake on the return. As they hashed out the plan, Audrey began to panic and after dinner she slipped back into her cabin, thinking of ways to back out.

But her father managed to roust her this morning, pumping her up with caffeine and guilt, telling her that the mission would fail without her, that she may never see Blake again. He successfully managed to quell her fears, all except for one.

In order to get from the submarine to the city's dome, they would need to enter the water. To avoid being crushed to death at that depth, they couldn't breathe compressed air, but a specialized oxygen-rich liquid, Stokes simply called "Liquid." Liquid was as dense as water, and when first drawn into the lungs and sinuses, it would feel like drowning.

Last night, she sneaked up to the ship's library and scoured the Internet for information on the deepest dives ever attempted. While there had been deeper dives successfully accomplished by a manned submarine, no one had ever *exited* a submarine at a depth of six thousand feet.

She laid awake all night believing her father was truly mad.

Stokes estimated it would take two minutes to walk fifty feet from the sub to the city's dome wall. One minute to negotiate passage into the city. Plus the return once they retrieved Blake.

Twice they would flood their lungs with Liquid and flush it from their lungs. Once when they were safely inside the city and again when they returned to the sub.

The flush was a potentially fatal process, thus the need for a small amount of compressed air, in a second tank specially designed to withstand the pressure. As the Liquid drained from their lungs, compressed air would fill the void in a delicate dance of equalized pressure to keep the lungs from collapsing. Too much air and the lungs would burst, too little and the delicate lining would collapse and stick together like wet tissue. In the latter case, suffocation and death would quickly follow without the necessary medical intervention. In the first case, well, there would be lots of agony and blood and little hope of surviving.

Stokes made it *sound* easy. So easy, he told her, that she wouldn't require a practice dive. But Audrey knew the truth. The more dives she took with Liquid, the higher the probability she would end up with an infection, permanent lung damage, or dead.

Audrey wore Sinto's necklace as a talisman. In truth she no longer needed the necklace to call to Sinto. The Mark did that in spades. But wearing it gave her comfort. She rubbed the claw between her fingers as she watched a crewman fill tanks with Liquid. The claw warmed in her fingers and a mild electrical current rippled through the silver links, warming the coils of the Mark in her arm and those running through her heart. If Sinto didn't know they were coming before, he would soon enough.

She tucked the necklace under her thermal top when Dr. Wickman sidled up to her side. "How are you feeling?" he asked.

"Scared shitless."

He pulled two hypodermic needles from his coat pocket. He held one up, "Antibiotic, to keep your lungs from getting infected, and this," he waved the second needle, "will take the edge off your nerves."

"Are you sure? I'd hate to do something stupid."

"I am confident you won't notice it at all. The adrenaline running in your system will offset the effects. Think of it as an anxiety equalizer."

She slipped her arm from her coat and pulled up the sleeve of her thermal top. He swiped her skin with alcohol and quickly administered both shots in her upper arm.

He applied a pair of Band-Aids and gave her a reassuring smile. "Try to relax." Then he pushed his way past her and repeated the same with Stokes and her father. Only they got one shot, the antibiotic.

It was time to suit up. Every crew member had a custom suit that fit like a glove, except her. She had to borrow one.

The tall guy who knocked her on her ass outside the cafeteria stepped forward with a black rubber suit in his hand. It literally looked like he had skinned a man for it—feet, hands, scalp and all.

He flashed her a grin. "I'm Dyer, sorry about the other day." His eyes fell to her chest, then her feet. "Time to lose the coat and slippers." She dropped the coat at her feet, stepped out of the slippers. She shivered in the cool air despite the wool socks, thermal leggings, and long-sleeved top.

He knelt and stretched the suit open. "In you go."

She wriggled her stocking-clad feet into the attached booties using Dyer's shoulder to steady herself. She struggled to get the skin-tight suit over her hips, shimmying them with little luck. Dyer softly whistled.

"Enjoying yourself?" she asked.

"Oh yeah." He grabbed the suit by the waist, hitched it up, jerking her off her feet. The action was so unexpected she gasped. To her chagrin, she slipped right in with it snugged tightly around her hips.

He bent, smoothing the suit against every inch of skin. "Don't want any air pockets."

A couple of guys across the chamber were watching with jealousy in their eyes.

"Halfway there." Dyer tucked her braid down her spine and held out the sleeves; she stuck her arms in one at a time. More wiggling and aggressive tugging and smoothing along every inch. Next, he folded a series of inner flaps across her stomach and chest, liberally using his fingers to tuck them smoothly inside, then he zipped it up with a special zipping system that sealed the opening completely. He checked the metal ring attached to the neck of the suit where her helmet would attach and lock into place.

"Last step." He affixed a tube to a port behind her neck. "This might feel a little weird but we've got to suck all the air out."

"Hey, what was all that business about patting the air pockets ah—ah—" The rubber contracted around the thermal layer and to every curve of her body, crushing down on her chest and bruised ribs. She now knew what it felt like to be vacuum sealed.

He unplugged the tube and gave her wry smile. "Oops. My bad. I forgot." He patted her all over, again. "Perfect fit."

She tried to glare, to look menacing, but found it difficult under the circumstances. She wheezed, "I can't breathe!"

"Put some effort into it."

Her eyes cut across the chamber to the guys who had been watching. "How did you get the honor to help me with my suit?"

He grinned. "We had a contest. I accurately guessed your measurements. Down to the millimeter." He leaned in and dropped his voice. "I slipped into your cabin last night. With a tape measure." Then, he winked.

Her cheeks flamed. She punched him in the arm. Her fist bounced back.

He laughed and shook his head. "Geez! Lighten up! That was *joke.*"

"Sorry," she said, sheepishly.

"No really, I did."

She gave him a dirty look.

"Maybe I didn't. Oh, I'm so confused! Did I or didn't I?" He laughed. "Guess we'll never know!"

His joking around finally cracked the tension. It was hard to laugh but the release felt good.

She flashed on the thought of her close friend Ryan, how he would appreciate Dyer's quirky humor—her heart pitched. *Shit!* She left Ryan in the lurch and had failed to contact him after her accident with Roy's boat. He had no idea what happened, where she was, that she was still alive. Everything had happened so fast, what with nearly drowning and ending up on her father's ship sailing for the North Pacific. She had been so distracted by the Mark, finding Sinto's city, and worrying about her father's intentions, that she simply forgot. She was certain he would be mightily pissed off and riddled with worry. First Blake and now her. On top of the fact she could barely breathe and that she was about to embark on a mission that may cost her her life, the guilt burrowed deep. She vowed that if she survived and they got Blake back, she would call him, ready to grovel.

Dyer was back to business, double checking the seal around her neck and the ring attachment lying across her collarbone. "Can you bend over and touch your toes?"

She bent over and stopped when she caught sight of her crotch. She pawed at the shriveled-up bulge between her legs. Not that she really cared what she looked like, but she was curious. She looked up at Dyer. "Whose suit am I wearing?"

Dyer chuckled. "Tucker's. He wanted me to be sure to tell you. You two are incredibly close to the same size." His eyes shifted to her crotch. "Except for that. Tucker's got one hell of a set of balls."

She rolled her eyes. "Of course he does. Be sure to tell him, I'm honored."

"You'll get the chance when you get back."

"I hope you're right."

He grabbed her by the shoulders and squeezed her gently. "Hey, nothing bad is gonna happen. Stokes won't allow it. I would give my left nut to be on that sub, just like every guy on this ship."

Audrey gave him a jittery nod. She had to admit that Dyer's lighthearted banter did help to quell her fear. But it didn't take long for that fear to slither back to her gut, and with a rumbling vengeance.

"Uh... I suppose it's too late to go to the bathroom?"

He laughed. "Affirmative, and if you make a mess in Tucker's suit, honored or not, he might cut you somewhere non-fatal, and in a very painful way. By the way, that's *not* a joke. I'd hold it if I were you."

"I'll try to remember that."

70

True Intent

Audrey's father approached, clad in his own suit of rubber armor, vacuum-sealed to his body. "Time to go."

They squeezed past the tender, tucked along the side of the cargo chamber, to the submarine, lying on the rails ready to launch.

The chamber's side door was open, with all six submersibles lined up and ready to launch. There was a flurry of activity around them, with stubby tubular-shaped payloads being strapped to their undercarriages. Audrey hadn't been privy to any discussions on why they would be needed nor what they might be carrying. She wasn't sure she wanted to know.

The submarine they would be using had been named and christened *Discovery* by the crew. *Discovery* looked like a pudgy fighter jet. Stubby wings protruded from the center of its body. A six-inch-thick transparent view port was seamlessly melded to the double-layered steel hull. It spanned across the first quarter of *Discovery*'s body, above the passenger chamber. Dual propellers were mounted in protective tubes aft of the stubby wings. Rudders provided steerage along with dual thrusters flaring out from the underbelly. *Discovery* was one-of-a-kind, designed and built by the

Larkians under the guise of Grey Industries. *Discovery* was stuffed with proprietary technological innovations, patented to the hilt.

Discovery was composed of two chambers. One up front for passengers, the other in the rear. The only means of entry was through the aft chamber. The aft chamber was designed to flood and drain quickly and would only allow passage to the passenger chamber once pressure was equalized.

The hatch to the aft chamber was open. A few easy steps up the ladder and she would be inside, or so she thought. She felt lightheaded. Between the vise-like crush of the suit around her chest and the ache of bruised ribs, she found it impossible to breathe freely. She took Dyer's advice and put some effort into it, drawing long and deep before taking the first step.

Her foot slipped on the second rung and she hung for a second from her arms as pain ripped through her chest. Someone shoved her up and pushed her through the hatch. She tumbled through the small round opening, landing on her knees. It took a moment for the shot of pain from her tender bruised ribs to subside.

She stood as best she could. The aft chamber was much smaller than she expected and she had to stoop. It would be a challenge for four bodies plus tanks to fit hunkered over. Four tanks of Liquid and compressed air cluttered the concave floor. Their helmets were hung above, along with an extra suit for Blake.

She squeezed past the equipment and through a second round hatch into the passenger chamber. This one was bigger, but not by much. She still had to hunker over. There were four seats configured in two rows with a narrow aisle running in between and not much else. Storage compartments and electronics were tucked into whatever remaining space was available. Small view ports the size of her fist were buried within the hull beside each seat.

Stokes was already seated at the helm, front and starboard. Audrey squeezed into the seat behind him. Her father was last to enter. Her ears popped when he closed the hatch and engaged the airtight seal. He squeezed into the seat opposite Stokes.

Stokes flipped switches. "Buckle up."

Audrey secured the five-point harness, making minor adjustments to the straps.

"Comm check," Stokes said.

Audrey was assigned communications. *Discovery's* radio was tucked sideways along the wall to her right. She switched it on, ran a quick test.

She looked out her view port. Dyer was visible, wearing a set of headphones with a microphone. She opened the channel. "Testing."

He gave her a thumbs up. Then he pointed at his wrist. Their suits included a built-in touch screen for communication.

She nodded back and tapped a message on the screen at her wrist: "Need to pee."

Dyer replied over the radio, "I'll instruct Tucker to sharpen his knives." She smiled at his response. She regretted Dyer wasn't with them; she needed a good laugh about now.

She smiled and tapped back: "Don't bother. I'll hold it."

"All systems check." Stokes twisted around in his seat. "Tell Dyer we're ready."

She flipped the radio switch. "Ready to roll."

Dyer gave her a thumbs up and disappeared from view.

Discovery lurched and rolled down the rails toward the sea. Audrey was thrown forward when they hit the water, thankful for the harness holding her tight in her seat. The sub bobbled violently in the wind-whipped seas. The slap of waves reverberated; sea spray splattered the dome above their heads.

"Ship clear," Dyer barked across the radio.

"Flooding ballast tanks." Stokes flipped a switch. There was a loud whoosh as air was flushed from the space between the specially formulated, double-layered inner and outer steel shells of *Discovery's* hull.

The sea swallowed them in a single gulp. Darkness quickly followed. Her father switched on the night vision lighting. An ominous red light filled the cabin.

Stokes guided the sub into a deep dive with a small joystick. Directly in front of him was a screen set in the forward bulkhead, displaying the same topographic chart she had worked with yesterday in Tucker's office. A glowing line led to a dot set within the triangle of sea mounts, a preprogrammed route to the city. At a descent rate of three hundred feet per minute, Tucker estimated it would take less than twenty minutes to reach the bottom, six thousand feet below.

Stokes engaged the autopilot, crossed his arms, and leaned back. "We're in for a smooth sail." The shadow cast by his brow hid his eyes and his smile twisted grotesquely in the eerie light.

Her father sat, eyes closed, meditating or something. She supposed she ought to be doing the same, but too much adrenaline was coursing through her veins. The shot Dr. Wickman gave her did nothing to quell her growing panic. Minutes passed. Her heart pounded and her eyes burned from staring at the depth meter showing their rapid descent. A shrill buzz filled her head.

"Audrey!" Stokes said.

"What?" She hadn't realized she was hyperventilating.

Stokes tapped the depth gauge; it read twenty-five hundred feet. "Time to check in with the ship."

"Right." She drew a deep breath before pressing the button. "Dyer, do you read?"

There was a snap of static followed by Dyer's voice. "Copy, we're tracking you at two-five-zero-zero, confirm."

"Confirmed."

"Right on schedule. Big Boy is receiving. Next check at five-zero-zero-zero, confirm."

"Big Boy" was a special sonobuoy Tucker designed and deployed at depth that connected to a chain of smaller sonobuoys and boosted transmissions coming from the deep to the surface, and vice versa.

"Confirmed."

"Roger." Pause. Then a message popped up on her wrist screen: *A, you okay?* Dyer asked.

She texted back. *Fine D.* Then as calmly as she could muster she said, "A, standing by."

It was a lie. She was panicked and struggled to even out her breathing.

Her father slipped into the seat across from her. He reached across and grasped her hand.

"Do as I say: deep breath in, deep breath out."

She stared into his eyes, so pale they looked pink in the red light. Concentrating on their dark centers, she breathed as he suggested. Their chests rose and fell in unison.

"I panicked the first time—deep breath in, good—ask Stokes, he had to talk me down—now out, slowly—just like I am helping you. It's natural to feel afraid. Remember your training. Focus on your fear, let it fuel you. Just like I taught you."

She didn't trust her voice so she nodded. *No problem, my tank is overflowing.*

"Good. I think now might be a good time to review our plan."

She sucked a deep breath. "Once we get into the city, we find Ianthe."

"And how do we get inside the city?"

"We all embrace and step through the dome wall as one—you, me, Stokes."

"Go on."

"Once we find Ianthe, you both agree to put the past behind you and part ways, peacefully. She hands over Blake, unharmed. Then we leave and never speak of the Merahvu again." The Mark flared in her arm. "And I never speak of *him* again."

He frowned. "I wish it was that simple."

"Dad, walk away from this before someone else gets hurt."

"I cannot do that."

"We're talking about Blake's life."

"Ianthe murdered my crew. Innocent men. Men who were like family to the rest of us. She murdered her own daughter and sent her son to murder your mother. Are you willing to let her get away with that? Let *Sinto* get away with that?"

"You don't know that for a fact. Besides, what did she have to gain?"

His jaw worked, chewing his words before he spit them out. "She wanted to hurt me. Killing your mother cut deeper than any knife."

"Why would she want to do that?"

He said nothing. In that moment of silence the truth became obvious. This new fact swirled, stirring up gritty loose ends she had forgotten from her confrontation with Ianthe. She had been overwhelmed by everything she learned that day and they didn't make sense at the time.

"Tell me everything about your relationship with Ianthe, starting from the day she saved your life."

He exhaled and gazed into the abyss through the transparent view port above their heads. "The winter storm took us by surprise. I had climbed the rigging, trying to sight land. It was coated in ice. When we struck the reef, I lost my grip."

"You were in love with her."

His gaze fell to his fisted hands. "I should have left her when I discovered that strange mark on her arm. She didn't have it at first. She tried to deny it, what it meant, but eventually confessed that she had been promised to another. *Ramasis*. She told me she didn't love him, that one day she would leave him to be with me. She made me vow not to tell anyone the extent of our relationship, not even my crew. So we feigned a strictly business relationship, trading news from the Sapien world in exchange for the secret source of her magical elixir and snippets she had gleaned of the future. She strung me along with her promises, then blamed me for what happened to her daughter. I had no idea the girl Thomas fell in love with was her daughter—she was dark-featured like the local natives."

He sucked a hard breath. "I had no idea of the power Ianthe possessed until that night. After she took her own daughter's life, she told us to leave and never come back.

"We sailed, hard and fast, toward the newly discovered Hawaiian Islands. But we were followed, attacked during the height of a tropical storm and severely disadvantaged. You saw what happened to Alvarez. Afterward, we made a pact to avenge the deaths of our fellow crewmen, tinkering with technology and accumulating wealth by capitalizing on Ianthe's predictions of the future. We searched for clues that would lead us to her secret city but found nothing. We began to wonder if they had disappeared entirely.

"Over the decades and centuries, we grew comfortable with our new lives. Then I met your mother. She made me feel free for the first time in my life. Before I met her, I was always running away from something or chasing my next prize, but the prize found me. Her. I embraced the idea of growing old and dying a natural death. It was your mother who gave me life, not Ianthe's cursed elixir.

"But I was the fool. Ianthe once told me, 'You will love no other.'" He paused, struggling to suppress his anger. "She sent her son to murder your mother and now..." He gazed at her arm. "She wants you."

"This never was about rescuing Blake, was it?"

He didn't answer. Their arrival to the city was announced by a blue glow. He slid from the seat beside her and joined Stokes to prepare for their landing.

Oh God, he's going to kill her.

71

Bait And Switch

AUDREY WAS FIRST TO enter *Discovery*'s rear chamber. Her father was last and sealed the hatch between the chambers once they were all inside. The small space quickly filled with their combined breath, stale from coffee and tainted with fear.

Stokes was hunched across from her and helped her pull up the hood of her suit. It was ridiculously tight and cupped her chin, leaving only an oval of her face exposed. It was so tight her ears ached and nose thrummed from the pressure cutting into the side of her face. Adding insult to injury he pulled a pair of swim goggles over her head and snugged them in place across her eyes and the tender bridge of her nose.

Her father was ready to go, staring at his reflection in the blade of a six-inch jagged-edged knife. A tool for dressing a recent kill, not negotiating a peaceful truce. When his eyes found hers, he slipped the knife into a concealed pocket at his thigh.

He handed her a mini-spear gun, auto-loading, with a barrel that spun to engage the next shot, like a six-shooter without the kick. Easy to reload: just eject the spent barrel, slip the new one into place, lock it down. Three steps, three seconds, and much more effective in water than bullets.

"You remember how to use this?"

"Yes," she answered with a tight smile.

Firing a spear gun underwater had been part of her training. Her father forced her to dunk her head under water to better see what she was targeting. Because of her fear of water she kept her eyes closed when firing, which infuriated him.

"And?"

She clinched her teeth. "Keep my eyes open."

He smiled. "Good girl." He clipped it to her hip. "Safety's on." Then he clipped three extra barrels of spears next to it.

He had been preparing her for this day. She didn't want this. It was his fight, not hers. He said her training was for her own protection, defense only. Lies. He had been preparing her to be a soldier in his war against the Merahvu. This starkly clear reality made her blood boil.

Stokes lifted her tank pack. She threaded her arms through the straps, stumbled under the weight. Fifty pounds of Liquid plus the canister of compressed air. He cinched the strap around her waist and looped a nasal cannula connected to the canister over her head and into her nose. He helped her slip on her helmet, clipping it into place. He double-checked the seal.

"Remember what I told you." His voice sounded distant and tinny through the rubber hood and sealed helmet.

She nodded nervously. "Relax, breathe naturally, let it slip inside. Think of it as really thick fog."

Stokes opened the valve. Liquid pooled around her neck, rolled across the bottom of her chin.

Move in harmony with force of life, flow as water, like stream around rock!

She convulsed when it reached her lips.

Not   water—not   drowning—perfluoro something—oxygen-rich—won't kill me—won't kill me—Stokes wouldn't let anything happen to me—Anything. Happen. To. Me. Right?

Cool Liquid rolled past her nose.

Ohgod ohgod ohgod!

Air escaped from her lungs. She pawed her helmet. Stokes grabbed her hands and pinned her to the side of the chamber. She opened her mouth, Liquid filled it. She swallowed. It tasted slightly sweet. She thought of her mother, the last seconds of her life. Was she afraid? Did she fight or surrender to her fate?

"Breathe!" Her father screamed.

Her lungs burned, her vision faltered, her legs buckled.

Her father hoisted her up. Stoke struck her in the solar plexus.

She gasped. Liquid roared down her throat and into her lungs. She froze with her mouth agape. She expelled that first liquid breath, then inhaled.

Fog my ass!

It was like breathing mud. She had to fight for every breath, primitive and unnatural. Nothing like the light and fizzy oxywater the Merahvu had perfected. *That* was like breathing fog, not mud.

Her father squeezed her hand. "Like running a marathon, pace yourself." She could barely hear him from the Liquid flooding her inner ears.

Once Audrey had settled into a strained rhythm of breathing, Stokes and her father flooded their helmets, sucking the Liquid into their lungs. She took pleasure watching her father squirm when he took his first watery breaths.

Stokes flipped a switch. Sea water filled the chamber. It swirled around their feet, the bitter cold seeping through the suit's thin rubber and her thermal layer beneath. Her hands and feet went instantly numb. Hypothermia was a real threat if they didn't hurry.

Stokes opened the aft hatch. The chamber filled with light emitted from the dome encapsulating the city. Her father pushed her through.

Her knees buckled when she landed on the marshy ocean floor. Marine snow exploded from beneath her feet, clouding the water. Numbness crawled up her arms and legs. She couldn't feel her extremities. Moving was impossible. Lungs sucked mud. Stokes encouraged her by pushing her foreword. Together they took baby steps toward the dome wall.

She set her gaze on flowers growing on the other side of the dome wall. *Step, suck. Step, suck.*

It took a minute to reach the dome wall but felt more like a day.

The Mark sprang to life and she was filled with Sinto's presence; the taste of him on her tongue and the warmth of electrified blood flowing through her veins. Her heart calmed and breath fell into a steady rhythm. She felt her extremities warm with his presence.

He knows I'm here!

Her heart thundered with hope and dread. Hope that the day would end peacefully. Dread, knowing of the deadly weapons they carried.

The dome wall soared before them. She pressed her gloved palm to the surface. It hummed and sparked. Electricity ran up her arm. The wall yielded and her hand popped through. Threads of electricity wrapped around her wrist, tugging her inside. She dug in her feet, resisting the pull, and signaled to Stokes and her father. As they had planned, the men embraced each other with her pressed between.

Electrical threads exploded from the dome and wrapped them in a blinding ball of light. Audrey closed her eyes as they pressed against the dome wall as one. It bent inward, stretching thinner and thinner, but refused to let them pass. It snapped back and they were hurled away from the dome wall, landing in an explosion of marine snow.

They untangled themselves, stood up, and gazed at each other confounded.

Stokes raised his wrist communicator but his finger never reached the screen. A bolt of lightning shot from the dome and struck him in the chest. He flew several yards back, landing next to *Discovery*. A second bolt shot out, wrapped around her father's waist, and sucked him inside the dome with a loud zap.

Audrey gaped in disbelief. Stokes lay on his back, unmoving. Her father knelt inside the dome, eyes wide with shock.

A third bolt shot out, grabbed her by the waist, and yanked her inside.

Stokes had managed to roll to his hands and knees. He got up, stumbled a few times, trying to make his way back to the dome. He reached out to touch it, but her father gestured wildly for him to stop. He pointed at his wrist communicator. Stokes nodded.

Her father typed something. Stokes read the message. He shook his head and held up his arm so they could see his screen. Gibberish. Interference from the city's dome. Communications cut off.

Peachy.

Her father pressed his shoulder against the dome. The surface rippled and bent, unyielding. He tried again, only harder. The dome bent outward, but snapped back. He was tossed into the air and landed in a sea of lavender.

Stokes waved to get their attention and held up his arm, revealing a message from the ship on his wrist screen. It read: "Blake here! Unharmed. Doesn't remember a thing."

Audrey looked at her father and their eyes locked. Concern etched his brow. He gave Stokes a set of simple hand gestures, the meaning clear: "Return to *Discovery*. Stand by."

Stokes acknowledged.

Her father pointed to the valve on the top of her tank. Audrey reached back and turned it. Compressed air burst through the tubes stuck in her nose. She unclipped her helmet, broke the seal. Liquid exploded from around her head and dissipated into the city's moist atmosphere. She dropped her helmet and bent over in shock, eyes watering. Liquid gushed from her mouth as air displaced Liquid from her lungs. Stokes said the flush would be a little unpleasant. It felt like regurgitating lungs. She would hate to experience what Stokes thought of as more than a little unpleasant.

She gasped and heaved and spit until she could draw a refreshing lungful of oxywater.

Her father seemed nearly as distressed with the process and it gave her pleasure to know she was not the only one to suffer.

She savored those first few breaths of oxywater. It felt like coming home but something was off. They were greeted by silence. The city was empty.

72

Trial

Audrey and her father had entered the city in the gardens surrounding the Great Tower. The mock sun blazed, lighting the metallic swirls on the curved wall, soaring above their heads, with its warm light. The tower's long shadow stretched beyond the dome, over jagged outcroppings and up the side of the mountain missing its top.

The Mark was going crazy in her arm and an unanticipated thought popped into her head. Sinto, offering guidance.

She told her father, "We enter on the other side of the tower."

The route Sinto dictated took them from the flats of the gardens and up a steep outcropping where the tower stood. They climbed along a narrow ledge, hugging the base of the tower; a sheer cliff inches from their feet. It was a challenging hike with heavy tanks strapped to their backs even with the extra lift of reduced gravity. Audrey appreciated the logic of Sinto's choice to round the back side of the tower. The route they took was inconspicuous, offering them cover from whatever prying eyes may remain in the city. Stokes followed closely in *Discovery* just outside the dome, hovering in the shadow of the tower.

Audrey stopped once they reached a tangle of overgrown vegetation. With their tanks strapped to their backs it would be impossible to swim over, so they had to go through. Her father stepped around her, karate-chopping his arms to clear a path.

A flashing light caught their attention. Stokes was sending a message in Morse code. Her father's jaw worked, then he waved back in acknowledgment.

"What did he say?"

"The ship is surrounded by Merahvu."

"They returned Blake unharmed. What would Ianthe gain by harming your crew? Maybe she sent them as protection."

He ignored her suggestion and resumed hacking his way forward. They broke through at the bottom of a zigzagged stairway that reached to the mouth of a cave carved into the rocky base of the tower. A ball of green light hovered in the entrance.

She pointed. "We go up and follow the light inside."

Her father stopped and studied the situation. The flat seabed outside the wall, the distance to the cave opening. Then he signaled for Stokes to land. *Discovery* settled softly next to the dome wall on a patch of flat seabed with minimal disturbance to marine snow.

Stokes acknowledged, "Standing by," in Morse code.

Her father said, "We leave the tanks here." They removed them along with their helmets and left them next to the dome wall.

The climb up the stairs was much easier without the added weight. They quickly hopped up, kicking their legs to help propel them upward. The ball of green light took off once they reached the mouth of the cave. They followed it through a meandering network of tunnels to an arched opening cut into the side of the tower's curved wall, buried deeply in rock.

The ball of green fire fizzed with a pop.

Her father pulled her back and entered the tower first.

Audrey followed, gazing up. Awe blossomed in her heart. The Great Tower was much more than just a gathering place where the Merahvu's governing Circle conducted business. An aura of peace and unity permeated its soaring walls, stretching ten or more stories high. Balconies ringed each level all the way to the top, enough to seat tens of thousands of spectators. Rays of light streamed from the open ceiling, lighting mosaics of gold, silver, and copper, and inlaid with semi-precious stones and diamonds. The mosaics told stories of historic events, like a great cathedral's stained-glass windows telling religious stories to ardent believers.

The most prominent mosaic represented the sealing of the peace agreement Sinto had told her about, a significant turning point in their history; the unification of three distinctly different warring tribes into one unified people: The Merahvu. The mosaic was of intermixed tribal members standing behind a youthful Queen Ianthe with her vitally handsome Terrakai mate, who's facial features were unmistakably inherited by Sinto. The symbol of their union prominently hovered between them—a trio of copper dots twined with a gold swirl, like the one Audrey saw pressed into the wall of Queen Ianthe's residence. If the Merahvu were a nation, this would be the symbol prominently displayed on their flag.

Other mosaics depicted all three tribes intermingling peacefully; of feasts and dancing; of families greeting the newly born and sharing coming-of-age celebrations; of romantic love and the Merahvu's version of matrimony; of the riches of a successful hunt shared with all; of healing and the acceptance of death as an integral part of the circle of life and not to be feared but celebrated. Inspiring stories of a people remade by setting aside a violent and bitter past and twining their differences into something new and rejuvenating. Stories of hope and promise.

As Audrey absorbed the Merahvu's history she wondered: *Is it really that simple to merely cast aside past grievances, to only look forward, to celebrate alongside your enemy while the blood of shared brothers and sisters still soaked the earth?*

Once she would have believed it possible, the Utopian world Sinto tried to sell the first time he brought her to this city. But life had a funny way of crushing simple dreams and opening one's eyes to harsh realities. She pondered what other, less pleasant, stories were not explicitly shared. Stories of angst and compromise, like Nawtuga blithely living in a cave carved beneath the seabed thousands of feet beneath the surface of the ocean, having never set foot on her terrestrial lands of Merluma and living in fear of what lay beyond the protection of her domed prison. The frustration of the senseless loss of life, like that young boy too sick to carry on and the Healer who could do nothing to save him, or the many others soon to get sick and die from Sapien-made toxins bleeding into the ocean and poisoning their city.

And what of *her* world? Of the young and innocent caught up in a maelstrom of power and oppression under the guise of progress and freedom. How grievances were passed along from one generation to the next, only to manifest long after the afflicted were dead and buried. The festering need for something better, where youthful invincibility trampled wisdom and sound reasoning, with history lessons cast aside and ignored. Where new grievances were spun by up-and-coming, charismatic, wannabe leaders offering hope and promise—a new future that could only be achieved once the old was destroyed. The ashes of which piled atop ashes from before. Layer by layer, century after century. Churn and burn. Lather, rinse, repeat.

How immune were the Merahvu to the mistakes made in Sapien history?

These thoughts swirled as her gaze fell to the tower floor where she stood beside her father, hellbent on vengeance. Was that what would become of today? Churn and burn? Or would they succeed in breaking the chain of tit for tat between her father and Ianthe. A conflict that had exposed past grievances buried long ago between Merahvu and Sapien... and between Terrakai and Seakai.

Unease riled as she ticked through her father's past grievances. The most troubling was his blind belief that Sinto had murdered her mother. Would he simply set his grievances aside in the name of peace? What about Ianthe? Was she entirely truthful when she asked Audrey to deliver her father?

Balls of purple fire hovered over a massive slab of stone. Six shell-shaped chairs were set around it, along with one other that stood out in particular; a giant conch, carved out of gold, sitting at its head. A throne fit for a queen. Transparent cups filled with pink liquid sat beside each seat, some more empty than others, as if whoever had been sipping from them had suddenly left.

A gathering of the queen and the Circle, interrupted.

"Where are they?" Audrey asked.

Her father pressed a finger to her lips, staring intently at the gold conch throne. "We are not alone," he whispered.

The Mark confirmed his suspicions. It snapped and sparked most suddenly. Sinto was near, very near.

"Ianthe," her father said. "I came as you asked, reveal yourself."

From the gold conch throne came a flicker of movement, shifting patterns and roiling heat waves in the shape of a woman standing up. Ianthe's face emerged from nothingness, her camouflage peeling off like a snake molting a skin until she stood proudly before them naked. The same raised swirled markings that covered her breasts curved around her hips, meeting in the space between her legs and tapering off at the top of her thighs.

Something brushed by Audrey. Another disturbance in the watery air, setting off a harmonic vibration in her arm. She reached out and Sinto's camouflaged fingers wrapped around her outstretched hand. A ripple of electricity launched a wave of goosebumps up her arms, to her neck, raising the hair atop her head.

"*I knew you would come.*" Sinto's voice threaded through her mind as freely as a thought, every nuance crystal clear. Like the instructions that lead them here. But it wasn't only his voice. Feelings flowed as freely as her own, visceral reactions co-mingling with hers. Wings aflutter in belly, hearts joyfully beating.

The oxywater rippled and Sinto appeared before her, her gloved fingers clasped in his hand. She stepped back, taking him in.

All of him.

She finally had the answer that had burned on the tip of her tongue that day long ago on Merluma when he revealed he was a Merahvu, how he differed from her. She was embarrassed to ask about more private things. Though he had been willing to show her, but she had stopped him.

His genitals were tucked within a protective sack of flesh decorated with his unique markings that spread from upper thigh to groin, around his hips, across his buttocks, up his spine, and down the length of his fluked tail. Naked, but not naked like a Sapien.

Audrey could imagine how the myth of scaled mermaids began. Sinto resembled some of the descriptions in mythological stories. Golden hair streaked with copper, tall and well-proportioned, with a mighty fluked tail. He had not scales but decorative markings adorning his body. A unique work of art that made her heart pump wildly and lungs gasp for air. Audrey circled, her finger tracing a raised swirl wrapping around his hip, her eyes gobbling up every detail.

Oh my, he is magnificent.

He smiled as if she had said her thought out loud.

She blinked. "You heard that?"

"*Shh, yes.*"

"How?" she whispered.

"*Think what you want me to hear.*" His eyes darted to her father briefly. "*Only I will hear you.*"

Audrey crinkled her brow in concentration and imagined, "Hello," floating in the air between them.

He gently squeezed her hand. "*You're trying too hard. Relax and try again. It might help if you look me in the eye.*"

She took a breath, not realizing she had been holding it. She gazed into his eyes and imagined the words rolling across her mind's tongue, rippling across the space between them. She imagined the words sinking into the darkness of his pupils and flying through the optic nerve to his brain. She thought, "*You freed Blake.*"

Sinto's face twitched, like an antenna receiving a signal. "*I told you he would not be harmed. I kept my promise, and so has my mother.*" His eyes fell to the bump on her nose and reached out and touched it. The deep ache she'd come to ignore faded instantly.

Recalling her earlier thoughts, she asked, "*Do you promise to let us go freely?*"

He withdrew his hand. "*That's up to them.*"

Audrey spun around. Ianthe and her father were practically touching noses, glaring at each other.

"Why did you kill her?" her father asked.

"I did not kill her," Ianthe replied.

"You're lying."

"I never lied to you. I sent my daughter and Ramasis to contact you in good faith. Why did you attack them?"

"Why did you attack my crew?"

"I was not responsible for that. But the incident with Leela... *that* was my fault. I made a terrible mistake."

"I didn't know she was your daughter."

"I know that... now. Please believe me, I had nothing to do with your wife's death." She touched his cheek. "Let me prove my sincerity."

He grabbed her hand, crushing the bones together. "Stay out of my head." Ianthe tried to pull her hand from his grip, but he held fast. "And stay away from my daughter." He released her hand and pointed at Sinto. "Especially you."

"All I seek is a truce," Ianthe said. "To put the past behind us so we can forge ahead, anew. I forgive you for attacking my daughter and Ramasis. I have brought no harm to your men, your wife, your daughter, or her friend, nor do I intend to in the future."

"Why should I trust you?"

Her face softened. "Please, let us end this senseless bloodshed..."

"Tell me who killed my wife."

She gestured toward Sinto. "I offer my son to find the true murderer, if indeed your wife was murdered, as you claim."

"Then what?"

"The murderer will be punished, of course. My people do not tolerate malice. Our justice is swift and deserving."

"What is *deserving* for murder?"

"Immediate death."

Her father grinned boldly. "Then we should be able to remedy our grievance at once."

"What do you mean?"

"With your gift to rifle any mind, no one can hide secrets from you, isn't that true?"

"Why yes, of course, it is one reason I am—"

"Then perhaps you should ask your son."

Ianthe startled.

Her father chuckled. "How could you not know? Did he not he tell you?" He pondered for a moment. "Interesting..."

He paced a slow circle around Sinto, hands clasped behind his back. "He met Audrey ten years ago. I watched him play with her on the beach. These little play dates went on for a month apparently. The two of them sneaking around while my wife naively swam nearby." He stopped pacing and faced Sinto. "The day she drowned, I had shooed young Sinto back to the sea from where he came and told him to stay away from my daughter and never return. Later, he called to me as he drowned my innocent and sweet wife, Teola, with great spectacle. He wanted me to watch him do it, for me to *suffer*."

Sinto's eyes darted to the chairs set around the stone table. Audrey gazed up to what she had presumed were vacant balconies. The blood rushed from her face. The city wasn't vacant—the Merahvu were still here, to witness, to *judge*.

But to judge what? she thought.

Desperation burned when she saw the vengeful twinkle of victory in her father's eyes.

The room spun. "*Sinto, what's happening?*"

"*Are you sure you want the truth?*"

She held her breath for a beat, did she? "Yes," she reluctantly whispered.

Sinto gave her a sad smile. "*Please know, you are my everything and a gift to the world. No matter what happens to me, go forth and be, live, fully and completely, even if I do not.*"

"*What are you saying? Sinto, stop—*"

He shut her voice from his mind, then gently pushed his mother aside and faced the stone table with its empty chairs that Audrey was certain were occupied by camouflaged bodies; the Circle. He said, "I address the Circle with a heavy heart. Your guidance was clear. Ever since I was a child, and I could understand the meanings, I accepted the importance of the sacred rules set forth by you many years ago. One in particular; it is forbidden to present our true selves to a Sapien." He gazed up at the balconies. "As we all know." He took a step toward his mother. "What Culliford says is true. I was there the day his wife died. She saw me, as Merahvu."

Ianthe gasped. "So you *killed* her?"

"She died in my arms."

73

Blood For Blood

SINTO COULD NOT FACE Audrey but he could the thousands of spectators, watching from above, still camouflaged and hesitant to reveal themselves. He raised his arms and addressed them.

"I claim full responsibility for the death of the Sapien woman, Culliford's wife, Teola. And being of the same flesh and blood as the queen I seek your judgment, free of her influence." He turned to face the stone table. "I am prepared to endure whatever punishment you deem fit based on the agreed-upon laws of the Merahvu."

The Circle dropped their camouflage and erupted into argument, peppered with harsh exclamations, squeals, and clicks. Witnesses in the balcony did the same, their accusing words and whispering voices echoing throughout the chamber.

His mother was screaming in his head. He slid steel walls around his mind, cutting off her arguments. His decision was final. He was expendable, she was not.

While he could close his mind to his mother, he could not ignore Audrey, because of the Mark they shared. Utter despair stabbed his heart. Her silence unraveled him.

The Mark was insistent, riling his blood and demanding he tell Audrey the *whole* truth. What he confessed was just a part of it. Her mother *did* in truth die in his arms. But it was not he who ensnared her in the net. He didn't kill her. She died while he was trying to save her.

He turned to Culliford, determined to see his decision to its fateful end. "I hope that satisfies your question."

"Not quite."

The chamber fell silent.

"What shall be his judgment?" Culliford demanded.

Ianthe leaped forward. "Please, have mercy, he was just a confused child!"

"There is a rumor that Sinto introduced this young Sapien woman to Merluma," stated Jabal, the lone Terrakai of the Circle.

Another outburst echoed from the witnesses above.

"Is this true, our queen?" asked Beech, a representative of the Seakai.

His mother turned to Sinto; confusion and fear filled her eyes.

Sinto whispered in her mind, "*Make me the sacrifice they seek. Prove you are still their queen. Show them strength!*"

She hesitated.

Her weakness appalled him. "*For Naiada, do it!*"

Her lips quivered when she said, "It is true, Sinto took the girl there, against my wishes."

"The severest penalty for which is the Undoing," said Jabal.

The witnesses in the balconies gasped.

"True," his mother said, "but considering his other confessed crime, I suggest you give final judgment to the one he has wronged most. Culliford must decide his fate. It is the only way to make peace between us."

Beech asked, "You have foreseen this?"

She hesitated. "Yes."

Sinto sensed she was lying. Naiada's suspicion was right, her foresight was fading.

The Circle huddled, conversing. Their fear of challenging his mother, especially in front of the people, outweighed the need to hold firm to the law. They voted, their decision unanimous.

Beech stood. "Culliford may decide Sinto's fate."

His mother turned to Culliford. "Robert... this is a mistake, one you will truly regret. Trust me, I know."

"What about your thugs circling my ship?"

Sinto cast his gaze to the far wall where Wantemo silently observed in the shadows. Wantemo had not said anything about Scouts sent to stand by Culliford's ship. They were to return to the city after returning Blake. From the confused look on his mother's face, that was her understanding as well.

"I have sent no one but my most trusted adviser to return the man we had captured. They must be rebels acting on their own."

"So that makes it *my* problem?" Culliford said.

"I understand your need to defend and will do everything in my power to protect you, but please use utmost discretion. We are aware of these rebels and will ferret out their leader and squelch their movement in one swift blow. They are few to our many and we mean you no harm. Please, consider a peaceful—"

Culliford's nostrils flared. "So be it." He withdrew a jagged-edged knife from a hidden sheath and anxiously tapped the six-inch blade against his thigh. "Give me the boy and we're even."

His mother stood before Sinto like a fortress. She grabbed Culliford's hand and pressed the tip of his knife to her chest. "No. Take me. I am the one who failed you, not my son."

Sinto spun her around to face him. "*Did you not foresee this?*"

Tears welled in her eyes. The answer was clear by the way she looked at him.

She had. Naiada was wrong.

It was in that moment he knew. His fate was cast long ago. He was never meant to be with Audrey or occupy his father's seat in the Circle or watch his sister become queen. His duty was to end this long-standing feud with Culliford with his sacrifice, freeing his mother and Naiada to thwart the rebel's movement and restore peace between Merahvu and Terrakai.

He squelched the desire to wallow in self-pity or to beg for mercy. It would do nothing to change the outcome. His future had been stolen the day he was born. The cursed son of an adulterous mother and a miserable and angry father, joined not of love, but against their will in the name of satisfying the needs of the people. The agreement of peace as flimsy as their forced relationship; one entered bitterly and reluctantly by the Terrakai, the source of the growing rebellion.

He embraced his mother, then kissed her on the forehead, nose, both cheeks, and finally her lips. Her tears were salty in his mouth. He gently pushed her trembling body aside.

He looked at Audrey longingly, standing behind her father. He saw desperation, not hatred, in her eyes, darting between Sinto and the knife in her father's hand.

"Will my sacrifice avenge your wife's death and end this feud between you and the Merahvu?"

Culliford nodded and flipped the knife in his hand, blade up ready to strike. "Blood for blood. I will honor an end to it."

Sinto splayed his arms and offered his chest. "Then take me before she changes her mind."

"No!" Audrey leaped for the knife but her father was quicker.

He ground his thumb into her hip flexor and she doubled over as if punched in the stomach; on the way down her elbow clipped his hand. The knife clanked when it hit the stone floor. They followed, grappling, arms and legs tangled, teeth gritted, eyes wild, a life-or-death fight for the weapon.

Culliford had the advantage with a longer reach and claimed it, rolling backwards over his shoulder and hopping onto his feet. Audrey was faster, flipping from arched back to her feet. In one fluid movement she jumped up, wrists grasped in a cross grip. With the aid of oxywater, she rose above her father's head from behind, then dropped, slipping her encircled arms around his chest, binding his arms.

Culliford stilled for a mere second, then spun his body within the circle of her arms. He delivered a head butt to her forehead, the force calculated for distraction, not injury. Stunned momentarily, Audrey lost her grip and Culliford broke free. He grabbed her wrist, whipped her around and pinned her arm behind her back. She winced. Her pain shot through the Mark. Culliford pulled her to his chest and hooked an arm around her neck. Before he could tighten the noose, she twisted and went liquid. Knees buckling, she slithered from his grip like a limp fish and dropped into a deep squat. Before he could react, she cradled one hand over the other's fist and drove up, bent elbow aiming for his sternum.

Culliford dodged. Knife still in one hand, he grabbed her elbow with the other, twisting it up and inward to the point of breaking. She screamed, tried to wriggle free and failed. He wedged her twisted arm into the pit of his arm wielding the knife. A ray of light glinted off its shiny surface as she struggled, pounding her free fist toward his face, his neck, even his groin. Culliford deflected her meager punches and held fast.

Audrey's brows crushed into an angry dark line. Frustration painted her aura bright red. She screamed, primal and fierce, then broke free and stole the knife from his hand. She froze a beat with an expression of pure surprise that he had given it up so easily.

She grasped the knife with both hands and stepped back. The violent dance between father and daughter had lasted less than a minute.

Culliford smiled, then he lurched and wrapped his hands around hers, gripping the knife. Dread filled her eyes when she realized her mistake.

She gasped.

Culliford coiled.

The blade flashed, whipping upward toward Sinto so fast he lost sight of it.

He felt a shocking jolt to the Mark.

Audrey looked up, eyes bugged with mouth agape, an expression of pure shock.

Sinto looked down. Entwined fists gripped the knife's handle, the shiny blade buried to the hilt inside his chest. His left knee had buckled but his body hung for a beat by a rib stuck on the jagged blade. Culliford yanked it out.

Sinto crumpled to the floor. Flueox bled from his merlux and spread through his chest like wildfire. His gills flared. He gasped. A cloud of blood erupted past his lips and lingered in the moist air like a stubborn bank of fog.

Then he felt it, the sudden eruption of pain and thick liquid filling his lung. His eyelids were stuck open. Faces blurred. His mind winked and Audrey's screams faded like a passing summer breeze.

74

All For Naught

Sinto's blood stained the knife Audrey held in her hand. He lay at her feet, gaze distant and unfocused. Green liquid spread from the hole in his chest. Death seeped from his still lips; a cloud of blood drifted across the chamber.

She dropped the knife. It fell with a *clang* on the stone floor. Daddy's deed was done. Blood for blood. Blood covered her hands. The taste of it filled her mouth with every breath. She gagged. Shards of glass ripped through her veins, tearing her apart piece by piece.

She fell to her knees. Someone was screaming.

Her.

Ianthe lay across Sinto's body, her face twisted in anguish, mouth frozen by grief. The smoldering fire was gone from her eyes. This once mighty and powerful woman, shriveled and broken.

Mayhem ensued. Angry arguments broke out. Nervous glances were exchanged. The Circle members hastily retreated. Witnesses sprang from the balconies and darted through the open ceiling.

Ianthe captured Audrey's gaze, tears welled in her eyes. "Get out while you still can." She pitched a ball of light toward the arched doorway. "Follow it. Now! Hurry!"

Her father yanked her to her feet. They bolted, following Ianthe's light, through meandering tunnels, leaping over holes, veering around corners.

They burst from the tunnel into the open. The mock sun blazed in the sky. Strange shadows were cast at their feet. From what was not obvious. They bolted down the stairs two at a time. Stokes had backed *Discovery* up near the dome wall, near where they had left their tanks and helmets just inside, ready for a quick escape. They ran to them.

She hung her goggles around her neck. Her father lifted her tank to her back. She clicked the straps in place. He handed her the helmet. She turned toward the dome wall unsure what to do, body numb and mind unresponsive.

Stokes frantically pointed at something behind her, his eyes big as saucers. Fearfully, she turned. Thousands of Merahvu hovered in the sky. The reason for the strange shadows was now clear. A mass of gathered bodies blocked the mock sun. Anger marred their faces. Their eyes were electrified. Oxywater crackled and sparked. Dark clouds formed in the sky above them, blocking out the remaining light from above. Lightning flashed and thunder rumbled, swirling gusts followed; a storm was brewing inside the dome.

Threads of electricity crackled and stretched from the dome wall to the sun, and from the sun to the collection of bodies, winding up for an attack.

Her father reached for his spear gun. "Helmet on. *Now.*"

Her hands shook uncontrollably, slipping across her helmet's slick surface. She finally grasped it and clicked the tube for the Liquid into its port. She pulled it over her head, locked it into place, and opened the valve at her shoulder.

Liquid flooded her helmet. Her nasal cannula rested beneath her chin; she forgot to stick it in her nose. The goggles bobbed freely against her face; she forgot to slip them on. Her vision blurred when the Liquid reached her eyes. She didn't care if her lungs collapsed and everything looked fuzzy. She decided it was for the best, to not see what was coming until it was already upon her.

She drew an agonizing breath. Liquid poured into her lungs and filled her sinus cavities. She deserved to die, wanted to end the misery; body and soul.

Her father wrapped his arm around her and pulled back until they were pressed against the dome wall. He pointed his spear gun to the sky. Before he could fire their feet slipped out from under them as they burst through the dome into the icy sea. Marine snow exploded when they landed on their backs.

Her father scrambled out from under her and yanked her to her feet. He cut the tank from her back with the same knife that had pierced Sinto's chest. Her tank fell to the sea floor in a fresh explosion of marine snow. Blind and clinging to her father, she stumbled toward *Discovery*.

Her father dropped down the ladder and opened the hatch. He jumped back down, pushed her up, and shoved her inside. She crumpled to the floor in a heap. He slipped in after, straddled her body, and sealed the hatch door.

Discovery lurched. Air bubbles roiled against the ceiling as water was replaced by air. Her father squatted beside her, pecking away at his wrist communicator. He stopped, gloved finger shaking. Held up his wrist. The message was blurred but the meaning was clear: "Ship attacked. 2 dead." Her father would surely retaliate.

Sinto died for nothing.

She felt sick to her stomach. The walls closed in. Dark spots danced before her eyes. She gasped, breathing Liquid faster and deeper, but it didn't help. What Liquid was left in her helmet was depleted of oxygen and now filled with carbon dioxide produced by her own lungs. She gaped like a fish, sucking for something not there.

She felt a tug, heard a *click* then a *whoosh*.

Cold air struck her face and startled her senses. Her helmet rang out when it hit the steel floor. Her father spun her around, pulled her back to his chest, wrapped his arms around her waist, then gave her a violent jerk. She folded. Warm Liquid shot from her nose and mouth. He shoved a nasal cannula in her nose and pressed her back to the floor. He straddled her and pinned her arms with his knees, his mouth set in a grimace. He clamped his hand over her nose and mouth, smothering her. She writhed in panic.

Now he's killing me!

She freed an arm and swung her fist at his head. He ducked and dodged, then let go of her mouth. She sucked a noisy breath, released it. A bloody mist splattered across his face. He pulled the tubes from her nose, held them to his cheek, tossed them aside.

"No air!" he screamed, rummaging for something.

She lay there, like a lifeless doll, with her lungs stuck and the light winking from her eyes.

He shoved a plastic mask over her face. Pressurized air forced its way into her mouth.

"Breathe!"

She gasped. Cool air trickled down her throat and no further. Stuck, like her lungs.

A deep ache spread across her chest. Her heart beat slower.

Her father grew frantic, eyes wide and full of panic. "Your lungs are collapsing, fight for me!"

He raised her up, arching her back, opening her chest. She fought as he asked, gasping and sucking. Everything went dark. Then a miracle. Painfully, her lungs filled, first one side then the other. He sat her up. She gulped air, coughed up Liquid, spat out blood.

He wedged her against the hull and peeled her suit down to her waist. The thermal layer underneath was soaked with sweat.

It came on slowly, then violently. Her whole body shook, shivering. She tried, but couldn't stop.

Her father swung open the inner hatch door. He lifted her quivering body to her feet and shoved her through the narrow hatchway into the main chamber. He set her in her seat and covered her with a scratchy wool blanket. The weight of the blanket helped; the shivering moved from her body to her teeth, chattering violently. That too, she couldn't stop.

Discovery circled the city high above the mountain peaks. Submersibles deployed from the ship hovered along the ridge line. The unmistakable shape of bombs were strapped to their mechanical bodies.

Her father turned to Stokes. "Get Alvarez on the radio."

She summoned the strength to calm her chattering teeth, and grabbed his arm. "Wasn't killing Sinto enough?"

Her father glared. "I made myself clear, blood for blood."

"You heard Ianthe. She's not the one attacking your ship!"

"You think this is the first time this has happened? She can't control her people nor can her Circle. Weak old fools, and so is she." His eyes cut to the radio.

"Radio live," Stokes said.

She dug her fingers into his flesh. "Don't. Don't do it."

"This is where it ends. We may never have another chance." He reached over her to the communication panel and punched the transmit switch with his index finger. A squeal of static broke the silence.

"Alvarez, blow those fuckers to hell."

75

Madness Descends

THE MERAHVU FOUGHT BACK. Blue threads of electricity burst from the city's mock sun, locked onto a singular point on the dome wall and gathered into a bundle of blinding light. A mighty bolt of lightning exploded from its surface and struck a submersible descending from above. The bomb the submersible carried exploded into a giant ball of white-hot fire. The bubble of fire expanded and burst, its fire instantaneously consumed by the sea, then disintegrated into a billion tiny bubbles.

It took a second, followed by a moment of blindness. There, then gone. But the destruction was not over. An invisible shock wave radiated from where it exploded. An unfathomable force that jolted a second submersible. It glanced across the top of a mountain and disappeared on the other side. The shock wave hit the dome. It buckled and sparks rippled across its surface, then it bounced back, resilient and formidable.

Bolts of lightning from the dome struck down three more submersibles lined-up for attack. They crashed into the side of the dome, exploding on impact with a spectacular flash of light. The dome shuddered, but bounced back.

Mayhem ensued inside the city.

Thousands of Merahvu swam for the dome wall. They clung to its surface like frogs, spinning electrified webs from their bodies, feeding the dome with their merluxes. The dome crackled and sparked with power. Threads of electricity shot from its surface to the mock sun, swelling like a star about to explode.

One more submersible was struck down. Another ball of fire and jolt of shock waves.

The dome buckled but bounced back. Inside, whirlpools sprang to life, tearing plants from their roots and bodies from homes, like tornadoes ripping through the central plains of North America. Bolts of lightning exploded from the mock sun, striking indiscriminately. Club Ballo collapsed, trees exploded, and the Great Tower teetered before sinking into a cloud of metallic dust. The dead fell from the sky, bursting into clouds of ash, snowing down.

Audrey gaped in horror. The dome held but at huge cost to the city and the Merahvu within. A desperate miscalculation by a peaceful civilization trying to protect their way of life.

"Go for the jellyfish!" her father barked into the radio.

The last submersible rose from behind the seamount where it had tumbled and raced toward the trio of giant jellyfish, now struggling to distance themselves from the doomed city. It swooped into a steep climb, dipped its nose, and dove straight for the red one.

Sensing doom, thousands of Merahvu burst from the dome, cutting tunnels through the sea. They zipped past *Discovery* as blinding streaks of light, fading like shooting stars once they passed. A thriving city, scattered.

Everything within the city had been destroyed. All that remained was the stubbornly resilient dome. Inside the mock sun continued to spin its storm of destruction.

What happened next was fruitless. The last submersible collided with the red jellyfish. At first it seemed nothing would happen. The bomb strapped to its belly a dud. Then *Discovery* was awash in blinding light and rattled by a thundering boom.

The dome disintegrated instantly. Shredded pieces radiated outward, lighting up the dark sea like an exploding firework. What was left of the dome fluttered down like giant pieces of confetti, lighting the destruction that followed. The sea roiled with angry bubbles racing for the surface. The tunnels and chambers carved beneath the city collapsed. The trio of mountains followed, awakening a fault in Earth's crust. The seabed quaked and split, sucking what remained of Tallamure down its throat. The massive drop in the sea floor unleashed a shock wave of incalculable energy; a silent killer, racing across the whole of the Pacific to unsuspecting shores, with *Discovery* in its path.

The blood drained from her father's face when he realized the magnitude of his mistake.

Audrey screamed. "What did you expect? You've unleashed a monster! Your blind rage will kill us all!"

He ignored her accusations and threw aside her blanket, clicked in three of the five points of her harness before securing his own. Stokes aimed for the surface, engines revving.

They were hit from behind. *Discovery* pitch-poled ass over nose. A second equally violent hit came from a surge of air bubbles. *Discovery* jostled and rolled like a toy cast into a vat of boiling water. The rear chamber hatch swung open. Tanks and helmets tumbled forward into the main chamber. Storage cabinets spilled their contents. A stainless-steel arrow whizzed past her face. A wrench struck her in the arm. The violence ended with a pop, a flash, and a roaring hiss. Then—

Utter and absolute darkness.

Audrey was jolted into action by the acrid smell of burning plastic. She covered her mouth and nose with her sleeve to filter out the smoke. She patted her lap for the blanket her father had given her. Her hand came back slick and smelled of blood. She realized she was hanging sideways in her seat, barely secured by three straps of her harness.

Discovery rolled upright, reverberating with the sound of stressed metal. Objects slid across the floor. She heard a rapid ticking like a bomb about to explode. She clawed at the darkness, feeling for her harness buckle. She sprung free and reached in the dark for her father. She found his leg and felt her way up to his shoulder, shook it.

He didn't respond.

"Stokes?"

He didn't respond either.

Her whole body trembled. She bent over hugging herself and rocking, afraid and utterly helpless.

We're gonna die, slowly and miserably.

Someone gasped and started coughing. She sat up with a start. "Dad?"

"Everything is fine, Teola. Go back to sleep."

Teola was her mother's name.

She heard Stokes stir, then a scrape and a click.

Red light flooded the cabin.

It looked like a war zone. A thick haze of smoke hung in the air. Dark splatters of blood painted the walls and ceiling. Her father bled profusely from a gash on his head and a spear lodged in his shoulder, pinning him to the seat.

He gazed over and smiled. Something about the way he looked at her was odd.

"Uh, Stokes, my father's acting funny. I think he's in shock or something."

"Help—" gasp, "me," Stokes said.

Audrey squeezed between the seats and knelt beside him. His arm hung to his side at a ghastly angle. A tank was wedged between his chest and the console where his hand still gripped the joystick.

His dark eyes found hers. "Get it—off."

She tried to lift it. It slipped through her blood-slicked hands and landed against his chest. Stokes clenched his teeth, stifling a scream. She wiped her hands on her shirt and tried again. Luckily, the tank was nearly empty. She wrestled it free, cast it aside.

"Unbuckle—me." He screamed when she tried to move his arm to reach the center point of his harness. The way he was blinking and gasping, she knew he was slipping toward unconsciousness. "Leave it," he finally said.

"What should I do?" Her eyes swept across the panel. Most of the gauges were out, except for the analog depth meter, slowly spinning numbers of their descent.

Stokes saw it too. "Shit. Give me—minute." His eyes fluttered shut and she thought she had lost him. He opened them and drew shallow breaths, fighting to stay conscious.

Hopeless, she thought. But watching Stokes fight for every breath gave her a jolt. *Grow up and deal!*

She rummaged through the debris for the first aid kit. One corner was crushed; she hit it with the heel of her hand several times to get it open. Inside were bandages of all sizes, a small splint, antibacterial cream, a surgical needle and thread, syringes, morphine, and more.

She analyzed the gash on her father's head. Her hands were shaking too much to attempt stitching it up. She rummaged through stuff littering the floor, found what she was looking for. She dabbed antibacterial cream on the wound, sealed it with a piece of duct tape. When she reached over to examine the spear in his shoulder, he grabbed her hand.

"Teola, rest, we have a long day tomorrow."

"I'm Audrey, your daughter, remember?"

He touched her chin and gazed lovingly into her eyes. "Nooo, you're *Teola*, my wife." She wrenched her chin from his fingers. "Now, now, no need to play coy with me." His eyes wandered to dark splatters on the ceiling. He got a confused look on his face. "Is that blood?"

She decided to leave the spear where it was.

"Audrey," Stokes said.

She went forward and crouched next to him. He didn't look good.

"Emergency switches." He raised a shaky finger, pointing to four red switches next to his knee. She flipped them. Nothing happened. He swore.

"Now what?"

He looked at the joystick wobbling in his hand, the warning light indicating that the engines were fried. The depth gauge continued ticking off their descent. His brow glistened with sweat. He tried to look hopeful. "Long shot. Risky."

"Tell me what to do."

Stokes talked her through the process. She drained the ballast tanks of seawater, that narrow space between the inner and outer skin of *Discovery*'s fuselage, and replaced it with the last of the air from their reserves.

Audrey grabbed Stokes' hand. Together they watched the depth gauge. It hovered, got stubbornly stuck. Like that place between heaven and hell no one wants to be. Purgatory. A minute passed. Nothing. She thought of Sinto's sacrifice and the Merahvu who gave their lives trying to protect their city. Was it selfish to ask for a miracle? Sweat trickled from her brow. She held her breath, reeling between hope and despair, anticipating what would come next. Up or down. Heaven or hell.

The gauge twitched. A jolt to the wheel stamped with numbers. It began rolling backwards. A tenth of a foot, then another, then it stopped and hovered. She held her breath as if that would help. An eternity passed. Then the gauge began to move again. Slowly *Discovery* ascended.

A collective sigh of relief. Stokes closed his eyes, his lips moved, whispering something to himself, then he gave her a weak smile. "Small victory—not clear—yet."

"What does that mean, exactly?"

He whispered, "Breathe shallow." His finger tapped the air gauge. It was teetering below half.

"How much time?"

He winced. "Maybe an hour. Less."

Her blood ran cold watching the slow spin of the depth gauge. It was questionable if they would reach the surface in time, if at all. After that, asphyxiation—a long and excruciating death.

Audrey gave Stokes' hand a squeeze. A tear snaked down his cheek. "I'm sorry," he said before looking away.

She slipped back into her seat. Her hands shook. She clasped them together trying to make them stop but it didn't help. She wanted to scream but it would waste precious air so she sat and quietly suffered, breathing lightly, waiting for the inevitable.

Her father was oblivious to their plight, talking to himself and telling tales from his past, and every so often he would reach for her hand or caress her face and give her a look entirely inappropriate for a father to give a daughter.

She tried to ignore him, wallowing in a sea of remorse. Sinto made a sacrifice, of that she was certain. Just before he died she felt it. He was innocent, the truth ringing clear through the Mark. He hadn't lied but held back, carefully choosing his words to make everyone believe it was he who murdered her mother. But why? Who was he protecting? What reason could possibly be worth more than his own life?

It ripped at her heart. The Mark in her arm lay dead. Sinto was dead. She would never know the answer why.

"Teola, please, no need to cry."

She turned her back to her father, seething at the unfairness. She hated him for killing Sinto and all those innocent people. But who was she to judge? Her hands were stained with Sinto's blood as well as the blood of the fallen. She led her father to Tallamure. She held the knife when it entered Sinto's chest. She deserved to die. All of them did.

The air grew weak. The temperature dropped. Condensation rained from the ceiling.

Audrey pictured Sinto's eyes, alive with green fire. His love of the natural world, his sister, his mother, the Merahvu. She relived racing through the sea cradled in his arms, hearing his contagious laughter when surfing with the dolphins, the way her stomach fluttered whenever he smiled. She hugged the blanket and sobbed. She would never again be challenged by his probing questions, smell the sea clinging to his hair, or feel his comforting embrace and electrified kisses. She would never know what special purpose they had been chosen to fulfill.

She clung to those enduring thoughts as she slumped forward and slipped into unconsciousness.

76

Reunited

AUDREY WAS JOLTED FROM her stupor by a sudden and violent motion. *Discovery* had reached the surface, pitching and rolling in a wild sea. Bright light filled the cabin; rays of sunlight, patches of blue sky, and broken clouds winked through the sea-splattered view port.

She wheezed at the irony. She was too weak to move and open the aft hatch for air.

A high-pitched buzz radiated through the hull, growing louder. Her oxygen-starved brain struggled to comprehend what would make that sound. A bee? A drone?

Discovery jolted, then she heard men's voices, the trample of feet, metal scraping, then a poof and a roaring hiss. A shower of sparks rained down. A thick chunk of metal clanked to the floor. A man's face filled a small hole in the ceiling. His pale eyes brightened when he saw her, gazing back.

"I'm Ensign Stuart with the United States Coast Guard. Glad to find you alive!"

He told her to stay where she was and hold tight, that they were in for a rough ride. Then he scampered away, the trample of many feet stopped, and men's voices faded.

Discovery jerked and the sound of rushing water resonated through the hull. They pitched to and fro in rough seas. Fresh air flowed through the hole, thick with the scent of the sea. Her stomach roiled from the motion but she welcomed it. It meant she was alive.

Stokes stirred and grunted, "Thank God."

Her father sighed. "Are we almost there?"

Pent-up emotion cracked and spilled, sobs intermingled with laughter—anger, guilt, and despair topped with a big dollop of disbelief; they had bucked the odds and were safe, and alive, and in the capable hands of Ensign Stuart. Stokes joined in as best as he could muster.

Her father looked a little confused by their outburst. He reached for her hand, patted it. "Now, now, no need to be upset. I've taken care of everything."

She wiped her nose, took back her hand.

Yeah, Daddy, you sure did.

The sides of a Coast Guard ship loomed beside them and there was a sudden flurry of activity; men shouting, the sound of metal clanking. Then *Discovery* stilled, became airborne, and landed with a sudden jolt.

Audrey rose on shaky legs and stumbled into the aft chamber. She swung open the hatch. The blast of cold air nearly knocked her over.

A ladder clanked against the hatch opening. Men clambered aboard, pressing past her. One stopped to check her pulse and shine a light in her eyes. He barked a quick set of commands. Another man helped her climb down a solid stainless-steel ladder and onto the deck of a Coast Guard cutter.

Off the starboard rail was the *Requiem Sea*, lying on her port side, settling low in the water. A salvage tug circled the wreckage. Coast Guard tenders ferried crewmen through wind-whipped waves.

Someone called her name. She turned. Dyer wrapped in a blanket. He was shivering in fits and starts. At his feet lay two occupied body bags. She ran to greet him. His face was smudged with grease. One of his ears was duct-taped to his skull. Dried blood ran down his neck. His knuckles were bruised and bloody.

He hugged her. "We thought you were dead."

Her gaze fell to the body bags. "What happened?"

"Those fuckers leaped from the sea, caught these two guys on deck unaware, turned 'em to toast. We locked down the ship. They gave up when they failed to find a way inside. Then something hit us from below. Some sort of tidal surge, then frickin' air bubbles came out of nowhere. Air bubbles! The sea swallowed us whole. We thought we were goners, but the ship popped back up. Some guys got busted up bad."

"Did you see Blake?"

"Yeah, before we were attacked. We found him lying on deck. The guy was hella confused."

Her eyes swept across the deck, scanning the faces of men waiting for first aid. "Do you know where he is?"

"He must be somewhere around here—he was one of the first off the ship."

Audrey bid Dyer farewell and wandered the deck, searching for Blake. Two men were helping Stokes climb down the ladder and away from the battered *Discovery*. His arm was in a sling and they had wrapped his chest tight with a stabilizing bandage. His face was ashen but he was walking on his own two feet.

Alvarez and Dr. Wickman were with her father, talking to Coast Guard officers. Dr. Wickman appeared unscathed, but Alvarez's glasses were skewed and his clothes were torn and bloody. Dr. Wickman waved her over.

"How is he?" she asked him.

"Delusional," he said, with a glance at the officers.

She stayed and listened. Her father was regaling them with a colorful tale about a mermaid queen who lived in a city at the bottom of the sea. Alvarez cut in, explaining that Mr. Culliford had been taking his daughter for a ride in his experimental submarine when the tidal surge from the underground earthquake struck and he hit his head. She stayed and listened to their remaining questions. She nodded in confirmation at all the right places but found her thoughts and eyes wandering. It was Dr. Wickman who cut the interview short citing the need to get her father immediate help for his injuries. When they moved her father off to the infirmary, she slipped away to look for Blake.

She found the young man, Ensign Stuart, rinsing off his dive suit on the fringe of the crowd. "Hey, your name's Stuart, right?"

"Yes, ma'am." His face radiated with youthful innocence.

Her heart ached in regret. She had youthful innocence once but it was incinerated along with Sinto's city.

"I'm looking for a guy, about my height with dark hair and blue eyes kind of like your—" The rest drowned in her throat.

Blake was walking determinedly toward her, a smile of relief slowly spreading across his face. He wore the same khaki-colored chinos and navy cashmere sweater as the day the orcas attacked *Annabelle*. He looked as if nothing had happened, as if his disappearance was merely a bad dream.

He engulfed her in his arms and she crumbled, overwhelmed with relief that he was safe and alive, that something good had come from the horror of the day.

He kissed her on the cheek and rocked her. "It's over, we're safe now."

She wanted to believe him. "So much has happened, things I've done, terrible things..." She couldn't say those terrible things, like how easily he was forgotten once she thought he was dead, or how easily the knife slipped into Sinto's chest.

"I don't care what you've done."

She bit back tears, desperate for his comforting embrace. Desperate to fill the growing void in her chest, for someone to lift her from the crushing guilt weighing down on her conscience. But it was she who did those terrible things. "I don't deserve you, or anyone."

"I heard you did some pretty crazy stuff to save me." He ran a knuckle across her fading bruises. She grabbed his hand and his gaze fell to her wrist. His brow furrowed when he stroked the place where he had tied the friendship bracelet. Yesterday to him, a lifetime to her.

"They said everyone thought I was dead."

"We did, I did."

He gave her that lopsided grin she had come to adore. "Well, you can't get rid of me that easily."

She looked away, afraid he would see the truth in her eyes. Sinto had claimed her heart, the core of her. Her very *essence*. And she was the one who gave it to him, unequivocally. Even with his death she could not imagine having another, not even—

Blake tipped up her chin, forcing her to face him.

"Blake, I'm—"

His lips were suddenly on hers. She hesitated at first, then fell under the spell of his kneading lips and the comfort of his cradling arms. A primal need to fill the utter emptiness she felt inside. She tried to imagine his lips were Sinto's and that his death was just but a bad dream, but Blake could never replace what she had lost and it would be wrong and unfair to him to pretend otherwise. When their lips parted she gently pushed him away.

"I can't do this."

"My feelings haven't changed."

"You can't love me. I—I am not the same person."

He laughed. "I'll take my chances." Then he grew more serious. "Audrey, I have loved you since the day I first saw you. Watching you grow, waiting until you were ready—"

"You don't understand. The ones who took you, they'll be back, for me, my father, and anyone we care about. It's not over."

"All the more reason you need me. You can't face them alone."

"And risk your life? I can't ask you to do that."

"I'm not afraid to die. I'm more afraid of losing you." He brushed her cheek. "Besides, you made me a promise, remember?"

"I did, but..."

She felt a twitch in her arm and pushed its sad reminder from her thoughts. The Mark lay cold in her arm. Dead like Sinto, along with a big piece of her heart. What remained quivered, in sadness and regret.

"I can't love you like you deserve."

He brushed her cheek with the back of his finger. "How will you know, if you don't try?"

She gazed into his eyes and felt that little tremor she had felt when he confessed his true feelings and kissed her for the first time. A big piece of her heart was dead, but maybe not all of it.

Blake held out his hand.

Her father taught her to fear the unknown, to live in a constant state of readiness to combat some horrible future threat. Because of that she felt fearful and suspicious of everyone. She had lived that way for half of her young life. Fear made her weak. She hated being weak. Suspicion bred loneliness. She hated being alone.

She gazed at Blake's outstretched hand. A new life beckoned. A future not to fear but embrace. Her heart would take time to heal. Maybe, at some point in the future, she would be ready to love again, but not now, not for a long time.

How will you know, if you don't try?

She closed her eyes and drew strength from the two people she had loved deeply and who were no longer of this world. The words they spoke that she would never forget.

She remembered—vividly—Sinto's last words: *No matter what happens to me, go forth and be, live, fully and completely, even if I do not.*

And the mantra her mother taught her threaded through her mind: *Move in harmony with force of life, flow as water, like stream around rock.* A simple string of words that helped her endure every challenge she had faced since her mother's death. Words of hope and wisdom; a promise that life goes on, and that it is the path she chooses that will define her.

Go forth.

Move in harmony.

Try...

She opened her eyes. Blake gazed back, patiently waiting for her reply. A tiny piece of her heart yearned for his presence, for his sincerity and the comfort he offered. "I'll try, but you may have to wait until I'm ready. I may take a very long time."

"I have all the time in the world. All I ask is that once you're ready, you'll try."

She twined her fingers through his. Raised his knuckles to her lips and kissed them, like Sinto had done with her so many times before.

"I promise. Someday. I'll try."

EPILOGUE

Choice

Sinto sat on a beach, hacking the flesh of his inner forearm with the sharp edge of a seashell. He cursed his sister for warning him to lean left and Wantemo for jettisoning him from the city before it crumbled.

Culliford's knife had found his merlux and a piece of his lung, narrowly missing his heart. Afterward, he spent a week on Merluma with Wantemo, who healed his near-fatal wounds.

He had begged Wantemo to let him die, not wanting to carry on a life in perpetual want for the woman he could not have. Wantemo agreed, but only as a rumor. *I will not let you die. You have much to do, that you are destined to do. Though I believe it wise to let them all believe you are dead. Deception will make your tasks much easier and lead to greater success.* When Sinto asked who needed to be deceived, Wantemo simply replied, *Everyone. Be careful who you trust. No one must learn you are still alive.*

Blood dripped from his elbow, staining the white sand. Skin, muscle, and gristle parted easily, but not the diamond-hard coils of the Mark. Neither steel, stone, nor fire could break its bond, only death. *Real* death, not pretended as Wantemo suggested.

He cried out in frustration. *Perhaps I should cut off my arm!*

He considered the idea, but knew it wouldn't make any difference. His lips would burn for her kiss, his heart for her love, his mind for her companionship, for as long as blood flowed through his veins.

He drew fire from his merlux, weak still, but sufficient and growing stronger with each passing hour. Wantemo forced him to consume vast quantities of sucuvita to help him quickly regain his strength and shared some of his flueox to replenish Sinto's losses.

Sinto traced the self-inflicted cuts on his arm with his electrified finger, wincing as fire cauterized the torn skin. Smoke and the nauseatingly sweet scent of his smoldering flesh swirled around his head.

He studied his handiwork. Scars masked the hardened ridges of the Mark. Angry and red like the one over his heart. He asked Wantemo not to smooth the puckered skin where the knife had entered his chest. He wanted to keep that scar to remind him of all he had lost.

After Wantemo healed Sinto he sent him here to this beach on the north shore of Oahu, an island rising from the waters of the mid-Pacific, with one last and critical assignment. Seven days had passed on Merluma while Sinto was there, healing, but only seven hours had passed here on Earth. Seven long hours since Culliford's bombs set off a great disruption at the bottom of the North Pacific, the consequence of which was quickly heading toward this shore.

Sinto set his sights to the sea, waiting for the reason he was here. It was unusually calm for this part of the island for this time of year. Still, impressively large waves rolled ashore, fetching up on the rocky shallows and breaking with a clean point in the center and curling into tubes on each side. The Scouts had shared stories about this beach, a prized place where Sapien surfers competed; a place they called *Pipeline*.

Surfers bobbed offshore on their flat pointy boards, waiting for the contest to begin. Voices squawked over tinny speakers; the names of the contestants, their credentials, and past victories.

A horn blared. The surfers were off, vying for spots on oncoming waves. They raced down the faces and slipped through the curl, punching a fist as they were spit out of the tube. Auras pulsed with exhilaration.

Sinto sat far from groups of Sapiens dotting the sand, laughing and drinking and bobbing to music blaring from tiny boxes; a cacophony of voices, notes, and rhythm, clashing between one group and another. A natural saltwater pool lay between Sinto and the shore, fed by larger waves surging over the bank of sand containing it. Children splashed and swam with joyous screams and laughter, safe from the tug of the sea. Mothers mingled. Couples held hands, walking along the shore. Pale-bodied Sapiens lay prone like monk seals, napping on the hot sand.

He had stolen a pair of swim trunks from an unlocked car, then manipulated his coloring to look like a local; black hair, brown skin, dark eyes. He tattooed an image of nipples on his chest. With his tail tucked tight against his back and his foot fins fully retracted, he looked like anybody and nobody, which suited him fine.

Three young females about his age paraded by, vying for his attention. He barely noticed them except the one who was Polynesian-born, long-limbed and graceful, with her hair secured in a long, dark braid with untamed curls escaping. He couldn't help stealing glances as she searched for shells in the wet sand, the way she carried herself... uncannily familiar. She noticed him watching, waved back and gave him a bright smile.

I knew a girl like you once; innocent and full of life before I crushed her hopes and dreams.

He felt an immediate and raw tug to his heart. A burst of fire coursed through his blood, the Mark lashing out, reminding him he was not dead, nor was she. Thinking of her jumbled his mind. He closed his eyes, breathing deep, until the fever subsided and his mind cleared.

Ignore it. I'm dead to her. Dead to everybody. Focus on the task.

He gazed past the dark-haired girl to the rising sea and the silent monster bearing down on the innocent Sapiens occupying this quiet beach and all along this vast shore, living their lives in fancy houses unaware of the danger launched by a man named Robert Culliford.

Wantemo had organized a team of his selected students to suppress the tidal surge from striking vulnerable locations around the Pacific Rim. They had stopped the surge from all except one, the Hawaiian Islands. The Hawaiians had withdrawn their tsunami warnings, believing the danger had passed.

They were wrong.

The dark-haired girl and her friends giggled, splashing each other in the pool's shallow water. Beautiful innocent creatures. Should they live or die? Wantemo told Sinto it was his decision but Sinto knew it was a test, his last and final one.

Sinto could sense it now, the surge of water, closing in fast, drawing an ebbing breath before exhaling.

Sapiens screamed in alarm when water sucked from around their legs, knocking some off their feet by a swift retreating tide. Surfers were sucked out to sea, frantically paddling against a force of nature from which they would never escape. The drawback exposed sand and the shallow rocky reef that created Pipeline's signature waves.

A siren wailed. Sapiens screamed. The burst of frantic announcements rang out over tinny speakers.

"Tsunami!"

"Run!"

Many Sapiens froze, mouths agape, unable to comprehend the imminent danger. The most primal of instincts were lost to them. Sinto was aghast at how easy it would be to eradicate thousands of Sapiens with a single swipe of the sea.

He reflected back to that day in Tallamure when Audrey begged him to give Sapiens a chance. That humanity had reached a critical point of discovery and understanding, that it was possible to change their ways if only the Merahvu would bravely come forward and share their knowledge. At first, he believed that her dream was impossible, that nature's way was the only way; that nature would eradicate the invasive and right imbalances, usually in a non-compassionate and indiscriminate way, as it had for millions of species for billions of years.

If I let the sea take them, would they understand the message?

Sinto wound his way through unmoving bodies to the edge of dry sand where the shoreline used to be. The sea prompted, seeking his answer. A chorus of many assorted voices—dolphin, seal, fish, whale, crab, turtle, shark, coral, and even the tiniest of creatures, invisible to the human eye—recited their grievances. Sapiens were on trial with Sinto as judge and jury. Since he was a compassionate man, he shared their pain and wallowed in indecision.

Time for judgment.

He summoned the language of the sea, a language stamped within the essence of every Merahvu from the day they were born. It was how they were able cut wormhole-like tunnels in the sea. When Sinto was thirteen, Wantemo taught him how to *fully* master the element of water, to control the ebb and flow, to stop a surge like the one fast approaching, no matter how great or small the volume.

The sea is a power unlike any other, and not to be abused, Wantemo had warned.

Those cherished lessons were taught only to a select few, like Sinto, fortunate to be the queen's son. A fortune he now viewed as a curse.

The vitality and purity of the sea filled him. Burning strong and fierce, it nourished his mind and body, and much to his surprise, was a great distraction. The fire of the Mark waned as did the ache in his heart.

Giddy from the Mark's reprieve and the power he possessed, he extended his hands to the sea. Revitalized flueox pumped through his veins. Sparks fell from his fingertips, hissing on the wet sand.

The sea swelled on the horizon, rushing with untold power toward shore. He summoned it. Its power thrummed throughout his body. He visualized his intention, raised his hands, palms flat toward the sea. He shared what he wanted; a great wall of blue water. The sea echoed his wishes, rushing up and towering two times his height, and stopping when it kissed his upraised hands. A magnificent power held in limbo by the flat of his palms and the will of his mind as far as he could see down the shore.

Sea creatures gathered in the liquid blue on the other side, coming face-to-face with the Sapiens frozen by shock and fear.

"Should I save them?" he asked of the sea.

Many voices spoke at once, pained and conflicted, weighing heavily against the Sapiens' favor. But one voice cut through all the rest, a voice of reason, sweet and innocent and wise, and so far, far away...

Naiada.

"Don't poison your essence, dear brother!"

He wavered, unsure if she meant to save the Sapiens or their comrades of the sea.

What would Audrey think of his uncertainty?

Would she think me a monster?

He flushed in anger at all he had sacrificed, and for what? Cast aside as dead. Audrey gone. Home destroyed. Merahvu scattered. The rebel's flex stronger than ever. More death sure to follow.

"I am not the monster!" he screamed.

He sucked grief and anger, compassion and hope, from the core of his essence and channeled it to his hands. His hands glowed bright with green fire, crackling and anxious to do his bidding.

He thought of Audrey and asked, *What would you have me do?*

The Mark responded and her essence filled him—mind, flesh, and bone—the whole of him. Fate intervened. And it was in that moment of clarity that the answer came. He made his choice, forcefully and confidently.

He pressed against the wall of water. Threads of electricity burst from his fingertips and rippled across its surface as far down the beach as he could see. A bolt of lightning shot to the sky from where his hands held the sea; a thunderhead bloomed and heavily wept.

The wall collapsed, stunning the creatures inside and scattering nearby Sapiens. A surge of water swept up the beach, scrubbing it of towels and books, phones and cameras, ice chests and empty bottles, and tiny speakers singing their last song.

The sea swept back from where it came, claiming not one life. The sun burned through the bloom of clouds and the sea calmed. The air was crisp with brine and clear from the sudden rain shower. Sapiens staggered to their feet on wobbly legs, stunned and mute. The bravest cautiously gathered around him, exchanging wild theories.

The dark-haired girl who reminded him of Audrey was one of them. Timidly, she asked, "Who *are* you? Where did you come from?"

He wondered if she, and the Sapiens surrounding him, would believe his story.

Sinto brushed her soft cheek with the back of his finger. He smiled. "Do you really want to know?"

The girl sucked a breath, then nodded, excitedly.

He spun toward the crowd. Those standing in front took a sudden step back.

"Do you want to know the truth of me?" he called out to them.

A burst of confused voices broke the silence. *Yes, yes we do*, they confirmed.

He raised his hands above his head to gasps of exclamation and nervous murmurs, and held them there until they quieted and he had their full attention. Then slowly he lowered his hands, peeling away his disguise. He saved his eyes for last. Green fire burned through the black curtain that hid the glow of his eyes.

Not a word was spoken as he fixed the crowd with his fiery gaze.

Then he burned through his swim trunks with the tip of a finger. When they fell to the sand he unfurled his tail. The crowd jumped when his mighty fluke slapped the wet sand. Proud and unafraid he let them stare. Some gaped, some gasped, others pointed, talking excitedly.

The dark-haired girl beamed with wonder and came forward, unafraid. Her eyes locked on his markings, swept across the flukes of his tail, lying at her feet, before capturing his gaze. The resemblance to Audrey's reaction was frighteningly similar.

"What *are* you?"

That same question he vividly remembered Audrey asking on that day on Merluma when he revealed to Audrey what and who he was.

He smiled. "I am a human, just like you, but our ancestors traveled a different evolutionary path. And this is for certain: We're more the same than not. And I am *real*, not a mythical fantasy."

Then he spun on his heel, ran into the surf, and dove into the sea. His fluke was the last to slip beneath the surface.

The Mark ignited, demanding and familiar. He accepted the fire of the Mark with fervor and focused on his renewed purpose. He intended to keep his promise to his mother: To find his father, for Naiada's sake, and once he did, he would help her quell the rebel uprising.

The Mark gave him renewed strength and determination. As long as he was alive, the Mark would continue to tug at Audrey's essence, insistent and unforgiving, until one day she answered its plea.

When that day came, there would be no more lies, and no more secrets.

NOT THE END...

The adventure continues with Swift as Wind

~ ~ ~

The war for two worlds has only just begun...

Presumed dead after a devastating attack, Sinto embarks on a dangerous mission: find his missing father and uncover the truth behind a surging rebellion. But when he discovers an army of engineered children being bred for war on Merluma, his quest takes a deadly turn.

Meanwhile, Audrey is drowning in grief, believing she caused Sinto's death. When research ships vanish in the Pacific Ocean, she jumps at the chance to investigate—unaware the strange orange fungus spreading across the ocean floor is fiercely guarded by an other-worldly army.

As Sinto follows a lead from an unlikely source as to the whereabouts of his father, Audrey is exiled to her childhood island home where long-buried truths await. Their separate journeys lead to shocking revelations: a powerful rebel with sinister plans, a wobble between worlds that threatens everything, and a love that transcends death itself.

Swift As Wind is the breathtaking second installment in Lisa Cram's *Earth Stones Trilogy*, where the stakes for control of Earth and Merluma ratchet higher.

~ ~ ~

Acknowledgments

EVERY SPARK NEEDS AIR to flame. Audrey Bordvick, you were my wind. Dana Cram, your love of story helped me find my own. My characters are richer because of your valuable advice on the human psyche. Derek Cram, I thank you for questioning everything.

To Dave Welker, my sea-wise technical adviser for a crash course on sonobuoys and designing a multipurpose ship with wings. Gregory Scott Houle, for teaching me how to defend and fight back. Greg Ewert for your endless support from the very beginning. You are greatly missed.

To all my early beta readers who helped shape this first book in the Earth Stones Trilogy and to whom I am forever grateful. You know who you are!

To Karen Fisher, my first editor who taught me to let go of words, to simplify, to find the love in the story no matter how painful the process. Dorothy Conway for teaching me grammar basics that I forgot, and shouldn't have.

A special thanks to Stephanie Cariker, my communications consultant, for spreading her magic—designing my website, building my brand, advising me on marketing strategy, and for being an awesome and inspiring person to know and work with.

To Lynn Nansen-Dale, my sister, editor extraordinaire, and so much more. You were, and continue to be, my guardian angel. You lifted me up and gave me the push I desperately needed to finish this story. Thank you for enduring that first draft and all the many cringe-worthy iterations after, with enthusiasm and encouragement.

To Dad and Mom (Ralph and Phyllis Nansen), who gave us wild, family adventures; who encouraged me to reach for the moon and raise a strong voice. I feel your love and support shining down on me every day.

And finally, my husband, muse, and soulmate, Doug, whose undying love and support keeps me going every day, and in everything I do.

May I ask you for a favor?

Reviews serve a dual purpose: to help readers find new authors, and independent authors, such as myself, connect to a community of new readers. I would be forever grateful if you could leave an honest review, if possible, wherever you acquired this book and/or on goodreads.com.

You can learn more of what I'm up to at my website: www.lisacram.com. Subscribe for important announcements and upcoming releases.

May you always find words to bring you joy, entertainment and wisdom!

Lisa

About the Author

Raised on a Louisiana bayou and the evergreen-cloaked shores of Puget Sound, Lisa Cram spent most of her life on the water, fantasizing about what lay beneath. The Earth Stones Trilogy is her debut as a writer. When not writing, you might find her reading, immersed in the outdoors, swinging a golf club, or her steel mace to raucous music. She divides her time between the Pacific Northwest and the California desert with her musician husband.

For news on upcoming releases from Lisa, visit www.lisacram.com